PRAISE FOR *THE AGE OF RA*

"However you label it, it's great stuff.
Mr. Lovegrove is one of the best writers out
there... Highly, highly recommended."
– *The Fantasy Book Critic*

"Impeccably researched, intricately plotted."
– *The Guardian*

"Lovegrove's bluntness about the gods' Jerry
Springer-like repugnance refreshingly reflects the
myths as they must appear to modern eyes."
– *Strange Horizons Magazine*

"Intelligent and provocative, it's yet more
proof that Lovegrove is one of the UK SF
scene's most interesting, challenging
and adventurous authors."
– Saxon Bullock, *SFX*

"Like no book I've ever read.
And I mean that in a good way...
In this day and age, huge dollops of originality
are hard to come by, but Lovegrove has managed
a feat of stunning creativity that will leave you
hungering for more. Read *The Age of Ra*.
It's an experience you won't regret!"
– Andy Remic,
author of the *Combat-K* novels

PRAISE FOR *THE PANTHEON SERIES*

"A compulsive, breakneck read by a master of
the craft, with stunning action sequences and
acute character observations. This is the kind
of complex, action-oriented SF Dan Brown
would write if Dan Brown could write."

– *The Guardian* on *The Age of Zeus*

"Lovegrove is vigorously carving out a godpunk
subgenre – rebellious underdog humans battling
an outmoded belief system. Guns help a bit,
but the real weapon is free will."

– *Pornokitsch* on *The Age of Odin*

"5 out of 5. I finished it in less than three hours,
yet have pondered the revelations found within for days
afterwards and plan to reread it soon."

– *Geek Syndicate* on *Age of Aztec*

"A fast-paced, thrill-filled ride... There's dry humour,
extreme gore, tension and large amounts of testosterone
flooding off the page – and a final confrontation that
leaves you with a wry smile."

– *Sci-Fi Bulletin* on *Age of Voodoo*

"A love poem to both comic books and the Hindu faith...
As always, Lovegrove's style is easy going and draws you in
quickly. A fine addition to one of the best series in
urban fantasy available today. "

– *Starburst Magazine* on *Age of Shiva*

"Lovegrove has very much made 'godpunk' his own thing...
Age of Anansi is enormous fun; *Age of Satan* is
entertaining and thought-provoking at the same time;
I loved the pace and energy of *Age of Gaia*.
Another great example of James Lovegrove's skills as
a writer of intelligent, fast-paced action adventure stories."

– *SF Crow's Nest* on *Age of Godpunk*

THE AGE OF RA

THE AGE OF RA

SPECIAL EDITION

JAMES LOVEGROVE

SOLARIS

This edition published 2015 by Solaris

First published 2009 by Solaris
an imprint of Rebellion Publishing Ltd,
Riverside House, Osney Mead,
Oxford, OX2 0ES, UK

www.solarisbooks.com

ISBN (UK): 978 1 78108 410 6
ISBN (US): 978 1 78108 409 0

10 9 8 7 6 5 4 3 2 1

A CIP catalogue record for this book is available from the
British Library.

Designed & typeset by Rebellion Publishing

Printed and bound by
CPI Group (UK) Ltd, Croydon, CR0 4YY

FOR

Theodore Finch Xavier Lovegrove
DoB: 27 July 2006

AUTHOR'S NOTE

I'M AWARE THAT in modern Egyptological circles there are preferred spellings of certain gods' names, e.g. Re for Ra, Seth for Set. I've gone for the traditional spellings, since they're more familiar to most people, including me.

FOREWORD

"HAPPY FAMILIES ARE all alike; every unhappy family is unhappy in its own way." So wrote a much better novelist than me. The essential truth he was hitting upon is that happy families do not make for good drama. They are identikit, bland; no one wants to read about them. Whereas unhappy families... That's the story motherlode. The right stuff. The grapes that make the wine.

No one can love more fiercely or hate more fiercely than close kin. Your family are the friends you'll always have and the enemies you'll never escape. They're the people you can trust the most and the people who can piss you off like no other. Want them or reject them, you're stuck with them for life, from the moment of your birth right up until your final croak. Others come and go, but your blood relations are under your skin. You can avoid them, sever ties with them, have no contact with them whatsoever – but they're still there. They have helped make you what you are, for better or worse. You have to give them credit for that, if nothing else.

What has this all got to do with a military-SF novel about the Ancient Egyptian gods? Everything.

Back in 2007 I was approached by George Mann, then commissioning editor of Solaris Books, who asked me if I'd be willing to pitch him ideas for an alternative history novel. I said, "Yes, of course," because I am a freelance writer and "Yes, of course" is my default reply to any work-related question. *Would you like to write something for us?* "Yes, of course." *Would you care to complete an article for us against an impossible deadline?* "Yes, of course." *Would you be willing to dance naked in Trafalgar Square in return for money?* "Yes, of – Wait a minute..."

I sent George paragraph-long synopses for three books, asking him to take his pick. One was called *The Unwinding* and was a futuristic story loosely revolving around Yeats's concept of the "Gyre" and the theoretical notion of the Singularity; it hasn't been written, and probably never will be. One was called *Redlaw*, and four years later that novel would indeed become a reality. The third, about a world ruled by the Egyptian gods, was called *Hieroglyph*, and it was the one George liked the most. Which was a joyful coincidence, because it was also the one I liked the most.

He commissioned it, I wrote it, the title was changed – and thus we have the novel you are holding in your hands right now.

I didn't know a great deal about the Egyptian pantheon before I started work on the book. I was aware that the deities themselves had animal heads; that the myth of Osiris's death and resurrection was a pagan precursor of the Christ story, predating it by some five thousand years; and that the Ancient Egyptians symbolised the Sun as Ra's Solar Barque travelling each day across the sky (I got that from an Alan Moore comic).

What I hadn't appreciated, until I began delving into the necessary background research, was that the bulk of the pantheon constituted a sprawling, internecine family. As soon as I realised this, I knew I had the novel's theme: a family at war. A family at war with itself. A family during wartime. The squabbles between the gods would be reflected in conflicts on Earth, the mundane mirroring the divine both on a worldwide scale and a personal level. The interplay between above and below would provide the book's backbone.

The Age of Ra first saw print while Solaris was undergoing a transition, changing hands between owners. Effectively it was, in the parlance of the publishing trade, "orphaned"; that is, sent out into the world and left to its own devices, without any editor rooting for it particularly or any publicist pushing it particularly. I don't blame anyone for that. People's minds were on other things. Such is fate.

But it did well. Word of mouth brought sales. Copies shifted. Such, too, is fate.

Solaris – now an imprint with a new big boss, Rebellion, and a new editorial team of handsome, thrusting, super-talented individuals (all adjectives suggested by themselves) – looked at the sales figures and proposed a sequel. I couldn't see how the story of *The Age of Ra* could be carried on. It seemed perfectly self-contained. It did occur to me, however, that there were other religions, other pantheons, each unique but having the dysfunctional family dynamic in common, so why not focus on those? Thus the *Pantheon* series was born.

Eight years on, the series now extends to seven titles, with more on the way. The books themselves are a family of sorts. They're all related, and all different. Their themes and styles argue with one another, as if engaged in a lively, sometimes stroppy debate around the dinner table. They're "unhappy in their own way" but, cumulatively, "all alike." They share the same DNA but, wow, the configurations it comes out in are pretty diverse.

Here is where it all started, in a brand spanking new edition. The text has been slightly revised, the cover smartened. Our decent, diffident hero David Westwynter awaits, with his close-combat crook and flail at the ready. *The Age of Ra* is all dolled up and eager to show you a good time. Enjoy!

JMHL
Eastbourne
March 2015

I. PETRA

THE SUN WENT down like a tin duck at a shooting gallery. Night stretched itself over the eastern Arabian desert, the light from a clear full moon creating a finely filigreed landscape of silver and black.

At an altitude of 1,000 feet a twin-engine Griffon-3 transporter plane released a stick of paratroopers in alternating door technique, ten on either side. Canopies flared immediately. The twenty men turned into the wind and dropped to the desert floor as silently as thistle seeds, each making a perfect five-point landing. Within minutes their chutes were buried and they were jogging towards Mount Hor and the dead city that nestled in its shadow, Petra.

They filed through the Siq, Petra's eastern gateway, a sheer-sided gorge hacked out by a long-ago earthquake and smoothed by water erosion. In places it was so narrow they could barely walk two abreast. Above, the sky was a distant strip of starshine, a glittering river meandering between black banks. The paratroopers moved carefully, wide-eyed in the near-total darkness of the gorge. The path sloped steeply, uneven underfoot. Each man held his ibis-headed *ba* lance at the ready, reassured by the warmth he could feel through the handgrips, the charge of divine essence that glowed within the weapon.

The Siq opened out onto a valley. Directly ahead lay the rendezvous point, a Romanesque temple hewn out of the face of a sandstone cliff and known as Al Khazneh, "the Treasury". Its colonnaded and porticoed entrance towered before the soldiers. Essentially a decorated cave mouth, it exuded a dusty silence, the breath of the ancient darkness within.

On the steps of the Treasury, Lieutenant David Westwynter lowered his lance and checked his watch. Precisely 8pm.

"Bang on time," he muttered. "At least, *we* are."

He gave the order to his men to fan out in a defensive formation. Sergeant Mal McAllister, his number two, relayed the order. The paratroopers broke off into small units and found what cover they could in this smooth-bottomed natural amphitheatre. They aimed their weapons in the direction an attack was most likely to come from, should one come: above.

"This can't be a trap," David said to Sergeant McAllister.

"Aye, but if it is," McAllister said, finishing his sentence, "they have us the ideal spot for an ambush."

"That's just what I'm trying not to think."

They waited. And waited. The cold desert wind sidled through the crags and canyons of the abandoned city, never louder than a sigh. In centuries past, Petra had been home to thousands. It had been a trading post, selling its principal resource, fresh water, which came from frequent flash floods and was husbanded in a network of dams and cisterns. The cave-dwelling citizens had worshipped deities who had been vanquished long ago, their names now forgotten, their effigies defaced. Christianity had briefly gained a toehold here, as had Islam. But in time those religions, too, had evaporated, leaving nothing but ruined monuments behind.

Petra, like so many other places, was a museum to the world's fallen gods. A museum and a mausoleum. Here lay their legacy, such as it was – a few broken idols and abandoned buildings, sacred to no one. Here were the sparse, scratched traces they had left behind, the only tangible proof that somewhere on earth they had once held sway. Now mankind belonged to the One True Pantheon, and the wind blowing through Petra sounded, to David Westwynter's ears, like a faint, mournful sob, the despair of defeated rivals. He was comforted by that.

"Sir."

A whispered warning from McAllister.

David turned.

Men were approaching from the far end of the valley. He counted at least a dozen. They were spread out in a line, and the moonlight showed them to be clothed in ragged camouflage fatigues, with turbans around their heads and scarves across their faces, so that just their eyes were visible. Only the falcon-head nozzles on their *ba* lances and the maces that hung by their sides marked them out as Horusites.

David drew himself up to his full height, which at 5'10" was a shade shorter than he might have liked.

The leader of the Horusite commandos halted in front of him and unveiled his face, revealing himself to be a broad-nosed black man with finely pitted skin. He stood an inch or so taller than David.

"Colonel Henry D. Wilkins, Eighth Infantry Division out of Cairo, Illinois," he said, snapping off a salute. "Cobra Force."

David returned the salute. "Lieutenant David Westwynter of His Pharaonic Majesty's Second Paratroop Regiment, stationed on Cyprus."

"By the light of Khons we have met…" said Wilkins.

"… by the wisdom of Thoth may we assist one another," David said, completing the password sequence.

It was a kind of verbal handshake. Wilkins stuck out his hand for the real thing.

"Pleasure to meet you, Loot' Westwynter."

"You too, sir. Related to Pastor-President Wilkins, I take it?"

Wilkins chuckled, amused. "How'd you guess? We don't talk about him much. White sheep of the family."

"The resemblance is marked," said David, also chuckling.

"Mind if I call you Dave?"

"David, preferably. I've only ever let one person call me Dave."

"Sure. Whatever." This was said with a slightly dismissive air. *You Brits and your formality.*

"And you're late," David pointed out.

Wilkins bristled. *You Brits...!*

"Listen, *Lieutenant*," he said. "It so happens we've been tramping around the desert for three months. Hiding from enemy patrols and Saqqara Birds. Living like animals. So we arrive a few minutes later'n we're supposed to. Cut us some goddamn slack!"

David frowned. The encounter had begun well, but things were deteriorating fast. He said, "You have some information for me regarding a concentration of enemy forces outside Amman and Damascus."

"Straight to business, huh?" said Wilkins. "Yep, we've got some good shit for you all right. Long-lens photos of Nephthysian infantry and heavy armour being marshalled. Major, major build-up. Ask me, it looks like the start of a push northward into the Ottoman Empire to take on the Osirisiac Hegemony's south-eastern flank."

David's eyes narrowed. "That'll be for the desk jockeys in Intelligence to decide. Our job isn't to speculate. It's to get the information back to them."

"Looks pretty cut and dried to me," replied Wilkins, adding sardonically, "But then what do I know? I'm just a dumb grunt on the ground who risks his life doing recon in hostile territory all day long. I sure as shit can't imagine what *else* the Nephs would be gathering their forces there for, but hey, let's do as you say and leave it to the big-brains. Ten'll get you one they agree with me."

"Where are they then?" said David. "The photos."

"Back that-a-ways." Wilkins gestured along the valley in the direction he and his Cobra Force cohorts had come from. "We're holed up in this place that's all towers and tombs. Ain't far, no more than a quarter-mile. You can come alone or bring your guys with you if you like."

David looked at Sergeant McAllister. "Let's all go. We'll be home by midnight."

McAllister nodded, his lip down-curling. "Men! Fall in. Home by midnight."

Wilkins had already walked off a few paces to rejoin his group. Now he stopped abruptly. His shoulders slumped. Not turning round, he cursed softly in a language that was not English. "*Khara.*" Arabic for *shit*.

David levelled his *ba* lance, training it on Wilkins' back.

"Who are you really, Colonel Wilkins?" he demanded softly.

"'Home by midnight'," said Wilkins. "That's your abort code. Mission compromised. Right?"

The paratroopers closed in on him and his men.

"I'll ask again," said David. "You're not Cobra Force. You're not even Americans. Are you Nephthysians? Setics?"

"The answer to that is fuck you, Dave."

"Brave talk, but you're surrounded and outnumbered. You have twenty fully charged god rods aimed at you. I suggest you try and be co-operative."

"What was it?" Wilkins said. "Where did I slip up? How did you rumble me?"

"The accent's pretty good," said David, "but you pronounced the name of your base 'Ky-ro', not 'Kay-ro' as the Yanks do. And you said the Osirisiac Hegemony, when most Horusites call it the Parent Hegemony. Either of those, on its own, I'd have passed off as harmless. An idiosyncrasy. But together…" He shrugged.

"Well, don't I just feel like the big shit-eating idiot. All those years at the Baghdad Special Ops Academy watching crappy Hollywood movies, and I blew it with a couple of careless mistakes. Thing is, Dave, I'm not the only one who's been careless."

"What?" said David.

"Look up," said Wilkins, adding, "sucker."

The rim of the valley was fringed with soldiers. They stood silhouetted against the stars. David could make out the distinctive jutting rectangle-and-semicircle insignia on their helmets and the baboon heads that capped their lances. Well, that settled that. Nephthysians. They were all fucking Nephthysians.

Wilkins' grin was bright and sickle-shaped in the gloom.

"You're surrounded and outnumbered," he said in a passable imitation of David's English accent. "You have forty fully charged god rods aimed at you. I suggest you try and be co-operative, or else we'll zap you all to the Field of Reeds."

David's response was to fire his lance at Wilkins.

Wilkins, however, had anticipated this and sprang out of the way. A beam of green *ba* light, pure godly essence, crackled out from the lance's mouth, striking the man who was standing behind Wilkins. It seared a hole through his chest and he fell to the ground, shuddering in death.

Wilkins rolled and came up firing. Golden light blazed from his Horusite lance, but it was a wild shot and missed its target, scorching the step at David's feet instead. David leapt back and took cover behind a column. McAllister joined him, firing as he went.

The Nephthysians started shooting from above, strafing the valley floor with purple beams. The paratroopers scattered, loosing off retaliatory shots. Wilkins' bogus Horusites also scattered. Shafts of light crisscrossed the valley at all angles, a cat's cradle of lethal, coruscating power. Men were shouting and screaming, their faces lit up by the rippling exchange of fire.

David took aim upward and shot at the origin points of the purple beams. His vision was laced with multicoloured afterimages, like slashes across his retinas. A *ba* lance fire-fight in darkness was inevitably short-lived. After a while your eyes became dazzled and you were firing more or less blind. It would come down to hand-to-hand soon. He was prepared for that.

He scored a hit. A Nephthysian shrieked and plummeted from his vantage point, hitting the ground two seconds later with a crunch. David then winged another, whose own blaster shot went astray and lanced through one of his colleagues in the valley. Enemy fire came David's way but struck the column harmlessly. At this range, the blaster beams could not penetrate solid stone.

A few of the paratroopers had retreated to the mouth of the Siq and were putting up a strong resistance from there. They took it in turns. One would shoot, eliciting return fire from the Nephthysians. Then the next paratrooper would aim a blast at where the enemy shot had come from.

The air was alive with the lightning-smell of ozone, along with a tang of burnt flesh. David sensed a lull was coming. The shooting was getting more sporadic. He slung his lance back over his shoulder on its strap and unhooked his hand weapons from his belt. Sergeant McAllister followed suit.

Colonel Wilkins, or whatever his name was, barked an order to his men in Arabic. All lance fire ceased. Then David heard the slithering sound of ropes being dropped, uncoiling as they fell. The Nephthysians on the valley rim were about to come down. This was his and his men's chance. They had to take out the handful of Horusites and flee down the valley before the additional Nephthysian soldiers weighed in with their greater numbers. It was the only hope they had of getting out of this clusterfuck alive.

"Crook and flail!" he called out. "Crook and flail!"

He and McAllister launched themselves from behind the column, hand weapons raised. The crook was a baton tipped with a crescent-shaped titanium blade. The flail was two lengths of ash wood linked by a short chain. Brandishing the one, whirling the other, David and McAllister made for the Horusite impostors. The other paratroopers were close behind, howling a war cry.

Colonel Wilkins and company rose to meet them, maces aloft. As the two groups engaged, David was appalled to see that they were more evenly matched than he had hoped. Only about half of his stick had survived the blaster fight. He knew they had taken casualties but not so many.

Then there was no time to think about any of that. There was only the immediacy of close-quarters combat, the brutal intimacy of standing toe to toe with an opponent and trying to kill him and not be killed, two people as physically near to each other as embracing lovers yet with the very opposite intention. David clinched with one of the Horusite commandos and let his training take over. The flail provided a diversion, preventing the man from swinging his mace properly. The crook meanwhile raked and slashed. Blood jetted, oil-black in the moonlight. The man went down, throat sliced open, gargling and drowning.

David spun to his left. One of his men, Private Langley, was being beleaguered by a pair of mace-wielding foes. Langley had lost his crook. A mace crashed into his chest and David heard ribs crack like far-off fireworks. He wrapped his flail around the attacker's forearm and tugged him off-balance. His crook blade sank into the man's eyeball and plucked it out like a plum from a pudding. A second, sideways jab with the crook cut short his scream.

Langley was on the ground, hissing with pain, struggling to get up. The other fake Horusite straddled him and lifted his mace with both hands to bring it down on Langley's head. Had he been a true Horusite soldier, more experienced with the weapon, he would have gone for a shorter-range blow to stun his victim first and then delivered the skull-crushing *coup de grâce*. As it was, he left David with a split-second window of opportunity.

David came in from behind the man and snapped the flail up between his legs. As the man collapsed to his knees, whimpering, David hooked the crook through his turban into the side of his head and yanked. The man's head jerked back. Most of his ear came away, along with a tangle of unravelling turban cloth. In an agonised frenzy the man aimed a backwards blow with the mace, which David was able to evade. Then Langley coshed him with his flail, knocking him sideways and concussing him.

David's blood was up. His heartbeat was pure pounding timpani. He looked around for Colonel Wilkins. The bastard needed to get what was coming to him, from one commanding officer to another.

Wilkins was clashing with McAllister, warding off the sergeant's dual-weapon assault with deft use of the mace. He, at least, knew how to wield one. Something else he'd learned at the Baghdad Special Ops Academy no doubt.

Then David saw that the other Nephthysians had arrived. Some were already in the valley and rushing to join in the mêlée; the rest were on their way, abseiling down.

Now he and what was left of his stick didn't have a prayer. Their only option was a tactical withdrawal.

"Retreat!" he yelled, stowing his hand weapons. "That way! Down the valley!"

He lunged past McAllister, barging Wilkins aside with his shoulder. McAllister came with him, running full tilt. The remaining paratroopers followed.

David had considered making an exit via the Siq, but it was too narrow, with too many potential bottlenecks. Wilkins might anyway have posted guards at the far end, and the paratroopers would be sitting ducks, coming up the gorge two by two.

Instead, all they could do was plunge deeper into the dead city and hope to find another way out.

Golden and purple beams of *ba* sizzled blisteringly around them. Private Robbins took one full in the spine. He arched backwards, slumping bottom-first onto the ground. Gasping and mewling, he groped for the hole in his back where several vertebrae had been fused together in a twisted mass of melted bone. His legs were splayed in front of him, useless. A second beam penetrated his skull from their rear. Briefly Robbins' head was lit up from the inside, like a crimson lantern, before his eyes burst and his teeth exploded from their gums and he keeled over, smoke pouring from his mouth and nostrils.

Colonel Wilkins was shouting again, giving more orders in Arabic.

It was just David now, and McAllister, and four other men, versus some thirty or so enemy soldiers.

They ran on.

Then, ahead, like dark ghosts, yet more of the enemy appeared. They emerged from behind rocks, from cave mouths, from ledges on the valley wall. They moved slowly, stiffly, shufflingly, as though every step was an arthritic effort.

David's breath caught.

Mummies.

He and his paratroopers skidded to a halt. The dead creatures in front of them advanced with a grim, swaying purposefulness, arms outstretched. They were wrapped from head to foot in cerecloths and linen bandages, which rustled as they walked. Their joints creaked, and their jaws worked, opening and closing with a terrible, empty clicking sound.

David felt nothing but a weary dread.

Mummies. He loathed mummies.

His men began firing. Fear – the innate, visceral fear of the undead – disrupted their aim. Shots went wild or else only clipped their targets. The mummies lumbered closer, little perturbed to have small chunks blown off them. Even the occasional direct hit in the body didn't faze them. They staggered, then resumed their advance, lacy fireglow chasing across the singed parts of bandage.

"Knees!" David yelled. It was elementary tactics. "Wide beam setting! Cut them off at the knees!"

He demonstrated with a blast that sheared a mummy's leg in two. The creature toppled onto its face. Even downed, it kept going, crawling along with its arms and one good leg.

The nearest of the mummies reached the paratroopers. It lunged for Private Carey, enfolding him in an embrace of hideous strength. Carey barely had time to cry out as the mummy crushed him to its chest, shattering his ribs and spine and bursting his heart.

Then Wilkins' voice rang out. A one-word command in Arabic halted the mummies in their tracks. Then, in English, he said, "Put down your weapons, Osirisiacs. Surrender. There's no way out of this. We have you pinned down. Surrender, or go to meet Anubis like dogs."

David glanced at McAllister and the other three.

He saw it in their eyes. They didn't want to die here, now, like this. They would if he asked them to. If that was his decision. But they didn't want to.

Neither did he.

He laid down his lance and raised his hands.

Within moments, he and his men were having their wrists bound tightly behind them. Colonel Wilkins strode up and looked David in the eye.

"Interesting," he said smugly. "I had you pegged as the go-down-fighting type. Clearly there's a streak of cowardice in the supposedly fearless British soldier."

"No," David replied. "It's just that, as long as I'm alive, I can still kill you."

"Ah," said Wilkins, as if musing on this. "Ah ha."

He gut-punched David, then kicked his legs out from under him.

"Kill me?" he spat, as David writhed in the dust. "I doubt it, Lieutenant Westwynter. But I'll tell you this. By the time I'm done with you, you'll be begging me to kill *you*."

2. EPOXY

WHEREVER PRIVATE MARTINEAU had been taken to be tortured, it was near enough for his agony to be heard easily. Every sob, every howl, every plea for mercy. Even, at the end, his soft imploring moans as he called for his mother.

The torture lasted half an hour, although seemed longer. When it finally stopped, the remaining four paratroopers could only look at one another and wonder which of them would be next.

All four – David, Sergeant McAllister, and Privates Henderson and Gibbs – were in bad shape. The Nephthysians had worked them over thoroughly before chucking them into this cave. David had suffered a particularly severe beating at the hands of the Nephthysian whose ear he had ripped off with his crook. Fair dos, he supposed, although every time he moved, the pain went from tolerable to excruciating and he was inclined to think far less charitable thoughts about the man.

Outside the cave entrance, daylight burned, too bright to look at. Three Nephthysians were on guard duty out there. They talked in low voices and smoked acrid-smelling cigarettes incessantly. Every so often one of them would come in to check on the captives and deliver the odd kick.

David wished there was something he could say to lift his men's spirits and give them hope. But there was nothing he could think of. It was all very well to believe that you would be brave in a situation like this, that you'd tap into some hidden reservoir of courage which would enable you to tough it out. But the truth was, a bunch of strangers intended to hurt them as cruelly as possible then kill them, and no amount of bravery could counterweigh that. Nor did it make any difference that David and his men had undergone capture scenarios as part of basic training. A capture scenario was an unpleasant experience, but was, all said and done, just theatre. Sitting there blindfolded while members of your own regiment yelled at you and battered you with sticks – it was like hard-boiling an egg in the hope that it might survive a hammer blow.

David was shit-scared. That was all there was to it. He was shit-scared and he knew it and he didn't mind admitting it to himself, and this was the only thing that made him feel the slightest bit less miserable. No false bravado. No illusions. He was man enough to acknowledge that most unmanning of emotions, plain terror.

Two Nephthysians came for Private Henderson.

Henderson's suffering went on for longer than Martineau's, perhaps three-quarters of an hour all told. At some point during that period, Private Gibbs pissed himself.

An hour after that it was David's turn. He was dragged out of the cave, hauled down some stone steps carved into the hillside, and deposited in a larger cave. This one had been hollowed out to form two adjoining chambers, a larger outer one and a smaller inner one, linked by a low doorway. The outer chamber had slit-like windows, several alcoves, and what had clearly once been a cooking area, with a flue for the fire smoke and a recessed hearth framed by the remains of a tiled surround.

Now, for additional homeliness, it had been furnished with a collapsible table and a pair of canvas chairs, in one of which sat the man who called himself Colonel Wilkins. He looked hot and bothered. Sweat sheened his forehead and his cheeks. Dried blood stippled the front of his fatigues.

David was made to sit in the other chair. The Nephthysians who had brought him took up position on either side of him, but Wilkins dismissed them with a flick of his fingers.

"The lieutenant and I are both civilised men," he said. "I am sure we can work things out through amicable discussion and nothing more."

Wilkins was now talking with a faint Middle Eastern inflection, no longer having to pretend to be American.

"Date?" he asked, proffering a plate of the fruits. They looked deliciously fat and plump, and David could imagine crushing one between his teeth, bursting open its sweetly fibrous flesh, gulping it down.

But he shook his head. "Under the..." he began. His voice was a papery rasp. He ran his tongue around his mouth and tried again. "Under the terms of the Global Convention for the Proper Treatment of Prisoners of War—"

"Let me stop you right there, lieutenant," said Wilkins, holding up a hand like a traffic policeman. "One, I know the wording of the Convention as well as you do. Two, I don't care about your name, rank, and serial number. Three, you and your men have been taken captive after illegally entering our territory, rather than in the course of battle, which renders the Convention null and void in this instance. You are not prisoners of war. You are *my* prisoners, and I will treat you however I wish."

David tried another tack. "Where are Martineau and Henderson? I want to see them. What have you done with them?"

"Take a look for yourself." Wilkins pointed to the doorway to the next chamber.

David glimpsed two bodies under blankets on the floor. Bloodstains had soaked through the material.

His stomach lurched with horror and disgust.

The disgust was good. Disgust contained anger. Anger gave strength.

He turned back to Wilkins and said, simply, "Cunt."

Wilkins sighed and rolled his eyes. "So free with the insults, Lieutenant Westwynter. It diminishes you in my eyes. A man who feels the need to belittle others all the time must have a very low opinion of himself."

"You're right," David said. "I take it back. You're not a cunt. You're a sanctimonious cunt."

Wilkins blinked slowly, looking for all the world like the aggrieved parent of a badly behaving child.

Then, in one swift movement, he stood and slapped David across the cheek, backhand.

His knuckles split open a bruise that the minus-an-ear Nephthysian had put there earlier. David hissed as warm blood trickled down his face and onto his neck.

Wilkins reseated himself. His two subordinates outside, glancing in, chuckled.

"I trust I won't have to do any more of that," he said. "I would much rather you co-operated. That was basically why I did what I did to your men. To let you know that I am someone who means business but would much prefer to *do* business, if you see what I mean."

"You could have left them alone," David said thickly. "They didn't know anything."

"Precisely. Whereas you, I am sure, do know something."

"What are you after? What the fuck do you want from me?"

"Information," said Wilkins. "Merely information. As much of it as possible. About troops. Locations. Numbers. Fortified positions. Plans. Anything and everything you can tell me."

"I'm just a soldier, doing a job," David said. "Just 'a dumb grunt on the ground', to coin a phrase."

"No. You are an officer and you are obviously an intelligent man. Someone who pays heed to what is going on around him; someone who considers the bigger picture."

"I'm flattered. But if I'm really so intelligent, how come I got myself and my men into a mess like this?"

"The trap was, if I say so myself, beautifully laid."

"You had all the right radio codes."

"Correct."

"Which you got from the Horusites whose uniforms and weapons you took."

"Correct again."

"By torture?"

A twitch of the eyebrows: *naturally*.

"And," David went on, "you then took those Horusites and had them embalmed and turned into mummies."

"What else does one do with dead foes?" said Wilkins. "We have a base camp nearby, and a Mobile Mummification Suite parked there, complete with priest. It seemed expedient. Although 'mummies' isn't the accepted term for them nowadays, is it? It's regarded in polite circles as somewhat coarse and dismissive. What must we call them? 'Reanimates'. Is that the word?"

"I'm a traditionalist," said David. "Mummies."

"Well, either way, as we're discussing mummies, perhaps that's where we can start. I'd be interested to know how many you have stockpiled at your garrison on Cyprus."

"And I'd be interested to know what your real name is. I don't want to keep thinking of you as Colonel Wilkins. Nice touch, by the way. Who'd be suspicious of a man with the same surname as the Pastor-President?"

"Indeed. If you must know – not that it's going to make any difference in the long run – I am Hasan Maradi, a captain in the Persian Tenth Infantry Brigade, Special Services Division."

"Nice. You gave yourself a promotion."

"Trying it on for size. It felt like a good fit."

"Well, Captain Maradi," David said, "as we're being candid with each other, perhaps I should tell you that because my squad has failed to radio back to base with a mission status by now, and missed its exfil window, alarm bells will have rung and a recovery team will be on its way to find out what's become of us. They're probably looking for us even as we speak. Your best bet is to up sticks and run while you can. The recovery team will be coming in gunships and you won't stand a chance."

Wilkins – Maradi – regarded David with frank scepticism. "Is that so? My understanding is that a mission like yours, a covert foray across enemy borders, carries full deniability. No one is coming to your aid. If your mission goes awry, your top brass will deny you were ever here or that you even existed."

"The army isn't going to leave twenty good soldiers stranded in the desert without mounting at least one rescue attempt."

"In that case," said Maradi wryly, "time is of the essence and we must hurry. I am going to give you one last opportunity to agree to answer my questions freely, without coercion. Then, I'm afraid, I will have to start being more persuasive. Let me show you what I mean."

He picked up what appeared to be a small tube of some kind of paste.

"What is this?" he said, holding it up for David to inspect.

David squinted. The markings on the tube were in Arabic script, but it could only be one thing.

"Glue."

"A very strong epoxy adhesive," said Maradi, nodding. "The kind used by hobbyists to assemble plastic aeroplane kits and the like. The kind that you are not supposed to bring into contact with your skin. See, there's a little warning notice here on the side. It says, 'Caustic. Severe irritant.' Now think how it might feel to have some of this glue squeezed into your ear canal. Think how it might feel if your eyelids were to be cemented together with it. Not painful. Well, not very. But the damage would, I fear, be considerable. Irreparable, in fact. Permanent deafness and blindness. And were I to apply some to your nostrils and mouth, sealing them shut with just a tiny hole left between the lips to breathe through – can you see how disagreeable an experience that might be? To be almost incapable of breathing? To feel slow suffocation, and the panic that comes with that? The awful, dizzying sensation of slow death? And I can slit your lips apart with this" – he held up a scalpel, the type with a replaceable blade; like the glue, something an artist or modeller might use – "to let the air in, and then reseal them as I please. Slit, reseal. Slit, reseal. After a while it would get messy but I suspect I will have made my point by then. Unlike your subordinates over there, you, Lieutenant Westwynter, have an imagination. For them, crude methods sufficed. For you, the ability to foresee the results of torture may be just as effective as torture itself. Am I not right?"

David tried a last desperate ploy, the only arrow he had left in his quiver. "Nephthys, Mistress of the House and Castle, Daughter of Earth and Sky, Mother of the Dead, may be married to Set but she is closer to Isis and Osiris than she is to him. We all know that. She helped Isis embalm Osiris's body after her husband slew him. She bore Osiris's child!"

"Indeed," said Maradi, smiling, "and you could likewise remind me that there have long been political and economic ties between her domain and that of her older brother and sister." His face hardened. "But it is all history. Now is now. We are at war. You and I are enemies. This is the only truth that matters. You cannot win me over by trying to appeal to a sense of commonality that I do not feel. I am not the sort to give much thought to the past – not when I have more pressing concerns in the present. So, one very final time, will you help me willingly, or must I summon Yusuf and Amal back in here to hold you down?"

David was out of answers, out of hope. He looked ahead to an hour or more of torment from which death would be the only release. The worst of it could all be avoided if he simply gave Maradi everything he asked for. David wasn't naïve. He realised he would be killed even if he did co-operate. But his death would at least be a quick, clean one.

This was the moment. This was the test that all soldiers knew they might one day have to face. Honour versus self-interest. Were you a dutiful servant of your country's armed forces or were you, when it came to the crunch, just a helpless, fallible human being?

If, David thought, he held out against Maradi and told him nothing, it was unlikely that this courageous stance would ever become known to the wider world. No one back home would ever be aware of what he had done. And the reverse was also true. If he sang like a canary, would anyone back home be any the wiser? Probably not.

Besides, it wasn't as if he knew anything vital. He had no information that the Nephthysians or the Setics couldn't have found out through their spy networks. Most likely he knew nothing they didn't know already. All he'd be doing was confirming their own observations.

"If I tell you as much as I can," he said, "will you agree to let the other two of my men go, unharmed? Anything I don't know, they definitely won't know."

"How noble. But alas…" Maradi shook his head, with what seemed like genuine regret. "That is not something I can offer."

"At the very least, you'll finish them off as painlessly as you can?"

"Now this, yes, I think I can manage."

"Promise?"

"You have my word."

It was better than nothing. By complying with Maradi, David would gain mercy for McAllister and Gibbs. He wasn't selling himself completely for free.

"So?" said the Nephthysian, cocking his head to one side. "Shall we begin?"

Before David could reply, he heard a rumbling. Maradi heard it too. It was low and distant, like a continuous peal of thunder several miles away. It rapidly grew louder, going from faint to ominous. Now it had a distinctive droning, whirring undertone. Maradi got up and went to the cave entrance to peer out. He muttered something to the two men outside.

David got up too, carefully, stealthily. Keeping an eye on Maradi, he began backing towards the inner chamber.

He knew what the sound was, what was making it.

RAF Eagles.

Two of them, he reckoned. Coming in low. Hedge-jumping. Under the radar.

There could be only one reason for that.

The noise had risen to near deafening now. Maradi turned to speak to David. He saw him ducking through the doorway in the inner chamber. A look of understanding dawned on his face. He began to shout out a warning to his men.

Then the jets roared by, skimming the valley's rim.

Then there was light. Milky jade-green brilliance. Blinding. Filling the world. And a detonation that punched the eardrums like knitting needles.

The cave convulsed. David was flung against the rear wall by a pressure wave. He fetched up sprawled across the corpses of his fellow paratroopers.

For a time, he couldn't move. Think. Feel.

HE STAGGERED TO his feet. The air was dense with dust. The inner chamber was more or less intact, but the cave's outer wall had been reduced to rubble. A ragged aperture remained, large enough to clamber through. David made for it. On the way he stumbled across something on the floor. Captain Maradi. The Nephthysian was lying on his back. His clothing was charred and tattered. Most of the skin had been burned off him.

He stirred.

Still alive. Just.

David knelt. Maradi blinked up with scarlet eyes. His mouth moved, wordlessly, or so it seemed.

"I told you I would kill you," David said. Or thought he said. His ears were ringing too loudly for him to hear even his own voice.

Maradi's expression was resigned – *the irony of it.*

David rammed the heel of his palm against the base of the man's nose, driving bone and cartilage upwards into the brain.

Outside, dust hung across the valley in a red-brown fog. Through its skeins and swirls David could see that the place had been devastated. This portion of Petra was more of a ruin than it had ever been. The temple façades were gone, a few spars of column jutting here and there from landslides of rock. The rest was red, cratered moonscape.

The Eagles had dropped dual-cell fusion bombs. Green Osirian *ba* in one half, white Isisian *ba* in the other. Within the casing, a thin dividing wall of ceramic that shattered on impact, bringing the two divine essences into sudden contact. The result: a violent melding of diverse powers and a half-kiloton yield.

Having delivered their payload, the jets were now gone. David doubted they would return. Job done.

He went in search of McAllister and Gibbs.

3. WEST

THE DESERT HISSED and shimmered. It was earth that had been flayed by the sun, a patch of planet stripped of all softness, peeled back to the bone. Wadis spoke of rain that came abruptly and in torrents, scored channels in the ground, then vanished, offering little relief. Plants here lived a half-existence, deep roots tapping for moisture while shoots were brittle to the point of crumbling. Snakes and scorpions raced from shade to shade.

Three men came walking. Two of them supported the third, who hobbled along on one leg. The other leg ended in a ragged mass of flesh, a thing that hung limp and useless and looked only vaguely like a foot. A belt was tied around the thigh in a tourniquet.

McAllister had insisted on being left behind at Petra. David had insisted that if McAllister didn't shut up, he would put a bolt of *ba* through his head. McAllister had asked him to do just that. David had hoisted the sergeant up by the armpits and set off.

They had no radio equipment. Theirs and the Nephthysians' had been buried by the bombs. They had no weapons except a single Horusite *ba* lance, which David had retrieved from the body of a dead Nephthysian. All of their own weaponry had, of course, been confiscated earlier, and the bombs had buried that too. They had no food or water. They had been deprived of their emergency rations and bottles by their captors.

All they had was themselves.

Getting far away from Petra was vital. The bombardment was bound to attract attention and the area would soon be teeming with Nephthysian troops.

They had to go west.

West would get them across the al-Jayb river and onto the Sinai Peninsula. Any other direction would take them deeper into hostile territory. West was their only hope. West, and the one neutral country left in the world.

"How far?"

This was Gibbs's question. David didn't know the answer for sure.

"Fifty, sixty miles," he replied confidently. "No more than that."

The sun towered down on them. David was already acutely thirsty and hungry.

They would never make it to Freegypt.

They kept going anyway.

NIGHT WAS BITTERLY cold, the stars like flecks of ice.

McAllister groaned dazedly in the dark. David sat with him, trying to distract him and keep him quiet by chatting to him in a low voice. Sound carried at night in the desert. A whisper was a shout.

"Ah'm such a heid-the-ball," McAllister complained in one of his lucid moments. "Getting my leg all mashed up an' that."

"Yes, it was your fault a chunk of cave roof collapsed on you," David said. "What an idiot."

"Ah'm just holding you up. You have to leave me."

"What, and miss your cheery Scottish temperament?"

"Go an' fuck yourself, sir."

"That's the spirit."

AT DAWN, as much through luck as skill, David managed to catch and kill a lizard. He chiselled off its head with a sharp stone and they took turns to drink drips of its blood. Then they took turns to vomit.

THE SUN BLAZED, Ra at his least forgiving. The paratroopers draped their battledress blouses over their heads and felt their bare backs and shoulders start to blister. The horizon was one long wavering line, melting into the blue of the sky. However far they trudged it never came any closer.

Soon David had almost stopped thinking. All that filled his mind was thirst. His tongue was a lumpen, desiccated object in his mouth; it no longer felt a part of him. His brain throbbed inside his skull like a prisoner beating on the walls of his cell.

McAllister was scarcely walking any more. David and Gibbs were carrying him, and every step they took with his extra weight seemed to drain one more ounce of hydration out of them, one more erg of strength.

Eventually they set him down in the feathery shade of a tamarisk bush. They knew they were not going to pick him up again. Their arms were too stiff to lift him any more, and McAllister was too pain-wracked and feverish to bear any more of being lifted.

A few words hissed from his parched lips.

David leaned close.

"Could murder a brew," McAllister said.

"Afraid we're all out," said David.

"Whisky?"

"I seem to have mislaid my hip flask."

Even more quietly, so that Gibbs couldn't hear, McAllister said, "They bombed us."

"I know."

"Our own planes. Cleansing the scene."

"I know," David said again.

"To shut us up. And so there'd be no bodies. No evidence. Nothing for the Nephs to parade on TV. Just a ruddy great mess of rubble that both sides can claim the other did."

The term that Captain Maradi had used popped up in David's mind: *deniability*. "We all know we're expendable."

"Still," said McAllister. "The stupid wee bastards."

"That's the military, Sergeant McAllister. That, in a nutshell, is who we work for. A bunch of stupid wee bastards. And some might say we're stupid wee bastards ourselves, for working for them. Look on the bright side. The bombing freed us."

"Not that that was the plan." McAllister gave a cough that was a laugh or a laugh that was a cough. He fumbled with the small, shatterproof glass phial that hung on a chain around his neck. "You'll... you'll do the necessary for me, sir?"

It was a last request. David nodded.

"You're not so bad, you know," McAllister said. "For a poncey English posho."

"I'll be sure to have that carved on my gravestone."

Within the hour, the sergeant was dead.

DAVID UNSTOPPERED THE phial and dribbled myrrh onto McAllister's bare chest. At the same time he murmured the Prayer of Anointment.

"Lord Osiris, Ruler of the Netherworld, I commend to you the ka of Malcolm McAllister, that his sins may be judged kindly by wise Maat in the Hall of Judgement at the Weighing of the Heart, and that he may pass on safely into the care of your nephew Anubis for all eternity."

The myrrh's sickly-sweet odour rose in David's nostrils, so cloying he wanted to gag.

"With this oil I purify and sanctify his mortal remains and raise him to a state of holy grace, that he may be worthy in your eyes, O Hundred-Named One."

He and Gibbs did not have the energy, or for that matter the tools, to bury the body. They had no choice but to leave it out in the open for the jackals to find and dispose of.

"You'll do the same for me," Gibbs said. "When the time comes. Won't you, sir?"

"The time isn't coming," said David, striding purposefully on.

FRIGID NIGHT. RELENTLESS day.

The landscape became no smoother, no less stone-strewn and rugged. Nothing changed except the amount of effort it took to keep going. They must have covered sixty miles by now. They must have covered far more. Gibbs kept casting sullen looks David's way, as if to say, *You lied to me.* David kept ignoring the looks, as if to say, *So fucking sue me.*

There was no one else. There was nothing here. Just desolation. You could have called the place Ra-forsaken, but for the fact that Ra was there most of the time, a pitiless shining presence, baking the sky, blast-furnacing the air.

Gibbs was flagging. For every twenty paces David took, he managed ten. David repeatedly had to stop and wait for him to catch up.

Gibbs was mumbling. Mostly he was cursing his luck, wishing he'd never joined the army, sometimes hurling veiled insults at David, sometimes talking to his own father as though Gibbs senior were strolling alongside him. It wasn't quite delirium but it wasn't far off.

Gibbs was refusing to take one more step. He had had enough. They weren't anywhere near Freegypt. They were never going to reach it. They were going to die here in this fucking desert where nobody would even find their bones.

He made a lunge for David, catching him off-guard. Before David could stop him he had snatched the Horusite *ba* lance off his back.

"Gibbs," David said, "give that back to me. Now. That's an order."

Wild-eyed, raw-skinned, Gibbs shook his head. "Can't do that, sir."

David moved carefully towards him, one hand extended. "Give me the god rod, Private Gibbs. Please."

"Don't come any closer." Gibbs twisted the lance's power regulator to narrow beam setting. His thumb quivered over the trigger.

"Killing me isn't going to help," David said. "We need each other. We need to do this together. We can make it, I promise."

"With all due respect, sir, I don't believe you. And anyway, it's not you I'm planning to kill."

"Gibbs..."

"I'm not going to spend days dying out here. Not when there's a better way."

"Gibbs! No!"

Gibbs flipped the *ba* lance to vertical, lodging its falcon-head nozzle under his chin. He pressed the trigger.

A flash of gold.

A mist of crimson.

A headless corpse crumpled to the ground.

One month ago, Private Gibbs had turned twenty years old.

ALONE, WESTWARD, DAVID Westwynter walked on.

And on.

Knowing that with every step, there would be just more desert. Over the next rise, and the next – just more desert.

4. STEVEN

ONE OF DAVID'S earliest memories was of his brother being born.

Not the birth itself. He was kept well out of the way while that happened, bundled off to his grandparents' for a night and a day.

But on returning home, he was keenly aware that everything had changed in the house. His father looked even more tired and preoccupied than he normally did, while the housekeeper, Mrs Plomley, was all grins and bosomy welcome, as though David had been away for weeks, not twenty-four hours. New toys – big primary-coloured plastic ones – littered the main hallway. In the library the butler, Jepps, was busy unwrapping more gifts for the new arrival and making a careful note of the donors' names.

Then there was the baby itself, lying in the bassinet by his mother's bedside, curled like a caterpillar on a leaf.

"His name is Steven," David's mother said. "Why don't you say hello?"

David leaned over the bassinet. Say hello? He couldn't see the point. The baby was sound asleep, scarcely moving. It wouldn't hear. Or it might hear and wake up, and David knew enough about babies to know that it was important to be quiet around them and not disturb them.

"He's your brother." Cleo Westwynter's face was doughy white, her smile blurry around the edges. "When he's a bit bigger you can play with him. He'll be your best friend."

David already had friends at nursery. He didn't need another.

He didn't say hello, or anything else, to little Steven. He simply turned and walked away from the bassinet and staggered across a desert plain on feet that were rubbed raw, constantly tripping over small rocks and stumbling in crevices. The sun seemed to have boiled his brainpan dry. No more headache, just a scoured-out emptiness behind his eyes. At one point he found himself face down in a patch of scrubby grass, and couldn't recall falling. All he knew was his six-year-old brother was jumping up and down on his back and whipping him with a dressing gown cord.

David was under strict orders not to retaliate when Steven got too rowdy. What he should do was remove himself from the situation. Calmly get up and walk away.

But he had had enough. A game of horsey had turned into something more violent, and this was after a morning in which Steven had broken the lid off David's favourite sarcophagus toy, the one with the articulated Tutankhamen figurine inside. With a growl he threw Steven off and started punching him, and Steven shrieked and bawled, and their mother came running and scolded David and sent him to his room, and it was unfair; it was so unfair; it was not fair at all that out of twenty paratroopers, twenty comrades, he should be the only one left alive. Of course he wanted to survive. Who wouldn't? But not like this, alone, the last of a stick. To make matters worse, he was the commanding officer, the one with responsibility. *His* stick. He'd always put his men first before. Their lives, he believed, were more important than his. Yet now, through no fault of his own, he remained while the rest of them had gone to the Field of Reeds. That wasn't right. That wasn't how it was supposed to be.

You looked out for those you were put in charge of. That was one of the fundamental, unshakeable rules. His father told him this the day Steven joined him at boarding school.

"Keep an eye on your brother," Jack Westwynter said, having drawn David aside for a private word, while around them cars pulled up and trunks were offloaded and sons said farewell to parents and cars pulled away. "He's not as sensible as you and he's not as bright as you. You've built a hell of a reputation at this place. You're a hard act to follow, and Steven may well not live up to the standards you've set. That'll make it tough for him, and you must help. Do you understand?"

David nodded.

"Good lad."

Jack Westwynter slipped his older son a twenty, then went back to the car, where Steven was trying to disentangle himself from their mother and her tight hug and her tears.

David put the money in his pocket. He was accustomed to his father paying him to do things. His father lived in a world of money. As current CEO of the family business, Jack Westwynter's life was one long series of fiscal exchanges. Cash and kin were synonymous to him. There was no difference.

Within a fortnight, Steven had got into trouble. He'd taken to sitting at the wrong table in the dining hall. There was an informal hierarchy in force. Certain areas of the hall were, by tradition, reserved for pupils of a certain seniority. A first-year did not eat where only sixth-formers were supposed to.

But Steven didn't care. Steven had no respect for this well-entrenched system of segregation. Steven declared that one table was as good as any other. He should be free to eat where he pleased.

Three boys in David's year took it upon themselves to teach Westwynter Minor the error of his ways. They beat him up quite badly, then for good measure hacked off his long, trendy side-lock of hair with a penknife.

Westwynter Major, in turn, felt obliged to demonstrate that if you attacked one brother, you attacked them both.

"Three against one?" David said as he kicked the living shit out of the bullies behind the cricket pavilion. "Fucking cowards!"

Afterwards he went to Steven and told him that this was the first and last time he would ever stand up for him like that. Steven had to develop some common sense. You didn't get anywhere by antagonising people.

"So keep my nose clean, huh, Dave?" Steven sneered through black eye and swollen lip. His head looked lopsided, thanks to the missing side-lock. He had been growing it since the age of ten. "Be a good little boy? Do as I'm told? And then I'll get to be a prefect, like you next term. And captain of the First Fifteen. And head of the school senet club. And, oh why not, head of the Upper Sixth as well. Everyone's all-round bloody hero."

"You've got five years to go, and I'm not going to be here to protect you for four of them."

"I don't need you to protect me."

"Fine. Then I won't."

"Fine."

Steven was a little more careful from then on, however. He flouted the school rules whenever possible and was a regular visitor to the headmaster's study and the regular bearer of the stripes of a good arse-thrashing. But he never again trespassed on the unwritten codes which the pupils themselves lived by. And after David left for university Steven prospered in his own way, setting himself up as a black marketeer and trafficking lucratively in such prohibited items as cigarettes, alcohol, and porn. He smuggled the contraband into school and sold it at inflated prices, and David often wondered what their father would have done if he'd ever found out. Would he have punished Steven, or congratulated him on his entrepreneurialism? Profit, after all, was what drove Jack Westwynter on. It was his pole star, his compass. It gave him a sense of direction, and David's own sense of direction was hopelessly confused. He should be heading west. He thought he was. But the sun would not stay still in the sky. It kept turning around, pirouetting, dancing tantalisingly. When it ought to be behind him, suddenly it was in front. When it ought to be directly overhead, suddenly it was somewhere to his left or right.

Ra's Solar Barque was no longer cruising in a straight line across the heavens. Someone was asleep at the tiller.

So David thought, although a precise voice deep inside him wanted him to know that the Solar Barque was sailing as true as ever. He was the one meandering, straying, circling. His course was wayward. Steven's course was wayward. He didn't do as David did and join the family firm. A seat on the board of AW Games had been waiting for David the moment he stood up from the exam-room desk having completed the last of his finals. He'd been welcomed in by the company executives. They'd said they had high hopes for him. A sound brain. His father's son. A chip off the old block. They were looking forward to working with him.

Steven, on the other hand, shunned further education and joined the navy.

He joined the navy because there was a war on and the armed services needed able bodies and the Parent Hegemony needed defending. Or so he said.

But it was obvious that he did it because it was the exact opposite of what everyone expected him to do and wished him to do.

Six months later, following the Battle of the Aegean, Steven was listed as missing in action.

Just as David would be. Probably was already.

He sat on a rocky outcrop overlooking a valley that was wide and brown, shot with pink by the rays of the setting sun. A bird wheeled above, wings outstretched, riding the evening thermals. At first David had taken it for a Saqqara Bird and had felt a faint stab of hope. Even now, some priest back in Cyprus was coming round from a fever-trance and informing David's superiors that he had found him. The army hadn't written him off after all. The government might have ordered Petra to be bombed but the Second Paratroop Regiment had refused to give up on its men.

But the bird was in fact a real bird, a vulture, and it was here for only one reason.

David felt empty. There was nothing left inside him. He was a shell, a brittle man-shaped crust enclosing a vast, exhausted void. He had gone as far as he was able to. There was no more distance to go.

He knew it. The vulture knew it too.

The Horusite *ba* lance lay across his lap. He was trying to summon up his last dregs of strength in order to pick up the weapon and place it against his head.

Gibbs had been right. There was no other way out. Death was inevitable. But at least, like this, you had some control over it. You could decide the when and the where and the snap-of-the-fingers how.

The life beyond awaited. In Iaru, the Field of Reeds, David would plough, sow, and harvest for all eternity. He would toil happily, with Steven beside him. There would be no more turmoil and dispute between the two of them. They would be as they were always meant to be, brothers who loved one another and forgave one another.

David tried to anoint himself from his phial but his hands were weak; his fingers couldn't grip the top to unscrew it. He gave up, thinking that simply saying the Prayer would suffice. But he couldn't manage that either. His lips were rigid, too cracked and flaked for speech, his throat too dry.

An unceremonised death, then. His ka would still make its way to Iaru, but perhaps not as swiftly as he'd have liked. There would be a time in limbo, before he at last found his way to the land of the dead.

He checked the *ba* meter on the lance. After Gibbs had used it, there was now just enough charge left for a single shot.

It would do.

The lance seemed to weigh as much as a bar of solid iron. David braced it beneath his chin and groped for the trigger.

There was light, golden light, and a spray of blood.

David lay on his back, feeling the blood cooling and congealing on his skin.

He could hear a babble of voices and knew they belonged to the souls of the dead in the Field of Reeds. The sound grew louder as his ka leapt free of his body.

Leapt free into the purpling sky.

Into the fading sun.

5. RA

Dawn, as always, *brings new hope.*

As Ra steps from Mandet, the night-time barque, to Mesektet, the Solar Barque, he feels a surge of reinvigoration. He stretches out his aching spine and works his stiff joints, and the cold of the night just gone by eases from his muscles, and the pains and woes of age recede. He does not feel young again – he never will – but neither does he feel so old any more.

Aker, at the helm of Mandet, bids him farewell. "Till this evening, my lord," he says with a toss of his leonine mane of hair.

Ra smiles. "Till then."

The Solar Barque sets sail. The voyage of day begins again.

Aboard the gleaming golden boat are Ra's regular diurnal companions. Maat, at the helm, gives her father a curt nod. Her expression is seldom anything less than grave, although Ra knows his daughter to have a wry sense of humour, which she reveals in unguarded moments. Her doglike companion Ammut squats at her heels, tongue lolling.

Meanwhile sly-eyed Bast is seated amidships on a divan, her upper body vertical, her legs stretched out sideways. Her shape is a languorous L. She purrs softly as Ra approaches and her eyelids close and open in greeting. He loves this daughter too. He loves her most of any of his family, for Bast is beautiful and untalkative and has never caused him any grief. He strokes her head and the cat-goddess preens pleasurably.

Proceeding to the bows, Ra finds Set, who is limbering up for the trials ahead. Set flexes his powerful physique, muscles snaking beneath his startlingly pale skin. He glances round at his great-great-uncle. He puffs a lock of red hair out of his eyes. He returns to his warm-up exercises.

The Solar Barque, the Boat of a Million Years, leaves the eastern gate of heaven, passing between the twin sycamores of turquoise. The river of day runs calm and smooth. The god of the primeval waters, Nun, can be felt beneath the keel, wafting the barque gently on its way.

Then, ahead, a disturbance on the surface. A patch of boiling turbidity from which, all at once, arises the terrible serpent Apophis. It rears from the water, towering above the barque, seething with evil. Its coils thrash and churn. It would swallow the boat. It would destroy the sun and snuff out all life.

But Set is here. Set is ready. His punishment, his penance, is to battle Apophis twice a day, every day. He launches himself at the creature, springing high to grapple with it. Arms around its neck, he strains every sinew to throttle it. Apophis hisses like a whirlwind and snaps its head from side to side in the hope of dislodging its assailant. Set clings on, digging his fingers into its sinuously glittering scales. He claws the serpent's throat open with his bare hands. Blood gushes out in cataracts. Apophis howls and plunges into the river, disappearing into the depths. Pink foam swirls on red water, and on earth the sky is stained with these colours.

Set swims back to the Solar Barque and his great-great-uncle reaches down to helps him aboard. Their gazes meet. Set's eyes are bright red, even brighter and redder than the blood he has just spilled. Ra's eyes are mismatched. The right is a lambent amber yellow, the left a pale pearly grey. This is a distinctive coloration he shares with many of his descendants – Osiris, Isis, Hathor, Horus, the ones he trusts most, the ones he is inclined to favour.

When Set looks into his great-great-uncle's eyes, it is a tangible reminder of his outcast status. He knows he will never be well loved by the senior god of the pantheon. He knows he will always be apart and different.

Ra knows it too, and is saddened. The first saddening of today. The first of many.

"Well fought," says Ra.

Set shrugs. "How much longer must this farce continue? How many more times do I have to slay that thing before you decide I've made amends?"

"For what you did to your brother? Your sentence is not nearly served, Set."

The two gods go their separate ways, and the barque sails on.

Soon a group of elder gods appear on deck: Sobek, Khnum, Ptah, Neith. Of these, only Neith has any vigour and vitality. She marches forward to hail her son.

"Ra," she says, her bows, arrows, and shield clanking. "How goes it?"

"You are strong in the world, mother," says Ra. "So am I."

"As long as those great-great-nephews and nieces of yours bicker, I will prosper," says the goddess of war. Her jaw has a mannish jut to it. Her hair is tightly braided and tied back so that there is no chance it will ever distract her by flapping in her face.

"Their bickering has a purpose beyond simple rivalry," Ra replies. "They must be worshipped, and worship requires sacrifice. The people of the world need to prove themselves worthy of the divine blessings they are given. The surrender of their mortal lives is that proof, and conflict supplies a convenient means of their dying." Ra says these words, but he isn't sure he believes them. Not any more.

"Am I complaining?" Neith's laughter rattles her armaments. "Of course not. I am flushed with power, unlike those pale shadows back there whom I have to spend most of my time with."

The other three elder gods shuffle their feet and look ashamed. They are ghosts of their former selves, sallow and emaciated. It is hard to imagine them ever having received the adoration of humans, ever imbibing the blood of slaughtered beasts and glowing with the flames of the ritual pyres lit in their names. Their ba is all but non-existent. They linger feebly, clinging to the lees of their lives, with little to say for themselves and less to do.

And Ra feels a tiny pang, his second saddening of the day.

For, looking at these four, he knows that even gods may fade. Even gods may die.

Now come his nephew and niece, Shu of the air and Tefnut of the rain, to pay their respects. Shu is an absent-minded sort. He would never remember to visit the barque if Tefnut did not drive him to do so.

These married siblings are joined by their children, Geb of the earth and Nut of the sky, also married.

All four of them, the First Family, make their obeisance to Ra. "As the children and grandchildren of Atum," they say, "from whose swirling chaos the universe was born, we salute you, O Sun God, Ruler of the Ennead."

"Big Chief Blazing Shorts," adds coarse-mannered Geb. His sister-wife digs an elbow in his ribs.

Ra laughs off the jibe, but inwardly laments Geb's insolence.

Thus, bit by bit, is his morning's happiness whittled.

There are other visitors to the Solar Barque during the course of the day. Minor members of the pantheon, lesser gods, a few demons. Ra receives them all civilly, as a ruler must. They are offered hospitality – sweetmeats and wine. There is idle chat. These duties bore Ra and tire him, but he tries not to let it show.

Thoth, his vizier, his dear old friend, he is always glad to see. The two of them repair to the stern, where only Maat may overhear their conversation.

"Tell me something to lift my mood," Ra asks of Thoth.

"You are not dead, Ra," comes the reply. "However dull and dim your life becomes, oblivion is worse. Never forget that."

"Ha!" Ra is almost amused. "I feel a chill, though. Why is that?"

"We are nearing the river's end," says Thoth. "The day is dwindling. Perhaps it is just the cool of the oncoming evening."

"No. No, I think not. It is a chill inside. A prickling in my heart. A cold presentiment. I fear, Thoth. I fear for the future, and don't know why."

Thoth beetles his hoary eyebrows. "We are old, you and I, Ra. Time grows short for us. The future is a strange monster. The less there is of it, the more it frightens."

"Is that all this is? An intimation of death?"

"Only you can know for certain, old friend."

Thoth leaves Ra pondering.

Finally, late in the day, the squabbling siblings come. They are the inheritors, the ones to whom the Earth was given whole and who have carved it up between them, parcelling it into separate dominions.

Osiris and Isis arrive hand in hand, giddy as newly-weds for all that they have been married for eons. Nephthys is with them, and only reluctantly leaves Isis's side to join Set. She much prefers the company of her sister to that of her brother-husband, who greets her coldly as she approaches and who places an arm around her shoulders much as a farmer might place a yoke on an ox's neck. Nephthys simpers in his embrace like a dutiful wife but in her eyes there is a yearning to be elsewhere.

Set and Nephthys's son, Anubis, puts in an appearance, scowling and brooding. Set nods to him. Anubis nods stiffly back, then moves off to stand at a distance from his parents, aloof, arms crossed. The Jackal-Headed One leads a solitary life. His dominion is death, and death is a lonely affair.

Following him comes his cousin and half-brother Horus, who winks at Ra with his one good eye, the left eye being covered by a patch. Horus has his four children in tow – Hapi, Imset, Duamutef and Kebechsenef – an unruly brood of godlings who scamper and brawl around the deck, paying little heed to their elders with whom they frequently and sometimes violently collide.

Set snaps at Horus, "Can't you keep your damn offspring under control?"

Horus glares back at him. There's enough venom in his one eye to fill two. "Want me to rip those balls of yours off again? I'll happily do it, you ginger freak. Come on." He clenches his hand at crotch height, gripping an imaginary pair of testicles. "Just give me an excuse."

"*Try it and I'll gouge your other eye out,*" Set retorts.

"*Loser.*"

"*Moron.*"

"*Liar.*"

"*Fool.*"

None of them stays long. It's a courtesy call, a formality. Ra is the ancient relative they come to see once a day more out of duty than love. They stay a brief while, exchanging pleasantries, managing to mask the divisions between them. They seem ill at ease, however. Perhaps it is the effort of maintaining an illusion of cordiality.

Or perhaps, Ra thinks sombrely, they sense what I sense, that my days are numbered, and it troubles them. Or else, which is worse, it doesn't *trouble them.*

They are soon gone, at any rate. Only Set remains, and that is because he has the second of his daily tasks to fulfil.

Apophis rises once more. The giant serpent, now healed, explodes from the river, and as ever Set leaps to wrestle with it. As ever, he is victorious. Apophis dies again, and for a time the river is all froth and crimson tumult.

And so the voyage is over. The Solar Barque reaches the western gate of heaven and moors there. Ra is by now weighed down with cares. A gloom has well and truly descended on him. He has nothing to look forward to but a night in the netherworld, Mandet drifting along a black river through caverns of utter darkness, the air glacially still, and only Aker for company, a stoic, uncommunicative presence, peering intently ahead at all times, his golden eyes like lamps in a tomb. No sleep, no rest, just a period of deathlike isolation, to counterbalance the brightness and gregariousness of day.

Ra steps off Mesektet and onto Mandet, heavily.

Dusk, as always, brings sorrow.

6. CARAVAN

THE CAMELS SPAT and grumbled, and the children laughed harshly and thrashed them all the harder with their switches. In a long line the beasts of burden picked their way across the desert, with a straggle of goats bleating behind. Their young drivers showed them little mercy.

Occasionally, during a rest stop, one of the fouler-tempered camels might take its revenge and bite. The children seemed to find this funny too. The bitten boy – it was always a boy – would giggle, rub the spot where the camel had sunk its teeth in, then turn on the offending animal and thrash it soundly. It was as if pain, giving it and receiving it, was all a game to them.

The adults of the Bedouin *goum* were no less hardy. They thought nothing of sitting ten, twelve hours in the saddle, remaining perfectly upright despite the swaying, arrhythmic lurch of the camels' motion. Their faces were imperturbable, their skin as finely folded as parchment maps, their eyes full of distance. During travel only the men spoke, and when they did, which was not often, it was to bark an order at the children or make some dusty, sardonic comment to which only the other men were expected to respond.

The women never spoke. At least, not in David's presence, although at night he heard voices coming from their tents and the sound was soft and tinkling, as refreshing as a drink of cool spring water.

This family tribe of Bedouin weren't just nomads, they were also merchants. Three of the camels did not carry people but had strongboxes hanging from their sides, two apiece. Whatever was inside the padlocked steel containers, which were stamped with hieroglyphs, was heavy and clinked metallically. These camels were the first to be unloaded each evening, and the strongboxes were kept overnight in a special tent guarded by men with rifles.

Jewellery? Weapons? Gold coins? Valuable merchandise of some sort, to be traded at the caravan's final destination.

David himself was valuable merchandise too. The ropes binding him told him this, as did the fact that he was never left on his own for a moment. When he needed to relieve himself he was always escorted by at least one armed guard, usually two, and when he was up in the saddle his wrists were secured tightly to the pommel so that he couldn't slide off even by accident. He was fed and he was given water, just enough to hold body and ka together, and he knew that the Bedouin wouldn't be keeping him alive if they didn't feel he was worth something to them. It would be a waste of precious provisions otherwise.

His memory was hazy, the recent past a blur, but little by little he pieced together what had happened.

The *ba* lance had slipped from his grasp at the crucial moment and the shot had gone astray. There had been a victim, but it was not him. Blood had been shed, but not his. The Bedouin caravan had been approaching just as he made his suicide attempt. He had been too preoccupied to hear, and he had, by some drastic fluke, killed not himself but the caravan's lead camel.

The sheikh of the tribe had finally managed, after several attempts, to explain this sorry mishap to him. David knew a smattering of Arabic, but these Bedouin used an unfamiliar dialect, one which had cross-pollinated with some glottal sub-Saharan language. With gesture and dumbshow the sheikh showed him a camel keeling over, and brandished the spent lance to make the point that this was the murder weapon.

So David had deprived them of a camel, and to make up for it they were going to have to sell him somehow. They seemed to have a buyer in mind.

"Osiris!" The sheikh indicated the embroidered emblem which made up part of David's battledress, a pair of phoenix wings enfolding his chest in a feathery embrace. Then the sheikh waved an arm in a southerly direction. "Nephthys! Khartoum!"

DAVID PONDERED ESCAPE. How to do it? He was never alone, never untied, watched at all times by his captors (although "owners" might be a more accurate description). Opportunities to make a bid for freedom seemed few and far between.

Then there was the desert. It was a kind of open-plan jail. Even if he managed to get away from the merchants, perhaps by making a desperate dash while someone's back was turned, he would only end up lost in the wilderness again. It had nearly destroyed him the last time. It would definitely do so this time.

Grabbing a gun, taking a hostage, demanding to be released?

Same problem. Where would he go?

Only one possible solution offered itself.

Steal a camel.

AT NIGHT HE shared a tent with six other men and four boys. It was a thing of rugs and striped blankets, cosy in its way, like a woven-walled room. David's designated sleeping space was right in the middle, and he had to lie there and make himself as comfortable as he could with his wrists tethered to one of the central upright poles, which was embedded in the ground between two of the rugs.

The smell inside the tent was noisome. One of the men did nothing but fart all night long, and all of them, including David, reeked of sweat and bad feet. The noise was pretty horrendous too, since there seemed to be a competition going on to see who could snore the loudest. If predators were roaming out there in the dark, it wasn't the light of the camel-dung campfire that would keep them at bay, it was the raucous massed snoring of the people.

It was horribly reminiscent of a boarding school dormitory. There was even buggery. Almost every night, during the small hours, David would be woken up by the sound of a certain man forcing himself on one of the boys. He would have to listen to several minutes of furtive grunting and groaning, followed by a slap which was presumably intended to remind the unwilling participant to keep quiet about what had been done to him. The boy would then, often as not, cry himself to sleep.

David knew who the rapist was. The man slept in the far right-hand corner of the tent and was a sort of semi-detached uncle, high up in the tribal hierarchy and a close confidant of the sheikh. In other words, too important to be called to account for his misdeeds, even if someone in the *goum* were to pluck up the nerve to denounce him. He had a twisted nose and a lush moustache and had somehow contrived to lose teeth in a diagonally alternating pattern, so that his smile resembled two rows of a chessboard. David would happily knock out all of the other teeth if the chance ever came.

But escape was his priority and he could let nothing interfere with that. Having settled on a plan, he bided his time, waiting till a moonless night came. By now he had recovered from his ordeal in Southern Arabia and regained much of his strength. The caravan had turned due south, and if Khartoum was where they were headed then that put them firmly in Freegypt, between the Nile and the Red Sea. This was the time to get away, before they crossed the border into the Sudan and were back on Nephthysian soil.

His hands were tied back to back, preventing him from reaching the knots with his fingers. There was nothing to stop him, though, from gnawing at them with his teeth.

It was a painstaking process, and at one point a pains-giving process, when a tooth that had been loosened during his beating by the Nephthysians, an upper molar, suddenly fell out. There was a tearing sensation in his gum, and what felt like a jolt of electricity went shooting up through his jaw into his sinuses. He stifled a scream. Blood filled his mouth, and he spat and spat until the wound sealed itself.

Then, in a somewhat more gingerly fashion, he resumed gnawing.

Around him the nocturnal cacophony of farts and snores continued. He froze as a man shouted out something. He'd been spotted. The game was up.

But the shout subsided to a murmur, then a smacking of the lips, a snuffle, then the man was snoring again.

Finally, the knots came loose.

He was free.

Well, almost.

He got up and tiptoed over slumbering bodies that he could barely see in the dark. He trod on someone's hand and expected a yelp of protest, but it was one of the boys and they slept more deeply than the men and were accustomed to physical abuse besides. The boy mumbled, David shushed him, and the boy rolled over and went back to sleep.

He reached the tent flap and eased himself through.

Firelight flickered, revealing all seven of the *goum*'s tents arranged in a semicircle. The goats were clustered at the mouth of the semicircle, and beyond them were the camels, lying with their legs folded under them, spectrally pale, like mountains on a horizon.

To David's left lay the tent where the valuable merchandise was stored. The men on guard looked drowsy. Their rifles drooped towards the earth.

He couldn't risk sneaking past them, however. He would have to circumnavigate the camp and come at the camels from the far side.

He crept away from the campfire, out into the indigo dark. The terrain the caravan was crossing had changed recently. The landscape was no longer rocks and hard-packed earth, but sand, nothing but sand. Scooped, ribbed, undulating, supple sand, mile upon mile of it, wave upon wave. Sand that got everywhere: in your socks, in your hair, up your nose. David had even found grains of it under his foreskin.

Keeping the tents to his right he went in a broad semicircle, slithery-footed on the dune slopes. Finally he began his approach on the camels. He had already singled out the one he was going to take: an elderly male, so beaten and worn down that there was no more obstinacy left in it. This docile creature would, he reckoned, accept an inexperienced rider at the reins and not try to throw him off at the first opportunity.

He checked the sleepy guards again. As he looked, one of them gave in completely to tiredness and slumped to the ground. The man ended up in a sitting position, head bowed over the rifle in his lap.

The other guard turned and eyed his colleague. He muttered something to him, then went over and nudged him with a toe. The sleeping man didn't stir. Another, firmer toe-nudge sent him tumbling over onto his side in a loose heap. The second guard bent and rapped him on the cheek. He looked closer. He straightened up in alarm.

Then David heard it: a soft *twang*. It came from out in the darkness.

At the same moment, he saw the guard clutch his neck and reel. The rifle fell to the sand with a muffled thud. A second later, and no less quietly, the guard fell too.

David hunched down and felt his heart rate pick up and the world grow slow around him. Figures appeared at the periphery of his vision, a couple of dozen of them descending from the brows of the dunes and stealing towards the camp. They wore form-fitting black and moved in two by two formation, each pair swapping the lead with another pair. Their weapons, as far as he could tell, were pistols and short-stemmed crossbows, strictly not *ba* tech.

The first two raiders to reach the camp inspected the downed guards, then signalled the all-clear. The rest came padding in and set up a perimeter around the tent entrance. The camels made a few uneasy grumbles, but the black-clad raiders were so silent and precise in their actions that the beasts weren't unduly disturbed. Two of the raiders went into the tent and came out with one of the strongboxes. They carried it carefully between them, holding it perfectly level. Another two went in, and another. Soon all six strongboxes had been retrieved and the raiders got ready to pull out from the camp with their booty.

Then two things happened at once.

The first was that David felt the barrel of a gun being pressed against the back of his neck.

The second was that a Bedouin man emerged from the tent next door to the one where the strongboxes were kept.

The raiders froze. As did David, for a different reason.

"Stay still," whispered a voice behind him. "Do not speak. Do not even breathe. Or I put a bullet in you."

Meanwhile the Bedouin hitched up his robes and began to relieve himself on the sand. He glanced casually around him and spotted the raiders crouching by the adjacent tent. His urine trickled to a halt mid-flow, spattering onto his feet.

One of the raiders rose and aimed a pistol at the Bedouin, who would no doubt have lifted his hands in surrender if he had been less startled and if his hands had been clasping anything less crucial.

"Shoot," the voice behind David hissed urgently, although the man with the pistol could not possibly have heard. "You have a silencer. Shoot the bastard."

Gunmetal ground into David's nape, and he prayed that if a trigger was going to be pulled in the next few seconds, it wouldn't be this one.

Over in the camp the Bedouin gaped at the raider, while the raider seemed hesitant, unsure whether or not to fire on an unarmed man.

Then the Bedouin let out a beseeching cry.

Then the pistol went off, with an almost apologetic *pfft*.

The Bedouin collapsed. But his cry had been enough. Other Bedouin were roused from their tents. They staggered blearily outside, took stock of the situation. Rifles appeared.

The person holding David at gunpoint yelled out an order in Arabic: "Fall back! Fall back!" Now he knew for sure what he had suspected before, that it was a woman. Her voice, when low, had been husky, of indeterminate gender, but when raised it was clearly, unmistakably, and authoritatively, female.

The raiders obeyed, laying down fire as they retreated with the strongboxes. The Bedouin answered with a volley of bullets, trumping the handguns' silencer-suppressed pops with sharp, loud rifle cracks. Their weapons had greater range and velocity, not to mention accuracy. The raiders started dropping. Meanwhile, the camels upped and fled in terror.

The woman behind David cursed. He heard the rasping squelch of a walkie-talkie channel being opened. The woman barked a command, and somewhere far off a car engine started up. Headlight beams forked through the darkness as the engine revved, getting rapidly louder.

Muzzle flashes flickered in the camp like firefly phosphorescence. Gun smoke drifted. The Bedouin had the majority of the raiders pinned down and were blazing away at them without let-up. The strongboxes had been dropped and the raiders were concentrating on self-defence. Plunder was no longer as important as survival.

Then, cresting a dune with a raucous diesel roar, came a jeep. It skidded to a halt fifty metres from the camp. A man sprang from the passenger seat and clambered back onto the flatbed, where a heavy-calibre machine gun was mounted on swivel bearings. He took up position at the machine gun's controls and started firing. Belt-fed rounds chugged into the chamber and were spat out at the camp, striking sand, tents, and Bedouin indiscriminately. The Bedouin took cover, returning fire as best they could. Several of their shots ricocheted off the jeep, but the machine gun's burping stutter continued unabated. David watched with increasing dismay as the tents again and again fell within its veering arc of discharge, their sides flapping and ripping under the bullet impacts.

Finally he couldn't help himself. "Stop," he told the woman. "Tell them to stop. There are women and children in those tents."

Just a brief hesitation, then she said, "So? I do not care."

"Well, I fucking do."

David leapt to his feet, heedless of the woman and her gun.

"Take one step towards that jeep," she warned, "and I will..."

Ignoring her, he ran headlong into the camp. All the way he expected to feel the smack of a bullet impact in his back. It didn't come. Perhaps the woman had decided that if he wasn't going for the jeep then he couldn't do any harm. Besides, down in the camp there were enough stray bullets flying around to do the job for her.

He lunged into one of the women's tents. There was shrieking and wailing inside, and he saw a wizened grandmother, possibly the oldest person in the *goum*, lying on the rugs with half her face missing. A middle-aged woman was prone over the corpse, sobbing. Others were hoisting up the back of the tent to create a gap to crawl out through. David bent and helped. The girls went first, then their mothers. He urged them to run, go as far as they could as fast as they could into the darkness. They didn't understand his words but they understood his tone. He grabbed the mourning woman and shoved her through the gap. Waiting arms on the other side seized her and bundled her away to safety.

Ducking low, David made for the next tent in line, which happened to be "his" tent.

Only the boys remained inside – and Uncle Chessboard Smile. He was on his knees, holding two of the boys to his chest and cowering behind them. They boys protested and squirmed but Uncle Chessboard Smile had a grip like iron. His human shield wasn't going anywhere.

Bullets whanged and thwacked through the tent's blanket walls. David made a dive for Chessboard, locking an arm around his neck. The Bedouin let go of the boys in order to reach backwards and grapple with David. He clawed at David's face, but he was not the only one with a grip like iron. David clung on, tightening the hold, pushing Chessboard's head forward with one arm and crushing his windpipe with the other. The two boys weighed in to help, grabbing their rapist relative's flailing hands. Chessboard choked and gurgled. His efforts to resist grew feebler. His eyes bugged. His tongue bulged. David did not let up until he heard and smelled bowels loosening. Then, to make doubly certain Chessboard was dead, he twisted the man's neck till it snapped.

Having seen the boys safely out of the camp, David prepared to move to the next tent. Then he noticed that the gunfire had slackened off. The rifles were shooting infrequently and the machine gun wasn't shooting at all. He surveyed the scene. The raiders appeared to have withdrawn completely. He couldn't see them or the jeep anywhere. They were gone, along with the strongboxes. The Bedouin were firing blind into the darkness, more in anger than in the hope of hitting anything.

It was time for him to make a getaway as well. David loped off into the dunes, intending to lie low for a while, then go in search of a camel. The beasts, though terrified, would not have gone far. They were too tame, too institutionalised, to want to live wild. Once everything was calm again, they might well begin to drift back towards the camp. He would intercept them before they go there.

A figure appeared in front of him, a black silhouette like a shadow.

"You," said the woman who had held him at gunpoint. She was holding him at gunpoint again. "A choice. Come with me or I kill you."

Her eyes glinted in the distant light of the campfire, as did the barrel of her pistol.

David weighed his options, such as they were.

"I'll come with you," he said, as though it was a decision.

7. ZAFIRAH

IT WAS ANOTHER kind of caravan, albeit a modern one consisting of a motley assortment of jeeps and other four-wheel drives, the majority of them converted to carry heavy-calibre machine guns and RPG launchers. They filed across the desert in a ragged line, travelling mostly at night. By day the vehicles would be parked in the lee of a rock formation or the shade of a palm oasis and have camouflage netting pulled over them. Their occupants would then sleep, or play cards, or roll cigarettes and aromatic joints and drink endless glasses of sweet mint tea, which David would share with them even though to him it tasted like liquid chewing gum.

After days of walking followed by weeks on camel back, David was finding it a relief simply to be in motorised transport. A bench seat in the rear of a canvas-topped Luaz ZT off-roader was the plushest armchair imaginable. The rumble of a Ukrainian-built engine was a lullaby. For a large portion of each journey he slept soundly, head angled against the canvas awning, feet perched on a case of grenades.

Zafirah, the group's leader, seemed amused by this.

"Stiff?" she asked him one morning as he stood beside the car massaging a crick out of his neck. "Perhaps I could arrange to get you a pillow."

"Sheets and blankets too, if you don't mind," David replied.

She didn't quite laugh but the skin around her lustrous green-and-brown eyes did crinkle slightly.

"You don't behave like a captive at all," she said. "You seem so calm."

"Am I a captive, Zafirah?"

"That depends. Maybe."

"Only, I've been taken prisoner twice in the past month or so, so I'm getting to be something of an expert. And this doesn't feel like captivity to me. You've even given me a change of clothes." His uniform was gone, replaced by a borrowed shirt and jeans.

"So if this isn't captivity, what does it feel like?"

David frowned. "Hard to put into words. It's more like you're letting me come along for the ride, rather than forcing me to. Besides, Freegyptian guerrillas aren't renowned for kidnapping foreigners, as far as I'm aware."

"Perhaps not. But we are always looking for ways to fund our efforts. What if we're taking you somewhere in order to ransom you back to the British army?"

"Then," said David, "I say go right ahead, and I hope you get a decent sum for me."

THEY WERE MEMBERS of the Liberators of Luxor, one of the dozen or more rogue paramilitary factions at large within Freegypt. Ostensibly the country was under the rule of the Secular People's Front, the dominant political party in the government, but it and Prime Minister Bayoumi controlled little more than a swathe of the north-east. South of Cairo all the way down to Abu Simbel, everything became a broiling free-for-all, particularly along the Nile's fertile banks. Up in Lower Freegypt, around the Nile Delta, they were welcome to fiddle about with democracy if they liked. They could do as they pleased there in the north, with their industry and their urbanisation and their trading ports. But down south, in the Upper part of the country, where poverty was rife and most people lived at subsistence level, democracy remained a notional concept at best, a nice idea but as unaffordable as silk. There was either lawlessness or there were warlords imposing their own regional dominion, which amounted to the same thing.

A land without gods is a land without order. This was the collective international consensus on Freegypt, and most Freegyptians would admit that their nation was not without its chaotic elements.

But look at the rest of the world, they would reply. *Look at the divine power blocs and their constant warring. Look at the death and madness that ravages the entire globe. And then tell us that lands* with *gods are doing any better.*

ZAFIRAH HAD NO surname that David knew of – none that she would tell him, at any rate. She seemed fascinated by *his* surname, however. She would use it at almost every opportunity. "West*ween*ter," laying marvellous, elongating emphasis on the middle syllable. He liked to watch her closely when she said it. Her lips would purse, then part in a shape that could be as equally a smile as a sneer, before coming together again at the end as if to kiss. Her soft accent made the fusty Englishness of the name exotic. In her mouth it became weird, unfamiliar, a kind of incantation. It seemed to mean something to her that it didn't to anyone else.

He also liked to watch Zafirah closely when she wasn't saying his name, or even talking to him. When she was ordering her men around, for instance. She would stand and issue rapid-fire instructions, her hand cocked on her hip, her head raised at an angle – jauntiness and haughtiness combined, a perfect blend of opposites. The men scurried when she spoke. They feared her but, more than that, they were besotted with her.

David could see why. It was the same reason he liked watching her so much. Zafirah had long sleek black hair, a figure made for the tight khaki shirts and chinos she liked to wear, and squarish features which offset one another nicely, the straight nose complementing the full lips, the full lips complementing the firm chin, and so on.

Above all she had those eyes, the green starring the brown of their irises, jade on topaz. She didn't surround them thickly with kohl, as all the fashionable women in England did. She left them bare, unframed, open, and their paleness contrasted hauntingly with the dark tawniness of her complexion.

No, he didn't feel like her captive. Not in the conventional sense.

But in another sense he did.

SHE CAUGHT HIM one afternoon studying the strongboxes which the Liberators had stolen from the Bedouin. It was five days since the raid on the camp, and the strongboxes hadn't yet been broached. They were stacked in the back of one of the cars, padlocks still in place.

"Curious?"

David jumped. He wasn't a nervy sort but she could move stealthily, could Zafirah.

"You lost men to get hold of these," he said. "Whatever's in them is clearly worth a great deal. I hope it is, at any rate."

She pointed to the markings. "Do you not read hieroglyph? Or did you stare out of the window all the time you were supposed to be learning it at school?"

"Mine's pretty rusty. I see the ideograms for 'god' and 'servant' joined together, meaning 'priest', so I'm assuming there's something *ba*-blessed inside. But as for the rest of it... Those are the names of the gods, aren't they? And the sign of a necklace can stand for any number of things – strength, happiness, gold. I can't put it all together in a way that makes sense."

"It's a puzzle for you, then. A challenge. You strike me as a man who likes challenges."

You're a challenge and I like you, David thought.

Then, to his shock, he realised he had actually said it out loud.

Zafirah blinked slowly, a deprivation of treasures.

"I don't think that's..." she began.

"Appropriate? Relevant? Proper? You're right, you're so right, absolutely. I didn't say it. It never happened."

Stupid, stupid, stupid...

David hated how easily embarrassed he could sometimes be. He knew he didn't lack courage, but in certain awkward situations he would always retreat in a hurry, taking refuge behind a barricade of diffidence or dry humour. Better to do that than press on with an attack that might leave him exposed, vulnerable.

"Well," said Zafirah. "Yes, then. Good."

To her relief, and David's, one of her men shouted for her attention.

"I must go," she said, turning away. "Something about the weather."

She paused, then turned back.

"You ran into that Bedouin camp, under heavy fire, to save people," she said. "People who'd been going to sell you to the Nephthysians."

"Yes. And?"

"Nothing. But as we're talking about challenges – why?"

"Seemed like the right thing to do. Seemed worth it."

She gazed at him. "Most challenges are," she said finally, and walked away.

"SOMETHING ABOUT THE weather" turned out to be a sandstorm blowing in from the east. But rather than batten down the hatches and stay put, the Liberators leapt into their cars and hared off in convoy.

The sky dimmed in an eerie twilight, the air browning as though burnt. David peeked through the rear flap of the ZT's awning to see a wall of dust approaching, like hills on the move. It filled the horizon, rising higher as it swept closer. It was coming fast, faster than the cars could go, and it gave off a monstrous moan, which David could hear even above the off-roader's roar.

The sandstorm engulfed the tail end of the convoy. One after another, vehicles were swallowed into its billowing mass, disappearing from sight. When it reached the ZT there was a *whump* that rocked the car on its shock absorbers. The awning clenched like a startled heart. Ahead and behind, visibility was reduced to a few yards. Sand swarmed and scratched all around, hissing like a million emery boards. The wind slammed itself in from every side, knocking the off-roader about. David clung onto the roll bars for support, while the driver and passenger up front, securely seatbelted, chortled and whooped. Their radio transceiver jabbered constantly, members of the group keeping one another updated on their whereabouts and making wild jokes about the driving conditions. As long as each car remained in view of the next in line, nobody would get lost.

They pressed on for hours through the seething storm. The ZT's windscreen wipers worked tirelessly, clumping the sand at the edges of the glass, until all at once they were no longer needed. The sky, like a miracle, cleared. The sandstorm had blown itself out.

The Liberators regrouped. Zafirah came over to the ZT just as a jolted and dazed David climbed out.

"Bet you didn't sleep through *that*," she said.

David clapped dust off his hair and clothing. The awning had been anything but airtight. "You lot have a strange sense of fun."

"Fun? You think that's why we did what we just did?"

"Looked that way to me."

"The sandstorm was cover. We travel at night for the same reason. So we won't be seen."

"By who? The Nephs? The Setics? Us? But Freegypt's a no-fly zone. There are no spotter planes here, no Saqqara Birds, none of that. It's not allowed."

"That's where you're wrong. We believe the Nephthysians are keeping an eye on us all the time. And not only them. We have to be incredibly careful."

"Paranoia. This is the only place on earth the major powers aren't interested in. The gods couldn't agree among themselves who should own the land where their worship first sprang up, so they decided it was best if none of them had it. Meaning none of the divine power blocs can lay claim to it. Even spying on Freegypt is against international law. Not just that, it's tantamount to heresy."

"Freegypt, the Unholy Land," said Zafirah with a trace of sarcasm. "The world's blind spot."

"Yes!" said David. He looked at her. "Or... no?"

She shook her head. "Not any more."

"What's happened?"

"More like what's happen*ing*. Have you not heard of Al Ashraqa? The Lightbringer?"

"The who?"

"Evidently not. I suspect the Hegemony governments know about him, even if they haven't shared that knowledge with the public. The Nephthysians have certainly heard of him, the Setics too. They've heard of him and they're very, very scared of him."

"The Lightbringer. Who is he?"

"A man."

"Does he have another name? A proper one?"

"He does, but very few people know it."

"What is he then, some local warlord with ambitions? He wants to take over all of Freegypt, and the Nephs are scared he'll destabilise the country even further and trouble will spill over the borders into their territory?"

"No."

"Could you be any more enigmatic?"

"Does it annoy you?"

"Frankly yes."

"Then I will try to be as enigmatic as I can possibly be," Zafirah said, and for the very first time he heard her laugh. It was taunting laughter but he liked it nonetheless.

"So you've massaged my curiosity and now you're going to leave me dangling, so to speak," David said.

"Yes."

"You could at least give me some clue about him."

"Why? You'll find out all you need to know soon enough."

"Eh?"

"Where do you think we are headed, David West*ween*ter? We are headed for the Valley of the Kings, and there we are going to meet the Lightbringer."

8. LUXOR

IN A RESTAURANT on Luxor's Corniche, which ran alongside the Nile, they ate shish kebab and pigeon stuffed with rice and washed it down with ice-cold Alexandrian beer. Feluccas plied the river, their lateen-rigged sails spread to catch the syrupy evening breeze. Mopeds farted up and down the street, swerving around donkey carts and battered old Mercedes Lotus taxis and filling the air with their two-stroke tang.

Luxor, the village-with-aspirations city, teemed. According to Zafirah it had never been so busy, not even during its heyday, back when Freegypt was more stable and tourists used to flood in from all over to view the temples and monuments and breathe in the dusty atmosphere of the cradle of the world's religion. Nowadays only a trickle of visitors came. You hardly saw a sunburned white face any more, and chances were it belonged to a journalist, down here to write some tone-piece on the Upper Freegypt "crisis". Either that or an executive from a holiday company on a jaunt sponsored by the national tourist board. The difference was easy to spot. The journalist came alone and looked intrepid. The holiday company exec came with an armed escort and looked scared.

"Visit Freegypt," David said. "You *probably* won't get caught in the crossfire."

Zafirah nodded as though not seeing the flippancy behind his deadpan tone. "It must be said, things have got a lot better. There are still territorial skirmishes between the militias now and then, but for the past three years we have known something close to peace. The south and the north are trading along the Nile again, and Cairo is supplying us with essentials such as medicine and baby milk, which it withheld during the worst of the fighting."

"You think one day this country will be whole again?" David asked, swatting away one of the many flies that were buzzing around his meal.

"I don't think it. I know it."

"Why?"

"Same reason Luxor is full right now."

"The bloke we've all come to see. Your mystery man, the Lightbringer. About whom you're not prepared to tell me any more. Or are you?"

Zafirah turned her gaze across the river, looking over towards the west bank, the place of tombs and dead pharaohs. Several of her men were clustered around a nearby table, two of them playing senet, the others looking on and offering advice on moves. One of the spectators made a coarse remark and everyone guffawed. Amid the general hilarity the tabletop was nudged and the game pieces were scattered across the board, much to the players' annoyance.

By the way Zafirah smiled, David had the feeling the remark had had nothing to do with the game and a lot to do with him and her.

"OK," he said, sensing a change of subject was in order. "Let me ask you this then. How does a nice girl like you end up in charge of a band of paramilitaries?"

"Am I a nice girl?"

"Educated, thoughtful, brave..."

"I could turn it around. How does a nice boy like you end up as a paratrooper, fighting on behalf of god, goddess, pharaoh, and country?"

"Because I enlisted," David said. "Because I felt I had to. Because... of other reasons."

"Personal reasons."

"More or less."

"So a sense of duty, coupled with a private need. Two motivations, inner and outer, converging."

"Yes."

"Same here," said Zafirah. "For one thing, I come from these parts, so signing up with a force that stands against outside aggression seemed a sensible thing to do. When I was a girl there were times when Luxor was under attack from three sides at once – the Red Sea Fellahin from the east, the Aswan Ulama from the south, and the Integrationist Army from the west. The Fellahin wanted to embrace us with their communist utopia, the Ulama wanted to convert us to their vestigial, politicised version of Islam, and the Integrationists, funded by Libya, wanted to incorporate us into a segment of the country they consider belongs to the Nephthysian states. Luxor didn't want to be any of these things. It just wanted to be Luxor. You've seen the price it paid for that."

On the way into the city David had passed countless buildings that were either husks pocked with shell holes or just plain ruins. They were still inhabited, many of them, stretched tarpaulins doing the job that missing roofs used to, corrugated iron for doors, sheets of polythene for windows.

"To preserve itself, to resist these attacks," Zafirah went on, "Luxor had to form its own guerrilla army."

"The Liberators."

"Yes. They had nothing, to begin with. No weapons, no vehicles, nothing except manpower and a will to survive. But with guile and subterfuge they captured enemy equipment and little by little gathered together the resources they needed. Whichever direction an assault came from, they were ready to meet and repel it. I grew up with the sound of gunfire and shelling. Year upon year, some faction or other would make a play for Luxor, usually around harvest time. I'd go to school watching raw recruits doing drill in the public parks, knowing many of them would be dead by the autumn. Boys and girls only slightly older than me were learning how to strip and clean a rifle, how to manufacture a roadside bomb, how to disable an enemy vehicle using only breezeblocks and barbed wire. This all seemed normal to me, commonplace, a way of life. Of course it did. I was a child, and as a child you take everything in your stride. I knew that Luxor had to be protected. I expected that one day I would be doing the protecting myself."

David caught the waiter's eye and ordered another round of beers. Zafirah was distantly related to the restaurant owner – a second cousin? – and as far as David could tell everything was on the house.

"My father, however, was keen for me to be a teacher," she continued. "He was determined that I should go to university, most likely in Cairo. I had a flair for languages. He saw me as an English teacher, perhaps after spending a couple of years in your country perfecting my syntax and grammar. He had high hopes for me, his only child. That was why he named me Zafirah. It means victorious, successful. That was also why he fought with the Liberators of Luxor, to keep me safe and give me the future he dreamed I would have. He was a Liberator commander, in fact. He was there at Karnak, nine years ago, seeing off a major offensive by the Fellahin…"

Zafirah's eyes glistened.

"Karnak," she said. "Its ancient name was Ipet-Isut: 'The most perfect of places'. Not any more."

David recalled seeing the temple at Karnak, on Luxor's outskirts. It had been devastated, its pylons and obelisks toppled, its hypostyle halls reduced to fields of shattered columns.

The fresh beers arrived and Zafirah took a swig. "The Fellahin nearly overwhelmed us that time. We won. We lost Karnak itself and hundreds of our soldiers, but we won."

"Your father…?" David asked, knowing the answer.

"The Fellahin had a Scarab tank. They'd captured it off the Integrationist Army, along with a priest who was being forced to perform the rites to keep recharging its *ba* cells. The tank was cutting a swathe through our ranks, scything them down with its blaster nozzles. Long-range conventional weapons couldn't pierce its armour, and it wasn't letting anyone get close enough to do anything at short range. My father found himself a shoulder-mounted rocket launcher and a horse. He rode at the tank, screaming at the top of his lungs. The tank took out the horse from under him. Took off my father's legs as well. But he'd got within a stone's throw of it, and that was all he needed. Somehow he managed to sit up. Somehow he managed to fire the rocket. The tank went up in a great ball of *ba* energy, vaporising everything within a two hundred foot radius, including a large number of Fellahin... and my father."

"A hero."

"Undoubtedly. But to me, also, a coward. Because he was my father. He should not have sacrificed himself. He should have lived so that he could continue to be my father and love me and my mother and look after us. He was a coward to throw away his life, when the heroic thing to do would have been come home alive."

"There are causes that matter more than individuals."

"You believe that," Zafirah said with a caustic laugh. "I suppose I believe it too. But not when I was eighteen."

"Your father saved the city, and you. He was giving you the future he promised he would."

"Not like that, though. I didn't want it like that." She sighed. "Anyway, it was impossible now. University? England? How could I even consider it when I had a new goal in life? One future had replaced another. I couldn't become a teacher. I had shoes to fill. The Liberators were down by hundreds of troops and one great, inspirational leader. How could I do anything else but volunteer my services and help make up the numbers that had been lost?"

"You make it sound like it wasn't a choice."

"It wasn't. The instant my father died, it was a calling."

With a wince, Zafirah finished her beer. David had the impression she hadn't revealed this much about her past to anyone in a long time. Alcohol was a factor, but it helped, too, that he was a foreigner and still something of a stranger. Often it was easier to unburden yourself to someone you didn't know too well.

Christians in the old days would pour their hearts out to their priests, telling them things they wouldn't have dared admit to their nearest and dearest.

David decided to make it a two-way street. "Five years ago I was helping to run a company with a multimillion-europound turnover," he said. "I was chauffeured to work every morning in a Rolls Royce Silver Ka. I entertained clients at five-star restaurants. I lived in a townhouse in Kensington, just around the corner from the Harrods Pyramid. All this by the age of twenty-five."

"And you gave it up for an officer's commission and paltry pay," Zafirah said. "Or did you lose it all and join the army because you were out of other options? Either way, that makes you a fool."

"Harsh."

"Although in one case slightly less of a fool than the other."

"Which one?"

"Which did you do?"

"Gave it up, voluntarily."

"That's the one. Because...?"

"Because, in the first place, none of it was my achievement," David said, smarting somewhat. "I inherited my position on the board of directors. I didn't have to work for it and earn it. The company was founded by my great-grandfather and the job of running it has been passed on through the generations like a hand-me-down suit."

"And what was this job? What did you actually do?"

He gestured at the nearby game of senet. "That."

She frowned exaggeratedly. "Play board games?"

"Make them. Specifically, senet boards and pieces and casting sticks. AW Games? Heard of them? That's us. Named after my great-grandfather, Archibald Westwynter, who took out the first and only worldwide patent on senet. This was back at the turn of the last century, during the Divine Diaspora, just when Carter, Carnavon and all the other evangelising archaeologists were busy bringing the gods of Old Egypt to the rest of the world. My great-grandfather was swept up in the fervour just like everyone else. He was mad keen on board games so he set about trying to fathom the rules of senet. There seem to be as many versions of the game as there are papyrus records mentioning it. Old Archibald read them all, synthesised them into one, and copyrighted that version, taking the game out of the public domain and firmly into his own hands. Then he started manufacturing copies and selling them, and in next to no time he was a millionaire. My family's been in the business of flogging senet ever since."

"I'd have thought that was a fun way to make a living."

"Hardly. The company's so big now it virtually runs itself. Junior executives make sure the suppliers keep supplying the raw materials we need as cheaply as possible and the factories keep turning out the required number of units per month. All the person at the top has to do is oversee the junior executives and count the profits and check the balance sheets to see that no one's ripping us off. That and mount the occasional intellectual property lawsuit against copycats and rivals. A trained monkey could do it, let alone a graduate with a degree in Economics and Business Studies."

"So you hated it."

"Hated's too strong. I got tired of it. At the start there was a feeling of heritage, of family responsibility, but it palled pretty quickly. After that, it was just drudgery. I suppose I could have stuck it out. Grinned and bore it. After all, if it was good enough for my dad, and his dad, it ought to have been good enough for me. But then…"

David paused, waiting to be prompted. This was the hard part of his story, mirroring the part about Zafirah's father in her story. He wanted to be sure she didn't fail to notice the equivalence.

"Then?" she said.

"My brother died," he said. "Younger brother by four years. Steven. He was a midshipman aboard HPMS *Immortal*. A dreadnought. She went down with all hands during the Battle of the Aegean. Torpedoed by a Setic Crocodile-class hunter-killer sub that had sailed down through the Bosporus to help out the Neph fleet. She sank in three minutes flat, according to eyewitnesses. Holed below the waterline. No one aboard stood a chance. A nine-hundred-strong crew, all gone. And the *Immortal* was just one of eighteen Osirisiac ships that were lost that day."

"Yet the Hegemony still won the battle."

"A Pyrrhic victory, like your Liberators at Karnak. Gained at such a price, you wonder if it was worth it. There was talk in government of approaching the Nephs and Setics with a peace plan after that. Pressure groups waged campaigns, saying we couldn't afford too many more Aegeans. The Nephs seemed amenable to the idea. They made the right noises, anyway. But of course it all came to nothing. All the high priests and holy royal advisors in Europe were counselling against peace, saying it was contrary to the will of Isis and Osiris. The Horusites were dead set against it, too. Jeb Wilkins threatened sanctions and trade embargos and the like. Good ol' Pastor-President Wilkins. Called a peace plan 'selling the cow to buy five magic beans'. And as for the Setics, the Commissariat of Holy Affairs forbade the Afro-Arabian Synodical Council even from considering the idea, so the Nephs, of course, bent the knee and complied, because that's the Bi-Continental Pact for you."

"An opportunity lost," said Zafirah.

David made a wry face. "It's out of our hands, isn't it? Whether or not we humans want war, the gods always do. It's their will, and if we didn't do their bidding we'd lose their favour, and that's unthinkable. They fight among themselves; therefore we have to too. Osiris and Isis will never forgive Set for what he did, so Europe will always be at loggerheads with Russia and China, and with Africa and the Middle East as well, because of Nephthys's love for Set. And the United States will always back Europe up because Horus is a good son, loyal to his parents, and loathes Set. Anubis isn't that fond of Set either, so Japan and South-East Asia are forever snapping at China's rear, while South America's gone to hell because Horus's kids can't see eye to eye on anything. The situation's never going to improve. We've had non-stop war for a century and we'll probably never not have war. So..." He shrugged. "So one naval battle, however disastrous, is hardly likely to be the start of a sea change in global affairs. You can applaud people for mentioning suing for peace, for even thinking the idea, but you know it's never going to happen."

"Very fatalistic," said Zafirah.

"Just realistic. Geopolitics is theopolitics, and there's nothing we can do about it."

"You don't think humankind has any say in its own destiny?"

"Collectively? None at all. Individually? I'm not so sure. Look at me. I changed my course, didn't I? Joined the army. Felt I had to do something more practical with my life, something that served a higher purpose, something that would actually count. Steven's death…"

A bitter time. A dark patch in David's memory, like an ink-stained page in a book, or a long, cloudy season. His mother withdrawn, uncommunicative, often heavily sedated. Spending far too much of the day in Steven's empty bedroom, which was pristine, just as he'd left it the morning he drove off to Dartmouth to volunteer. A shrine to him. Either that or she was visiting an actual shrine, the local temple to Isis, where she'd offer sacrifices of milk and bread and pray to the Protector of Children for strength and guidance. Jack Westwynter, meanwhile, going through the motions of his life, walking as though in a dream. Drinking. Drinking slowly, steadily, stalwartly, from breakfast through till midnight. Each of them, husband and wife, struggling to fathom why Steven's death had happened and what either of them could have done to prevent it happening. Each, with hooded, accusing stares, blaming the other, and at the same time accepting the other's blame, feeling it might be merited. And David staying at the periphery of it all, leaving his parents to deal with their grief in their way while he dealt with his in his. Resenting Steven. Steven, for being such a wayward, rebellious sod. Steven, for turning his back on the golden opportunities he'd been presented with and going off to fight a war that would have no end. Steven, for being so…

So…

So *right*.

"I saw it," he said to Zafirah. "I saw it in a flash on the way to work one morning. This was maybe a month after we got the letter of notification from the Admiralty, along with Steven's posthumous medal, a Golden Bee for, I don't know, Bravery While Drowning or whatever. I saw that Steven had had the right idea after all. Up till then I'd spent my life thinking he was a born pain in the arse, always doing the opposite of what he should, always going against the grain. Why be such a troublemaker? Why rock the boat? But then it struck me. He hadn't joined the navy to get away from his family and shirk his responsibilities. He'd done it so that he could be himself, not what someone else wanted him to be."

"And you felt you needed that too," said Zafirah.

"That's it. That's pretty much it. Nail on the head. All my life, everyone else had been making choices for me. Now it was my turn to choose. So I tapped on the glass partition in the Roller. I told the chauffeur we weren't going to the office. I had him take a right turn at the Howard Carter Memorial instead of a left. Pretty soon we were outside a recruitment bureau. And that was that."

"The poor little rich boy signed up with the army and started jumping out of aeroplanes. I bet Mummy and Daddy weren't pleased about that."

"Furious."

"One son killed in action, now the other looking like he wanted to go the same way..."

"My father tried to pay them to de-enlist me. Offered them who knows how much. They wouldn't take it. They didn't need the money. They needed the warm bodies."

"But were you being selfless or selfish?"

"Honestly?" David frowned. "I don't know. A bit of both, probably. What I do know is, I make a decent soldier. The army certainly thought so, packing me off to Sandhurst straight away for six months to earn my commission. That shows confidence in me, and I deserve it. This is one job I can do with almost no doubts about my motives or capabilities. I enjoy it – the comradeship, the regimented life, the sense of purpose, all of it. This is, I think, what I'm meant for, and I'll do it for as long as I can. I'm content with that."

"Even though, as you point out, the war is unlikely to end?" Zafirah said. "Even though taking part in it has come close to killing you?"

David pondered this. "Better to do what you want to do and be happy than do what you don't and be unhappy. That's what Steven showed me. And hey..."

He raised his beer bottle.

"I'm still here, aren't I?"

LATER, THERE WAS a moment. Just a moment. Zafirah had scored them accommodation in a fleapit hotel opposite the Medinat Habu temple. Her Liberators of Luxor staggered drunkenly to bed. She and David were the last two left standing. The time came for them to say goodnight and go off to their separate rooms. Or perhaps not.

They had exchanged truths about themselves over the meal. They'd reached out to each other, tendering painful reminiscences like olive branches. There was, now, something established between them, although David could not say for sure what it was. Not quite intimacy but almost.

They faced each other in the flickeringly lit corridor. Zafirah looked up at him. He noticed a stippling of downy hair across her upper lip, a moustache so thin and faint it could only be seen at this proximity. It wasn't a turn-off. If anything, the opposite. He almost put out a hand to touch her. He almost lowered his face to kiss her. He sensed it would be OK if he did. It would be the most natural thing in the world.

A moment.

Zafirah shied away.

"Big day tomorrow," she said, heading across creaking floorboards to her room. "We need our sleep."

The door closed behind her.

David felt the temptation to go over and knock on it.

But the temptation wasn't strong enough. It was a seed that needed deeper soil.

He went to bed. Mosquitoes whined around him infuriatingly all night long.

9. PALACE

THERE ARE WORLDS *within worlds within worlds. A god may be in any of them and all of them. A god may, to take an example, be voyaging aboard his Solar Barque, that aspect of him fully present there, conversing, laughing, brooding. He may at the same time be elsewhere, in another aspect. To be a god is not to be limited to one specific location or moment. Even the least among the Pantheon may manifest in two or more places at once, and Ra is anything but the least among the Pantheon.*

Ra is at the palace of Osiris and Isis. He stands in a courtyard that is both as large as might be imagined and as large as can be imagined. Colonnades surround him in a rectangle, leading to halls, which lead to countless other halls. The columns are topped with palm-leaf capitals. Their sides are plated with electrum. Garlands of white jasmine are wreathed around them.

At the centre of the courtyard a fountain plays, and in its crystal-clear arcs and jets of water can be seen glimpses of life on earth. Images of humans appear and disappear, shimmering within this limpid liquid screen. A baby being born. A child at school. A pair of young lovers, coupling. A man and woman getting married. A worker receiving a promotion. A mother paying tribute at a temple.

A grandfather on his deathbed. Fleeting moments, there then gone. Like human lives. Over in a blink.

Osiris and Isis enter the courtyard hand in hand. At home they prefer to go naked, apart from their headdresses, which are things of golden light that float above them rather than things that are worn, more halo than hat. Osiris bears the Atef crown, a double-plumed mitre with a small solar disc at the tip. Isis's headdress shifts between a throne and a vulture, depending on which angle it is viewed from.

The couple kneel in obeisance to their great-great-uncle.

"You honour us with your presence, O Giver of Life," says Osiris.

Isis claps her hands. "Mead!" she commands. "Olives! Dates! Figs! Okra!"

The victuals are brought in immediately on salvers, which are carried by childlike creatures, darting, nebulous beings, sibilant-footed and with something of the bird of prey about them.

The three gods sit, eat and drink.

"You are heavy-hearted, Great-Great-Uncle," Isis says at last, once the obligations of both host and guest have been discharged – stomachs are full, cups are empty. "Tell us what is on your mind."

Ra heaves a sigh. "In truth I do not know where to begin."

"So many sorrows?"

"Just one, but it is formless and seems to have neither head nor tail nor middle. I cannot fathom the shape of it."

"Is it us, All-Father?" asks Osiris. "Your family? That would be my guess." Across Osiris's bare skin can be seen a series of fierce red scars. One encircles his arm, just below the shoulder. Another rings his neck. Several crisscross his torso. His body was torn asunder, split into fourteen pieces, and those pieces flung to different locations across what was once called Egypt. They were eventually reunited, the flesh fused together again, but the imprint of the ghastly dismemberment remains. Osiris possesses a perfect physique, gorgeous in itself. The scars add a strange, savage beauty of their own.

"Our disagreements have always pained you, Ra," Isis says, taking up her brother-husband's theme. "I see it in both of your eyes when

*you watch us. Your sun eye dims. Your moon eye wanes. You wish
we could learn to set aside our differences and live in harmony."*

"That may be it," says Ra. "I had thought myself resigned to
your endless grudges and enmities, but perhaps, in my dotage, I am
finding them more upsetting than I used to."

The word dotage *sparks a flurry of polite protest from the
married siblings:* no, no, you are not old, your mind is as sharp as
ever, you have many an eon left in you.

Ra swats the supportive comments aside. "It aggrieves me that the
very act which was intended to beget unity has merely exacerbated
the divisions between you. When the First Family handed control
of the earth to all of you, it was meant to bring you together, a
shared responsibility. Instead, it seems to have had the opposite
effect, providing you with yet another bone of contention."

"It is early days still," Isis points out. "Barely a century has
passed since the First Family finally destroyed the last of the
other gods. A hundred years – you might say that our reign is
only in its infancy. Perhaps in another hundred years things will
have settled down."

Osiris looks unconvinced. "I would never wish to contradict my
beloved bride, She At Whose Teat Every Newborn Suckles," he
says. "However, I, for one, cannot foresee a time when I shall not
hold my brother Set in utter contempt. How can I contemplate
forgiving what he did to me, let alone forgetting? That son of a
hyena tried to overthrow me. He tricked me into a coffin he'd had
made for me. He told me it was a gift, built to fit only me. I climbed
in, he slammed the lid and nailed it down, and then he threw the
coffin into the Nile and left me to drown. And that was just the
start of it."

*Isis pats her husband's knee. She has heard this tirade of his
a thousand thousand times. Osiris never tires of it, nor of the
righteous indignation it allows him to feel.*

"You have to admit, my husband, it was partly your own fault,"
she says, *in a tone of gentle wifely mockery.* "It was rather obvious
that our brother was setting you up for something. Do you not
know Set? Deceit is second nature to him."

"Pardon me for being so trusting!" Osiris snaps. "You might have seen a trap. All I saw was a gesture of fraternal kindness."

"But you knew how jealous Set was of you. You knew how he resented the way the people of Egypt loved and worshipped you. Anyway, you weren't stuck in that coffin for long. I came and found you at Byblos, on the Lebanese shore. The moment I heard about a mystical, miraculous tree growing there, I knew it was you. I took the coffin back to Egypt and was preparing to give you a proper burial..."

"When Set turned up again," says Osiris, "and snatched the coffin and cut me up into pieces." Reliving the memory brings a hardness to his face and voice. "Do you know what that feels like? Trust me, you don't want to."

"But then we found you again, dear. Nephthys and I. We searched high and low and we gathered all the bits of you together and we made you whole once more."

"Nearly whole." Osiris peers sullenly down at his lap, where used to reside the one piece of his body that the two goddesses failed to recover. A fish devoured his penis. Now in its place a wooden phallus has been fitted. Handsomely proportioned, a fine specimen of polished cedar, but not, of course, the real thing. A fully functioning substitute but not the same.

"And I," says Ra, "breathed life back into you, so that you and Isis might lie together again, an event from which issued a son. The tale has a happy ending, Osiris. Harm was done but not, I feel, irreparable harm."

"Not irreparable!?" scoffs his great-great-nephew. "I have a fake cock that might argue otherwise."

"Well, I have no complaints in that department," says Isis with a sly smile. "None at all."

The comment soothes her husband. "Thank you, my love," says the ever-uxorious Osiris. "I live to please you. But even so, were it not for Set I would be intact, a whole person."

"And Set is doing his best to atone for it," says Ra. "It and many other crimes. Can you not be content with that? Can you not simply let the matter lie now?"

Osiris considers the suggestion – for all of a second.

"By killing me Set condemned me to be ruler of the dead," he says. "It's a position I am honoured to hold and I discharge my duties gladly."

What duties? *Ra thinks to himself.* Anubis does all the work. You are nominally in charge but it's your nephew who actually supervises the labourers in the Field of Reeds.

"But," Osiris goes on, "it's something I'd rather have accepted by choice than had thrust upon me. Given that and Set's other offences against me, am I willing to let bygones be bygones with the so-called Lord of the Desert? No." He thumps his fist on the bench. "No I am not."

"And in the meantime," says Ra, "down on earth, humankind is engulfed in a maelstrom of conflict, largely because you and Set cannot sort things out between you."

"So be it," says Osiris. "The mortals worship us, hence they must act in accordance with our wishes and desires. That is the way it is and must be."

Spoken with finality. No room for compromise.

Ra stands and takes his leave. Osiris and Isis escort him off the premises with every courtesy and good wish.

Ra is back on the Solar Barque. Ra is a single being in a single place. He always has been.

Maat, at the tiller, says, "My lord? All is well?"

Sombrely Ra nods. "I now know what I have to do. It is a hard undertaking, perhaps an impossible one, but I must attempt it anyway. Somehow I must end my descendants' warring. It has all gone far enough. I must unite them in peace."

Maat smiles to herself, a calm, wise smile. Ra has decreed it. So will it come to pass.

Ra rubs his face.

"Peace?" *he says to himself.* "I must be mad."

10. LIGHTBRINGER

IT WAS EARLY evening, and people crossed the river like pilgrims. Passenger ferries groaned with the weight of them. Feluccas zigzagged back and forth, riding low in the water on the outbound journey, packed to the gunwales with human cargo. It seemed as if the entire population of Luxor was making the trip from one side of the Nile to the other, a mass migration. Everyone shouted, everyone looked eager, even the children too small to understand what was going on. There was an atmosphere of festival, and an undertow of solemn urgency.

Having reached the west bank, David walked with Zafirah and the Liberators and the crowd, through the bottleneck that was the bridge over the El Fadiyah Canal, then across the plain towards the Ramesseum, through the Valley of the Nobles and on to the Temple of Hatshepsut. This was where the pilgrimage ended, where people stopped and congregated, in the flat causeway in front of that huge mortuary edifice, which rose in a series of terraces against the face of a sheer limestone cliff.

A broad ramp led up to the temple's second tier. David saw floodlights arrayed around the temple, and a sound system was in place, all centred on the podium which stood at the head of the ramp between a pair of stone lions. He looked around him. The crowd already numbered around a thousand, and more and more were arriving, swarming in from all directions, with still half an hour to go before the event was due to begin. The sun was setting over the Theban Mountain. The babble of excited voices was deafening.

"Taking mental notes?" asked Zafirah. "Compiling a report for your superiors?"

David started, a little guiltily. "Just observing. You make it sound like I'm a spy or something. Don't you remember? You invited me along. You wanted me to see all this."

"I'm only teasing. You look full of curiosity, that's all."

"Well, I am curious. Who wouldn't be? This is interesting."

"Is that why you haven't checked in with headquarters?"

"What do you mean?"

"You've had all of today to yourself. There are payphones all over Luxor. There's one in the lobby of our hotel. Yet you haven't tried to contact anyone to tell them you're alive."

"How do you know that? Maybe you're the one who's been spying."

"Isn't it true?"

"So what if it is?"

"Then I'm intrigued," Zafirah said. "Surely the good little soldier's first duty, if he's missing believed dead, is to let his commanding officers know he's alive. Unless, of course, he doesn't want them to know he's gone AWOL."

"I'm not AWOL. As far as the army's aware, I'm KIA."

"As of today," said Zafirah, "I'd say you were AWOL."

David thought briefly. "Put it this way. Everyone thinks I'm dead. For the top brass, that's a desirable outcome. Awkward for them otherwise. So for the time being I might as well remain dead. It's not doing anyone any harm, and it's strangely invigorating."

She looked wry. "Being dead – invigorating?"

"Yes, I know."

"What about your parents? Don't they deserve to know you're all right?"

"My parents…"

Jack Westwynter: "I have no son. Do you hear me, David? As of now, unless you recant this ridiculous decision of yours, I have no son. Go off and get yourself killed. See if I care."

"I haven't spoken to them in five years," David told her. "If I called them now, my dad would be too drunk to pick up the phone and my mum would be too away with the sedative fairies even to hear it ringing."

"Sad."

"Yeah, the cord of the Westwynter dynasty has pretty much unravelled." His laugh was eggshell-brittle. "I'm the last frayed, loose end of it."

"It's never too late, David Westwynter. You'd be surprised. Nothing is beyond repair."

"Where does this boundless optimism of yours come from, Zafirah?"

"From experience. From faith in people. From having met despair and seeing it to be the enemy of life."

"And from the revered Lightbringer as well?"

"Oh yes," Zafirah said earnestly. "Him most of all."

"Then I can't wait to hear what he has to say," said David.

And he didn't have to wait long. Within twenty minutes the sky was dark, the area in front of the temple was thronged, and the show began.

First, with a fusillade of clunks, the floodlights came on. A few thousand voices hushed. Then recorded music emerged from the huge banks of speakers – the supple skirl of an arghul, long reedy notes rising and falling with flickering trills in between. David couldn't help think of a snake charmer enticing a cobra from a basket. The arghul was joined by the shiver of a sistrum rattle and the shimmer of a tambourine, which together created an understated but insistent rhythm.

There was no crescendo. Slowly the volume was turned down, the music faded away, and then a man stepped out from within the temple and strode casually up to the podium. A few among the crowd whistled and cheered, but for the most part people were quiet. Rather than come out with a bang, as David had been anticipating, the Lightbringer had made a subdued entrance. This wasn't just some rabble-rousing demagogue, he realised. This was something different, subtler – perhaps even more potent.

He peered at the Lightbringer. From a distance of a hundred feet or so he could make out a reasonably tall man. He was wearing a plain green jumpsuit that revealed a trim figure. His posture was relaxed and self-assured. As for the face...

It was no face.

The Lightbringer's entire head was sheathed tightly by some kind of thin white material, muslin or gauze. His features were mere indentations. No protrusions. No hair, no ears. There was just a pale, oblate sphere above the collar of the jumpsuit, somewhat like a moon. The Lightbringer's hands were leather-gloved. None of his skin was exposed. Nothing distinguished him. He could have been anyone. No one. Everyone. And David could tell that that was the point. The Lightbringer was anonymous. He was universal. He was a Freegyptian Everyman.

When he spoke his voice was warm and mellifluous, reminiscent of the arghul in its sinuous ebb and flow. There was a depth to it, a resonance, that made it very easy on the ear.

Zafirah translated.

"My friends," the Lightbringer said, "my fellow Freegyptians. I thank you all for coming. You have travelled here from all four corners of our beautiful, independent nation, from desert and town and coast and mountain, to share in a glorious moment."

The amplified boom of his oratory rolled across the crowd, echoing afar.

"Many of you have until not so long ago been implacable enemies. Now you come here as allies, in a spirit of togetherness, willing to set aside hostility in the name of a greater good. The infighting which has plagued Freegypt for years and prevented her from becoming the mighty state we know she can be, is at an end. Your presence here proves it. Foes are now as brothers. Factions are no more. I have brokered truces among you. I have brought warlord face to face with warlord and established common ground. I have worked hard and tirelessly to show you all that the greatest threat facing us is not ourselves, it's the world beyond our borders. Man should not struggle endlessly against man. Man, instead, should be standing up against his common foe – the gods."

David felt a frisson of shock as Zafirah relayed these words. He glanced at the sky, half expecting a bolt of lightning to descend from the heavens and fry the Lightbringer on the spot.

"Infidels they call us," the Lightbringer went on, unfried. "They mean it as an insult, but to me it is a badge of honour. Do we toil under the yoke of divine domination? No, we do not. Do we pander to deities, cravenly begging for their blessing and sacrificing to them in the hope that our crops will grow and our children will be healthy and we may be granted *ba* to power our weapons? No, we do not. Do we live in constant fear of offending these aloof, supreme rulers, to the point where we send off generations of young men and women to fight and die in wars waged unceasingly in their names? No, we do not. Are we victims of their whims and caprices? No! We are Freegyptians and we thrive without assistance from above and we are nobody's slaves!"

This brought ragged hoots of assent from the crowd. The Lightbringer made a calming gesture, keen to show that he wanted things to remain low-key. It was almost as though he was chatting to a roomful of people, not addressing a rally of thousands. Yet still he was able to hold everyone's attention. That, thought David, took some doing. No doubt about it: the man had charisma.

"So listen. Listen well. The time is coming. Our forces are gathering. We are an army and soon we will make our move. We are going to provoke the gods. We are going to thrust a stick into the hornets' nest that is the Pantheon, and we are going to rouse their anger. It will not be easy and it will not be safe. There will be consequences, dangerous ones. But it must be done. And why must it be done? Because the gods are destroying the world. Their feuds ravage every continent. Their wars murder millions. This has been going on for a hundred years and it cannot continue. Someone must rise against them and dethrone them, and that someone is – and can only be – us. And I tell you this, my friends: when it is all over, when our crusade is done, when we are victorious, the entire human race will thank us for it. Better yet, they will remember us for it, for all time."

He spread his arms.

"Look around you. This temple and all the others nearby, these tombs, these resting places of ancient kings and queens, were built with just one aim, to ensure immortality for the people they contain. Seti, Hatshepsut, Tuthmosis, Ramses after Ramses, they raised these mausoleums so that after they died we would always know their names and their deeds. But time passed. Statues crumbled. Inscriptions were defaced. Treasures were robbed. Wind and rain eroded. Sand drifted and buried. Most of these monuments ended up lost and forgotten. The vanity of pharaohs' dreams."

He lowered his arms.

"You, Freegyptians. I promise you. Unlike them, you will never be forgotten. Once you have helped rid the world of the pestilential Pantheon, your fame will be celebrated down through the centuries. You will be known forever as peacemakers, creators of harmony, builders of utopia, of paradise on earth. You will be the ones who ended a dark age of violence and servitude. You, I, all of us... will be Lightbringers!"

Applause came. It rippled through the crowd like rain, and up on the podium the Lightbringer acknowledged it modestly, standing back from the microphone with his head slightly bowed. David studied the faces around him, looking for manic fervour. All he saw was stolid conviction, a belief that was neither wide-eyed nor narrow-minded. The Lightbringer's speech hadn't been intended to whip up emotions. He wasn't here to make converts or gain new recruits. He had won these people over already, and the aim of the rally was simply to remind them of their purpose and stiffen their resolve.

Soon he withdrew into the temple, and the crowd broke up.

On the way back to Luxor, Zafirah asked David what he'd made of it all.

"Frankly?"

"All right."

"I think the man's mad, and so are you. Provoking the gods? Ever heard of the word hubris?"

Anger flashed in her eyes. "Tell me, do you really think the gods care about you? Isis, Osiris, they want nothing from you except worship and obedience. Your faith in them gives them power, and they pay it back in dribs and drabs, a bit of *ba* here, a prayer answered there, that's all. It isn't even a relationship. It's a dictatorship."

"It works."

"It could work without them too. Man, for the first time in history, could rule himself. He could be master of his own destiny."

"But even assuming that were possible, do you reckon it would usher in a golden age? No war, no suffering, no inequality? Do you really, truly think we humans could do a better job of running things?"

"I don't know," said Zafirah. "But we could at least try."

SHE DIDN'T TALK to him for the rest of that evening, and he didn't see her for any of the next morning. He spent the time making enquiries, figuring out the best way of leaving Luxor and going north. An English-speaking felucca pilot offered him passage to Cairo but the price was steep and David had no money. A train ticket was marginally less costly but the problem, lack of funds, remained.

To remedy this, he went in search of somewhere where senet was played competitively for cash. He found a small square near a souk, filled with old, rickety trestle tables and old, rickety men. He had nothing to stake except the phial of myrrh around his neck, but someone took pity on him and agreed to a best of three. The Luxorian clearly felt this Osirisiac outsider was going to be a pushover and a few fluid ounces of myrrh wouldn't be a bad return on a few minutes' playing time.

So as not to hurt the man's feelings, David let him win the first game. Then he trounced him comprehensively on the next two. The Luxorian was horrified but he paid up without quibble.

David took his small winnings and, over the course of the next few hours, parlayed it into a considerable sum. A buzz built up around the square as he took on all comers and beat them. Soon the locals were queuing up to challenge him, and others stood around his table betting on the outcome of the games or simply enjoying the novelty. Senet was, after all, Ancient Egyptian in origin, and a traditional local pastime. How could this Englishman be so unvanquishably good at it?

None of them could have known that senet was in David's blood. It was the family game. At his father's knee he had learned tactics and strategies, and Jack Westwynter would always, of course, play for money, never for matchsticks or other tokens or even for fun, so David had had to become proficient at the game pretty quickly or else he would see his weekly allowance get wiped out in a matter of moments.

Again and again David threw the six casting sticks, chose a counter, moved it the appropriate number of squares, and bumped back one of his opponent's counters or else built up an unassailable three-counters-in-a-row formation. Again and again he reached the last squares on the board first and occupied four of the five Houses marked there, making sure to leave the House of Humiliation open so that his opponent kept being forced to land on it and have his counter sent back to the nearest unoccupied square. Again and again he cleared all five of his counters off the board first while the other man managed to remove, at most, two of his own. For David it was almost a mechanical skill, senet, a process governed by logic and statistics, with the casting sticks providing an element of randomness but not a significant one. There wasn't a variable the sticks could bring to the game that David couldn't adapt to his advantage through sheer familiarity with the workings of the board. Luck was scarcely a factor if you had a potential move in mind for each of the six possible outcomes of a throw. He was never without permutations.

DAVID LEFT THE square a couple of hundred *guinay* to the better, plenty to cover the cost of his trip to Cairo. Once in the capital he planned on presenting himself at the Hegemony consulate and asking their advice on what to do. If the army wanted him back, no questions asked, that was fine. But there might be difficulties. Zafirah had been right. He was on the verge of being Absent Without Leave, if indeed he hadn't crossed that line already. The question was, did he owe the army his loyalty any more, given that they had deliberately dropped a fusion bomb on him? For the first time in a long time, perhaps ever, he was feeling rudderless, unsure of his place in the scheme of things. Hierarchy and discipline gave shape to the world; that was what he had always believed. Life was made easy by adherence to a rigid structure. But maybe that only really worked when you were at the top of the ladder, when you were doing well. The further down the rungs you went, the more of a victim of circumstances you became and the less it mattered whether or not you were in control.

Not that that was necessarily terrible. There was something to be said for being without responsibilities, for not having to answer to the army or his family or anyone except himself. David had a weird, free-floating sense of possibility – infinite possibility. As he'd said to Zafirah, being "dead" was strangely invigorating. He could do as he chose, especially now that he had a fat wad of local currency in his back pocket. He could go home or not go home. He could be Lieutenant David Westwynter again or, if he liked, if he dared, something completely different.

He stopped for a coffee at a cafe on the Sharia al Mahattit. The coffee turned into a fresh orange juice and the orange juice into a couple of bottles of beer, and it was as he was halfway through the second of those that Zafirah and two of her Liberators found him. The two Liberators, called Saeed and Salim, looked like twins but were in fact cousins.

"Where have you been?" she snapped. "We've been looking all over. Come on. There's no time to waste."

"What? What's going on?"

"The Lightbringer. He wishes to meet you."

"Me? Why?"

"He just does. Now come with us."

David glanced at Saeed and Salim, both large men, both wearing impenetrably dark sunglasses. He had a feeling Zafirah hadn't brought them along just for company.

He picked up his beer bottle, drained it, set it down again.

He wasn't really in the mood for trouble.

Besides, infinite possibility...

Why the hell not?

11. AMULETS

THEY WENT IN procession up the ramp to the Temple of Hatshepsut, Zafirah leading the way, David following close behind, Saeed and Salim at the rear.

The terrace at the top of the ramp led to a second ramp, which in turn led to a courtyard. Everywhere, there were brightly coloured reliefs depicting birds and trees and gods and goddesses and a great deal else that David didn't have time to take in. Across the courtyard lay a pink granite doorway, hewn out from the rock face. Passing through this they entered a long subterranean chamber, gloomily lit, blessedly cool.

The Lightbringer was seated at the far end, in heavy shadow, his masked head ghostly in the darkness. Zafirah strode up to him and the two of them spoke for a while in low tones, the Lightbringer casting frequent glances over Zafirah's shoulder at David. It was impossible to tell what the glances meant. That all-white oval of a face was utterly indecipherable, a blank sheet of paper.

While they were talking, David spotted the six Bedouin strongboxes stacked in a corner of the chamber. One of them lay open, its padlock having been prised off with a crowbar.

He craned his neck. His eyes widened.

Inside were amulets, dozens of them. They were the sort of trinkets you could buy at any shop or temple, made of die-cut steel, machine tooled, the sort that factories in Formosa and the Crimea churned out by the million. Each was slung on a cord of knotted leather and was designed to be worn around the neck as a fashion accessory or a symbol of faith or both. David saw an ankh, a scarab, a crown, a hand, an eye, a representation of cow-headed Hathor, and countless others, all jumbled together. They were the most ordinary-looking objects imaginable.

Except, these ones weren't ordinary. You could tell. These amulets had *ba*. They were infused with it. Together, en masse, they pulsated with it. It radiated out of the strongbox like an aura. Somewhere deep in his head, deeper than his ears, David could hear a throbbing. At the back of his throat, he could taste the power.

The Lightbringer noticed him staring and let out a small, mask-muffled laugh. He said something to Zafirah, which she translated into English.

"The Lightbringer wishes to know what you think of our gift to him."

"Well, since he asks," David said, "those things are completely illegal."

As Zafirah relayed the answer, the Lightbringer shrugged and laughed. His reply, via her, was: "Illegal they might be, but highly useful too. Saqqara Birds are everywhere, and some of us don't always wish to be seen. A man wearing one of these amulets is blurred to a priest's inner eye, all but invisible. He may act in secret, without arousing attention. Spies from every power bloc, not least the Hegemony, use them as a matter of course, although no government would ever admit it. So, they can only ever be transported from place to place by people like those Bedouin, in secret. To traffic in *ba*-charged amulets is a crime under international law, and no nation wants to be *seen* to be breaking the law."

"They're unholy," David added.

"Some would say the same about me," said the Lightbringer. "Including, I suspect, you."

"I wouldn't put it that strongly."

"Then how would you put it?"

David said, "I think you're foolhardy, that's for certain, taking on the gods. You're picking a fight you can't hope to win."

"Gods aren't invincible. How can they be? The One True Pantheon managed to wipe out its rivals, after all. If Jehovah and Allah and Odin and Zeus and the rest were so almighty, how come they're not still around, worshipped everywhere?"

"That was gods defeating gods, in a struggle that lasted centuries. You, if you don't mind my saying so, aren't in nearly the same league."

The Lightbringer started chuckling even before Zafirah had translated that last remark. David got the impression that the man understood more English than he was prepared to let on.

"The First Family won their victory on two fronts," the Lightbringer replied. "Yes, they battled the other pantheons on a plane beyond our comprehension, but the war was waged down here as well. Men were involved, knowingly or otherwise. All those clashes between the faiths – Christians hounding so-called pagans, Muslims persecuting Jews – were fostered behind the scenes by followers of the One True Religion. We know this now. The Freemasons, the Knights Templar, and the other cults and secret societies famous for their Ancient Egyptian iconography – that was their task, to install acolytes in high places and have them exert influence over governments and monarchs. It was done to keep the other religions at one another's throats constantly. With every battle, every pogrom, every massacre, the other gods lost worshippers and were weakened. They were also distracted, making them easier targets for attack on the divine plane. It was a long, sustained campaign that went on till the last of the First Family's enemies was exhausted, drained of all power, and could be picked off easily."

"And then the First Family stepped back and passed the world on to their offspring, and here we all are." David snorted. "So? It doesn't change the fact that you're human and they're divine, and thinking you stand a chance against them is like an ant thinking it could topple *you*."

"Enough ants, employing the right tactics and leverage, probably could topple me," said the Lightbringer. "My point is that the gods conducted part of their war on earth and I intend to use the same battleground. I doubt I'm going to be able to convince you of this, though."

"I don't think so."

"A pity. From what I've been told about you, I could do with somebody like you by my side."

"Me?"

"A true soldier. A man who understands how to take and give orders."

"Oh no. No, no, no." David shook his head vehemently. "I'm not up for that. Not at all. I can't defy the gods. I'm a believer."

"Are you?"

"Of course I am. I was raised that way, I've lived that way all my life..."

"That doesn't mean you *are* one," said the Lightbringer. "All it means is you've been conditioned to think you are."

"I trust in Isis and Osiris. I respect them as rulers. I have faith in them to guide our leaders wisely and do what's best for us."

"Did Isis and Osiris, I wonder, sanction the bombing of you and your fellow paratroopers at Petra?"

David kept his voice even. "It was a military decision, made for the general good. And in a roundabout way it saved my life."

"But the gods aren't involved in military decisions?"

"They speak to priests and kings, not field marshals."

"But field marshals are answerable to priests and kings, are they not?"

"Zafirah," David said, "I've had enough of this. Please tell Mister No Face here that I'm not prepared to argue the rights and wrongs of theocracy with him. I'm not going to be able to persuade him to see my point of view and he's not going to be able to persuade me to see his, and that's an end of it. Oh, and by the way, thanks for telling him absolutely everything you know about me. I love being put at a disadvantage when I'm meeting a complete stranger."

"He asked," she said. "He's very interested in you, in case you hadn't noticed."

"Well, if he wants a boyfriend, he's barking up the wrong tree."

David judged that to be a pretty good exit line, and turned on his heel to go.

Immediately Saeed and Salim closed ranks, blocking the way out.

"All right," David said, "which one of you plug-uglies wants it first?"

The two Liberators folded their arms. David reckoned he could take them down pretty easily. Though both were stockily well built, neither radiated the calm, ready-for-anything aura of an experienced fighter. Street muscle. They would go for obvious blows – face, chest, belly. He would jab at nerve clusters and soft spots – throat, eyes, genitals. No contest.

The Lightbringer spoke, and Saeed and Salim unfolded their arms and stepped aside.

He spoke again, and Zafirah said, "David, the Lightbringer says you are free to leave if you wish. He will not stop you. But," she continued, "he has heard rumours that you are an accomplished senet player."

"Oh, has he? News travels fast."

"Luxor is a small place and the Lightbringer likes to stay informed. He wants to know if you will sit with him in private and play a few games."

"What for? I can't see the point."

"Indulge me," the Lightbringer said through Zafirah. "I fancy myself a pretty good player too. In fact, I've yet to meet my equal in the game. Maybe that's you?"

"Not interested."

"Not interested? Or do you simply fear losing?"

David knew, with an inward sigh, that that was that. A gauntlet had just been thrown down and there was no way he couldn't pick it up. Nobody called David Westwynter a coward. Or even implied it.

TEN MINUTES LATER, he and the Lightbringer were alone in the chamber. Everyone else had been dismissed, including Zafirah. Without her as interpreter there would be no conversation, no interaction other than through the game itself. It was just the two of them, hunched on wooden chairs, with the board laid out on an upturned crate between them.

David noted that it was a proper AW Games board, not a crude knock-off like the ones he'd played on earlier in the day. Freegypt was exempt from international patent law, much as it was exempt from all the other rules the rest of the world lived by, so bogus copies of the game could be produced and sold with impunity. The Lightbringer, however, clearly preferred the quality and craftsmanship of the genuine article. The version he owned was actually the deluxe edition, carved from teak, with counters made of polished marble and a small drawer inset into the board in which to stow them. Everything was scratched and scuffed with age and use.

As the Lightbringer set out the counters for the first game, David took the opportunity to study him at close range. The mask was sewn to fit, with seams down both sides, and gathered at the neck. Whatever material it was made from, it was thin enough that the wearer could see out without much difficulty. Seeing in, though, was much harder. David could just make out the glitter of the man's eyes as they flicked to and fro. The mouth was a dim oval. He thought he spied a patch of strange, ribbed roughness covering the skin of most of one cheek, but it might have been shadows cast by tiny pleats and folds in the fabric.

The Lightbringer looked up and David ended his scrutiny. The Lightbringer proffered the casting sticks. David took them and threw them. He got a 1, meaning he was playing black and went first.

And the game commenced.

And David lost.

It happened so fast he could barely believe it. He'd succeeded in getting just one of his counters to Square 30 and off the board. He'd had a hard time even manoeuvring them onto the last row.

The Lightbringer gave a grunt of satisfaction, then made a gesture: perhaps David would like a second chance.

David certainly did.

The game began again, and again David lost. He made a better fist of it this time, installing counters on both the House of Beauty and the House of Three Truths, but it wasn't enough to foil the Lightbringer's efforts. He won while David still had three counters left to remove.

The Lightbringer might have been pleased to have had two victories on the trot. He might have been annoyed that David wasn't proving to be much competition after all. It was impossible to know.

They knuckled down to a third game, David now more determined than ever to beat the other man.

It was a close-fought contest. Luck was definitely on David's side this time, in as much as luck meant anything. The sticks kept giving him fours and sixes, allowing him turn after turn after turn. He built up a commanding lead. He removed one counter from the board.

Then the Lightbringer came from behind, gained the upper hand, and in fewer than ten moves had all his counters off and yet another victory under his belt.

David looked at the board aghast, as if somehow it had betrayed him. Three games. He had lost three whole games. And badly too. They'd not even been marginal defeats. They'd been crushing ones.

He hadn't had such a poor run at senet since... he couldn't remember when. He could think of only two people who'd ever been able to best him at the game quite so convincingly. One was his father, and the other was dead.

He debated whether to agree to a fourth game. He wasn't sure his ego could handle it. However, when the Lightbringer held out the sticks to him, he took them, and shook them, and threw them, and once again board-game battle was joined.

Now David began to notice something. He hadn't realised it before, but the Lightbringer's playing strategies were very familiar. They mirrored his own. Every move the other man made was the move he too would have made had he been in that position. The Lightbringer followed game patterns he himself favoured. It was as though he was up against another David Westwynter, and that was why he was losing. The same skills he used to beat others were being used to beat him.

Accordingly he changed tactics. He abandoned formal play. All the permutations he knew by rote, he avoided. He went for wild-card moves instead, doing what he least expected of himself and therefore what his opponent would least expect too. Given a choice between safe and unpredictable, he chose the latter every time. His only rule was recklessness. Chaos was the order of the day.

He didn't care that this probably meant he would lose. It was also the only hope he had of winning. If he continued to play as before, he would simply be handing the Lightbringer a fourth victory.

To his surprise, the gamble paid off. As he plucked his fifth and final counter off the board, David could barely suppress a grin of glee.

The Lightbringer nodded, perhaps in appreciation, perhaps in bemusement, perhaps both.

Then, in perfect English, with no trace of an accent, he said: "Well done."

David's jaw dropped.

"You figured it out," the Lightbringer went on. "Took you long enough, but you got there. Go mad. Take absurd risks. It's the only defence against tightly structured play."

"You're... you're British."

"Yes, but you can do better than that."

"What do you mean?"

"What do you think I mean? Dave."

David didn't understand.

Then he did.

All at once the chamber seemed tiny, constrictingly small. David felt as though the world were telescoping down, zeroing in on this point in space and time, this moment, this impossible event. Nothing else was happening anywhere, just this. There was just this stone room, these two chairs, the two people sitting on them. Everything outside the immediate vicinity had ceased to matter, ceased to be.

He stared at the Lightbringer. And stared and stared.

The features behind the mask remained hidden. Unknowable.

But the voice...

Oh gods. Oh Osiris of Djed-pillar. Oh Isis of the Blood Knot. That voice.

Huskily, querulously, not even in a whisper, more an exhalation, David spoke the name.

"Steven?"

12. AEGEAN

LET ME TELL you this, Dave. All the advance planning in the world, all the preparation, all the well-formulated tactics, it doesn't amount to a bucket of shit once the fighting starts. That's true of any battle and it's truer than true of naval battles. The moment you and the enemy engage, everything goes to pieces. All you can do is hang in there, keep hammering away at the other guy, and hope there are more of your ships left afloat at the end than there are of his. That's while contending with sea conditions, tides, weather, all of that as well. It's a wonder the admirals even bother with strategy meetings. They might as well sit in a circle wanking each other off for all the difference it makes. They probably do that anyway.

So there we were, three days out of Marseilles, steaming up through the Dodecanese to take on the Nephs, who were harrying merchant shipping all along the east coast of Greece from Thessaloniki to Athens. It was a classic piece of sabre-rattling from them. Things had been pretty quiet on the Mediterranean front for a couple of years and someone high up at Neph Fleet HQ must've got bored and fancied some action. You can bet the Setics were egging them on from the sidelines, too. Moscow in particular had been itching to reopen hostilities in the Med arena. All those battleships docked at

Odessa and Sevastopol – couldn't have them sitting there gathering barnacles, now could we? Besides, there's nothing worse than sailors in port with nothing to do. They drink the bars dry, wear out the whores, and start fights. So it was in the Setics' interest if the Nephs stirred it up with us. Then they could come whizzing to the rescue from the Black Sea, bingo, everyone happy.

On the day of the battle itself, I was on Forenoon Watch and eight bells were about to toll. Which means, landlubber, my shift was nearly over and it was coming up to midday. It had been a beautiful morning. I remember telling myself to try and take it all in, how the sky looked, how the sea looked, the smell of the air, because I knew we were likely to encounter the Nephs that day and I mightn't have the chance to enjoy another morning ever again. The sky was sapphire. The sea was purple, choppy, frenetic. We were sailing with a strong southerly bumping us along from behind, so I was inhaling plenty of fumes from the funnel but I didn't mind. Barely noticed. Everywhere on a warship smells of diesel. Your clothes stink of it, your hair. It's a sailor's perfume.

Lovely morning, like I say, and it felt good to be part of a fleet heading towards a battle zone. From my starboard watch post I could see at least half a dozen other ships – a couple of frigates, a destroyer, our fellow dreadnought the *Indomitable*, and the corvettes that were escorting her and us. Our corvette was the *Serapis*, and personally I blame her imbecile of a captain for what happened to the *Immortal*. I mean, his one and only job was to stop a submarine getting a shot off at us, and did he do that? Did he arse!

But until he let us down so grievously, it was comforting to see his ship and the others, all forging along on the same heading at a rate of knots. It really gave me a feeling of invincibility. His Pharaonic Majesty's Mediterranean Fleet in full force, backed up by some French and German cruisers, with a Spaniard or two somewhere in the mix, all of us with our battle ensigns flying. The Hegemony out for blood, happy to take the bait the Nephs had dangled before us, eager to in fact, with Britain of course leading the way as usual, belligerent and bloodthirsty bunch that we are. I thought nothing could beat us. I'd accepted the fact that this could be my last day on earth but I didn't really anticipate that being the case.

Just as the watch was over, a Saqqara Bird came scooting in from the north. The ship's priest had been sitting cross-legged for an hour at the bows, little spot he had there that he liked to occupy while in trance. He stood up, straightening out his cloak and adjusting his gold silk head-cloth, and held up his hands to catch the bird. It glided to him and he cradled it in his arms and stroked it like a pet, like it was a real feathered creature and not just a *ba*-animated piece of carved willow. Priests, I ask you! It's not a profession for a sane person, is it? Some of them are born communing with the gods, in which case they don't start out normal, and the rest learn how to commune with the gods at seminary, in which case they inevitably end up a bit bonkers. Either way, they're doomed to a life of mental wonkiness. Hearing voices, seeing visions – it soon loosens your grip on reality.

Anyway, I could tell that our guy's bird had shown him where the Nephs were while it was out on its scouting mission, because he wasn't looking any too happy. And judging by the way he scurried aft to the bridge to report to the captain, they weren't too far off.

A few minutes after that the battle stations klaxon sounded and everything went crazy. A whole lot of ship-to-ship heliographing went on – no radio communication so that the Nephs couldn't intercept the transmissions – and the fleet closed together in battle formation, becoming this moving wall of armour and firepower, ironclad, unstoppable. Or seemingly unstoppable.

Then they appeared on the horizon, the Nephthysian fleet, coming towards us, another moving wall of armour and firepower. Their smoke hung above them, a long, dark grey stain in the sky. It was the smoke I could see, more than the ships themselves, which were little more than dots. But I could still tell that there were as many of them as there were of us. There seemed to be more, in fact.

By this point I was belowdecks, overseeing the manning of the for'ard guns. But there's a viewplate in the turret just next to the barrels, to help with range-finding and observation, so I could watch from there as we bore down on the Nephs and vice versa.

They were well within range of our sixteen-inchers, and us of theirs, when the firing started. Ten thousand yards or less between the two fleets when the *ba* shells started flying.

The madness of battle...

Well, you must know about it as well as I do, Dave, now that you're a soldier boy. Honestly, who'd have thought it? The Westwynter heirs, both of them joining military service. Never in a million years would anyone have predicted that about us. Least of all you, bro, turning your back on the cushy lifestyle, giving Dad the two fingers and buggering off to the army. Zafirah tells me I'm to blame for that, indirectly. You'll have to tell me more about it later. You want to know what happened to me, so I'll carry on. Here's the rest of the story.

Guns fucking blazing. The turret rocking with each shell that we fired. A boom that was deafening despite ear defenders. A noise so loud it left you feeling dizzy each time. And no other thought, no other purpose in mind, but to lob as many of those shells as you could, as quickly as you could, and pound the bastards over there to bits. Radar and the gunnery obs post telling us what to do, where to aim. Shooting at a foe we could barely see. Men loading charge and projectile, yelling at each other. Gunners calling out their firing solutions. A chaotic machine.

I'd been in skirmishes before aboard *Immortal*, random encounters with stray Neph craft where the odd shot was exchanged, usually a low-level tit-for-tat zapping with *ba* bolts, never anything like this, with the big guns in play. The incoming fire was terrific. The sea around us kept exploding in huge white geysers of water, lit from within by *ba*. I saw, with my own eyes, one of the frigates go up, less than five hundred yards from us. It was there one moment. The next, it was this fragmented thing, barely a ship, more a rough outline of one, aflame, listing over, rolling like a wounded whale.

The initial bombardment lasted an hour all told, and by then we'd got close enough to the enemy for our destroyers to turn broadside and unleash torpedoes. Their torpedo tubes revolved and ripple-fired, while we dreadnoughts kept the artillery salvoes going.

What none of us had any idea of then was that a torpedo was coming our way, courtesy of a Setic sub half a mile to port. The captain of the *Serapis* had no idea either, though he bloody well should have. He should have been hunting down that sub with his sonar and depth-charging it to oblivion, instead of which he was fannying about doing something, anything, other than what he was fucking supposed to.

It hit us amidships, bang on the aft boiler room. It broke *Immortal*'s keel in two – snapped her spine. It had to have been a fusion-head torpedo, to do that much damage. Red and purple *ba* uniting, the power of Set and Nephthys coming together, an even more volatile mix than that of Isis and Osiris. Any other kind of torpedo, striking anywhere else, and *Immortal* might have been able to carry on. The bulkhead seals would have contained the inrushing water and she'd have been reeling but still able to fight, like a punch-drunk boxer. But the engines were blown up, the hull lost integrity... the technical term for her status is "fucked".

And so the call came to abandon ship. Horns whooped. Men scarpered for the lifeboats, and believe me, I was scarpering as fast and as frantically as any of them. Disaster drill? Calm and orderly evacuation? Forget it. Everyone was trampling over everyone else to get the fuck out of there, clawing, scrabbling, fighting. Rank meant nothing. We were all of us equals in our terror. We clambered out onto deck, in our lifejackets, and *Immortal* was shrieking and groaning and shuddering. The whole of her midsection was engulfed in smoke and flames, and she was letting out these bellows of tormented metal, which mingled with the dull thudding detonations of exploding fuel holds.

Then – and this is the truly shit part – I felt the deck start to rise under me at an angle. Everyone around me was finding it hard to keep their balance. Me too. The bow of the ship was coming up out of the water. The stern was as well. *Immortal* was collapsing in on herself, her two halves bending together in a massive V, and not a single lifeboat had been launched yet, not a single crewman had got safely off her. It was all happening too fast. Suddenly the deck was canted at forty-five degrees and getting steeper, and men started slithering and tumbling down it, heading for the inferno at the crux of the V. I happened to be standing near the anchor capstan and I managed to grab on to it and clung on, but I knew I wasn't going to able to keep hold of it forever. And the ship was starting to sink. No, sink's too gentle a word. She was starting to *plummet*. This beautiful big boat that I'd come to trust, that I'd come to believe was the sturdiest thing in the world, was going down as swiftly as though something was dragging her below, some leviathan or kraken of myth, wrenching her down into the depths. I hurtled down with her, still clutching that capstan. The surface of the sea below me was boiling white, seething, steaming, with an orange glow deep within, the fuel holds still alight even underwater. I remember wondering whether the water was going to be scalding hot or freezing cold when I hit it, and I remember thinking I probably wouldn't know either way because at this speed the impact was bound to knock me out.

I did lose consciousness, but not quite that way. One moment I was descending. Next, a flash of light and I was flying. I had no idea at the time what was happening, but I've found out since, by reading eyewitness reports. The fire reached one of *Immortal*'s for'ard magazines. Her bow end convulsed in this immense explosion that blew me off my perch and outward, away from the ship. I must have looked like a flea being flung off a shaking dog. I have this dim recollection of weightlessness, of not knowing which way was up or down. It was weirdly pleasant, like a funfair ride. Remember that time we went to the funfair, you and me? With Mrs Plomley. And we went on the waltzer ten times in a row, and at the end I got off and was sick down Mrs Plomley's coat. Felt a bit like that. The waltzer part, not the being sick part.

I have no memory of landing in the water. I have no memory of anything from the next few hours. I came round sometime towards evening. The sky was pink, clouds were swelling overhead, and I was floating in the water, my lifejacket like this constricting puffy collar around my neck. My brain felt fragmented, my thoughts all over the place and I couldn't pull them back together. I couldn't hear anything except the lapping of the water around me, the heave and surge of the sea.

Gradually I began making sense of things, and I listened out for the sound of guns, because I assumed the battle must be going on somewhere within earshot, even if somewhere meant ten miles away. But the battle had moved on. The fleets, the Nephs' and ours, had gone off in one direction and I'd gone off in another, and I was all alone out there on the ocean. Just me, the Aegean, and nothing else. Oh, a couple of corpses bobbing nearby, ratings from the *Immortal*, but they weren't much for company and we soon went our separate ways. Otherwise, alone.

I became aware of the left side of my face feeling odd. Tight. Stretched. Painful in a dull, tingly kind of way. I tried touching it to find out what was the matter but my fingers were numb. Been in the water so long they'd lost all sensitivity. I guessed I'd struck something or been struck by something, debris perhaps, and my face was swollen and bruised.

Night came. Rain started to fall – great hissing sheets of it. I lay there floating, thinking maybe I should try and make the effort to swim. But swim where? Which way? It would be a waste of energy. If I conserved my strength instead, I might just stay alive that little bit longer. I was probably in a current and the current would be taking me somewhere, maybe to land, maybe further out to sea. Whichever it was, swimming wasn't going to make a gnat's fart of difference. So I just hung there, suspended in the water, the rain rattling down on my head, drumming on the roof of my skull.

I'm not ashamed to admit I bawled like a baby several times during the first part of that night. I was lost and terrified, and the rain was doing what the sea couldn't and half-drowning me. I longed to be home, safe and dry, and see you again, and Mum, and even Dad. I'd have given anything for a chance to be with my family, everyone on good terms with everyone else, all differences set aside, forgiven, forgotten, a clean slate.

The rain stopped around midnight, I'd say. The sky cleared. The stars came out. By that point the pain from my face had faded, I couldn't feel my limbs at all, and I was shivering uncontrollably. Exposure, hypothermia, delayed shock – I knew I was suffering from any or all of them, and I knew, no two ways about it, I was going to die.

But the stars, Dave... I couldn't stop gazing up at them. They were so beautiful and so many. I identified the constellations. Astronomy was about the only lesson I ever paid any attention in at school. I knew all the names, both the old Roman ones and the modern ones. Orion's Belt, for instance, which we now call the Three Pyramids, with the Milky Way representing the Nile. And Draco, a.k.a. the Crocodile. And Leo, the Sphinx. They glittered above me and somehow it was hugely reassuring. Not in any spiritual way, just the fact that there were so many stars up there, so many millions of them. And here was little me down here, on my own, with just hours to live, if that, and the stars were sparing a fraction of their light to create this rich, brilliant display in the heavens, and they were doing it for me, that's how it seemed. I felt I was the only person who was appreciating or had ever appreciated the show they were putting on, and I was determined to enjoy it for as long, or as little, as I had left.

That was when I first began to sense it: the size, the scale, the scope of the universe. Staring up at the stars, I had an inkling of something significant. I'm going to use a Christian term here: epiphany. It's fallen into disuse but it fits better than any other word I can think of. Epiphany.

Our physics teacher, what was his name? Him with the stammer and the lick-and-spit comb-over. Perkins. Mr Perkins. "Puh-Puh-Puh-Perkins", as we used to call him. To his face. Fuck, we were cruel. He once said that the universe isn't just big, it's infinite. There's no measuring it. There's no way of quantifying everything it contains. You just have to accept that it goes on forever and is mostly full of nothing.

"A buh-buh-buh-bit like your head, Westwynter Minor," he added. The old wuh-wuh-wisecracker.

But it didn't seem empty to me then, the universe. Quite the opposite. It was full. Jam-packed with stars, and each of those stars a sun like our own. And our sun is Ra, we all know that. Science tells us it's a gigantic ball of burning matter, an explosion in the sky. But it's also a physical manifestation of Ra's essence. His *ba* suffuses it and makes it shine. Without him animating it, the sun would cease to be. That's what we know. That's what we're led to believe. Those are reconciled facts.

But what about all those other stars? Is there a Ra for each of them?

If so, then our Ra is only one of an uncountable number of other supreme deities.

If not, then Ra is just a single supreme deity in one remote corner of a vast, unending nothingness.

Meaning, one way or the other, Ra is less than we think. Far less.

He is, in fact, insignificant, and so by definition are all his descendants.

Those were my thoughts. It was barely an idea, more the preliminary sketch for an idea. But still it struck me as being profound and extraordinarily powerful.

Not that I stood to gain anything by it. What use is enlightenment when your life is zooming to a close?

The stars wheeled giddyingly, and I blacked out.

When I came to, I was on a beach. It was morning. The sun was hot on my back. I had sand up my nose and I was being bitten all over by sand flies.

I wobbled upright. My face, the left side of it, was agony. I felt sick and thirsty. I had a headache like you wouldn't believe, a right royal brain-splitter. I've never been in worse shape.

But – ecstasy.

I was alive.

I was fucking well alive!

Turned out I'd washed up on one of the hundreds of islands that dot that part of the Aegean. It was a tiny knob of land jutting up from the sea, probably smaller in surface area than Courtdene, which is, what, the whole estate, a hundred acres? You could have walked around its perimeter in less than an hour, not that that was possible. Most of the shoreline was steep, jagged rocks forming coves and crags, especially on the windward side. It had one sandy beach, though, the one I'd woken up on, and a couple of pebbly ones.

It also had wild olive groves. And a freshwater stream that ran down in a series of falls and eddying pools. And a colony of rabbits. And a small, smooth-floored cave.

It had, in other words, everything a person could need in order to survive. Food. Water. Shelter.

And survive is what I did on that island, for the best part of six weeks. It was the most remarkable stroke of good fortune winding up where I did, and I took full advantage of it. I'd been as good as dead, and now through some fluke of wind and tide I found myself in a place with enough in the way of natural resources for a subsistence level of living. How had the olive trees come to grow there? Seeds carried by birds or the ocean currents, I suppose. Where had the rabbits come from? Perhaps a pet, a pregnant doe, had survived a shipwreck. Or perhaps it was simply the case that once in the dim and distant past the island had had human inhabitants and the olives and the rabbits were their legacy. I didn't know. I *don't* know. I didn't want to probe the matter too deeply, either. I was scared that if I started questioning the origin of these amenities, they might just, you know, vanish in a puff of smoke. Gift-horses and mouths and all that.

Six weeks of Robinson Crusoe, and I won't pretend it wasn't hard. The worst of it was my face. I'd figured out that it had got burnt, scorched when *Immortal*'s bow end blew up. I couldn't tell how badly, though. I had no mirror, and the stream and the sea weren't able to provide a smooth enough reflection to check. My fingers explored blisters and wet sore patches and could feel the heat of inflammation, not to mention scrubby bits on my scalp where the hair was gone, but unless you can actually see your injuries for yourself, it's hard to know the full extent of them. It's all a bit hypothetical. I imagined terrible scarring and equally I imagined mild singeing. The only treatment I could think of was bathing the affected area in salt water, so day after day, every couple of hours or so, I'd kneel in the shallows and rinse my face. Never pleasant. Fucking horrible, in fact. But it began to do the trick. Gradually it hurt less each time. The inflammation went down. The sores healed up. But the damage had been done and was, I knew, permanent.

Catching and eating the rabbits wasn't much of a problem. The buggers were as tame as anything. They'd lived there for generations without a natural predator, so they would come lolloping up to me when I approached, more or less ready to sniff my hand. Then – grab, hold, twist, snap neck. Easy peasy. And they never learned, the stupid things. Never got wise. Every time I went up to their warren, another bunny would hop trustingly forward and offer itself as lunch.

I'd skin 'em and gut 'em with a sharp stone, then lay the meat out on a rock to cure in the sun. It wasn't delicious but it wasn't the worst meal I'd had either. Ship's food could be a damn sight less tasty.

And olives; never my favourite vegetable, or is it fruit? But they were edible and filled a hole. Mind you, after a steady diet of them for six weeks I never want to touch one again as long as I live.

It was bearable, though, that was the thing. I knew I could stick it out, this whole ordeal, because I was convinced I was going to be found and rescued. I never had any doubt about that. It wasn't as though I was stuck on a coral atoll in the middle of the Pacific, after all. I was on an island in the Aegean, in one of the busiest parts of the Aegean what's more, an area laced with shipping lanes. Time and again I saw ships pass by, freighters, tankers, ferries, too far away to spot me, certainly too far away to be hailed, not that that stopped me from trying or from feeling crushed and despondent when they steamed on out of sight. But I remained sure that it was only a matter of time before one of them sailed close enough and I was seen and picked up. The odds were in my favour. All I had to do was sit tight and wait.

In the end a rescuer didn't just pass nearby. He landed virtually on my doorstep.

His name was Iannis, and he was a smuggler, and he owned a small but surprisingly nippy fishing boat which he'd inherited from his father and used to run drugs between Europe and North Africa. Normally he did this without much interference. He'd dart back and forth across the Med and the authorities on both sides were mostly preoccupied with other things, too busy keeping an eye on the enemy's manoeuvres to worry about one little boat and its comings and goings. Sometimes, though, he did fall foul of the coastguard and either had to bribe his way out of trouble or else make a run for it and lie low for a while till the heat died down.

My island was one of Iannis's boltholes. It was also a handy stopover, a secluded spot where he could put in for the night to break up the journey.

I was fast asleep when he anchored at my beach late one evening. I woke up in the morning, left my cave, strode down the sand... and bugger me, there was this boat sitting there, and this middle-aged man in a string vest standing on deck taking a leak over the side.

He stared at me. I stared at him. To his credit, he didn't stop peeing. Me, I'd have been so startled my flow would have seized up. I mean, it must have been quite a sight, some scrawny fellow in a ragged sailor's outfit, looking half-crazed, with an injured face and some clumps of hair missing, growing back as stubble. Me, tottering towards him out of the blue, on an island where he had every right to believe he was perfectly alone. But Iannis, he just kept on pissing till he was done, then tucked himself away and buttoned up, still staring at me, surprised but somehow managing to stay casual, as if he'd had far stranger encounters than this in his lifetime.

Then he asked me, in English, if I was English. I said yes, how could you tell? He said it was the uniform. Royal Navy. A midshipman, judging by the jacket cuffs. And then he said the thing that told me I was going to be all right with him. He said, "Also known as a 'snotty'."

I laughed. "That's the nickname for my rank. How'd you know?"

Iannis gave a hefty, big-shouldered shrug. "I know many information. Fifty years I am sailing these seas, since a boy. All that time, war. Navies, uniforms, nicknames – I pick up all these things and have them in the memory, here." He tapped his grizzled head. "Languages too. I speak many very good, some not so good."

I didn't ask which of those categories he put his English in. That's exactly how he sounded, by the way. I know you think I'm crap at accents, Dave, but really, I've nailed Iannis's. Look sceptical if you want. Suit yourself.

Point is, he was basically a decent bloke, and he could tell my whole sorry story just by looking at me, and he knew he wasn't going to leave me there on that island, and I knew it too by the way he'd spoken. So it wasn't long before I was on board his boat and we were putt-putting out to sea and I was enjoying a swig of paint-stripper whisky and feeling relieved and redeemed and about as happy as a man can hope to be.

Iannis told me he was heading to Tangiers, "on business", but he could drop me off at Gibraltar on the way if I didn't mind. Did I mind? How could I mind! He also said he'd try and find a doctor to take a look at my – he didn't say what. Just circled a finger around one side of his face and looked sorry and grim.

Later, I found a shaving mirror in the cabin below and had a squint at myself...

I don't want to talk about it. Not now. All I'll say is, it wasn't terrible scarring and it wasn't mild singeing either. If one's ten and the other's zero, then let's rate the damage a seven. Really, I don't want to talk about it any more than that. Maybe some other time.

So south-west towards Morocco we went. It didn't take me long to work out that Iannis's "business" was less than legit. For starters, he was piloting a fishing boat that wasn't doing any fishing. The nets were bone dry and new-looking, like they'd never even been in the water. But also, whenever he spotted any other vessel, no matter what sort of boat it was he'd change course and steer clear. And then there was the little matter of the secret cargo hold I accidentally discovered, with an access hatch hidden beneath a section of false floor in the head. It was a crawlspace that ran nearly the entire length of the boat, well caulked and dry, empty but smelling strongly of hashish. I didn't mention finding it but Iannis knew I had because I'd failed to lay the floor section back quite as snugly as I should. He produced a pistol and told me that as I'd uncovered his secret he was going to have to shoot me and toss me overboard. I said there was no need for that. I didn't care how he chose to make a living. I admitted I was fond of a bit of dope myself, and added that I'd been something of a smuggler myself at school, which is true as we both know. He could shoot me if he wanted, I went on, but he'd surely be better off taking me on as a deckhand instead. With me assisting him, he could do his runs in half the time because he wouldn't have to stop for rests. We'd take the helm in shifts, travel through the night, and he could do twice as much business but I would only ask for a quarter of his profits. Ergo, he stood to gain half as much money again as he was making now, for the same amount of effort.

The maths impressed him. Next thing I knew, the pistol had been put away, the whisky was out, and we sealed the deal by getting roaring drunk.

Iannis was as good as his word. He got me to a doctor in Gibraltar, who didn't speak a word of English but had a face that was as expressive of his diagnosis as any words could be, if not more so. Essentially, there was nothing *señor médico* could do for me except give me some kind of salve that might have helped had I had it six weeks earlier. He suggested plastic surgery but didn't hold out much hope of success. At least now I know the Spanish for "disfigured": *desfigurado*.

For the next year, Iannis and I plied our not-so-reputable trade up and down the Med, the old Greek seadog and his English seapup sidekick. I can't deny it was fun. We had our fair share of scrapes, of course. Fired on by coastguards outside Naples. Rammed by rival drug runners off Malta. Not to mention the time we strayed into a mine-seeded zone not far from Tunis harbour. My fault, that one. Didn't read the charts properly. Hairiest half-hour of my life as Iannis gentled the boat around and back while I leaned over the bows peering into the water for those huge conker shapes. We actually nudged one of them with our hull, though somehow it didn't go off. It was clean underpants time afterwards, as you can imagine.

We became firm pals, the two of us. And I know what you're thinking. A Greek sailor, and lithe, well-muscled young me. Well, belay that foul thought, big brother. It wasn't like that. None of that sort of thing went on, no hanky-panky belowdecks. Mostly what we did in our spare time was get blisteringly blotto together. Whisky was our preferred tipple, but Iannis got me onto retsina too. Here's an interesting fact about retsina: it tastes the same coming back up as it does going down. I experienced that more times than I care to remember.

All that time, I was thinking hard about the insight I'd had while floating in the sea that night. I'd talk about it with Iannis now and again. He was a great one for the deep and meaningful discussion. The deep and meaningful discussion with an ever-emptying bottle in your hand.

Iannis liked to hark back to the days of the "old religion" in Greece, and I don't mean Orthodox Christianity. Before that. The days of the Olympian pantheon, Zeus and all his relatives and cronies.

"Gods who were like us," he said. "Gods you can understand. Fighting, fucking, falling over, fouling up. Zeus, always being caught with the pants down. Dionysus, never sober. The Furies, hounding the men, driving them mad. I have known many women like that, it's true. I even married with one, for too many years. Gods you feel you could sit down, have chitchat with. They would be interested in you, like you in them. They never left the people alone, always making mess in lives. But because they wanted to be with us. They liked humans. This lot, the One True Pantheon. Pfah!"

Imagine someone spitting at their feet here.

"They use us, that's all. What is the saying? A means to an end. For getting their own back on each other. They have no respect for us, even though we keep them going. Without worship from us they are nothing. And do they thank us? Do they even notice us any more?"

His conclusion was always this. Somebody should take a stand against them. Somebody should show them the contempt they show us. See how they like it.

"Freegypt," he'd say. "If only the whole of the world was like Freegypt."

He didn't mean at war with itself. In that respect the whole world *was* like Freegypt. He meant, simply, independent of the gods. Freegypt might be troubled but at least its troubles were of its own making. Secular troubles.

We often stopped off at Freegypt on our travels. Nothing I saw of the place made me think here was some humanist paradise.

Alexandria, Port Said, El Alamein – I found them to be typically fly-ridden North African seaports, where baksheesh for the harbourmaster meant you could get away with loading or offloading just about anything, if you were reasonably discreet. No one there looked to me any happier or more enlightened than anywhere else. Not even the foreign apostates who'd come from abroad seeking a life without theocracy. They just seemed kind of disappointed, as if they'd been expecting more. This wasn't the promised land, just another fucking fucked-up country. The dockers were lazy, the hookers surly, the sailors ready to stick a knife between your ribs as soon as look at you... The main difference I did notice was the absence of hieroglyphics. All signage came in Arabic, or sometimes Arabic and English. Officials didn't have cartouches on their uniforms telling you who they worked for and how important they were. But apart from that, Freegypt never struck me as being particularly, well, free.

But there was *something* there, I thought. If Iannis was right – and I was more and more sure that he was – and somebody had to make a stand against the gods, Freegypt was where to do it. It was the place to start.

And I was the man for the job.

Destiny calling. A year, almost to the day, after I met Iannis, we parted ways. The big old fellow hugged me and blubbed like a baby. Told me losing me was like losing the son he'd never had. I didn't point out that you can't lose a son you've never had. Truth be told, I was a little choked up and teary myself. We'd had some great times together. But I'd found something more important to do now. Iannis understood. He gave me some extra money, on top of the money I already had, the drug earnings I'd carefully saved up and hardly spent any of.

"For the doing of good work," he told me. "To free the world."

I stood on the dockside at Port Said and watched his boat chunter off into the distance, till it was lost in the sparkle of the sea.

Then I turned and went south.

A disfigured white man in an Arabic country wasn't going to get far unless he learned the local lingo. So first thing I did was get a job with a private English-language school in Cairo, which I managed without having a passport or any form of ID, let alone a qualification. The school head was as open to unsolicited cash windfalls as anyone. In theory I was teaching middle-class Freegyptian kids to speak English. In practice, I was doing my best to pick up their tongue. I struggled with the glottal stops and the long consonants and the superheavy syllables, but I got there in the end. In fact I've been told my "teachers" succeeded too well. Zafirah says my Arabic is horribly slangy. I slur and elide like a slack-jawed teenager. But I like to think that gives me the demotic touch, which I'd never have back home, say, speaking with this posh accent of mine, dontcha know, toodle-pip, what-what.

Then, once I was conversational in Arabic, if not quite fluent, I headed down to Luxor, because here was where the infighting was at its worst. When you set out to cure a disease, you don't bother yourself with the secondary symptoms. You go straight to the source of the problem, and Luxor was it, a festering wound in Freegypt's gut.

I realised something right away. Basically, all that the factions who were slugging away at one another wanted was to be top dog. Each of them had no aim other than that, to rule the region and be boss. It sounds obvious, but in all the confusion they themselves seemed to have forgotten the causes they'd started fighting for all the decades ago. Now it was just rhetoric and entrenched positions, with motive and logic long lost. It was gang mentality. Each side knew all the others were their enemies and wanted to beat them, and that was it.

A go-between was needed. Someone non-aligned. Someone who could mediate among the factions and show them that there was a greater prize available to them than just crushing their foes.

That was how the Lightbringer came into being. My alter ego. The jumpsuit – it was straightforward, non-threatening, mundane. The gloves? So my lily-white hands wouldn't show. And the mask… well, I settled on that so that my *desfigurado* fizzog wouldn't put anyone off and also so that I wouldn't be just some meddling foreigner, a European colonialist coming and telling everyone else what to do. They'd had enough of that back in Victorian times, when the map of Egypt was British imperial red. The mask anonymised me. Is that a word, anonymised? It should be. Effaced me. Made me distinctive and at the same time less distinct.

It took ten months – ten long months of bloody hard slog. I convinced the Liberators to give me a chance first of all. The lovely Zafirah helped out there. She put her trust in me almost before anyone else did. And once I had the Liberators in the bag, I used their ground-knowledge and their strategic resources to get to the enemy camps and win hearts and minds there as well. Not easy. I've lost count of the number of times I wound up kneeling with a gun to my head and some sweaty guerrilla commander yelling at me that he was going to blow my brains out, and all I could do was talk and keep talking and pray that no one ripped my mask off and saw the mangled face underneath. Which did happen a couple of times, as a matter of fact, and luckily the result worked in my favour. Everyone was so startled by what they saw, they stopped and heard me out.

What I was offering them was both less and more. Less in terms of tangible military conquest, more in terms of status. I was offering them a new ideology to replace the ones they'd pretty much allowed to lapse. I was telling these local warlords that they could continue fighting over Upper Freegypt and maybe one day end up with a slightly larger chunk of land to call their own, but never the whole region. That was not going to happen. It had been stalemate here for a century. How was that likely to change? Or they could break the cycle and start afresh.

You'd be surprised how well the message went down. I know I was. Seems there was a real appetite for an end to the hostilities, or else the paramilitaries had had their fill of relentless, grinding conflict and couldn't stomach any more. They were tired of killing their own countrymen, but none of them wanted to be the first to say enough. None of them had the nerve to raise the white flag and tender the olive branch. Their leaders couldn't afford to do that, as a matter of pride, until I came along and presented them with a dignified, face-saving excuse. Throwing in their lot with the Lightbringer wasn't a climb-down. It was the opposite, a way up and out of the morass of partisanship they'd become bogged down in.

The day came when there was a big powwow between me and every one of the faction leaders, just us sitting down in a room to seal our alliance once and for all. All of them knew by then that I was a displaced Englishman with complexion issues, and they had got past it. It didn't matter to them. I kept the mask on anyway at all times, because I knew it was helping to build a mystique around me. Across the region the Lightbringer was becoming this strange, not quite human figure, unknowable, a little monstrous perhaps, someone people talked about in slightly disbelieving whispers, an object of speculation and wondering, and that all served to foster my reputation and further my cause.

But in that room, as we formally agreed to work together as a united force of Upper Freegyptians, it gradually became clear that the faction leaders were deferring to me. They kept looking to me to confirm or disagree with whatever they said. I realised that I was making all the running, setting the tone, and they were happily going along with it. When we got up from the table it was bear hugs and handclasps all round, and I could tell that quite without meaning to or trying to, I'd taken charge. I was the big shot now. I was top dog. There'd not been any election, any show of hands. I hadn't had to arm-wrestle a rival into submission or kill one of them just to show the others I meant business. By unspoken consent all the warlords had deferred to me. They seemed only too happy to pass the burden of command on to someone else. They were waiting for me to tell them what to do next. So I told them.

"We start training our men, together. We instil them with discipline. We forge them into a unit, a single army. And we gather weapons. As much as we can. Every type that we can."

That was three years ago. And here we are now.

13. CACHE

"HERE WE ARE now," echoed David, as the jeep they were riding in plunged into and out of a pothole the size of a small crater. Steven crunched gears and cursed. He was driving at least fifteen miles an hour faster than was wise on a road this badly made, but seemed of the opinion that it was the road that should mend its ways, not him.

"So what do you make of it?" Steven asked, or rather the Lightbringer asked. For the past half an hour David had been listening to this masked man in the seat beside him talking in Steven's voice, using Steven's intonation and turn of phrase, sounding exactly like Steven… Cognitively he knew it was his brother under that mask. He had no doubts on that score. Who else could it be? Nobody but Steven could have told that anecdote about throwing up all over Mrs Plomley, or conjured up the speech-impedimented shade of Mr Perkins quite so accurately.

For all that, David could not shake off the impression that he was sitting next to an impostor, or perhaps a psychic channelling Steven's dead spirit. He longed for a peek beneath the mask, for final irrefutable confirmation of what he knew to be true, but he'd decided to let Steven choose to show him his face in his own time. He would do it when he wanted to, if he wanted to.

"What do I make of it?" David said. "Well, it's quite a tale."

"I know! I wouldn't believe it myself if I hadn't lived through it. But actually what I meant was, what do you make of us meeting up again like this?"

"Fluke. Happy coincidence."

"Me, I think it was meant to be. I mean, my own brother pitching up here in Freegypt – what are the odds? Astronomical. But as soon as I heard from Zafirah that she'd picked up this British soldier in the desert and his name was David Westwynter, I felt this click inside. Like, of course Dave's here. Why shouldn't he be? You didn't get the same feeling, though."

"No."

"Well, you always were the hard-headed, practical one, weren't you?"

"Perhaps our meeting would have had more significance for me if you hadn't spent all that time arsing around, stringing me along, pretending you didn't know me. Was it really necessary, that whole charade?"

"To start with, yes. I'm the Lightbringer, remember."

"So?"

"Well, I couldn't just walk up to you and say, 'Hi, Dave, how's it going? Long time no see, big brother.' I'd no idea how you'd react. You might have punched me in the face, and that wouldn't have looked good in front of all those people. Instead, I thought it'd be better if I got you on your own, then did the big reveal."

"Except you didn't. You made me play senet with you first."

"Yes, that, I admit, was for a laugh. I was waiting to see how long it'd take for the penny to drop. Your face, Dave!" Steven chuckled and slapped the steering wheel. "What a sight. Haven't seen you look so shocked since the time we found that polished mahogany Osiris Special in Mum's bedside cabinet."

"Glad it amused you."

"Look, I'm sorry, all right?" It was one of those apologies that didn't sound very apologetic. "You know me. If there's temptation, I always give in to it."

David frowned sternly at him, but couldn't maintain the expression for long. Right now he felt he could forgive his brother almost anything. Besides, it had been a harmless little deception, Steven just being his typical, slippery, prankish self. If the roles had been reversed, David might well have done the same. No, who was he kidding? That was the difference between them. *He* seldom, if ever, gave in to temptation.

"And I know what you're going to say next," Steven said, holding up a warding-off finger.

"Yes?"

"Yes. You're going to ask why didn't I get word home that I wasn't dead, as soon as I could."

"I wasn't going to—"

"You were. Come on."

"OK. Maybe I was. Well?"

"It's not that easy to explain. The thing is, by the time I got off that island, I knew you and Mum and Dad would have already given me up for lost and mourned me. Then I sort of fell into a life of crime with Iannis and realised it suited me to be officially an ex-person. And now that I'm the Lightbringer, Steven Westwynter might as well not exist any more. That's just the way my life has gone – my afterlife, my second life, whatever you want to call it. That's how it's had to be."

"But a letter, a phone call home, even an anonymous one…"

"… might have been the right thing to do but it would have brought complications. Which isn't to say I didn't think about it. I thought about it a lot. But the longer I left it, the more unhelpful it became to me. It was something I kept putting off until it, all of a sudden, it was too late. Can you imagine what would have happened anyway? Dad gets wind that I haven't gone down with the *Immortal* after all. Knowing him, he'd alert the authorities, have them hunt me down and haul me home to face a naval tribunal for desertion or dereliction of duty or whatever. Wouldn't he? Am I right?"

Reluctantly David nodded.

"I know I am. I'd pissed him off by signing up. It'd have pissed him off even more if it turned out I'd publicly screwed up being in the navy. He'd want to see me doing time in a military prison and getting farmed out with a dishonourable discharge. 'Teach the lad a lesson.' Whereas this way, posthumously, Jack Westwynter has got the best son he could hope for: a war hero. The black sheep who came good. Died fighting for his country, and so on. Something to brag about at the country club. Again, am I right?"

David could not deny it. Once their father had got over the shock of bereavement, he'd come to terms with Steven's death by accommodating it into his personal understanding of how the world should be. Jack Westwynter was not a man who accepted failure or disgrace. He'd never had to. So, by listening to his peers when they told him how proud he should be of Steven, and by carefully recalibrating his memories of his wayward disappointment of a son, he was able to present himself as the grieving parent of a young man whose life had not been wasted but rather sacrificed in a good cause. This attitude made him absurdly happy and served him longer than any black armband.

"And Mum..." Steven began, then shrugged. "Well, tough on her, but there you go. Same with you too. I'm sorry about it, Dave." Unlike the last apology, this one sounded more or less sincere. "But to be brutally honest, I'm a grown-up and shouldn't have to worry about what anyone else thinks, my parents least of all. More than that, I'm a man with a mission now, and men with missions need to be free from all other responsibilities, all encumbrances."

"Family isn't an encumbrance."

"Unless your surname's Westwynter."

David didn't have an answer to that.

"Anyway," Steven went on, "from what I hear, you've not exactly been in a hurry to return to the bosom of home and country, have you? You've gone rogue yourself."

"Circumstances."

"Yeah, yeah. You're enjoying it, aren't you? Come on; admit it. Nearly thirty years old, and this is the first time in your life you've ever known anything like real independence, and you're having a ball. It's exciting. Scary too, but mainly exciting. No?"

David shook his head, but the jeep jolted heavily over a bump and the shake somehow turned into a nod.

"Free agent, Dave." Steven clapped him on the knee. "That's you. Me too. We're free agents, and the past is a big door shut behind us and the future is a million doors waiting to be opened. And now we can open them together. Side by side. You and me. How brilliant is that?"

David half smiled, remembering how his brother had never lacked for enthusiasm. He himself, born cautious and dutiful, had always found it hard to come by, so had resented Steven for having so much of it. Envied him, too.

Now he saw that enthusiasm was something that could be shared. Like champagne in a champagne tower, it spilled over from the top glass and could be caught in the glasses below.

He looked sidelong at his brother, five years dead, only not so after all. The Lightbringer's body language was Steven's, definitely. The profile, though softened by the mask, was Steven's too.

David ached with joy, and also regret.

Regret because, although he believed Steven's account of how he had spent the past five years, he believed it only up to a point. He knew his brother. He knew when he was hiding something or lying. Steven's story had been the truth, but far from the whole truth.

Whether or not it mattered, though – that was something David couldn't decide.

THIRTY-ODD MILES SOUTH-WEST of Luxor they came to a small town. It looked like an ordinary enough place: wide, dusty streets, low whitewashed houses with flat roofs and painted doors and shutters, high-kerbed concrete pavements, a cat's cradle of power lines threading from building to building, a communal well, here and there a stand of palms, all of it parched and pounded by an oven-hot wind. Hundreds of towns like this one dotted the desert wilderness, tenacious outposts of humanity, like limpets on a rock.

The moment the jeep pulled up in the main square, a horde of children appeared from nowhere and surrounded the vehicle.

"Al Ashraqa! Al Ashraqa!"

Along with the clamour of their voices came begging hands thrusting in from all directions. Steven stood up on the driving seat and dug out handfuls of boiled sweets from his pockets. He hurled them around, and the children went diving and scurrying to retrieve them. One little girl with a club foot wasn't agile enough to compete, and as the other children hurried off with their cheeks bulging, she was left prizeless. Steven strode over to her, ruffled her hair, and dropped three of the sweets into her cupped palms. He'd saved them specially for her.

"*Shokran*," the girl said with a dainty bob of her head, and hobbled off.

"Steven Westwynter the great philanthropist," said David wryly. "Who'd have thought?"

"Ah shut up, Dave."

"But you've never liked kids."

"These ones I do. They're not just any old kids, anyway. They're my people. You could even call them my employees."

"Child labour, eh?"

"You'll see. Oh, and by the way. While we're in public, I'm the Lightbringer, OK? Not Steven. Not brother. Lightbringer."

"I see. OK."

"Don't take it personally. I'm not embarrassed that we're related or anything. It's just, like I said, Steven Westwynter doesn't really exist any more. No one knows me by that name, not even Zafirah. I am what I am now. The mighty, mysterious leader. The man with no face, no past, no ties. You understand?"

Funnily enough, David thought he did.

They walked through the town. A passing pick-up truck honked its horn. Steven waved in response and called out, "*Assalaamu aleikum!*" A pair of plump women sitting in the shade of a shop awning smiled at him. He nodded back graciously. David noted an ease and comfort to his brother's movements. Steven was right at home here. He was known and liked, and liked it.

Choosing a house apparently at random, Steven went up and knocked on the door. A old man with a lazy left eye invited him in, all smiles and obsequies. Inside, a just-as-old woman, the man's wife, was peeling onions at a small table with a worn Formica top.

She greeted Steven with a cry of delight and a hug, then chatted to him for several minutes while her husband plonked himself down in front of the TV set that was blaring at top volume in the corner. The news was on, and every other item, as far as David could tell, was a piece from a war correspondent, much like the news back home. There was a report from the Bering Sea, where Horusite and Setic naval divisions were clashing among the floes of springtime brash ice. Another from the Indian subcontinent, where tensions in Kashmir were rising. Another from the suburbs of divided Warsaw, where Osirisiac forces were skirmishing with Setic forces along the fortified banks of the river Vistula. Freegypt wasn't involved in the global conflict, but the global conflict still impinged on Freegypt. People here wanted to know what was going on outside their borders, perhaps if only to remind themselves how lucky they were that it didn't directly affect them. For now.

The old man asked David a question, pointing at the TV screen.

"Kareem thinks you're a journalist," Steven said. "He wants to know if you've come to do a report on me. Not a bad idea if you play along, just for now. Nod and look interested in me."

David tried to do as instructed.

The old man grinned and spoke triumphantly, grinning at Steven.

"He's saying I'm a hero," Steven said. "I brought peace to Freegypt, and I'm going to bring peace to the whole world. He's saying you should tell people that."

"You tell Kareem not to worry. I may be very new to this journalism lark but I'm sure I already have a clear picture of what the Lightbringer's like."

Steven relayed this to the old man, though probably not giving an exact translation of David's words.

Shortly, just as David was beginning to wonder what the point of this visit was, the old woman stood up and produced a key from around her neck. She and Steven invited David through a bead-curtained doorway and along to a back room.

David was expecting a bedroom, a pantry, something like that. He was not expecting the old woman to unlock a door and usher him into an armoury.

There were guns everywhere. Rifles in open crates. Machine guns and sub-machine guns racked on the walls. Pistols piled high. Ammunition of every calibre lying around singly or belted or in boxes. The air reeked of gunmetal and grease.

There were grenades too, and landmines, and antipersonnel devices, and bundles of high explosive. Everywhere he looked, David saw weaponry and more weaponry. There were even *ba* lances – Setic, Horusite, Nephthysian, Osirisiac, Anubian, the whole gamut.

"Holy shit," he breathed.

"Yeah," said Steven. "Kareem and Fatima seem such a sweet, ordinary old couple, don't they? Who'd suspect they're hoarding a mini arsenal on the premises? And that's not all. This way."

He led David through the house and outside. At the back there was an enclosure, walled on the right and left, the rear opening out onto the desert. Laundry flapped on a line, root vegetables grew in a well-tended kitchen garden... and occupying more than half of the available space, swathed in a large pegged-down tarpaulin, was a Scarab tank.

Steven dragged the tarpaulin off to expose the tank in all its fearsome glory. It was parked with its drive sphere butting up against the rear of the house and its quartet of blaster nozzles aiming out towards the horizon. Its smooth, rounded contours contrasted with the four-square regularity of its surroundings. The photovoltaic plates that covered its back, like a carapace, gleamed a soft, faintly iridescent blue.

"Captured from the Nephs by the Red Sea Fellahin," Steven said, "then passed on to us. The *ba* cell's at about half capacity, which isn't bad. The Fellahin didn't squander it. And all that's needed is a day's charging in the sunshine to get the thing rolling again. The radiance of Ra is free *ba* for everyone. You don't have to pray for it."

David ignored the tinge of sarcasm in his brother's voice. He was recalling the first time he ever saw Scarab tanks in action at first hand, during exercises on Salisbury Plain. They'd moved so lightly, that was what had surprised him. For such large vehicles they scrambled and bounced like dune buggies. That was thanks to their relatively thin armour and their drive spheres which, mounted on dual-axis gimbals, gave them turn-on-a-sixpence manoeuvrability. The downside, as he learned from one tank commander later, was that they were a pig of a ride. If you wanted to know how it felt to be the beads in maracas, spend some time in a Scarab.

"We have eighteen of them including this one," Steven went on. "All solar powered, naturally. Round here you don't get any other kind, and anyway they're cheaper and easier to run than your North European diesel models. Some say they're inferior to the diesels but I disagree. They don't need refuelling every couple of hours, for one thing, and the power to weight ratio's roughly the same – solar cells have a lower b.h.p. output than an engine but aren't nearly as heavy, so it evens out. The only drawback with the solar version is that it's useless past midnight if you've run it too hard during the daytime. But that's not the end of the world, especially if you're up against other solar Scarabs. Then everyone's in the same boat, or rather tank."

"Eighteen," said David. It seemed like a lot, and yet not nearly enough for what Steven apparently had in mind.

"We've some armoured personnel carriers as well, and a couple of half-tracks which are pretty much antiques but still going strong. I think they date back to the Belgian Congo campaign. Mid-1950s at any rate, but they built things to last in those days."

"All embedded around the town."

"Correct. Along with a good twenty or so weapons dumps, each as big as Kareem and Fatima's, some of them bigger. The fruits of three years of diligent stockpiling. As you've seen we've got some *ba* tech but most of the guns are conventional. Imported from South America, where else? The South Americans love their bullets and cordite, don't they? Have to, I suppose, given how thrifty with their *ba* the children of Horus are. Minor gods, less divine essence to spare – stands to reason. If the gods won't provide, there's always human ingenuity to fall back on, and Brazilian and Peruvian gunsmithery is second to none."

"So this whole town..."

"... is one big arms cache, yes," said Steven. "Our own quartermaster's stores, based in a tiny little flyspeck in the middle of nowhere. The last place anyone would think to look, if they were looking."

"I'm impressed."

"Thought you might be."

"But..."

"But what?" Steven said sharply, a flint-spark of irritation in his voice. "What's the problem, Dave?"

"No problem."

"You've got some criticism, though. I know it. I can tell. Something's niggling. Out with it."

"It's just..." David groped for the right words. "You've plenty of materiel here to fight a localised war. But from what I've gathered, your plans are more ambitious than that."

"You're saying I'm underprepared."

"Not exactly, no. Well, sort of. I think maybe you've underestimated just how much weaponry you're going to need – by quite a large margin. You're taking on the whole world, Steven, that's what it comes down to. And however much you've got in the way of resources, it's just not going to be adequate."

"Oh, Dave. Dave, Dave, Dave. This is bloody typical of you, isn't it?" The irritation had flared into a flame of anger. "Typical patronising older brother. To you I'm still little Steven, still Westwynter Minor who could never do anything right and was never as smart or as sporty or generally as *good* as you. You assume I haven't thought this through properly because that's how the old Steven was, the Steven you once knew. He never thought things through. He just did whatever came into his head and hang the consequences."

"That wasn't what I—"

"Well, newsflash," Steven said, steamrollering on. "I'm not him any more. It's been five years, and I've seen and done a lot during that time. A lot's happened to me. I'm not the same creature I used to be. And I resent you treating me like that, like nothing's changed and you still know best."

"But I—"

Steven jabbed a finger in David's chest. "You have no idea what my plans are. No idea! You just think it's going to be some half-arsed, cockeyed scheme that's never going to work. It's doomed to fail, and I'm going to wind up dead."

"Yes!" David exclaimed. "That's precisely it. That's what I'm worried about."

"But how can you—"

Now it was David's turn to interrupt. "If you'll just let me get a word in edgewise," he said, "if you'll shut up and listen for a second, you fuckwit…"

His brother leaned back, cocking his head. "Come on then. Tell me where I'm going wrong. Give me the benefit of your great wisdom."

"I only want to know if you're sure, really sure, this is what you want to do."

"You're trying to get me to back out?" Steven shook his head. "No way."

"Steven, up until a couple of hours ago I believed you were dead," said David. "No, not believed. You were dead. Now, suddenly, here you are, alive, and it's great. I'm thrilled. Couldn't be more delighted. Only, it turns out you're hell-bent on throwing your life away on this, this campaign of yours. So try and see it from my point of view. I've only just been given my brother back and already I'm facing the prospect of losing him again. I'm trying hard to take it all in, all this, what's happened today, it's a lot to deal with, but right now my honest reaction is I don't want you to go to war against the Pantheon. Not because they're gods and you oughtn't defy them. Simply because, selfishly, you're my brother and I don't want you to die. Again."

The Lightbringer's mask was impassive, frozen for a moment, blanker than ever. Then the material shifted in a way that indicated a broad smile had broken out underneath.

"That's the nicest thing anyone's said to me in a long time," Steven said. "You actually care about me."

"Of course I do."

"Never mind *me* changing. You've changed, Dave."

"Have I? I always cared about you."

"Maybe, but you never showed it. Not as obviously as you've just done."

David shrugged, a little embarrassed, even though he knew he had nothing to be embarrassed about.

"Thing is," his brother went on, "I couldn't back out even if I wanted to. People are counting on me. They've invested in me. I can't let them down."

"You could disappear tomorrow," David replied matter-of-factly. "Up and leave. Your followers would be disappointed, perhaps, but they'd get over it. There'd be no comebacks. No one knows who you really are. You could take off that mask and go anywhere, and that would be an end of it."

"Do a moonlight flit? And what about everything I've established here? You think I can just walk away and leave it?"

"Someone else could take over."

"No one else could."

"Then without you in charge it might all simply fade away and be forgotten."

"You're missing the point. You've seen how people react to the Lightbringer. This isn't some flash-in-the-pan political movement, here today, gone the next. This is a bona fide revolution, the beginning of something big, seismically big. It's begun, it's grown, it's still growing, and it's about to explode across the world stage. I created it. I'm spearheading it. I'm not going to abandon it, not for any reason."

"Even if it might – no, will – kill you?"

"I'm not afraid of dying. If I die defeating the gods, it won't have been in vain."

David detected no hint of bravado in the statement. Steven meant it. He believed it.

"All right then," he said. "That leaves me with only one option."

"What?" said Steven with a wary laugh. "You're going to clonk me on the head, knock me out and carry me off over your shoulder? Spirit me out of the country?"

The thought had crossed David's mind, if only flickeringly briefly.

"No," he said. "I'm going to join you."

"Come again?"

"I said—"

"I heard. I just... Really? Join me?"

"Someone needs to keep an eye out for you. Someone has to watch your back. Someone to make sure you don't do something really, truly stupid. Might as well be me."

Steven was momentarily dumbfounded. "Dave, I hoped... Well, that's why I brought you here. I thought I might be able to convince you to... And now you... Fuck. This is great. You're on board? Seriously?"

"Seriously."

Steven cheered, grabbed his brother in a fierce embrace, punched him manfully on the shoulder, did a little dance on the dusty earth.

David let him celebrate, feeling pleased that he had given Steven what he wanted. Pleased, too, that he had put himself in a good position to try to steer his brother away from the suicidal course he was on.

But not happy.

Far from happy.

14. RELATIONS

THE FIRST FAMILY *are a confusing lot, especially when at home, in their Palace of Unity. There, in a building that appears to have an infinite number of floors but actually has only one, they dwell together, inseparable – father, mother, son, daughter, all seemingly alike, hard to tell apart despite their many differences. Shu, of the air, is married to his sister Tefnut, of the rain, and their son Geb, of the earth, is married to his sister Nut, of the sky. But Geb is effeminate, so much so that he and Nut could almost be twins. And Geb is also a mummy's boy, so enamoured of Tefnut that he once even raped her. For this crime he was never punished, and it has been speculated that the rape was not perhaps a one-sided affair, that Tefnut was at least a half-willing participant. So they are a close family in many ways. Too many, perhaps.*

All this passes through Ra's mind as he manifests in the First Family's living quarters and eyes the bed which dominates the room. It is a bed of enormous dimensions, a world unto itself, and it is festooned with mountainous cushions and oceanic counterpanes of damasked silk, upon which the four members of the Family recline, naked, entwined, semi-asleep. It takes him a moment to distinguish one from the other, to identify this leg as Shu's and that breast as Tefnut's, this hip as Geb's and that shoulder as Nut's. They are a mass of disrobed divinity, like some protean, many-limbed organism. Even their glowing headdresses, though varied, seem similar.

Roused by Ra's arrival the Family members separate, out of politeness. They sit apart on the bed, at each of its corners, and Shu shows himself to be a wizened, weak-eyed old man, crowned with a feather, and Tefnut a flowing-haired old woman with a cobra shimmering above her. Geb, meanwhile, takes the form of a young man who, though girlishly handsome, has a goose-like cast to his features, and Nut becomes a beautiful young woman in a night-blue, star-spangled dress, her head haloed with the outline of a water pitcher.

As one, they formally greet their visitor, who responds no less formally even though he is impatient to get down to business.

"First Family," Ra says, "upholders of all there is, I come in supplication, craving a boon."

"From us?" says Shu in his thin, wispy voice. "The almighty Ra, seeking our help?"

Geb cackles gleefully and chants, "Ra, Ra, he's come far, he wants our help, he's asked our pa."

Both his sister-wife and his sometime-lover mother hiss at him to be quiet.

"Forgive my son, O Sun God whose secret name is known only to Isis," said Tefnut. "You know how lacking in self-restraint Geb is," she adds with an indulgent smile.

Ra bows in a manner that implies understanding, if not absolution.

Nut yawns and stretches languorously, arching her back, and briefly she is a firmament, the glittering heavens, spreading vast and forever. Then, a woman once more, she says, "Whatever is in our power to do, Ra, we shall."

"I'm grateful," says Ra. "I should warn you, though, that the favour I require of you is one that, simple as it sounds, may well prove impossible."

"Name it anyway, Uncle," says Shu.

"I wish you to bring peace among your offspring."

No sooner have the words left Ra's lips than the First Family burst out laughing.

"You could more easily bid the wind to stop blowing," says Shu.

"Or the rain not to fall," says Tefnut.

"Or the stars not to shine," says Nut.

"Or the ground not to tremble when there's a great big rumbling earthquake!" cries Geb.

"I understand," says Ra, "and I agree. The enmities that exist between them, between Osiris and Set particularly, seem implacable and irreconcilable. However, if anyone were able to find a way of resolving the matter, it would surely be you four, who are the very essence of oneness. You have set an example by overcoming your own disagreements. That places you well to persuade your descendants to follow suit."

"Undoubtedly," says Shu. "But the truth is, we are unable to help."

"We would like to," says Tefnut, "but cannot."

"Too tired," says Nut.

"Too bored," says Geb.

"We are old, like you, Ra," says Shu. "Old and very weary. Our battles with the other pantheons have left us worn out and drained."

"We continue to exist," says Tefnut, "but zest for life, for anything, is beyond us."

"That's why we bequeathed the earth to our descendants," says Nut.

"Too much like hard work, running that place," says Geb.

"It seemed wise to let them inherit it," says Shu. "It seemed no less wise to divide it up between them in more or less equal portions, for the sake of fairness."

"In hindsight," says Tefnut, "a mistake."

"Their old animosities and rivalries would not stay buried," says Nut.

"Like Osiris himself!" says Geb. "Can't keep him underground for long!"

"We hoped that they would learn to work together," says Shu, "instead of which their arguments only grew more vehement."

"It wasn't our intention that the world should suffer the consequences, either," says Tefnut.

"But events on earth mirror events in the heavens," says Nut. "That's how it's always been."

"As above, so below," says Geb.

"It's a misfortune of our own making," admits Shu.

"We feel responsible," adds Tefnut. "But not guilty."

"And we cannot become involved," says Nut. "We've done what we have done. Our struggles are over. Our lives are now rest and repose, and we wish them to stay that way."

"So take your boon and stick it where you don't shine!" chortles Geb.

His mother reaches across and clouts him.

"Owww!"

Shu glares at his son, eyes as icy as an arctic breeze. "Apologise to the Light Over All That Is," he says. "At once."

"Sorry," Geb mumbles to Ra.

Ra feels the heat of indignation building inside him. Geb's rudeness is bad enough, but it is the First Family's general apathy that really grates.

"I suppose it was too much to hope for," he says, "that you would show a scintilla of interest in the affairs of your fractious progeny. I realise now that it is much better to laze about here in perfumed splendour, caring little about what goes on around you, than feel in any way troubled by the mess you have created. The mortal realm lies in disarray, humans in their millions suffer, war and wanton destruction rule the day. But" – he sighs theatrically – "as long as it doesn't affect you, that's fine."

"We care about the mortals," Shu retorts. "Of course we do. Their worship sustains us, just as it sustains you."

"It may not be formal worship," Tefnut adds, "but we value it nonetheless."

"As long as there is someone thankful for a cooling wind or a breath of fresh air..." says Shu.

"... or a fall of rain that fills a reservoir or brings life to crops..." says Tefnut.

"... or the fertility of the soil that the crops grow in..." says Geb.

"... or the sight of a clear blue sky or the stars..." says Nut.

"... *then we four will have strength in our hearts and live,*" concludes Shu. "*In the same way that you, Ra, live because mortals cherish your brightness and warmth. Their joy in you is a prayer. They turn their faces up to you and bask, and your ba is replenished by their appreciation.*"

"*So do not presume,*" says Tefnut, "*to tell us how much or how little mortals matter to us. It insults us and demeans you.*"

The First Family have risen from their shared bed. They are affronted, but also galvanized. Ra sees that he might use this to his advantage. If he can annoy them further, perhaps they just might stir themselves to comply with his wishes, to spite him if nothing else.

"*You know, looking at you now, it's hard to imagine that you managed to vanquish all those other pantheons,*" he says. "*How can four such listless and self-obsessed individuals ever have managed such a feat? It's a wonder you can even get out of bed in the morning. Oh wait, you seldom do, do you? You just loll around here, writhing in one another's embraces.*"

"*What hypocrisy, coming from the former King of the Earth who retired to his Solar Barque when he'd had enough of ruling the mortal plane!*" This snarled riposte from Shu comes like the blast of a hurricane.

"*How dare you, Ra!*" Tefnut chimes in, monsoon-fierce. "*To denigrate our achievement like that! We gave every ounce of ourselves in that conflict. It was long, hard-fought, hard-won.*"

"*We strained, we heaved,*" says Geb.

"*We shone!*" declares Nut.

And now they are all speaking at once, their voices overlapping, their words colliding, unified by rage. It is a litany of their victories, a roll call of the defeated:

"*All those gods of war... the many-armed destroyers... the ones with dragon bodies... the warrior deities... the laughing gods who just wouldn't stand still... the solo gods perched in their lofty cloudtop citadels, defended by archangels, djinns, serpents, sword-bearing armies... the thunder gods... the luck gods who kept on escaping us, against all the odds... the fire gods... the archer gods...*"

*the demons... the ineffable gods who were near impossible to find...
the mischief gods who tried to trick their way out of trouble... the
mad-eyed protective mother goddesses... you think it was easy?...
Furies... Valkyries... frost giants... Oni... fairies... demigods too...
it was gruelling... punishing... relentless... centuries... all our
energies... we deserve our relaxation... we've earned it!"*

As one, shouting, the four reach a climax. Silence follows, as in the
wake of a storm that has battered the land and torn the sky to shreds.

Ra finds himself reeling in the aftermath. He knows he has had a
glimpse, the merest glimpse, of the full power that is these four's to
command, and it is awesome indeed. They are all of Creation. They
are Everything. Those other gods, even the mightiest among them,
never stood a chance against the Family's theocidal onslaught.

As the echoes of their tirade fade away, Ra says softly, "Well, you
can certainly muster up some vigour when you want to. Would that
you could apply that same vigour to the matter at hand..."

But the First Family draw together in a sullen huddle, and he
senses he has miscalculated. He has peeved rather than piqued them.

"No," says Shu, adamant. "It's out of the question."

"You have asked too much," says Tefnut. "Presumed too much."

"You should leave," suggests Nut, her dress sparkling so
dazzlingly it makes Ra's eyes ache.

"Yeah," says Geb. "Sod off."

This time, no one chastises him. Geb has spoken for all four of
them.

"I apologise," says Ra, bending low from the waist. "This has
been a regrettable episode. Let us forget it ever happened. Next
time we meet, it shall be on cordial terms, as in the light of a new
dawn after a troubled night."

Courteous, ever the diplomat, Ra knows how to mollify when
he has to. The First Family's umbrage is lessened somewhat. Their
backs grow a little less stiff, their eyes a little less narrow.

"Yes, well," says Shu. "Bygones."

"Bygones," repeats Ra.

The Family retreat to their bed, merging back into one atop
that great silk-swathed mound. Soon all four of them are fast

asleep, breathing deeply, their chests rising and falling in unison. Ra, meanwhile, is back aboard the Solar Barque, where Thoth greets him.

"How went it?" he enquires.

"Not well," replies Ra. "I made little progress. None, to be honest – unless you count invoking the First Family's wrath."

"Not a sensible thing to do."

"Tell me about it. Old friend, I'm stymied. What should be my next move?"

"Continue as you are, for now," counsels Thoth. "That is all I can suggest. Keep on with your quest to bring peace. Only good can come of that."

Ra rubs his brow. "I am a god, Thoth. How come I cannot simply snap my fingers and have anything that I desire?"

"Even gods have their limitations," his vizier replies with a sad smile. "We are as the mortals imagined us. They shaped us in their own image, imbued us with their own traits. They saw us as imperfect, fallible, prone to foibles, as they are. They raised us up on pedestals and at the same time gave us feet of clay. We have had no choice but to go along with that. We are their creations as much as they are ours. It is one of the immutable laws of the universe. And truth to tell" – Thoth's smile broadens and brightens – "would you have it any other way? Would you wish for everything to come easily to you? Would that not make life unbearably dull?"

"At this moment, O Wise One," says a rueful Ra, "at this precise moment I would give anything for a dull life!"

15. SORTIE

THEY ENTERED LIBYA around midnight, after a long trek across Freegypt's Western Desert. There were three vehicles in all – a ZT and a pair of flatbed trucks with guns mounted on the back. The full personnel complement was eight, including David and Zafirah. They made the crossing from one country to the other off-road, in a remote, uninhabited area, to avoid checkpoints and lessen the chances of encountering a border patrol.

As big moments went it was low-key, even anticlimactic.

"We've done it," David said to Zafirah, glancing up from the map. "We're officially on Neph soil. This is it. No turning back now."

"We can always turn back, any time," Zafirah replied, peering ahead at the landscape picked out by the headlamp beams. "If we choose to."

"Do you want to?"

"No."

Thus was an act of war begun.

THE EASTERN fringes of Libya played host to an assortment of Nephthysian sub-sects, which were tolerated if not sanctioned by the authorities in Tripoli. Littered across the wastes and wildernesses of the region were shrines, temples, even monasteries, each dedicated to a lesser member of the Pantheon. They had been established during the Divine Diaspora, when Pantheonic worship spilled out from what was then just plain Egypt like fruit from a cornucopia. While the renowned foreign archaeologists went racing back to their homelands with their arms full of tomb treasure and their hearts full of gnostic revelation, Egyptians themselves began spreading the good news to their immediate neighbours and to more distant nations as well. Most of the attention was on the major deities and the philosophies they represented, but the Egyptians didn't want the minor ones to be neglected. The One True Pantheon was rich and diverse. It would be a shame if, in the worldwide rush to embrace Isis, Osiris, Set, and their ilk, their less celebrated relatives ended up trampled underfoot and forgotten. In a frenzy of proselytising zeal, Egypt gave away every last one of its gods, draining its religious reservoir, leaving nothing behind for itself. In hindsight it was clear that this was what the gods themselves had willed, and so were laid the foundations of the world's one and only lay state.

Some of the sub-sects took root; some did not. None flourished to any meaningful degree, and the few that survived did so by virtue of gaining a purchase in territory that was sympathetic, or at least not hostile. This was the case in, for example, South America, where the children of Horus would never have succeeded in obtaining joint custodianship had that part of the continent not been so strongly under the sway of its neighbour to the north, their father's realm.

The same was true in Africa, where toeholds were available only to lesser gods who had some connection, however tenuous, to Nephthys or her husband.

The Lightbringer's orders to David, Zafirah, and their team were simple. Go into Libya. Find sites sacred to lesser gods. Blow them up.

THEY LOCATED A Wepwawetian monastery on the very first day.

It was a primitive, semi-subterranean edifice, more tomb than dwelling, more cave than tomb. A dozen monks occupied it, pallid creatures, their modesty barely preserved by the tattered remnants of black robes. Their bodies were so thin as to be almost skeletal, emaciated by a meagre diet of jackal flesh and baked dung beetle. Wepwawet was Anubis's son and a regular chip off the old block, pure darkness and annihilation, so his worshippers delighted in mortifying themselves, spending their lives teetering as close to the brink of death as possible.

Consequently the monks were too feeble to put up any resistance as the Lightbringer's troops rousted them from their sarcophagus-style beds and dragged them blinking into the sunlight. Held at gunpoint, they stood in line like living scarecrows, swaying and moaning while David supervised the laying of charges inside the monastery.

When the blast happened, the monks cried out in a strange sort of ecstasy. As their holy home collapsed in on itself in a vast billow of dust, they looked both aghast and perversely gratified, as though this act of violent desecration confirmed everything they believed in. All was ruin and decay. Life was a bleak catastrophe. Here – here was the proof.

One of them, apparently the abbot, hissed a command to the rest. The monks immediately began advancing on their captors, ignoring requests to stay put or be shot.

David realised what they were up to. He shouted to Zafirah, telling her to tell the others: on no account were they to open fire.

But too late. They did.

Bullets flew. The Wepwawetian monks went down happily, willingly. It was an act of mass suicide. They died with blissful smiles on their skull-like faces.

"They could see no need to carry on," Zafirah said later. "What we did, destroying the monastery – it made their lives complete."

"Yes, well," said David, guiding the ZT around a rock outcrop. The off-roader's initials stood for Zemlya Tantsovschik, Land

Dancer, but it hardly lived up to the name. It was murder to drive, the steering wheel asking for effort all the way from your shoulders to your wrists before it would rotate even a few degrees. The ZT could be said to dance in the same way that a portly octogenarian babushka could be said to dance. "Nobody else dies. Not if we can help it. That's not what we're here for. Our targets aren't civilians, remember. Or even enemy troops."

"No. The gods. Only the gods." Zafirah smiled grimly. "I wonder if we're not insane, David West*ween*ter. What are we doing, provoking them like this? It's asking for trouble."

"Of course it is. But the Lightbringer" – he nearly said *Steven* – "has calculated the risks. He thinks he knows how this is going to play out."

"And do you trust him?"

"I do."

"You sound surprised."

"I am, a little. But only a little."

"Is it because he's an Englishman like you? You wouldn't have gone along with this if he was from any other country? Compatriots sticking together."

"That's not it. I just feel…"

David wasn't sure what he felt. He knew only that he felt *something*. Whenever Steven spoke about his plans, his grand scheme, his crusade, it sounded right. Sounded plausible. Sounded like a cause worth fighting for and a confrontation that could be won.

"I don't know," he said. "I mean, this goes against everything I believe in. Used to believe in. Somewhere inside me a faint little voice is going 'Don't!' But there's another voice, a louder one, and it's saying 'Why not?' I've never heard it before, I don't recognise it – but I quite like it."

"I hear that voice," Zafirah said. "I think it may be the voice of freedom."

David adjusted his grip on the steering wheel. "I think it may be too."

IT WAS A tiny village, a handful of houses clustered around a water hollow. In the hollow, a stone effigy of the hippopotamus-headed goddess Tawaret squatted, thigh-deep in the muddy water, belly bulging, breasts heavily pendulous.

"Ugly bitch," Zafirah commented. "I hope someone will shoot me if I ever let myself get that fat."

"Fertile, though," said David. "Isn't that the point? Tawaret's all about the babies." He gestured at the largest of the nearby buildings, into which the villagers had all been herded, as much for their own safety as anything. They were howling with rage and indignation from inside this makeshift corral. "At least half the women are pregnant, and I've never seen such a high child-to-adult ratio as in this place."

"The women lie beside the statue for a day," said Zafirah, "then lie beside their husbands at night."

"Stinking of brackish water..."

"But it still works. Perhaps it's the only time they do lie with their husbands. The poor men are so desperate, they'll forgive the smell."

David inserted a blasting cap into the last of the charges, then waded out of the hollow, unspooling wires as he went.

There was a massed scream from the house as the effigy exploded, followed by high-pitched ululations of despair.

The Freegyptian vehicles were pursued as they left the village. Women chased them down the road, cursing and hurling rocks.

Only women, though, David noted. The village menfolk had looked... relieved?

AN INTIMIDATED LOCAL gave them directions. Follow the river, three miles, where it bends, there is the shrine to Sobek.

What they found was an altar stone on the riverbank and a heavily tattooed priest holding down a young sheep, barely a lamb, preparing to sacrifice it. A cluster of onlookers chanted rhythmic prayers. The sheep's terrified bleating sounded close to a scream.

The priest raised his left arm. He had no hand, only a stump with a hook attached. He brought the hook down towards the sheep's throat.

David fired into the air, and everyone shrieked and froze. The priest remonstrated with the new arrivals, furious that the ritual had been interrupted. While he was shouting at them the sheep wriggled out of his grasp and skittered away, tossing its head.

"Not much to destroy here," Zafirah observed. "That altar stone will have to do."

Then there was a thrashing in the water, and a ten-foot-long crocodile emerged, clawing its way up the bank.

The locals retreated in alarm. Even the priest backed off, rubbing his hook-ended arm. He, it seemed, had better reason than anyone to be wary of this beast.

The crocodile eyed them all with a slow, yellowy stare. It shuffled over to the altar and opened its jaws wide, revealing tooth upon tooth. It thrashed its tail, eager for the offering of a meal, which the sheep's bleating had promised.

The rifle David was carrying was a Brazilian-made Anaconda, loaded with .303 brass-jacketed fragmentation rounds. He brought it up to his shoulder and took careful aim.

The crocodile turned towards him.

A sacred animal. For an uncanny moment David felt as though he was looking down the gunsights straight into gaze of Sobek himself, son of Neith the goddess of war. Set once hid briefly inside a crocodile, hoping to escape being punished for the murder of Osiris. Apophis, the serpent Set fought twice daily, was the son of Sobek.

He was conscious of all these associations, the linkage of god to god embodied within the reptile in front of him. His finger squeezed the trigger but not all the way.

He couldn't do it.

It was more than sacrilege. It felt like cold-blooded murder.

Blam!

Zafirah lowered her rifle.

The crocodile writhed and rolled, grunting horribly as the message passed along its nervous system from its bullet-smashed brain – *you are dead.*

It lay on its back, soft pale underside exposed, as the last few twitches of life ran through it.

The priest and the crowd of locals were on their knees, weeping.

"It was just a fucking crocodile," Zafirah said tersely, striding back to the cars.

ON THE EVENING of their fifth day in Libya, as they were making camp for the night, one of the team spied a Saqqara Bird in the distance. It was flying in a criss-cross pattern, searching the area by grid.

"Looking for us?" Zafirah wondered, peering at the bird's small black silhouette as it glided to and fro against the twilight sky.

"You can count on it," David said. "Word of what we've been up to will have reached Tripoli by now."

"What should we do? Shoot it out of the air?"

"And give away exactly where we are? No, for the moment we stay put. The vehicles are camouflaged, and we personally are getting a measure of invisibility from these." He tapped the amulet around his neck. All of the team were wearing them. "But I think our time here is coming to an end. The Lightbringer said we should avoid direct engagement with Neph forces if we can, and that's going to become inevitable if we stay much longer."

"So our little jaunt is over."

"Jaunt?" David laughed. "Don't you mean hostile sortie? Act of deliberate provocation?"

"That's what I said." Zafirah laughed too, and it occurred to David that this was an all too rare sound from her. She didn't laugh enough. Neither did he. They both took themselves too seriously. It was something they had in common and something, he felt, that was keeping them apart.

He wanted her. He desired her. She, he was certain, felt the same about him. But unless he did away with the reserve which he wore like a suit of armour and she stopped using her ability to wrong-foot him as though it were a weapon, nothing was ever going to happen.

"How many Anubians does it take to change a light bulb?" he said.

Zafirah frowned. "What?"

"It's a joke. Go on. How many Anubians does it take to change a light bulb?"

"I don't know. One?"

"'What's a light bulb?'"

Zafirah looked blank.

"You know. Anubians. Their thing about darkness. They don't like bright light. Try to avoid it. Therefore... they don't have..." He trailed off.

"Oh. I see. Funny," said Zafirah, and she wandered off to talk to one of the Freegyptians.

David cursed himself for an idiot. He'd only wanted to hear her laugh again, and now he felt like a teenager on a fumbled first date.

What did it take to win this woman?

Whatever it was, he was now all the more determined to do it.

He was David Westwynter. Back in England, in his old life, in the circles he'd moved in, that had meant something. It had meant he could have just about any woman he set his cap at.

Here, the same rules did not apply. But that was fine. It upped the challenge, and the stakes. Here, where the name Westwynter and the reputation attached meant nothing, everything came down to the man himself. With Zafirah it was about admiration and lust, a combination David recognised as being the cornerstones of love, but it was about more than that too. It was about him finding out whether there was anything more to him than the sum of his upbringing.

Was he a somebody, as in England? Or was he *somebody*?

THEIR LUCK HELD for another two days, during which time they found and eliminated another six holy sites dotted among the Chinese-owned oilfields of Libya's south-eastern Al Kufrah municipality.

Then, just as David was thinking that the time had come to cut and run, a spotter plane located them. It flew directly over the three vehicles, returned for a second pass, then hurtled off into the blue.

The Freegyptians sent trails of machine-gun fire after it, nipping at its tail.

"Saqqara Birds not working, so the Libyans have gone conventional," said David. "Pilot's radioing base right now, relaying our position."

"We should make for the border," said Zafirah.

"Too damn right we should. They'll be scrambling jet fighters from Maaten al-Sarra. Say twenty minutes for them to get here. We're about fifteen miles from Freegypt. It's going to be tight."

The ZT and the two trucks tore across the desert at a mean sixty miles an hour, ploughing straight over rocks, clefts, and other obstacles normally best avoided at that sort of speed. Axles grumbled, suspension groaned. Everyone kept one eye on the sky. David reflexively sent up a small prayer to Osiris, asking for protection, while the Freegyptians, with no gods to importune, put their faith in the laws of probability. It was probable that they would reach the border in time. It was probable that the planes would arrive too late to catch them.

Probability, however, had little regard for human wishes, and Osiris, if he was listening today, turned a deaf ear.

A pair of Nephthysian jets appeared on the horizon to the rear, flying low – Locusts, to judge by the swept-back wings and the twin-bubble cockpit canopy. David's map and compass told him that he and his team were on Freegyptian soil, or at any rate so close you'd hardly notice the difference. Borders, however, were tricky things to define, especially from the air, and he suspected the Neph pilots' orders didn't involve giving the interlopers the benefit of the doubt. Two or three miles further into Freegypt, and there would have been no question of attacking. It would have been an overt infringement of Freegypt's sovereignty. But here, at the point of contiguity, in a stretch of desolate no-man's-land, there was room for uncertainty. Margin for error.

A bolt of purple *ba* hit the ground a few yards to the left of the ZT. The vehicle rocked. Debris from a freshly drilled crater rained down on the roof and bonnet. A second bolt struck just in front, and the ZT reared and came down with neck-jarring force.

The windscreen shattered. Glass fragments flew everywhere inside the cab. Zafirah fought to maintain control, pulling out of a skid that threatened to turn into a somersault. The off-roader slewed and slalomed but kept going.

The Locusts shot ahead in side-by-side formation. Afterburners glowed as the planes went into a steep ascent, peeled off in different directions, and came round for a second run.

"Faster!" David yelled, wind slamming into his face. "We've got to go faster! It's our only hope!"

"No shit!" Zafirah shouted back, shifting down a gear and flooring the accelerator.

In one of the trucks behind, a Freegyptian clambered out through the cab's rear window and loosed off a volley of bullets at the oncoming jets from the machine gun mounted on the flatbed. He might as well have been spitting at the planes for all the good it did. *Ba* crackled outward from under their wings. Zafirah swerved hard left, then hard right. Two of the *ba* blasts struck either side, missing narrowly both times. There was a loud detonation from behind, and in the wing mirror David saw the rearmost of the two trucks erupt, blown apart by purple light. Orange flame billowed a split-second later as the truck's fuel tank went up. Bodies and bits of bodies were hurled clear as the wreckage spun end over end, disintegrating a little more with each impact. When the truck finally came to rest, it barely looked like anything that might once have rolled off a production line. It was several sections of twisted, charred metal that were somehow still clinging on to one another, like an animal carcase after flaying and evisceration, held together by sinews alone.

Zafirah swore loudly and angrily. The two Freegyptians in the back seat of the ZT swore too.

The Locusts veered around for a third pass, but this time they did not open fire. As they thundered overhead they see-sawed their wings in a victory salute, then peeled off in a 180-degree turn, heading back to base.

"Bastards," David hissed, but in his heart he knew the pilots had let them off lightly. They could have kept on strafing till all three vehicles were gone. This way, honour was served and there were survivors left to carry the message back home: *That's how we treat people who come into our country and cause trouble.*

The ZT and the remaining truck drove the rest of the way to Luxor at a sombre pace, much like a funeral cortege.

16. FRATERNITY

THE INNER CHAMBER of the Temple of Hatshepsut had been transformed since David's first visit. Now there were maps tacked to the walls, showing Africa north of the equator, most of Arabia and even the southern reaches of the Ottoman Empire. There were trestle tables and canvas chairs. There was electric lighting, a TV set, a shortwave radio, a phone. Cables snaked around the floor, all leading to a side chamber where a generator hummed. A mausoleum, a place of the dead, had become a place of activity, a base of operations – a command bunker.

When David walked in, the Lightbringer was busy conferring with half a dozen of the local faction leaders. Glancing round, the Lightbringer held up a hand – *won't be a second* – and continued his discussion. David stood by and listened. He barely understood a word being said but it was clear who was in charge here. He marvelled at the authority his brother commanded. The warlords were a slab-faced, rough-and-ready lot, the sort of men who were very hard to impress. The Lightbringer had them hanging on his every word.

David was still finding it hard to reconcile the Steven he used to know with the masked figure before him, this self-made icon, this sweet-talking demagogue. Five years was a long time. People changed. But they tended to change into slightly different but still recognisable forms of themselves. They didn't, as a rule, undergo a complete metamorphosis, as from caterpillar to butterfly. Watching Steven at work, he was filled with a sense of pride. He imagined this was how younger brothers felt about older brothers, how Steven had once felt about him: pleased to be able to look up to him, glad to be related by blood, conscious that what was great about the other might be great about himself as well.

The meeting ended. The Lightbringer dismissed his confederates. They filed out, most of them giving David a nod of acknowledgement as they passed. One of them patted him on the shoulder, a gesture of congratulation and of commiseration too. He had done well in Libya. Such a shame that Freegyptian lives had been lost.

"Beer?"

Once it was just the two of them left in the chamber, the Lightbringer relaxed his shoulders, eased out his spine. Mask notwithstanding, he was Steven once more.

"Why not?" said David.

Steven fetched two bottles from a small refrigerator. He uncapped them and handed one to David. Then he rolled up his mask to just below his nose and took a sip from his bottle. David drank too, sneaking a sidelong, surreptitious glance at his brother. A small portion of Steven's left cheek was exposed and he could see the bottom of the burn-damaged area, hard, waxy scar tissue puckering the unmarred skin next to it. The edge of the scarring formed a surprisingly rounded, neat curve. It looked almost like a cattle brand.

"Don't stare," Steven said. "It's rude."

"Sorry. I just… One day you'll show me your whole face, won't you? I'm sure I can take it."

"I'm sure you can, and maybe one day I will. For now, though, it's not something I'm happy about sharing with others. You understand. I used to be a good-looking young lad. Handsome, I'd even go so far as to say."

"Hey, you are my brother."

"And you, Dave, are still good-looking. Try to imagine suddenly losing that, becoming the opposite of handsome, having a face that makes people wince and turn away. You wouldn't like it, trust me."

"I'm sorry it happened, Steven. I'm... I'm sorry about a lot of things that have happened."

"You mean between us? Ah, fuck it. It's all in the past."

"I don't think I was the best of brothers to you."

"What are you talking about?" Steven exclaimed.

"You know, I wasn't very tolerant. I didn't—"

"Don't talk bollocks. You were a brilliant brother. You looked after me. I know Dad often paid you to, but you could have just taken the money and ignored me. He wouldn't have known. And I was a proper little shit. I'm not afraid to admit it. I was a pest to start with, and I grew up into a pain in the arse. *I* wouldn't have looked after me if I'd been you. I'd have told me to fuck off."

"I more or less did at school."

"And I had it coming, and it was probably the best thing you could have done. You're talking about the day you beat up those three boys who beat me up, right? What you said afterwards, that this was the last time you'd do anything like that for me – bang, a revelation. I realised I'd always been counting on you to protect me and it meant I could get away with anything. I'm a born troublemaker, but I was safe because big brother Dave would always be there to mop up my messes. And then, all at once, it seemed he wasn't going to any more. I knew then that I had to sort myself out and think about the consequences of my actions in future and take responsibility for them, because otherwise I was going to keep screwing up and there'd be nobody to bail me out. That was the day – I'm not kidding – when I started to become an adult. You shouldn't feel guilty about what you did. You should give yourself a thumping great pat on the back."

"Really? OK then, I will."

"And speaking of pats on the back," Steven said, "excellent job in Libya, Dave. Fucking fantastic. I've been watching one of the Libyan national networks." He nodded at the television. "Reception's crap but the message is loud and clear. Our little invasion is all over the news. Tripoli's up in arms. They've lodged a formal complaint with Cairo and they're lobbying the Afro-Arabian Synodical Council to take action. The hawks on the Council are arguing for military retaliation and even the doves are cooing about some form of 'robust response', which is liberal-speak for the same thing. Whether they end up approving reprisals is open to debate, but it's looking likely. The Libyans are pretty hot under the collar about it all and say their priests have been having visions of disgruntlement from on high, which, if true, is hardly surprising. We've stopped worshippers worshipping. It's only temporary but that doesn't stop the gods feeling the pinch. Meanwhile the parliament in Cairo is strenuously denying any involvement in the attacks and blaming a terrorist element in Upper Freegypt."

"That'd be us."

"It would. They've even named me, in the hope of diverting the blame. For the first time Freegyptian politicians have publicly acknowledged the Lightbringer's existence. They're pointing the finger of blame right at me, but it's not helping. They still look bad, weak, because it appears they're not in full control of their own country."

"Which they aren't."

"Not down here they aren't. Down here, I am. So Cairo can whimper all it wants about its innocence but Libyan tempers aren't going to be soothed, and if retaliation is sanctioned, you can bet the Libyans won't do it by halves. They'll mobilise everything they've got, and they'll have backup from the Sudan and Chad, who're scared we might go in and do something similar to them and would like to pre-empt that if possible. All in all it's looking good. We tweaked the Nephs' noses and they're going to react exactly as hoped, lashing out. And it's thanks to you, Dave."

Steven clinked the neck of his bottle against David's.

"You don't look completely delighted," he said. "Why not?"

"I'm exhausted," David replied. "A week on the move, without a decent night's rest…"

"And?"

"And we lost four men, don't forget that."

"I regret it, truly I do," said Steven, sounding sincere. "I've already sent my condolences to their families. But we knew, going in, there'd be casualties. I was hoping it wouldn't be so soon, but still. Troops die. Leaders have to be prepared to accept that, otherwise they have no business starting a war."

"I know. But I saw those men die, with my own eyes. You weren't there. I was. You can talk casually about casualties, but watching it happen is a whole different thing. It's not something anyone can ever get used to. I just want you to bear that in mind, Steven. You sent four of your men out to their deaths. And they're only the first. There will be others."

"Fair point," said Steven. "Duly noted. What you haven't mentioned is that I nearly send *you* out to your death."

"You didn't send me. I volunteered."

"Even so, I could have said no. Would have, if you hadn't been so damn insistent."

"The mission needed someone in charge who had proper military experience."

"Well, for the record, I was worried sick all week. If you'd been killed, I'd never have forgiven myself. What was I thinking? I must have been crazy to let you talk me into it. Zafirah would have managed fine without you. Fuck it, I shouldn't even have sent her. She's not expendable. Neither are you."

"No one is," David said firmly. "That's what I'm getting at."

"OK, OK." Steven put up his hands, surrendering. "Enough of the lecturing. I understand where you're coming from. I don't disagree."

"Just as I promised, I'm here to make sure you don't do anything rash."

"My brother, my conscience."

"Bingo." David drained his beer. "And now I'm going to stop giving advice and ask for some instead."

"Advice? From me? Well, there's a turn-up. Fire away."

David hesitated, then said, "Zafirah."

"Zafirah? What do you—?" Steven stopped, and his mouth curled into a sly smile. "Oh, don't tell me. You're smitten. Dave's smitten with Zafirah. Who'd have thought?"

"I wouldn't say I was—"

"It's written all over your face," Steven said, the smile turning gleeful. "And I can't honestly say I blame you. She's a looker all right. Nice tits. Firm, round arse. And those eyes…"

"You know her. Pretty well. Don't you?"

"Could say that. As well as anyone can get to know Zafirah. It's been three years – more – and I like to think she and I have a pretty good understanding of each other. Even so, I feel I've only scratched the surface with her. She doesn't let people in easily."

"I've noticed."

"Desert girl. Hard, hot, beautiful, inhospitable. And so now you're the mole-rat, wanting to make himself a burrow."

"Don't take the piss."

"I'm not taking the piss. I am surprised, though. She doesn't seem your type."

"I don't have a type. Do I have a type?"

"Blonde. Wealthy. Brittle. That's the woman I always remember you going for."

David cast his mind back over his past relationships. Girls like Kismet, Aida, 'Titi, Alex. Each had seemed as different from the others as trees in a forest. But they had all belonged to the same forest; that was undoubtedly true. The same species of tree, moreover.

"Alex wasn't blonde," he said, adding, "Well, not naturally."

Steven chuckled. "A collar-cuff mismatch, huh? Well, be that as it may. Your choices were never anything less than classy. Never anything less than frosty, either. The kind of women you could keep at arm's length, because they didn't mind. That's how they kept you. Zafirah, though, she's a whole different proposition. And if you really want my advice…"

"I do."

"I'd steer clear."

"What?" David was startled.

"For one thing, that's a father-fixated girl you're dealing with. She told you about her daddy, the great freedom fighter and martyr? She still worships him. He's dead and no man will ever live up to him in her estimation. So you're competing against his ghost, and you're unlikely to win. Plus, she's wedded to the cause. This cause. My cause. It's what drives her on. It's all she really cares about. There's an emptiness inside her and this is what fills it. This is what gives shape and meaning to her life."

"Oh."

"Oh? You haven't noticed?"

"I knew she was... committed," David said. "I didn't see it as anything more than that."

"Committed to the hilt. She wants the Pantheon's hold over the world broken as much as I do, maybe even more."

"And in the meantime she's not interested in anything else?"

"Nothing *you* can offer."

David pondered this. He supposed Steven was right. Steven had had three years to get the measure of Zafirah's character. By all accounts they had been working closely together.

Yet, at the restaurant the other night, Zafirah had referred to her father in disparaging terms, as a "coward", and had shown a trace of scepticism when talking about causes.

Perhaps Steven saw things that he, David, did not. Equally, perhaps he was mistaken.

There was a third possibility, and it put David in mind of Steven's account of his adventures after the sinking of the *Immortal*.

Perhaps he was lying.

David trusted his brother. On the big issues, not least his crusade against the gods, he believed Steven meant everything he said. But on lesser issues, personal matters, he was not so sure. When it was just the two of them together, Steven didn't always seem to be entirely on the level.

He realised, in a flash of insight, that there was a clear distinction here.

He trusted *the Lightbringer*. Steven, on the other hand, he wasn't so sure about.

What did that mean?

"Can I ask a question?" he said.

"Of course," said Steven.

"Do *you* fancy Zafirah?"

"Sure. Why not? Who wouldn't?" This was said dismissively, as if David had wanted to know whether he liked sandwiches.

"So you wouldn't be trying to put me off her for any specific reason?"

"Such as?"

"Well, to, you know, keep her for yourself."

"Dave, you wound me," Steven said, mock-hurt. But not wholly convincingly mock-hurt. "I'm your brother. I'm just looking out for your best interests, and I'm telling you – listen to me – Zafirah isn't for you." He repeated it, in case David hadn't got the message – "She isn't for you" – and his voice took on a strange, resonant timbre as he spoke. The words seemed to penetrate deep inside David's head and lodge themselves there.

"Anyway, for your information, I've bigger fish to fry than Zafirah," Steven added, sounding more like himself again. He yanked the Lightbringer mask down, tucking the base of it inside the collar of his undershirt. "In case you haven't noticed, I'm rather busy saving the world at present."

"I understand. I'm sorry."

"You'd better leave." Steven's posture had shifted. Stiffened. "Go get some rest. You said it yourself: you're exhausted. 'Bye, Dave."

David, dismissed, walked back through the Valley of Kings to Luxor, and with every step he took through the necropolis he could think only of his brother's advice that he should leave Zafirah be. He could hardly think of anything else.

It made a kind of sense. Steven knew her. He was trying to protect David. He didn't see them as a good match.

Zafirah isn't for you.

She wasn't for him. That was all there was to it.

17. AIRSTRIKE

DAVID WAS HOME.

Home wasn't his London pad. Pleasant and well furnished as that was, it served as a convenient place to live, nothing more.

Home was Courtdene, the family estate on the Sussex Downs, the flint-and-brick manor house with its walled gardens and its long, valley-hemmed views of the Channel, the sheep-cropped fields, the oak copses and hawthorn thickets, the wide expanses of grassland that were treelessly bleak and bare, the curving driveway, the main gates capped with sphinxes, the pyramid folly which Archibald Westwynter commissioned to be built the day after he bought the property, the lake with its replica Solar Barque dinghies and small overgrown island, this secure and private world where nothing intruded from the outside that wasn't permitted by the family within.

Home was always the place where life was at its simplest.

David strode up to the front door, pausing to glance up at the family cartouche that was carved into the lintel. It was the best kind, a compact, logogrammatic one. You could spell out any name in the uniliteral manner and get a string of simple demotic hieroglyphs, but that was little better than an alphabetical substitution code and looked ungainly. For real class, you paid the priesthood a small fortune – the current asking price was €50,000 – and had your surname translated officially into hieratic logograms. The cartouche for Westwynter consisted, logically enough, of the logograms for west (a bird crown and a sun setting over hills) and winter (four assorted geometric shapes), arranged one above the other and enclosed in a box.

David had always thought of a cartouche as a sign of vanity, but a necessary one. No family that was held in high regard could do without.

He passed under it and entered the house.

The hallway was empty. A clock ticked. Dust motes hung in a shaft of sunlight, swirled by a draught. He smelled the familiar musk of waxed floorboards, mixed with the hint of damp which hung around the draughty old building constantly, even in high summer.

No one.

He was home from war. He had a right to expect some kind of reception, a welcoming committee. Didn't he? He had been away for weeks. He was presumed dead. Why wasn't anyone waiting in the hallway to greet him, rejoicing? His mother at least, even if his father had chosen to disown him.

"Hello?"

Echoes echoed echoingly. No answer.

"Mum? Dad?"

Nothing.

"Jepps? Mrs Plomley?"

Silence.

He searched the ground floor: all the drawing rooms, the library, the dining room, the billiard-room, kitchen, scullery, pantry. Everything exactly as it should be, spotlessly tidy. Not a soul to be seen.

He went upstairs. He tried Steven's bedroom, then his own. The beds were tightly made, sheets turned down, awaiting occupancy. Finally he approached his parents' bedroom at the far end of the corridor.

The door was ajar. He nudged it open.

His mother and father lay in bed together, naked, entwined, locked in a fervent kiss. Jack Westwynter was kneading Cleo

Westwynter's breast. Cleo Westwynter's hand was under the covers, working away at Jack Westwynter's crotch.

David stood and stared. He wanted to back away, pull the door to behind him, steal off down the corridor before his parents realised he was there. But he couldn't move. He was paralysed with embarrassment... and fascination.

Nobody in their right mind wanted to see their parents making love, or even to think about it.

But then, as David had realised, these weren't actually his parents.

Around their heads golden auras glowed, and each aura had a distinct shape. His father's was a double-plumed mitre, his mother's a weird blend of vulture and throne.

Dreaming.

David continued to watch as his father's hand moved down his mother's body, sliding over her belly and beneath the bedcovers to stroke between her legs. His mother, Isis, moaned. His father, Osiris, grunted softly and stroked harder.

Then, as if on some unspoken cue, the two of them calmly turned their heads and looked round to where David stood. They smiled. They kept their hands on each other's genitals, rubbing, caressing, but their gazes were focused on David. Their expressions were kindly but stern.

"Why are you doing this, son?" his father asked.

"Why are you helping your brother?" his mother asked.

"Because..."

He was dreaming.

"Because he needs me. And because he's right. I really think he is."

"We're your parents," said Osiris. "We watch over you. We care for you."

"Don't you think this is hurting us," said Isis, "this rebellion of yours?"

"It's not rebellion," David replied defensively. He couldn't think of a better name for what the Lightbringer was up to but *rebellion* sounded so childish, the way his mother had said it, a hormonal-teenager thing, like getting a piercing or a tattoo.

"If you want to hurt us, you're going the right way about it," his father said sternly.

"Come back home," said his mother. "Come back and all will be forgiven."

David thought he had come back. He was home. Wasn't he?

He was having a dream, and outside the hotel room...

"We love you," said Isis, still fondling his father's cock.

"Don't make us angry," said Osiris, still fingering his mother's cunt.

Lightning flickered at the bedroom window. Thunder growled. The sky had been cloudless a few moments earlier, but now—

David snapped awake.

He had been having a dream, and outside the hotel room there were flashes of bright red-purple light and the rumble of distant explosions.

He went to the window and drew back the curtain.

The bombardment of Luxor had begun.

FOR TWO WEEKS the Nephthysians had been threatening an assault. The Afro-Arabian Synodical Council had debated and fulminated. There had been deputations to both the parliament in Cairo and the Kommissariat Svyatoy Dyela, the Setics' Commissariat of Holy Affairs, or KSD. From Freegypt's Prime Minister Bayoumi, nothing less than a full acceptance of liability had been demanded, along with a promise to track down the instigator of the temple attacks, the Lightbringer, and hand him over to Libya. Neither of these things could Bayoumi do. It was impossible for him to admit that his country was responsible, since that would be tantamount to a declaration of war on Libya. It was equally impossible to find and extradite the Lightbringer since Lower Freegypt had little say over what went on in lawless Upper Freegypt. Politically and practically, Cairo was stymied and the Nephthysians knew it and relished it and had no problem taking advantage of it.

As for the Setics, the KSD happily huffed and puffed on the Nephthysians' behalf and made all sorts of statements about unity, alliance, standing shoulder to shoulder against a common foe, the sanctity of the Bi-Continental Pact, et cetera, et cetera. "To harm a single Nephthysian," said Vladimir Chang, KSD High Commissar, "is to harm us all, Nephthysians and Setics alike. Just as the millions of us stand firm against Osirisiac expansionism, Anubian aggression, and Horusite interventionism, so we stand firm against this unprovoked and unprincipled violation of Libya and its people. Freegypt, like a viper in our midst, has bitten our flesh and the poison must not be allowed to spread." The Setics guaranteed to give the Nephthysians their full backing, diplomatically and, if necessary, militarily.

The Osirisiac Hegemony was more cautious in its condemnation. Pharaoh Benedikt II of Germany, the country to which the revolving control of the Hegemonic Ecclesiastical Polyarchy had fallen this year, released a joint statement with his sister Queen Dagmar. "Terrorism is ugly in any form," the statement ran, "and terrorism against religion is the ugliest of all. Freegypt's political leadership must be held to account for the actions of its people. At the same time, the Hegemony would counsel the Nephthysians to take a measured view on this incursion. We recommend a programme of political sanctions and trade embargos. Any more forceful response runs the risk of adding new converts to the cause of this so-called Lightbringer, whoever he is. For terrorists to prosper, we need only greet their violence with more violence."

The Horusites broadly supported the Osirisiac stance, although Pastor-President Wilkins was heard to comment that if this Lightbringer guy had trashed a few Neph-related temples, so what? In a way he was doing America and Europe a favour, and what the heck, maybe he could give some of those Setics a damn good butt-kicking while he was about it.

The Anubians, for their part, said very little, officially at least, although where death and destruction were concerned the mood of that introverted Pacific Rim empire was never hard to gauge. War had waxed and waned across the planet for the past hundred years, and recently the levels of fighting had been relatively subdued. The

Lightbringer's actions seemed likely to trigger a fresh rise in the tide of conflict, and for the thanatophiliac Anubians that could only be good news. Slaughter suited the Jackal-Headed One, their dark deity. It brought more souls to his realm and boosted his status. The suicide rate in Japan went up significantly, a reliable indicator of Anubian cheerfulness.

The intensity of the Nephthysian sabre-rattling grew and grew. The Setics egged them on from the sidelines. The other religious power blocs looked on with interest and perhaps an element of smug glee. It did appear that Freegypt, godless Freegypt, the Unholy Land, for this first time in its heathen history, was about to take a hammering. Arguably, it was long overdue.

EVEN AS HE watched the bombs rain down on the northern outskirts of Luxor, David could not shake off the last lingering traces of his dream. It wasn't at all uncommon for Europeans to dream of Osiris and Isis and, moreover, dream of them in the role of parents. Supposedly such sleep visions were a visitation from the two gods themselves and that any message they imparted should be taken seriously and paid attention to.

So the priests said, anyway. David himself was minded to think that in this instance it *had* been just a dream, his subconscious working through the anxieties of his present situation and urging a return to the safety and security of the life he used to know.

He just wished the content of the dream hadn't been quite so explicit. It would take days for the image of his parents *doing it* to fade from memory.

The bombs burst in crimson hemispheres of light tinged with shimmering coronas of purple. The Libyan planes were striking at Luxor's commercial district. Steven had predicted this, saying the Nephthysians were likely to try to keep casualties to a minimum, at least to begin with. Property damage, yes. Human damage, no. All the same David feared that the blasts were straying near residential areas, and even hitting them.

The airstrike went on for another twenty minutes, a rippling, overlapping cascade of incandescent eruptions, each accompanied by a rolling rumble of impact that rattled the hotel windows. It was darkly, devastatingly, coruscatingly beautiful.

THE LIGHTBRINGER TOURED the bombsites the next morning. He sighed over the flattened buildings, the factories and business premises turned to rubble, the great smoking holes that had once been shops and livelihoods. He lamented the deaths, of which there had been ten in total. Night watchmen mostly. A taxi driver. A family whose house had stood just a fraction too close to the target zone.

He comforted the bereaved in person. Then he addressed the crowds that were following him. He reassured them that none of the deaths would be in vain. This appalling attack demonstrated the enemy's absolute callousness, their and their goddess's lack of regard for human life. He stated his belief that the airstrike was only the beginning. The Nephthysians would mount further assaults, perhaps even a land invasion. It was time to put the next phase of his plan into action.

The citizens of Luxor were in full, vociferous agreement. They chanted the Lightbringer's name – "Al Ashraqa! Al Ashraqa!" They hoisted him up on their shoulders and paraded through the streets, declaring undying loyalty to him and death to all who opposed him.

Reporting the episode to David later, in private, he said, "They were passing me around and shaking me up and down like a football trophy. I nearly got dropped on my arse several times."

"Ah, the perils of being a beloved leader."

"They do love me, though, don't they? It's true."

"Just don't let them down," David said. "Let them down, and being dropped on your arse will be the least of your worries. Today's adoring crowd can be tomorrow's baying-for-blood mob if you're not careful."

"Oh, it's nag, nag, nag with you all the time, isn't it?"

"Only sounding a note of caution."

"Why would I let them down, Dave?" Steven asked brusquely. "Why would you even think of saying that? Trust me, the Lightbringer is no false messiah. I've vowed to lead the world out of a Dark Age, into enlightenment, and that's what I'm going to do. Anyway, enough of that. We've a busy couple of days ahead of us. Pack your belongings."

"I've no belongings to pack."

"Good. Neither have I. We can start all the more quickly. Let's get to work."

A LITTLE OVER seventy-two hours after the airstrike, Nephthysian forces moved in on Freegypt from three sides. Libyan armoured divisions rolled across the border and into the Western Desert, kicking up a towering plume of dust behind them, while Sudanese troops pushed up from the south along the course of the Nile, past Aswan, and Arabian warships took up position along the Red Sea coast, blockading ports and harbours from Hurghada to Foul Bay.

The Libyans arrived at Luxor the following day, halting at the river. Their Scarab tanks blasted *ba* across the water, not with a view to hitting anything in particular, more as a way of announcing that they were there.

The lack of answering fire from the town was disappointing to say the least. Unsettling, too. Not even the crackle of a machine gun. Nothing.

By arrangement, it was left to the Sudanese to make the first forays into Luxor on foot. Troops darted along the streets, going from house to house, kicking down doors and entering. At any moment they anticipated being ambushed and shot at with conventional weapons. They held their baboon-head *ba* lances at the ready.

Silence hung over everything. In the streets stray dogs sniffed and roamed with unusual boldness. In the houses the Sudanese discovered grandparents and children cowering in corners or behind furniture. All morning and afternoon the soldiers encountered only the town's infirm, the very elderly, and the young with their mothers. There appeared to be nobody else left in Luxor. Virtually everyone of sound body and arms-bearing age was gone.

18. ANUBIS

THE PALACE OF *the god of the dead is built of bones, high on a snowy mountain peak. Its gateway is formed from the ribcage of a whale. Its floors are tiled with human teeth, toe joints, and knuckles. Femurs and shins make up its walls, interleaved like brickwork. Its windows are framed with skulls and elephant tusks. Its towers are, literally, ivory towers.*

Anubis dwells here, alone. Alone, he sits and broods, a dark presence at the heart of this white place.

Ra arrives with trepidation. It is never easy to predict what sort of mood his thrice-great-nephew will be in, but the safe bet is it won't be a good one. Added to that, Ra has a perennial dread of the realm of the dead. He spends half his time voyaging through its bleakest, blackest regions, and its lightlessness distresses and repels him. It is everything that he is not. He shines; it overshadows. He is filled with life; it is oppressive. He gives; it takes.

Anubis, on his throne, looks up and sombrely assesses his visitor. He squints somewhat, Ra's inherent radiance irksome to his gloom-adapted eyes.

"Great Ra," he says, and something in his tone of voice tells Ra that – miracle of miracles – Anubis is actually not displeased to see

him. His mien is a few notches below its usual level of grimness. He is, by his own glum standards, almost jovial.

"He Who Belongs To The Cerecloths," says Ra, "I'm here to—"

"I know why you are here," says Anubis. "I know of your self-appointed peace mission. We all do. Talk amongst the Pantheon has been about little else of late."

"Then that spares me the effort of a lengthy explanation."

"I confess I am slightly surprised you did not come to see me sooner."

"Really?"

"I occupy a unique position," says Anubis. "To all intents and purpose I am the son of Set and Nephthys. However, it's common knowledge that my real father is Osiris. My mother visited him in the night, he mistook her for Isis, and I am the bastard product of that adulterous union."

"It has never been proven..."

"It has never been *admitted, which is not the same thing. Osiris refuses to accept that he could have been so careless. My mother adamantly denies that she would seduce another woman's husband. Their efforts to cover up the whole sordid business are as strenuous as they are ludicrous. But dignity must be preserved at all costs, mustn't it?" Anubis barks a laugh. "Really, though, it's pathetic. How can Osiris not have known that he was lying with a woman other than his wife? Mind you, he has to say that. Otherwise Isis would doubtless see to it that he was going around with a pair of wooden balls to go with that wooden cock of his."*

"You blame him solely for the indiscretion? Surely Nephthys must bear some responsibility too."

"Oh no, I blame her equally. She was no less guilty."

"But my impression," says Ra, "is that you don't hate your mother as much as you do Osiris."

"Your impression would be erroneous. I hate her. I hate Osiris. I hate my adoptive father, dear old Set, who feigns not to be aware that I am not his blood son and yet still holds me at a distance. I hate all of them for their lies and their hypocrisy. I decry everything they stand for. And now you have come here to ask me to heal the *rift between them, to act as the glue to reunite my true father and my adoptive father. Because, nominally, I belong to both Osiris and Set, I ought to be well placed to prick their consciences and bring them to the negotiating table. Am I not wrong? That's what you're after? That is the task you wish to enlist me to carry out?"*

"You are not wrong," says Ra.

"So why did you not approach me earlier? You have spoken to Osiris and Isis and to the First Family. Why me now? Why was I not top of the list?"

"I..." Ra hesitates. "I would have solicited your aid sooner, had I not believed that I could discharge this mission on my own. I did not wish to burden anyone else."

"But you have failed so far, and this is the next step, talking to me. An act of desperation, one might perhaps call it."

"No."

"How am I not supposed to feel second-rate, though? An afterthought?"

Anubis, thinks Ra, is sensitive when it comes to feeling wanted. Like many a child of dubious parentage he is insecure at heart, forever afraid of rejection. His brooding demeanour masks fragility. I must tread carefully.

"One avenue of approach has proved unsuccessful," he says. "This fresh direction, which I was initially loath to take for fear of troubling you, may yet be the one that bears fruit."

"For fear of troubling me?" Anubis's grin looks very much like a baring of fangs. "Or for fear of me?"

"O Chief Of The Necropolis, Lord Of The Hallowed Lands, He Who Stands Guard At The Head Of The Bier..."

This litany of epithets is begun by Ra on a note of protest. Then he realises he is not being honest, and did not Anubis just now state his abhorrence of dishonesty in all its forms?

So, with humble straightforwardness, he says, "Yes, I do fear you. I cannot deny it. I wish it were otherwise, but it isn't. I am the sun, light, life, and you – you are not."

Anubis nods, approving of Ra's plain speaking. "We cannot all be alike, or sympathetic to one another. It would be boring and *absurd if we were. But alas, Great Ra, for all your most welcome frankness, I'm afraid I must decline your invitation to help. And before you remonstrate, let me explain my reasons why. Come."*

They go to a balcony high in the palace, from which vantage point nearly all of the realm of the dead lies visible before them. Iaru, the Field of Reeds, stretches as far as the eye can see, an endless glittering green expanse beneath a low, thunder-purple sky. The souls of the dead are hard at work down there, ankle-deep in the marshy water, million upon million of them. Bent-backed, they plant and sow. They wield hoe and scythe. They reap and gather. Some of them sing toil-songs in thin, high voices. The sound drifts up to Ra's ears like the warbling of birds in a far-off forest, and it speaks of contentment and certainty. For all eternity the dead will labour here among these reed-beds. For all eternity they will watch seeds grow to shoots and the shoots become crops to be harvested, and they will never tire of the endless repetition of the process. For the dead, the cycle of life will never lose its fascination.

"What do you see?" Anubis asks.

"You know what I see. Your realm. Your subjects. The ever-growing ranks of mortal souls."

"Ever-growing," says Anubis, seizing on the word. "Indeed. With each new arrival my kingdom expands and is augmented. Moment by moment, Iaru gets larger. Its bounds increase and so does my power and influence. I am the lord of all this. Do you not understand what that means?"

Ra looks blank, deliberately.

"You don't, do you? Neither did my real father. Osiris had the chance to be ruler of the dead. If Isis had not resurrected him and breathed life back into him, he would be here now, at my side if not in my stead. He still insists he is god of the netherworld or some such, but it's an honorary title at best. He claims some form of authority here, but in truth he has none. For him, the soft comforts of wife and hearth and bed are far preferable. Osiris is a sensualist. The solitude and austerity of this existence, which I find congenial, he would find unbearable. Little does he realise what he has passed up."

Anubis gazes out over Iaru, a tiny spark appearing in each of his black, black eyes.

"When it comes down to it," he says, "there is only death. Death is all that is and all that ever will be. In their lives, mortals struggle and compete, but when it's over they all of them wind up here, the same, united in co-operation, subject to me. I am here for them, after their bodies have crumbled and failed. And like their bodies, the world they live in is frail and finite. It will not continue to support them forever. They ruin it and ravage it, and a day will come when it will no longer be habitable. Centuries from now, perhaps millennia, the human race will dwindle and sputter out like a spent candle. So then which of us gods will still be around, as the dregs of mankind breathe their last and expire? Which of us will still have any power? Who among the Pantheon will remain, once mortals become extinct?"

Rhetorical questions, but Ra supplies the answer nonetheless. "You, O Anubis."

"I," intones the dark god. "Precisely. I, and only I. The rest of you will be long gone while I continue to preside over the eternal dead. And thus I will endure, until the stars wink out and the very last trace of heat ebbs from the cosmos and there is nothing but eternal icy nothingness. Here, in my realm of souls, I will outlast you all. You may burn brightly now, great Ra, but you cannot burn forever, whereas I in all my coldness and restraint have countless eons ahead of me."

"So you do not care, is that what you're telling me?" says Ra. "You do not care about family or happiness or peace in the world?"

"Why? Why should I? Eventually, in time, I will have no family left. Happiness is a fleeting emotion and, in my judgement, overrated. As for peace in the world, it is a figment, an illusion, a desert mirage. Unattainable. Humans fight. It is what they do. What they do best, moreover. Even if by some miracle you were able to stop the Pantheon's quarrelling, humans would simply find other justifications to hate and kill one another. There would still be wars, waged for reasons of money, philosophy, skin colour, territorial gain, any or all of these."

"Perhaps the wars would not be so intense, or so continuous. Perhaps there would be periods of relative calm. Lulls in the bloodshed."

"I doubt it."

Ra tries a fresh tack. "So you will not intercede between Osiris and Set, and you do not see the point in peace," he says. "At the very least, would you consider looking a little more kindly on your fellow gods? I know you hate all of us—"

"Not all, Ra. You, for example, I am merely indifferent to."

From Anubis, this is tantamount to a declaration of love.

"I'm honoured," says Ra. "Still, what I'm asking is—"

"Could I try not to resent my relatives quite so much?"

"I'd be happy if you could manage it with even just one of them."

"Which one, though? Not Osiris, the hypocrite. Not Isis or Nephthys, those deceitful shrews. Horus? Huh. There's nothing to Horus. He's hollow, a thing of bluff and bluster. And as for those wretched children of his..." Anubis mimes a shudder.

"That leaves one person. Set."

"Him?" The god of the dead sneers, and his teeth are many and they are sharp. "'Daddy'? Him I would find it hardest of all not to dislike."

"You're similar in many ways."

"That would be why, then. Ever heard of magnets? Aligned alike, we repel each other."

Ra heaves a sigh. His third attempt to bring about a change of mood within the Pantheon, his third failure. It's useless. It really does seem that his quest is futile. Perhaps he should simply give up. Doubtless that's what Thoth would counsel. Maat too. Wisdom is knowing when you're defeated.

Then Anubis says, "Try not to be so downcast."

"Is it that obvious?"

"Your light has dimmed. I can almost bear to look directly at you. You're aware, aren't you, that unusual events are occurring on earth?"

"I've been somewhat preoccupied. What events are these? Tell me."

"In the place they call Freegypt. Look there. What do you see?"

Ra is the sun, the ever-open eye. Ra gazes down in rays and

beams, and the world lies spread out below him, laid bare, and he sees into every corner of it. He focuses his attention on Freegypt, where no member of the Pantheon holds sway, the land where their worship arose and where by mutual agreement they leave no tread. A birthplace for all, a home to none. The empty nest. The tiny speck of territory that reminds them of their origins and of how far they have come.

Freegypt's entire history, its recent past, what has happened there during the last few days – in an instant Ra perceives it all. He takes it all in. He observes and comprehends.

"Ha," he says. "Ho. Interesting."

"Is it not?" says Anubis. "A small but significant shift in the status quo. I only noticed it myself when a handful of Freegyptian souls appeared in Iaru. Unbelievers always make their presence felt when they come here. They just aren't expecting it. I sense their startlement – like an itch in my extremities – though it soon subsides as they adjust and fall to work alongside their fellow dead. These ones, however, were killed by Nephthysians. They bore the mark of Nephthys's ba on them, which naturally made me curious. Investigating, I learned the whys and wherefores of their dying, and that led me to discover the desecration of temples belonging to Wepwawet, Sobek and others, and thence to the existence of this man calling himself the Lightbringer."

"The Lightbringer," Ra says. He frowns, pensively. "Yes. I can discern very little about him. I can hardly see him at all, in fact. There is something about him, a – a kind of pearlescent aura. It shifts and shimmers, like fog. He disguises himself. How?"

"This troubles you."

"Of course it troubles me. As does his chosen name. Am I not the one who brings light?"

"There is an element of hubris there, I agree. Perhaps of challenge too."

"The situation," Ra says, "merits further enquiry. Thank you, Anubis. This hasn't been a wasted trip after all."

"I am, O Ra, indifferent to you, remember?"

"And I feel the same way about you, Anubis," Ra says, with warmth.

19. SHEEPDOGS

DAVID GUNNED THE throttle, and the trail bike responded with a tremendous tinny roar, fishtailing in the sand as it accelerated. Zafirah was parked ahead, waiting for him to catch up. She sat astride her bike domineeringly, comfortable in the saddle. She rode it much the same way.

David wished he was half so confident. Back home he'd owned a motorbike once, a Norton Mongoose. It was a touring model, sturdy, stately and sedate, a prudent choice of machine, promising a safe level of adventure for the not-very-adventurous. Its 1150cc engine was great for cruising along A-roads and motorways, but around town the Mongoose was sluggish, nothing like as nippy as its animal namesake. At times David, reclining in the seat, felt as though he might as well be at the controls of a car. He'd had no regrets about selling the bike back to the dealership after three weeks.

The trail bike was another story. Lighter, livelier, it skittered around on its narrow, knobbly tyres, sensitive to the slightest shift of its rider's weight. Its unpredictable handling meant you could over-steer without intending to and skid onto your side. You could also, because of its lack of weight, easily over-brake and risk pitching yourself headfirst over the handlebars. In the first hour of riding, David had fallen off three times, much to Zafirah's amusement. He had since mastered the bike but he was still wary of it and would drop cautiously into third or even second gear if the going got rugged.

As the Lightbringer's army trundled north, it was David and Zafirah's job to scoot back and forth alongside the column of vehicles, making sure all was well. If a car broke down, they alerted a mechanic via shortwave. If they found stragglers, they guided them back to rejoin the main body of the column. David likened their role to that of sheepdogs. They kept the flock together and travelling in the same direction. Sheepdogs with two-stroke engines.

It was some flock, too. The column stretched a good five miles from the Lightbringer's lead car to the petrol tankers that brought up the rear. In between was a hodgepodge of civilian automobilia – rusty taxis, vans, pickups, off-roaders, puttering family saloons and station wagons, several motorhomes, a limousine that had seen better days but still exuded an air of battered, imperturbable elegance, and even a couple of buses – all overloaded with passengers, weaponry, plastic water kegs, tents, and non-perishable food. The captured military vehicles rolled in their midst, the half-tracks and the APCs, and of course the Scarab tanks, incongruous in all their roundness and their photovoltaic shimmer. The tanks' whirling drive spheres churned up great gobbets of earth and flung them high, meaning there was a gap of at least twenty yards between each one and the next vehicle in line. Otherwise, people drove pretty much nose to tail.

In all, David estimated that over three thousand people were on the move, perhaps as many as three and a half thousand. It was a fair-sized force. It was also hopelessly ragtag, as ill-equipped and under-trained as an army could be. Seen from a distance the column resembled nothing so much as a line of refugees, an exodus from persecution or conflict. Military transport notwithstanding, this looked like a march *away* from battle, not towards.

He braked to a halt beside Zafirah, switched off the engine, heeled down the kickstand and pulled his riding goggles up onto his forehead. Like her he was wearing a cloth turban, secured under the chin, with a flap drawn across the lower half of the face to act as a dust filter. He pulled this down, to speak.

"Murder on the knees, these bikes," he said. "And the backside."

"Old man," she retorted.

He offered her his water flask. She drank. David then slaked his own thirst, his throat feeling so parched it ached.

Squinting, he surveyed the passing column. "How far to Suez, do you reckon?"

"Sixty, seventy miles," Zafirah replied, with the merest of shrugs. "Why?"

"Just wondering how long till we get attacked. Suez is where the Nephs will most likely hit us. We're making good progress but we'll have to slow down in order to cross the canal. It's a chokepoint, and we'll be sitting ducks."

"Why not hit us sooner? Why not now? Aren't we sitting ducks out here in the open?"

"The Nephs aren't sure where we are. They know which way we went out of Luxor and where we're headed, because the people we left behind will have told them."

"Then surely they're following us."

"We have a couple of days' head start on them, and the desert's a damn big place and we're out of range of Saqqara Bird surveillance. So all they can do is send warships up to the head of the Gulf of Suez to lie in wait for us, with Saqqara Birds patrolling onshore. Soon as they get a glimpse of us they'll let loose with the heavy artillery."

"We could cross the canal further inland, couldn't we?"

"Further inland there aren't any road bridges, and then you reach the Great Bitter Lakes and you're virtually at the Mediterranean coast. Suez is the only place where we can get onto the Sinai Peninsula easily, and the best chance the Nephs have of stopping us."

It had occurred to David, more than once, that he was in the process of retracing the major portion of his journey from Petra to Luxor, and he felt that in a way this was helping him come to terms with the whole dreadful experience. A volunteer now rather than a captive, someone with a purpose more than merely surviving, he was erasing his own tracks, undoing what had been done.

"You've mentioned all this to the Lightbringer, I suppose," Zafirah said. "Of course you have. You two are as thick as thieves. Is that the right saying in English?"

"It'll do. And yes, I've discussed it with him. Last night, in fact. He doesn't seem too worried."

"He has a plan?"

"He says it's a contingency he's ready for. He disagrees with me about the possibility of a naval bombardment, though. He thinks the Nephs have upset the Freegyptian government too much already with the airstrike on Luxor. He says Prime Minister Bayoumi won't wear another Freegyptian town getting bombed, especially as Suez is so much closer to Cairo than Luxor is – practically next door – not to mention economically vital to Lower Freegypt."

"The Nephthysians hardly care what Bayoumi thinks."

"They might now, because he's made a public plea to the Hegemony and the Horusites to do something to help."

"Help Freegypt? No one helps Freegypt." Zafirah said this with pride and some contempt. "No one's ever given two figs what happens in my country. We've always been an ignorant, infidel backwater republic, and that isn't going to change."

"But now the Nephs have stepped in," David said. "They've done what nobody else has in a hundred years and invaded. Whatever else Freegypt is, it's a sovereign state, and the Nephs have broken international law. Never mind that they were provoked. They've still done the unthinkable. In crossing the Freegyptian border with a military force, they've crossed a line."

"The Hegemony will intervene?" Zafirah sounded doubtful.

"They might. Osirisiacs never need much of an excuse to take a pop at their enemies, and the Horusites will certainly be keen for them to. Jeb Wilkins likes conducting wars by proxy if he can get away with it. No Americans and Canadians coming home in bodybags always plays well with the voters. So he'll be goading the Hegemony on, talking about common interests and the importance of maintaining strategic effectiveness in the Middle Eastern theatre, or some such. If the Hegemony does get involved, that may or may not be to our advantage. We'll have to see. The real question is what the Setics will do."

"Obvious. Support the Nephthysians."

"Maybe. There's been plenty of talk coming from the KSD but precious little concrete action so far."

"Give them time."

David acknowledged this with a nod, not a full one.

"It's interesting," said Zafirah.

"What is?"

"How you've come round to the Lightbringer. How close the two of you have become. He's always conferring with you."

David nearly blurted it all out then: *That's because he's Steven, he's my brother, my long-thought-lost little bro*. The secret seemed desperate to leap out of him and latch itself onto someone else, like it was a living entity with a mind of its own, a kind of virus. He only just managed to keep it contained.

"Perhaps he enjoys having someone around he can speak his native tongue with," he said.

"He has me," Zafirah pointed out.

"Jealous?"

"No. But I remember how sceptical you were to begin with. How hostile. Now look at you – his right-hand man."

David smirked. "I saw the light."

This flippant remark drew unexpected scorn.

"Oh, so now you're so cosy with him, you can make fun of him behind his back," Zafirah snapped. "Is that supposed to impress me?"

"I didn't mean anything by it. It seemed like a witty thing to say."

"Some of us respect Al Ashraqa deeply, you know. Even revere him."

"I know."

"He may be a man, not a god, but this is a land where idols have been in short supply."

Again the secret squirmed within David. Again he fought to hold it in.

"I meant no offence," he said. "Sorry."

"Apology accepted – just." Zafirah frowned. "What is it with you, though? I don't get it. Most of the time you're so self-assured, completely in control of whatever you do, and then all of a sudden you're this awkward little boy who doesn't know how to act around grown-ups."

It stung, because it was true.

"Aren't all men that way?"

"Perhaps, but with you the difference is so marked." She fixed her jade-and-topaz gaze on him. "All I'm trying to say is, I can't figure you out, David West*ween*ter."

"But you want to?"

"I think so. For a long time I've felt like I shouldn't be interested in you. I've needed to keep you at a distance. I don't know why. In denial, I suppose."

"In de Nile," David said, regretting it the instant he said it.

"That's just it!" Zafirah exclaimed. "That – that pathetic schoolboy humour of yours. Here I am, trying to say something serious, and you just make a joke. I don't know why I bother."

"No, please bother."

Somewhere inside herself she found the reserves of tolerance she needed to keep going. "All I want is for you to understand that I know I have been difficult with you. I admit it. Stand-offish. That's a real word, right? I have been that way. But I don't think I can do that any more. I don't think I want to. You confuse me, you infuriate me sometimes, but..."

That was his cue. That was a come-on line if ever David had heard one. And all at once he was reminded, acutely, how good Zafirah looked. Even with her features hemmed in by the turban and seamed with road grime, she was nothing less than striking. And the way she straddled the bike – arms folded, legs straight out in an inverted V, holding the machine upright with the clench of her thighs – was impossibly sexy. He felt a bead of sweat trickling down his torso under his shirt, working its way from collarbone to crotch.

He could reach out to her now. Should. Must. This was it. Now or never.

But then Steven's admonition flashed through his head: *Zafirah isn't for you*. He could see the words in his mind's eye, as though they were written in letters of fire ten feet tall. They formed a barricade in his thoughts. He couldn't seem to push past them. Steven had put Zafirah off-limits, had made her forbidden territory for him. The two of them could still work together, that was acceptable to him, but nothing more. And somehow David couldn't help but comply with his brother's wishes.

Why? he asked himself as his arms remained limp by his sides and the bead of sweat was absorbed untraceably into his waistband. *Why am I letting Steven dictate what I can and can't do regarding this woman?*

Zafirah was watching him, waiting for him to make his move.

David felt abject. Helpless.

Seconds passed.

Zafirah turned her face away. Something in the middle distance caught her attention.

"There," she said coolly. "Look. A car in trouble."

A dinky little runabout had strayed off the hard-packed dirt track the column was following. It had driven onto the soft sand at the edges. It had become bogged down.

Zafirah lowered her goggles and stamped down on the kick-starter. David did the same. He rode after her towards the stricken car, steering his bike along the snaky double-groove her tyres left behind.

The car had to be unloaded. They dug the wheels out. It still couldn't free itself. They used planks so that it could gain traction. Finally, revving hard, the car lurched clear.

An hour's work in the blazing sunshine, David and Zafirah barely exchanging a word.

And that was how it remained with them for the rest of that day and into the next, all the way to Suez. Awkward. Strained. The air between them heavy with silence and disappointment.

Then came the Nephthysian attack. Not the naval bombardment David had predicted. Something much more insidious.

20. MUMMIES

THE PROCESS OF recycling dead troops in mass quantities had become quite industrialised. There was something of the production line about it.

First, freshly killed corpses were gathered from the battlefield and transported to a Reanimation Facility, usually to be found at a military base as part of its extensive temple complex. In the Reanimation Facility, a pyramidal building naturally, the bodies were sorted into two categories, the relatively intact and the unusable. The latter were discarded; incinerated. The former were cleansed and purified with oils, then sliced open so that certain major organs – liver, lungs, stomach, intestine – could be excised and removed. Each crop of viscera was sealed in a set of Canopic jars, the military-issue version of which was a cubic canister with four separate compartments, designed for compactness and utility.

The corpses' brains were extracted next, scraped out through the nose with hooks and destroyed. Not only was this customary, as the Ancient Egyptians had always believed that the purpose of the brain was nothing more than to provide lubrication for the sinuses, but the last thing unliving shock troops needed was the potential capacity for autonomous thought.

Up until the middle of the twentieth century, natron had been used to dry the bodies out. They were covered with the substance, a kind of salt mixture, and left for forty days while it did its work. Natron, however, was expensive to procure, as well as slow acting, so a cheaper, faster method had been devised. The bodies were hung on racks and rolled into an enormous kiln, to be fired like wet clay. Once they were desiccated, entirely without moisture, they were allowed to cool and then wrapped from head to foot in cerecloths, with an extra layer of plain linen bandage forming a tight, tidy outer casing.

The entire process took less than twenty-four hours, and could be performed by trainee acolytes or even workers drawn from the laity. For the final stage, however, a fully-fledged priest was required.

The priest prayed over the withered bodies, chanted, made animal sacrifices, invoking divine power, summoning down *ba* to instil life in these husks, to make them capable of standing up, walking, even wielding mêlée weaponry. The Canopic jars, and the associated innards they contained, were *ba*-infused at the same time.

Mummies could be kept in storage till needed. Then, as many as were required could be activated and sent into the field. The mummies would do their masters' bidding as long as they remained within reasonably close range of the Canopic jars, at a distance of no greater than five miles. Outside that radius they ground to a halt and became lifeless, insensible things again – true corpses – and could not be resurrected a second time.

To intercept the Lightbringer as he neared Suez, the Nephthysians deployed an entire regiment of mummies, approximately 600 undead "units". The intention was to sow fear and discord, and rout the Freegyptian desecrator-terrorists. The Nephthysians wished to demonstrate to the infidels what happened when you opposed those with a god on their side.

ADVANCE SCOUTS CAME back to the Lightbringer with the news. The western outskirts of Suez teemed with mummies. There were throngs of them around the town's petrochemical refineries and concrete and fertiliser plants. There were more in the desert itself. They were just standing there in rough formation, clutching the Nephthysian choice of close-combat weapon, the short sword. They were completely still, like statues. It was eerie – hundreds of bandage-swathed figures stationed out in the hot sun, waiting. Just waiting.

"The Nephs are trying to spook us," said the Lightbringer. "They think that that many mummies will scare us off. We won't dare advance. Me personally, though, I'm insulted. They're sending the undead to take care of us? That's how seriously they take us, that they won't even commit living troops? If it wasn't for this mask, I'd spit on the ground."

Troops were marshalled. Weapons were readied for an assault.

Meanwhile, David was despatched with Zafirah and several of her Liberators on a subsidiary mission.

𓂀

SIMPLE TRIANGULATION DETERMINED the likeliest location for the Canopic jars. Given the maximum five-mile range and the sheer number of mummies involved, the jars had to be on a ship, a largish one, close to shore, somewhere inside the curve of the Bay of Suez.

Sure enough, a freighter flying the Nephthysian colours lay at anchor at Port Tawfiq, a spit of land jutting out into the confluence of the canal and the Red Sea. Through binoculars David spied three priests on deck, taking the late-afternoon air. That clinched it. Battleships invariably carried a priest, sometimes two. But a merchant navy vessel? The Canopic jars were on board. The freighter was the hub of the Nephs' mummy operation.

Darkness fell. David, Zafirah and the Liberators approached along the shoreline, keeping low. The freighter loomed before them, her bulk haloed by the dockyard floodlights. She was manned – perhaps fittingly, given her cargo – by a skeleton crew. The watch at the base of the gangplank consisted of just a pair of junior ratings, who were more interested in the Pan-African Tournament football match they were listening to on a transistor radio than in the possibility of a sneak attack on their vessel. Two of the Liberators, the twin-like cousins Saeed and Salim, stole up behind them and briskly and efficiently slit their throats. The watch on deck were no more vigilant, and no more difficult to catch unawares, and then just no more.

Nephthysian overconfidence. They really had not got the full measure of the Lightbringer yet.

On the bridge the chief officer was keeping a sleepy eye on things. David put a gun to his head and demanded to be taken below. The man spoke excellent English. He begged not to be killed. He had a wife and six daughters back home in Dar es Salaam.

"Six?" David said.

"Too many," said the chief officer, with feeling. "I am overjoyed to see them when I am on leave, but within a week I am always overjoyed at the prospect of returning to sea."

"Think about them, then, and everything will be OK."

The chief officer promised he would keep his family uppermost in his mind and do whatever David asked.

Belowdecks, he led David and the others along a catwalk that ran almost the entire 500-foot length of the freighter's hull. Beneath their feet lay a couple of dozen open-topped holds, laid out in a grid pattern, each large enough to accommodate perhaps twenty of the undead creatures stacked upright. Overhead ran a system of pulleys and winches for hauling the mummies up onto a cargo elevator. All of the holds were empty.

A sound of singing grew louder, drifting through the cavernous space from a doorway at the far end of the catwalk. A trio of male voices were entwined in liturgical harmony, intoning praise for Nephthys, Queen of the Hot Lands, Consort of Set, Guardian-Goddess With the Wings of a Kite. David took a quick glance at his watch. Past 10pm. Spot-on timing. The Lightbringer's forces would have just begun engaging with the mummies. Steven wanted to give his troops a taste of combat. He wanted them blooded. He also wanted them to learn that mummies, strong as they were, loathsome as they were, were not as indomitable as their reputation suggested. Much of their effectiveness came from the natural revulsion people felt towards them. If that could be overcome, then what was left was a bunch of stiffly moving, somewhat clumsy opponents who responded slowly to commands and could be neutralised by the simple expedient of blowing their legs off. The ship's priests were aware that battle had begun. They were beseeching Nephthys to grant a favourable outcome.

They broke off from their song as David entered with the chief officer, followed by Zafirah and the two cousins. The holy men were startled, then outraged. They launched into a tirade of protest, and one didn't need Arabic to know what they were saying. We were in the middle of conducting a religious rite. How dare you people come barging in like that? This is blasphemy! Sacrilege!

Zafirah waved a gun at them. That shut them up. In the space of a second the priests went from barking hounds to whipped curs. They seemed to deflate within their robes.

"Not so keen to visit Iaru just yet, eh?" she jeered. "Doesn't surprise me. Life – this life – is good for a priest. Wealth, respect, status, why give it up?"

Other than a small altar with votive candles on it, there was nothing in the room but brushed-steel canisters, the sets of Canopic jars. They were piled neatly on shelves like tinned goods in a store cupboard, each stamped with the date of excision and a serial number. David fancied he could detect a faint whiff of rotting flesh in the air, but that was doubtless his imagination.

While Saeed and Salim got busy laying charges, the priests and the chief officer were shepherded towards the ship's living quarters and locked in the wardroom. David, Zafirah, and the Liberators then set about rounding up every other crewmember they could find, including the captain who was fast asleep in his cabin. By 10.45pm everything was ready. The crew and priests were escorted down the gangplank. To the west the night sky was lit up by flashes. Distant detonations rumbled and pealed. The Lightbringer's army, laying into the mummies. David could picture the looks of growing delight on the Freegyptians' faces as they scythed through the ranks of the undead, realising that it wasn't so hard to destroy these monsters, especially if you could get over thinking of them as things that had formerly been human. It helped that none of the mummies was likely to have been a Freegyptian once. As David knew, mummies were that much more difficult to deal with when there was every chance that some of them used to be your own allies, your own countrymen, perhaps even close comrades.

Saeed – or it could have been Salim – handed David the remote detonator. He passed it on to Zafirah.

"You do the honours," he said.

"A gift," she replied sardonically. "How kind."

He didn't want her to look at him like that, so bruised, so resentful. He hated how her eyes became narrow, dimming their usual gemlike lustre. But what could he do? He kept wrestling with his conscience. He kept trying to overcome his need to please his brother by abiding by the taboo Steven had imposed on her. He kept losing.

Zafirah raised the detonator and, with an emphatic set of her jaw, pressed the button.

The explosion was muffled, like someone slamming a heavy door in a room downstairs, but the whole freighter jolted with the force of it. She rocked as though some vital organ had gone into spasm. Deep ripples eddied out from her hull. A short while later smoke appeared, seeping out from under her cargo hatches.

At much the same time the sounds of far-off combat waned. The flashes and rumbles grew further apart, then ceased.

One of the priests fixed David with a glare and began muttering.

"What's he saying?" David asked Zafirah.

"Oh, just cursing you. Summoning the wrath of Nephthys down on your head. Calling you a heathen and a godless monkey and a follower of a false prophet."

Had David been in a better, more even-tempered frame of mine just then, he might have shrugged it off. In the event, fury welled up. He saw himself reaching for the priest, grabbing him by the robes, knocking him to the ground, kicking him in the face as he lay there. He saw himself, and then realised he was actually doing all this. It was as though he was not the author of his own actions, he was a bystander, someone else was responsible.

He stopped then, when the truth dawned. Leaving the priest moaning and spitting out blood and teeth, he turned on his heel and strode off in a cloud of self-disgust.

AT THE SITE of the battle, jubilation reigned. Half the mummies had been felled by gunfire and grenade. The rest had collapsed abruptly, turning to heaps of bandage and powdered flesh the moment the Canopic jars had been destroyed.

"The Nephthysians thought us cowards and fools," the Lightbringer told his troops, who hadn't suffered a single casualty. "They treated us with contempt. They thought all it would take to make us turn back was a few mummies. How severely they underestimated us! How wrong they were!"

The cavalcade of vehicles traversed the canal without further interruption, passing onto the Sinai Peninsula, the immense triangular tract of land that would take them to the eastern border of Arabia. David, in the back seat of the Lightbringer's car, closed his eyes and did something he hadn't done in weeks: he prayed.

He called on Osiris and Isis. He asked them to hear him. He begged for their understanding. He was looking out for his brother, that was all he was doing. He had allowed himself to become swept up in the Lightbringer's crusade but it was Steven he was helping. He wasn't a heathen. He was not. He was still a true son of the Parent Hegemony. He still had faith.

Didn't he?

For the first time in his life David felt no certainty that the Benevolent Father and the Mother of All were listening. His prayer seemed to go nowhere, sounding hollow in his head, dull and echoless. He wondered if that was the fate of all the prayers he had ever prayed. He couldn't recall a time when any of the wishes he had articulated in them had actually been granted. He'd prayed mainly because praying had made him feel better.

It didn't now. Quite the opposite.

He opened his eyes.

Heathen.

How had that happened? When? At what moment had his faith deserted him?

In the desert. When he was lost. When he had been close to death and all too acutely aware of the gods' indifference, not to mention that of his military superiors, who had thought it preferable to kill him and his men rather than leave them the possibility of escaping and surviving. When he had never felt quite so abandoned and alone.

It wasn't that he no longer believed the One True Pantheon existed. Of course it did.

He no longer believed *in* the Pantheon. He no longer trusted the gods, any of them, to do what was right by their worshippers.

So damn them.

Heathen he was, then.

And as such, he would stick with the Lightbringer – with Steven – to the bitter end.

21. ANUBIANS

At dawn, not far from the border, David found Steven atop a low ridge, facing east. Behind them the encampment was coming to life, the Lightbringer's army getting ready for the push into Arabia. Ahead, the desert was lit in shades of virgin pink and baby blue. The camp was filled with clatter and bustle as meals were eaten and tents put away, but from the landscape ahead came a tremendous, primordial silence that seemed to sweep all before it, the engulfing soundlessness that must have existed at the world's beginning and would be all that remained at its end.

Steven, hearing the crunch of footfalls, twitched his head. He had been lost in contemplation of the sunrise. He turned.

"Dave," he said. "Glad it's you. Don't feel up to talking to anyone else just at this moment."

"What's the matter?" David asked.

"Nothing," his brother said. He rubbed a hand back and forth over the top of his mask, as though trying to carve the white sphere of his head even smoother. "Nothing. Just... vertigo, that's all."

David glanced around. The ridge they were standing on was a bump in the earth, barely twenty feet high. "This is hardly Everest."

"Not actual vertigo, dimwit. Metaphorical. We're about to take an immense step. A step over a precipice, it feels like."

"Doubt? You?"

"Not so much doubt. A sense of... I'd say destiny, except you'd laugh."

"I would, too."

"This is it, Dave. Today we make the move that'll bring the full wrath of the Nephs down on our heads. The Setics probably as well. Once we cross the Arabian border there's no going back. We go from nuisance to threat. We'll no longer be something the Nephs try to brush off, we'll be something they're duty-bound to crush."

"But that's what you want, isn't it? That's why we've come all this way. To draw the Nephs out. To face them in open battle."

"Absolutely. And if we can get them to confront us on the particular battleground I have in mind, then we stand every chance of winning. After all, he who chooses the battleground has half won the battle already, as some wise man once said. Probably me. If they go for us before then, though, we're pretty much buggered."

"The way I see it, we're pretty much buggered whatever happens. We're taking on one holy power bloc, possibly two, with three-thousand-odd men and largely outmoded weaponry. Chances of outright victory? Nil, I'd say."

"Remember your Classical Civilisation at school?" Steven said. "Three hundred Spartans defeated a million Persians at Thermopylae. The right tactics in the right location can work wonders."

"As I recall, the Spartans all died."

"But they saved Greece, and their memory lives on."

"You're not in this for posthumous fame, though," David pointed out.

"No. I'm after the world's freedom, nothing else. Your freedom, mine, everyone's. An end to religious wars. An end to multiple, fractious divine dictatorship. A better future. Getting the human race up off its knees and standing on its own two feet. We may well die achieving it but I'd prefer not to. I'd much rather live to enjoy the benefits of what I've done."

"But still," David said, "you're feeling that this is the moment you could back out, if you were going to."

Through the mask Steven scratched one side of his face, the scarred side, pensively.

"I'm feeling like Caesar must have when he was about to invade Rome and spark civil war," he said. "This is my Rubicon. I have to forge ahead, knowing that there's no real alternative. Happy, in a way, that there's no real alternative. Why are you talking like this anyway? You thinking *you'd* like to back out?"

"Not me."

"I wouldn't blame you. I wouldn't hold it against you either. If you want to call it a day, Dave, feel free. I mean it. You've done all that I could have expected or asked for. More. You can bow out now with my complete blessing. I'd be disappointed but I'd understand."

"No," David said firmly. "I'm here to see this through – all the way through."

"Spoken like a true Westwynter."

"Spoken like a true brother, I think you'll find."

The Lightbringer mask creased into a smile. "If we were the hugging kind we'd hug right now, wouldn't we?"

"But we're not the hugging kind."

"I know. Born British, boarding school education, emotionally constipated parents – it's a recipe for repression. I think even a manly bonding handshake is beyond us."

"How about a clap on the shoulder?" David offered.

"A mutual infliction of slight pain? That'll do."

David clapped him on the shoulder. Steven clapped back.

"And don't worry about what's coming," Steven said. "It's like a game of senet. Whatever the other fellow does, there's always at least one move you can make to counteract it. And then there's the throw of the sticks, the element of randomness that can bring you a stroke of good fortune when you're least expecting it and most need it, and hang on a tick, what in the name of hell are those?"

Steven leaned forward, peering at the horizon.

Out of the low orange sun seven black dots had appeared. A sound could be heard, all but swallowed by the vast desert stillness, a throbbing bassy pulse that resonated through the bones of the skull. The black dots grew larger, each taking on a recognisable outline.

"Helicopter gunships," Steven breathed. "Shit. The Nephs aren't messing about. They're coming for us already. Right! We need to get those Scarab tanks front and centre, pronto!" He snatched the shortwave handset from his belt and switched it on.

"Wait." David laid a hand on his arm. "Just hold on."

"Hold on? The fucking things'll be on us in no time!"

"They're not Nephthysian. Profile's wrong. No Neph choppers have wheel farings like that. Those ones haven't got camouflage paintjobs either. Not khaki desert-pattern. Plain black."

"Black?"

"Anubian."

STEVEN'S NEXT QUESTION was "What the fuck are Anubian gunships doing all the way over here, about a million miles from home?"

David was wondering the same thing, and he was minded to think that Steven was right. The tanks with their *ba* artillery should be brought into play to defend the encampment.

Instinct was telling him something different, however. The choppers were not flying at top speed and they were taking an all too obvious line of approach. If this were a sneak attack, they'd be coming in from two sides at once and would almost certainly have opened fire already. They were well within range. The element of surprise had been theirs. They had chosen not to take advantage of it.

Why?

David had a sneaking suspicion he knew why.

The gunships roared over his and Steven's heads in a chevron formation, then over the camp. Down there, people were milling about in confusion. David could see armaments being broached, men running to the Scarab tanks.

"Order everyone to stand down, Steven," he said. "It isn't what it looks like."

"You sure?"

"If it were, we wouldn't be alive and having this conversation."

Steven barked into the shortwave in Arabic. Then, together, the two brothers set off down the hill at a run.

THE HELICOPTERS LANDED a mile beyond the camp, their downdraught kicking up a small sandstorm. Steven and David commandeered a jeep and drove out to greet them. By the time they got there the choppers' engines were powering down, their rotors resolving from disc-shaped blurs to sets of whirling vanes and finally coming to a rest. They were C39 Cranes, superb aircraft, Japanese-conceived and Indonesian-built, sizeable yet agile beasts, sporting a full suite of conventional and *ba*-tech offensive capability. In design they were all smooth planes and sharp angles. Even their undercarriage was cowled for extra sleekness and aerodynamicity. Viewed side on, their shape was reminiscent of a meat cleaver. Their function was much the same.

David's guess was that they had flown up from the Indian Ocean. Anubian aircraft carriers prowled the international waters there, keeping an eye on things across the way from the Malay Archipelago. Refuelling stops could have been made in Ethiopia and Arabia, at commercial airports and most likely at gunpoint.

This was a rogue unit. The helicopters would not, could not, be here under official sanction. The men in them were deserters.

A door opened outward from one of the choppers and a black-clad soldier emerged. He jogged through the thinning dust clouds holding his hands high to show he was unarmed.

Reaching the jeep, he saluted the Lightbringer.

"Squadron Leader Hideo Nonomura," he said, his black leather flight gear creaking as he gave a tiny, tight bow. "Former subject of the Demigod Emperor of the Anubian States. Former member of the Imperial Navy 'Sea Dragon' Special Airborne Regiment. Now wishing to be a loyal disciple of the Lightbringer of Freegypt. My men and aircraft are at your disposal, sir. We wish nothing except to meet death in your name."

Steven turned to David. "What was I saying?" he said in tones of barely restrained delight. "The sticks in senet. We've only just gone and thrown a bloody six!"

22. GODSEND

THE ARRIVAL OF the renegade Anubians and their gunships buoyed up the Freegyptians' morale, for a time. All at once, the Lightbringer's army had some airpower, an edge that the Nephthysians were unaware of. The convoy of vehicles travelled onward, up through the Negev Desert, up through the Wilderness of Judaea, along the shores of the Dead Sea, and beyond, feeling a little less vulnerable than before. The Anubians kept pace, hopping ahead in their C39s to meet up again at prearranged rendezvous points. If air support were called for, the helicopters could be summoned back at a moment's notice. After all, a Nephthysian attack of some kind was surely in the offing.

But it didn't come. No airstrike on the convoy, no ground assault, no ambush, nothing. The Lightbringer and his band of followers drove unmolested through the western fringes of Arabia, and with every mile their mood began to darken, turning warier and more apprehensive. After the mummies at Suez, why were the Nephs now ignoring them? Were they trying to lull them into a false sense of security? Was a trap waiting for them further up the line?

If the news broadcasts on local radio stations were to be believed, the Nephthysians weren't being anywhere near so canny. Their inactivity stemmed from indecision. The Afro-Arabian Synodical Council was itching to make a move against the Lightbringer, who had had the temerity to march across the border onto Nephthysian turf. The Kommissariat Svyatoy Dyela, however, had begun urging the Nephthysians to bide their time and hold their fire. The auguries received by the Setic high priests were, it seemed, sending a mixed message. There was confusion in the bowels of the animals they cut open, a vatic vagueness. Some of the innards were in good condition, suggesting Set regarded the KSD's original, censorious policy towards the Lightbringer with favour. Others contained horrendous abnormalities, suggesting the opposite. The priests' dream-visions were inconsistent as well, sometimes undeniably in favour of attacking the infidels, sometimes not. For every hierophant who was visited in his trance by the image of, say, a hawk swooping on a rabbit and tearing it to bits, there was another who came round remembering nothing but a flock of doves gliding in the sky.

In other words, the Setics, having at first offered unstinting support for whatever the Nephthysians wished to do with regard to the Lightbringer, had subtly shifted their stance. Publicly, High Commissar Chang was no longer using the kind of inflammatory language he had before, with his talk of vipers and poison. Now, in more measured tones, he was comparing the Lightbringer and his Freegyptian army to cockroaches, rats, and the like – pests rather than dangerous beasts. He was also suggesting that an all-out blitz on these vermin, of the kind the Synodical Council was desperate to launch, would be overkill and would make the Nephthysians look intemperate and vindictive. Best to wait, for now. Wait and see what the Lightbringer was up to in Arabia. Where he was headed. How far he would go.

The Synodical Council complained to the KSD during a long and tetchy teleconference. Chang and colleagues listened over the occasionally crackly dedicated-landline connection as the Synodical Council members begged to be allowed to attack the Lightbringer and rebuked the Setics for telling them to hold back. Then, after they had aired their grievances, Chang proceeded, with great patience and restraint, to remind them that this was not the

Osirisiac Hegemony, which was so equal a merging of blocs that they were to all intents and purposes a single entity. Who could tell where Northern Europe ended and Southern Europe began? Whereas the balance of power between Setics and Nephthysians was of a wholly different order. Economically speaking, they were well matched, with the Nephthysian states' mineral mines and oil reserves more than making up for their lack of industrial base and scarcity of other resources. However, it was doubtful whether they would ever have been able to exploit this natural wealth without Setic business leadership and technological know-how, and it was even more doubtful they would be able to survive in the modern world without the manufactured goods, including arms, which the Setics sold to them at special, subsidised rates. Put simply, were it not for the Bi-Continental Pact, the Nephthysian bloc would be stuck in a dark age, eking a meagre livelihood from agriculture and safari tours. Was that not, Chang concluded, a fair assessment of the situation? And furthermore, would the Synodical Council be keen to see a – for want of a better word – change in that situation?

Having thus firmly put the Nephthysians in their place, the High Commissar enquired if there were any further objections. The Synodical Council members grumbled but could come up with none. All they could do was acquiesce, reluctantly, to the Setics' wishes. The Lightbringer would be left alone. For now.

Hearing the news reports, nobody in the Lightbringer's army was convinced they were being told the whole and unvarnished truth. Someone was playing a game here. Someone was bluffing. The Freegyptians had ventured a couple of hundred miles into Arabia, and the Nephs were just letting them get away with it? All on the Setics' say-so? No, there was something going on behind the scenes. Had to be.

The Lightbringer himself agreed. "Don't be fooled," he told his people. "This grace period isn't going to last. Sooner or later the Nephs are going to come down on us. Hard. The Setics can't keep them on the leash forever. They'll act independently if they have to. In the meantime, all this dithering is to our advantage. It's, if you will, a godsend. It's giving us the opportunity to get to exactly where we want to be. The Nephs don't realise it but the longer they leave us alone, the more difficult they're making it for themselves in the long run."

On the third day, the convoy was passing through farmland. Metalled highways rumbled beneath their tyres and caterpillar tracks. Locals watched them go by, and some just stared in a kind of indignant astonishment, while others hurled abuse and occasionally stones. All around was ordered greenness, irrigated fields of safflower, groundnut, and chickpea sheathing the slopes of gentle hills. The sun beat down just as fiercely here as in the desert but its force was mitigated by the manmade verdancy of the landscape.

They came, eventually, to a broad plain overlooked by low mountains. The Anubian helicopters were already there, waiting. The convoy trundled to a halt. The bedraggled, road-weary army stepped out of their vehicles. This was where the Lightbringer wanted them to be. This was it. They had arrived.

"Perfect spot for a battle," David opined, surveying the terrain. "Flat. Open. Good lines of sight. Plenty of high, defensible positions."

"I know," said his brother, looking around too. "I'm not the first to realise that either. There've been battles here, way back in the past. Ancient Egyptians fought the Canaanites over three thousand years ago on this spot, and then a few centuries later they had a bash at the armies of the Kingdom of Judah. The earth beneath our feet is soaked with their blood. The place has history. It has precedent. *Form.*"

"So now we dig in, set up our lines, and brace ourselves. Is that the plan?"

"That is the plan." The Lightbringer drew in a breath and exhaled. "The moment's coming," he said. "There's going to be one hell of a clash, right here. I can feel it. I know it. It's almost as if it's been preordained."

They had halted at a point roughly equidistant between the River Jordan and the Mediterranean. They were twenty-five miles south-west of the Sea of Galilee and sixty north of Jerusalem.

They were standing on the Plain of Megiddo.

23. NEPHTHYS

RA IS DRAWN to a corner of his Solar Barque by the sound of weeping. Nephthys is crouched on deck, her face in her hands. Each sob that passes through her is like a small death. Her body jerks as though stabbed.

"Come, come," says Ra gently, kneeling beside his great-great-niece. "What's this? I won't have people crying on my boat. It's not allowed."

Nephthys looks up, pink-eyed. As the tears spill down her face, Ra thinks of a flash flood, a river bursting its banks in rainy season, arid land inundated. With his thumbs he wipes her cheeks dry. The sobs subside. Nephthys regains her composure.

"Forgive me, O Ra," she says, sniffing. "You weren't supposed to see me like this. I came to talk to you, to ask your advice, but then... it all got too much... overwhelming..."

She seems on the verge of crumpling, but manages to maintain control of her emotions.

"Hush," soothes Ra. "It's all right. Don't be upset. What's the matter?"

"Can we go somewhere private?"

Ra looks round. Maat and Thoth are within earshot, but both

of them are discreetly minding their own business. Maat keeps a steady hand on the tiller, guiding the Boat of a Million Years along the river of day, with faithful Ammut as ever at her feet. Thoth is studying the ripples on the water's surface, seemingly absorbed in contemplation. Amidships, Bast lies curled on her divan, asleep. In the bows, Set is likewise asleep, exhausted after his latest bout with the serpent Apophis.

"You can rest assured, nothing you say to me here will go any further."

"Even so," says Nephthys, with a glance towards her brother-husband.

Ra nods, and he leans back and opens his heart to her, and all is light and heat. They are surrounded by perfect white fire. They are standing at the centre of the sun. It's a place to which none may go unless invited by Ra, and into which none may pry. Here, atoms crackle and bubble like eggs on a skillet, and everything is a swirl of blazing creation. This is the crucible of life, the furnace that forges existence.

"Tell me then," says Ra. "Why the tears?"

Nephthys is not a relative Ra has any strong feelings for, or against. She is, he has always felt, a little too in thrall to others to be truly interesting, and there is an air of duplicity about her, a kind of meek maliciousness which her sweet, heart-shaped face only just disguises. Nonetheless he regards her with fondness, as he does almost everyone, and he hates to see her upset.

"You're aware," she begins, "of the infidel attacks on my domain."

"I am."

"And of how Wepwawet has suffered the indignity of seeing one of his few shrines despoiled by these unbelievers."

"Sobek was a victim too, I understand. And there were others."

"Wepwawet is unwell as a result."

"I'm sorry to hear that."

"My grandson has always been sickly," says Nephthys. "His worshippers are few and far between, and he is overshadowed by his father. His dearest wish is to follow in Anubis's footsteps and rule over legions of death-lovers, but I'm afraid he lacks the drive and the

influence. He will never be anything but a pale imitation. And now, poor creature, he is ailing, so thin you can almost see through him. It's heartbreaking. How I would love to see these wicked, faithless humans destroyed. I would gladly have them erased from the earth."

She is close to crying once more. Only with great effort does she steel herself and stem the flow of tears.

Why do women cry when they are angry? It is a mystery even to great Ra. The fact that they do, however, makes their anger all the more devastating. They appear vulnerable just when they are at their most dangerous.

"O Nephthys," he says, "your desire for vengeance is well warranted, and if it is your intention to visit retribution upon this Lightbringer and his cohorts, far be it from me to stand in your way. The blow that they have struck against you and your near kin is an offence of great magnitude. Although it is my belief that there is altogether too much strife and suffering among the mortals at present, in this instance I feel I can make an exception. The Lightbringer is not fighting at the behest of any god, he is fighting against us, all of us, and that must not be permitted. So if you and your husband wish to set about eliminating him—"

"My husband?" Nephthys lets out a hollow, corroded laugh. "Set? What do you think I'm doing here, talking to you? Set isn't paying attention to this matter. Set, in fact, doesn't seem to care. Wepwawet..."

She halts, and Ra realises she cannot bring herself to say what she would like to. Wepwawet, son of Anubis, is unquestionably her grandson. But is he Set's also? Strictly speaking, no. Not if, as is widely accepted, Anubis's real father is Osiris.

"Well," she says, "Set does not seem to be able to find a great deal of time for Wepwawet."

Nephthys cannot admit the truth, at least not out loud. Shame and decorum prevent her. She and Set and Osiris and even Isis are all entangled in the coils of a deception. They share in a family secret which they have covered up but which none of them can fully forget, or forgive. It is at the core of all their arguments. It is the root cause of the rift that divides them.

"Set..." says Ra, ruminating.

All at once he perceives that he has penetrated to the heart of the matter, and with the realisation comes the possibility of a solution to the deadlock that exists between his descendants. As with any sudden flash of insight, it seems obvious, an answer that has been sitting there in plain view, waiting to be stumbled upon.

"Nephthys," he says, placing his hands upon her shoulders, "let us be honest with each other, shall we?"

The goddess blinks and nods.

"Your brother-husband is difficult to get on with. I understand that. Set is a sullen creature, prone to fits of pique and envy. He resents it when things do not go his way. His manner is cool towards you, sometimes cruel. But remember this. You did betray him."

Nephthys opens her mouth to protest. The graveness in Ra's eyes makes her close it again without uttering a word.

"You slept with Osiris," he continues. "Whether or not Osiris knowingly slept with you, that's between him and his conscience. Either you fooled him or he fooled himself. Let's not get into that now. The fact remains, adultery was committed and a bastard son was the result. You and Set have maintained a careful façade ever since, a unified front. Set knows Anubis isn't his son but has tried to treat him as though he is. Hasn't succeeded, but at least, to his credit, has tried. You, meanwhile, continue to cosy up to Osiris and Isis – Isis particularly, since you and she are as close as any sisters could be. You would rather spend time with the two of them than with your own spouse, and that's perhaps not surprising. But it deepens Set's hatred of them. I am not defending Set here. I am not making a case to justify his behaviour. I am merely pointing out that he has a legitimate grudge against you, and against Osiris, and if he doesn't share you sense of righteous grievance right now, it is perhaps explicable. However..."

Ra beams.

"However, all that being said, I am willing to talk to Set for you. I will do my utmost to persuade him to do something about the Lightbringer, in tandem with you. It would give me great pleasure to see you and him standing shoulder to shoulder against this human interloper, this self-styled enemy of the Pantheon."

"Together," says Nephthys, "how easy it would be for us to get rid of him."

"Indeed. And when you do, you will be doing us all a favour. But – there is a condition. A quid pro quo."

"Yes?"

"In return, you have to confess all."

Her face falls. "You mean...?"

"About how you duped Osiris. About how Anubis is Osiris's son. Make a clean breast of it. Get it all out in the open. So that there are no more lies. No more secrets festering away. Announce it to the entire Pantheon. Tell everyone. Tell, above all else, Isis."

"But Isis already knows. Sort of."

"Sort of. Strongly suspects, I'd say."

"She'll kill me."

"I think not. She has remained your friend all this time, in spite of having a pretty shrewd idea what you did. I think she will still be your friend after you reveal the truth. She may even love you all the more for your bravery and honesty in owning up to what you did."

Nephthys looks doubtful – and yet hopeful. "Ra, it will be hard."

"But worth it," says Ra, and he kisses her forehead, and they are aboard the Solar Barque once more, whose gleaming effulgence, dazzling though it may be, is but a candle compared to the brilliance that burns within Ra's heart.

Nephthys departs, brimming with promises and good intentions. Ra pivots on the spot, directing his gaze towards where Set lies, still asleep. Both Maat and Thoth watch him as he strides towards the slumbering figure. They note resolve and satisfaction in his gait. They, these two divine pillars of wisdom, understand that Ra has at last come by a solution to the conundrum that has been vexing him, and they exchange a wink. The best progress is the progress one makes by oneself, unassisted. They knew he would get there in the end.

Bast stirs as Ra passes, opening one eye, then the other. She sniffs the air, catching wind of a change of mood. She is content. She tucks her head onto her forearms and dozes off again.

Ra has hitherto baulked at approaching Set as part of his peace mission. He has deemed the Lord of the Desert too intransigent, too hotheaded, to be worth dealing with. Now, however, he has a bargaining chip in his back pocket, something to offer Set in exchange for his co-operation. It could make all the difference.

"Set?" he says.

Set awakes. He rises.

"Ra?"

"Walk with me."

And they walk.

They walk, as gods may, across the universe. Side by side they stride through the gulfs between worlds, through the dark vastnesses that separate the stars. In a matter of moments they have journeyed to the outermost reaches of Creation, the point at which light and life run out and beyond which lies nothing but an abyss, pure, cold, perfect emptiness. From this vantage, looking back, the entire cosmos seems so small that it could be cupped in the palm of one hand, and crushed in the clenching of a fist.

Set gazes around him, shivering. "Why are we here, Ra? Why have you brought me to this place?" His voice has no echo. The surrounding void swallows it, deadeningly. "I don't like it. We're too far from anything that means anything."

Faced with oblivion, even a god may quail.

"Have you – have you brought me here as punishment? Do you mean to exile me?"

Ra does not calm Set's fears, not immediately. "We are here to gain perspective," he says.

"Perspective?"

"To establish what is important and what is not. Set, I shall speak plainly. You have done bad things in your time. You have tricked; you have deceived. You have fought and harmed. You have made enemies and harboured grudges."

"O Great Ra, I admit I am not perfect. I'd be the first to say I have not led a blameless life. But in my defence—"

"Let me finish, Set. You'll get your turn. Among your many crimes is the murder – I should say attempted murder – of Osiris."

"He had it coming."

Ra holds up a hand. "Patience. I told you, you'll get your turn.

Then there is the matter of your feud with Horus. Who knows what the origins of that are. Everyone seems to have a different opinion. I know that at one stage you raped him. I know also that he tore off your testicles in a fight. There's certainly a strange sort of antagonism going on between the two of you."

Set's face reddens, almost matching the hue of his eyes and hair. "I despise Horus," he says. "I wish to see him humiliated."

"And he you. And yet you and he are so alike in many ways."

"No one can get under your skin quite like kin," says Set.

"Perhaps so. But we shan't dwell on that now. Your final crime is simply one of neglect. You neglect your wife, Set, while she still cleaves submissively to you. You are callous towards your son, not to mention your grandson."

"I have my reasons."

"Indeed. Perhaps they are even forgivable ones. But people need their parents whatever age they are. They need the reassurance of knowing their mothers and fathers are always there to be turned to and consulted, or rejected if necessary. They need their unconditional love."

"I'm a busy man," Set says. "If I neglect my family, it's hardly my fault. I have precious little time to spare even for myself. In case you haven't noticed, I am a permanent 'guest' aboard your barque and have a twice-daily penance to serve."

"Justice must be done."

"Injustice, more like."

"You do not accept responsibility for the wrongs you have done, or the need to atone for them?"

"I claim that there were extenuating circumstances. I have been a victim of slights and offences myself. No one seems to remember that. It's always 'Set insulted me, Set assaulted me', conveniently overlooking the fact that I only did any of those things because someone did something to me first. I have a reputation, I'm the bad apple, so it's open-and-shut as far as the rest of you are concerned. Nobody cares that I've been provoked, that I've been cuckolded and denied high position and publicly embarrassed, that my actions are reactions. Nobody sees my side of the argument. Once you become the villain of the piece, you're the villain of the piece for all time. You don't get the chance to be seen in any other light."

"Your temper plays a part."

"True, I do get a little out of hand from time to time."

"You call tearing Osiris to pieces 'a little out of hand'?"

"I see red. I get carried away. It just happens. It's how I'm made."

"And here we get to the nub of it," says Ra. "How you're made. Set, do you think it's at all possible that you could change?"

Set is taken aback by the question. It seems that the thought has never occurred to him before.

"Change?" he says, eyebrows knotting. "In what way? And, more to the point, why?"

"The way is simple," says Ra. "Be a better person, that's all. Control yourself. Be kind to others. And as for the why, see that?" He gestures towards the tiny twinkling ember that is the universe, all but lost amid the blackness of the abyss. "See how small and remote and fragile it looks? As though a casual breath could snuff it out? We are gods, Set, and we are powerful and we live for eons, but still, in the grand scheme of things, we are insignificant. Ultimately, nothing we do is of consequence. We may be big but the eternal void is infinitely bigger."

"So why bother changing? Why bother doing anything? Isn't that the appropriate response when faced with your own insignificance? If existence is meaningless, it doesn't matter how you behave."

"That's one way of looking at it, I suppose. The other way is: if existence is meaningless, then why not change? Why not alter your attitude, if only to create meaning?"

"Of a very limited kind."

"In a limited environment, that's the best you can hope for."

Set acknowledges this, and Ra detects, or thinks he detects, a glimmer of interest in those scarlet eyes. Set is actually considering the proposal laid before him. Set is intrigued by the idea of changing.

"I wouldn't be me," he says, "if I didn't ask what's in it for me."

"For a start, if you did sincerely make an effort to improve and become a kinder, gentler, more thoughtful and forgiving Set, I would release you from your penance."

"Who would battle Apophis in my stead?"

"I would attempt to broker a truce with Apophis. I imagine he is as weary of the relentless conflict as you are, especially given that he comes off worse every time. Failing that, I would fight him myself."

"An onerous burden for you."

"Then I pray that negotiation with him succeeds," says Ra. "I think it will. The other benefit for you would be improved relations with all of your family. No longer would you feel this sense of estrangement, of victimhood, that keeps you apart from your kin. If you resolve to become a reformed character, and strive your hardest to keep to that resolution, I think you'll find that attitudes towards you will alter. Others will respond in kind. Most of all your sister-wife will actively enjoy spending time with you, rather than running off to be with Isis at every opportunity. I'm offering you a chance to improve your lot radically. All you have to do is be a new god. Put your past self behind you."

"I change, and yet no one else has to make the effort to. Hardly seems fair."

"Nephthys has agreed to change too. She is to confess her adultery with Osiris to all. She will admit she instigated it."

"Really? After so long, with her falsehood so well entrenched, that will take some courage."

"And yet she is willing to do it, in order to clear the air between you all, and in order to regain the full love and respect of her husband."

"Hmm," says Set. "And for my part, how should I begin this process of reform? Any suggestions?"

"Ah, I have a tailor-made solution for you. The Lightbringer."

"Who? Oh yes. Him."

"Him. Join with Nephthys and vanquish him. Smash the little mortal upstart. Wipe him and his army off the map."

Set looks at Ra askance, a smile twitching at his lips. "The Lightbringer seems to have got under your skin, O Sun God. You sound positively aggravated by him, and you such a mild-mannered type normally."

"I..." Ra bows his head. "I do find him bothersome. I'm not sure why. It may be because I can't 'see' him properly. I look at him and don't know who he is or anything about him. Something is keeping me from identifying and understanding the man. Perhaps it is his Freegyptian genesis, perhaps that mask he wears, I don't know. Some power is... is eclipsing him in my perceptions, and I do not like that, not at all."

"He is an unknown."

"Yes. Just so. An unknown. An anomaly. And on those grounds alone I want him off the world. I want him swept away. Him and all his followers."

"I can arrange that for you."

"You and Nephthys."

"Yes. We can rid you of this turbulent human. It would be an honour."

"And a good start to your bid to improve your standing among the gods."

"That too. Mutually beneficial."

Ra appraises Set, and is pleased. The younger god seems truly to be seizing this opportunity. He is eager to chart a new course for himself. And that, in turn, will chart a new course for the rest of the Pantheon, Ra is sure of it. Set is the key. Once he aligns himself with the other gods, universal harmony will ensue.

24. NONOMURA

DAVID WAS EXHAUSTED, but couldn't sleep.

He had spent the past two days helping to arrange the Lightbringer's forces around the plain in the most strategically effective manner and establish a fortified position on Mount Megiddo. Atop the mountain – a sharply rising 700-foot-high plateau – lay the ruins of the city of Megiddo itself. Narrow streets running between the remnants of stone walls made for perfect trenches and gun emplacements, while a high, vaulted chamber with arched alcoves, which had once been a storehouse, was easily put to use as a command post. From the plateau's perimeter the entire plain could be seen, spread between the slopes of its valley, and the view stretched all the way to Mount Carmel in the west and Mount Tabor in the east.

The troops were divided into units, each a hundred strong, which were distributed at intervals along three lines radiating southward from Mount Megiddo. Each unit was accompanied by a Scarab tank or a conventionally armed vehicle. The indigenous smallholders were none too happy at having men and machines trampling across their fields and bedding down among their crops, but few raised any objections. The wise ones, sensing what was coming, simply packed up their valuables and got out with their families while they could.

The Anubian C39s occupied a central position at the foot of the mountain, and it was here that a restless David went, picking his way down a steep footpath by moonlight. The Anubians were night owls, and he had spied them from above, gathered around a campfire close to their gunships, drinking. Awake in the small hours, jangling with pre-battle nerves, he craved company.

Squadron Leader Nonomura invited him to sit. Nonomura and his men were pink-eyed drunk. A saucepan of sake was warming over the flames, and David was passed a porcelain cup full of the steaming liquor. It burned his throat in more ways than one, but he chugged it down and asked for another. Nonomura approved.

"The only way to drink sake is carelessly," he said. "Like there's no tomorrow."

"There may well not be," David said. "It's the eve of battle. The Nephs are on their way. If they don't reach us later today, then definitely the day after."

"A toast to that," said Nonomura. "*Kampai.*"

His men raised their cups and echoed, "*Kampai.*" Among them were a couple of Australians, who followed up with "Good on yer" and "Down the hatch".

"You say the Nephthysians are on their way, Lieutenant Westwynter," said Nonomura. "You know this?"

"Intelligence is sketchy. We're relying on radio newscasts as much as anything. But it looks like the Setics have relented and told the Nephs to go ahead and attack. Whatever was troubling their high priests isn't troubling them any more. So we've got Neph infantry battalions amassing to the north of us in Damascus, and a whole lot more troops moving in from Baghdad and Riyadh. And that's not the worst of it."

"No?"

"We reckon the Setics are going to get involved after all. Chang's making noises about sending several battalions'-worth of reinforcements down through the Caucasus and Persia."

"The gods have changed their minds?"

"Set, apparently, has. Or maybe it's just politics. All the sabre-rattling that the Horusites and the Hegemony were doing. They've stopped now, but it seems to have galvanised the Setics into action. Suddenly it's high priority for them that the Lightbringer is stamped on, most likely so as to prevent the Hegemony taking matters into its own hands. Last thing anyone in the region wants is an Osirisiac invasion of Arabia."

"Something is going on up there," said Nonomura, pointing to the starry heavens.

"Something always is."

"But don't you feel it? I do. Everything seems uncertain, shifting, one day this, the next day that. It's as though the Pantheon is no longer setting the agenda. They're trying to keep up with events down here. Mortals, for once, are influencing the gods rather than the other way round. The Lightbringer has reversed the order of things."

"Is that why you've defected to his cause?" David asked. "You think we're the winning team?"

Nonomura chuckled, and his men chimed in. "Oh no, Lieutenant. We're not here for that. The Lightbringer hasn't a hope of success. The gods are too powerful to let him win. We're here to die, simple as that. This whole enterprise has an air of glorious futility about it. It looks like being as pointless and meaningless a sacrifice of life as it is possible to imagine. So naturally we want to be a part of that."

David frowned, then held his cup out for a refill. "That doesn't make any sense, but then maybe I need a bit more alcohol inside me." In truth, he was already buzzing from the sake and was starting to relish the clarity and calmness that being drunk brought.

"It makes sense to any Anubian, with or without the aid of alcohol," said Nonomura. "We live to die. Life has no goal for us beyond taking us to the point at which we leave it. We despise life. We endure it while it lasts, but death is where we wish to be. Our ruler is Anubis, so why would we not want to be closer to him, in his realm?"

One of the Australians, a lanky giant with dyed black hair and skin that had seldom seen the sun, said, "We all wind up in Iaru eventually.

It's just that some of us want to get there sooner than the rest. You know what they call us in Oz, me and my type, the ones who go along with the Asians? We're the 'can't wait, mate' brigade."

"But surely," David said, "if you're keen to die, you at least want your deaths to mean something? To achieve something?"

"Forgive me, but that is Osirisiac thinking," said Nonomura. "You are with the Lightbringer, you have come this far with him, so I can only assume you're aware that there's a good chance you may perish fighting on his behalf."

"I'd prefer not to, but yes, it may well happen."

"And if it does, you'd like to sell your death as dearly as you can. You don't want to throw your life away."

"Of course."

"There's the difference," said the Asian. "For us, a good death is a cheap death. We show our contempt for life by dispensing with it as we might a... a..."

"A pair of old underpants," said the Australian.

"Thank you, Gunner Coburn," said Nonomura. "Not as elegant a simile as I was looking for, but it'll do."

"No worries."

"So," David said, "you're here effectively to commit suicide?"

"Yes. In the vainest and most fatalistic of circumstances. The moment we learned about the Lightbringer, we knew we had to come and take part. The Nephthysians are going to slaughter this little army of yours. You're doomed. That appeals to us greatly."

"You're not even going to try to fight?" David felt cold disgust snaking through him, counteracting the heat of the sake. "So what's the good of you? You've brought us seven abso-bloody-lutely lethal helicopters and you're just going to, what, crash them into the enemy the moment you see them? Thanks a lot!"

"No, no, please don't misunderstand, Lieutenant. We will fight. We will fight till every last one of our bullets, missiles, and *ba* bolts is gone. That is the only honourable and fair thing to do. But after that our lives are forfeit. *Then* we will crash our aircraft into the enemy, and take as many of them with us as we can."

"Oh." David unclenched. "Well, that's more like it."

"Your enemy isn't strictly speaking our enemy," said Nonomura, "so we gain nothing and lose nothing by killing them."

"Adding to the meaninglessness of your deaths."

"Indeed."

"Well, you're all mad," David said, raising his cup, "but I salute you."

The Anubians reciprocated, saluting him with their cups.

DAVID STAYED WITH the Anubians a while longer, till a sliver of pre-dawn grey appeared behind Mount Tabor, levering sky and land apart. He got steadily drunker, and when the Australian, Gunner Coburn, started singing a song in praise of Anubis, he joined in. He wasn't familiar with the verses, but the chorus had a catchy tune and was easy to pick up:

> *Oh, a knife to the heart*
> *Or a bullet in the back'll*
> *Get you quick-smart*
> *To the kingdom of the Jackal.*

The Asian Anubians sang along too with this death-affirming ditty, swaying to the rhythm and slurring the words merrily.

When, finally, David stood up to leave, his head rushed down to his boots. The world whirled and wobbled, and he knew he was going to be sick. It was a matter of when, not if.

"Got to... got to go now," he told Nonomura.

The squadron leader nodded vaguely, like someone dropping off to sleep.

"I'll see you around."

"Yes," said Nonomura. "Yes. We shall meet again in the Field of Reeds." The Anubian for farewell.

"Not too soon, I hope," David said, staggering away.

Moving like a sailor on deck in high seas, he made his way back to the footpath that led up the mountainside. Halfway up, he stopped and puked, so violently it felt as though he was turning himself inside out. He couldn't recall when he had last been quite so severely, so incapacitatingly inebriated. Not since he'd learned the news of Steven's "death" and had gone out on a bender with a couple of friends in London and woken up in an alley with a policeman prodding him and advising him to move on or be arrested. Even the vomiting brought no relief. He cursed himself for being so careless and rice wine for being so beguilingly potent. He continued the uphill journey bent double, sometimes on hands and knees. He planned on crawling into his little camp bed before anyone saw him and catching a few hours' sleep. If war came today, he'd be in no fit state to face it without some shuteye beforehand.

Gaining the summit, he looked around. Sunrise was still several minutes away. Everything was grey and bleary. He could see his little bivouac, perched with several others among the rubble of shattered, ancient houses. Not far. A few hundred paces.

He blinked, and the sun was nearly up, and his bivouac was still a few hundred paces away. He stood up on the spot where he had briefly passed out. He tottered forwards. Then he passed out again.

He half-opened his eyes, hearing voices. He was lying on his side, cheek in the dust. Two people were talking softly nearby, a man and a woman, in Arabic. Dimly David knew that he knew both voices. They were so familiar, it seemed absurd to him that he couldn't for the moment identify them. There was a time lag between what he was thinking and what he wanted to think.

Steven. And... Zafirah?

He tried to stand, so that he could see them. Standing, however, had become a skill as hard to master as juggling. The best he could manage was hauling himself up onto all fours, from which position he was able to peer over the top of an old stone rain-cistern.

His brother and Zafirah weren't as close by as he'd thought. They were at the entrance to the command post, perhaps 200 yards from where he was crouching. In the dawn stillness their voices, though low, carried far.

He couldn't make out their words, and anyway his Arabic wasn't up to translating. He focused on their body language. What did it tell him? Might it reveal what Zafirah was doing up here, talking to the Lightbringer at this hour?

Zafirah looked perplexed, to him. Her usual swagger was gone. There was a hapless hunch to her shoulders. Afraid? Maybe. Almost everyone in the Lightbringer's army was tense, anxious, and understandably so. Attack was imminent. But somehow he didn't feel Zafirah belonged in that category. This was a fight she'd long been spoiling for, and if she harboured any fears, she was the type to keep them to herself.

What, then? What was the reason for the stooped stance, the one foot toeing the other, the hands that didn't seem to know where to put themselves?

And Steven. He was looking concerned. Conciliatory. His head was canted to one side. The patient listener. The man who cared.

Then something he said made Zafirah wheel away abruptly. He caught her by the arm. He turned her back round. His head bent to hers and his voice dropped to an inaudible whisper.

David watched as Zafirah leaned in with her ear close to Steven's mask-veiled mouth – intimately close. He watched as Steven murmured to her, still holding her. He watched her body start to unstiffen. She relaxed. He thought, although he was too far away to be sure, that she even smiled.

And now he thought, or imagined he thought, that Steven's hand was caressing Zafirah's hair.

And now he imagined, or thought he imagined, that Zafirah was pressing her cheek against Steven's face. Had the mask not been there, this would have been a kiss. A lingering touch of lips to cheek. Even with the mask it was still a kiss, of sorts.

Then Zafirah was walking away, confidence restored. She strode straight past David's place of concealment. She didn't see him. He didn't make his presence known. She disappeared down the footpath. Steven turned and ducked in through the command post entrance.

David slumped to the ground, his sake-soused brain struggling to digest what he had just witnessed. It couldn't have been what it had appeared to be, and yet it couldn't have been anything else. Steven and Zafirah in a clinch. Well, not quite a clinch, but as near as made no difference. An embrace too close to be that of just-friends. She had been unsure about something, and Steven had soothed her, as tenderly as a lover would, and they had parted with a kiss.

And where had the pair of them been immediately before that conversation? Indoors? In the command post? Alone together? Was that why Zafirah had needed soothing? To set her mind at ease over something that had happened in there? Something they had done?

It was all leading to one conclusion. David kept trying to reinterpret the evidence, direct it onto a more innocent track. Again and again it steered itself inexorably back towards that same conclusion.

His head swam. The rim of the sun crested the horizon, Ra on the rise. He wanted to get up, go and confront his brother. His eyelids were as heavy as old sash windows. The hard earth felt extraordinarily comfortable beneath him, soft as a feather bed. Steven, the liar. Steven, the traitor. The dawn sky was red. Blood of Apophis, shed by Set. Just a few minutes' rest. Steven, the devious, selfish bastard. Fucked her. Fucker.

"Fkrrr," David mumbled, and lapsed into unconsciousness.

AND CAME AWAKE to the scream of jets and the crackle of explosions. A Nephthysian Locust passed a couple of hundred of feet overhead, its roar making the whole of Mount Megiddo tremble. Cluster bombs tumbled from its wings. Rippling patches of *ba* swelled and popped across the plain like blisters.

David scrambled to his feet, suddenly and brutally sober.

Battle had begun.

25. BOMBARDMENT

CLUSTER BOMBS WERE a notoriously imprecise and inaccurate form of antipersonnel hardware. Each tennis-ball-sized bomblet had so little mass that it tended to float down rather than fall and was subject to the whims and vagaries of the wind. The primary purpose of cluster bombs, over and above than the taking of life, was to cause panic and disarray. This, at Megiddo, they did not achieve. The Lightbringer's forces were so thinly spread out that the hails of bomblets mostly missed. Crops were destroyed but precious few people. The Freegyptians were amazed and relieved, and consequently kept their nerve. As the planes rumbled into the distance, they steadied themselves to meet them on their next run. The Scarab tanks lofted their blaster nozzles. The Anubian C39s took to the air.

On their second sortie the Locusts were joined by some weightier air cavalry, a brace of Russian-made Typhon bombers backed up by three Serpent attack helicopters, also from Russia. The Typhons, named after the strange doglike beast that was symbolic of Set, were fat, cumbersome things that looked about as likely to get airborne as bumblebees. But then their role wasn't to flit around and look elegant. It was to carry fusion warheads. Lots of them. And deliver them.

The Locusts bombarded the Lightbringer's lines again, but this time the Scarab tanks were ready. *Ba* spat into the sky in rippling four-shot sequence from their blaster nozzle quartets. The heavy-calibre machine guns were also brought to bear. Tracer rounds marked the trajectory of their bullets in lines of glowing dots, much like the patterns made by the tanks' phased *ba* fire. The air above the plain was filled with crisscrossing stitches of light, and not all the Locusts came through it unscathed. Planes reeled away with wings and tails alight. One spun cartwheel-fashion, crashing into the side of the valley. Another hurtled past Mount Megiddo and pancaked explosively on the far side, ploughing a fiery furrow through fields.

The Typhons entered the fray shortly afterwards, with their Serpent escorts strafing the ground madly, trying to clear a path for them through the thickets of flak. By this time, however, the C39s were aloft and out for blood. Squadron Leader Nonomura and his men closed in on the Serpents and...

... the only word David could think of to describe it as he looked on from the mountaintop...

... *pulverised* them.

The Serpents never stood a chance. The C39s took them out with almost arrogant ease. Beams of black *ba* knocked out their tail rotors, sending them into a terminal spin. Heat-seeking missiles finished them off, like the punchline to a cruel joke.

The Anubians then turned their attention on the Typhons. Thicker armour made the bombers a tougher proposition than the Serpents. So did dedicated defensive gunnery.

The leading Typhon already had its bomb bay doors open and was starting to empty its payload onto the plain below. Two of the C39s attacked its flanks. Red *ba* sparked from the bomber's mid-fuselage blaster turrets. One of the helicopters bulged with scarlet brilliance and disintegrated. The shielding on the other held out, and it retaliated with a *ba* bolt of its own that blew the offending turret, and the gunner within, to smithereens.

A third C39 – and somehow David knew it was Nonomura's – tackled the Typhon head-on, flying in reverse and disgorging vast amounts of *ba* and rocketry at the plane. Anubians did not have access to fusion weaponry, being under the aegis of only one god, not two. But what they lacked in quality of destructive capability, they made up for in quantity. The sheer amount of firepower emanating from the gunship was breathtaking, an almost solid barrage of conventional ordnance and divine essence leaping from it to the front of the Typhon. Bit by bit the bomber's nosecone was flayed, metal skin flaking off in shards till the ribs of the airframe showed through. Its windshield shattered, turning from clear glass to white ice. The Typhon lumbered on, but its bombs were no longer falling. The bomber itself was falling, gradually and inexorably losing height and speed. The C39 continued to hammer at it all the way down, till the Typhon, now rotating around its longitudinal axis, scraped the ground with one wingtip and instantly slammed flat onto its nose, teetered, then keeled over onto its back with a tremendous, dust-billowing thump. Nonomura's C39 sprang triumphantly away into the sky.

The second Typhon, similarly harried by Anubians, tried to get out of its predicament by gaining altitude. This, though, enticed a C39 to nip in under it and blast upwards at its belly. A shot penetrated into the bomb bay. What happened next was as inevitable as it was spectacular. A huge tonnage of Setic-Nephthysian fusion warheads ignited at once. The ensuing ball of light spanned a quarter of a mile in diameter, scarlet shot through with shimmering bands and vortices of purple. The ball erupted then contracted in the space of a couple of seconds, engulfing not only the Typhon but the C39 that had triggered the blast and also another of the helicopters that had been attacking the bomber. What remained, after the dazzling sphere was gone and the echoes of its deafening detonation had faded, was a surprisingly small amount of debris and wreckage, which rained down to earth, trailing ribbons of smoke.

The Locusts returned in a third and final wave but were warier this time around, chastened by the punishment they had taken previously. They came in at greater altitude, which further hampered their accuracy. They dropped whatever was left beneath their wings to drop, then hightailed for home, with the four surviving C39s giving chase. Nonomura's men secured three more kills before the much faster jets poured on speed and disappeared over the horizon.

David, still blinking to clear the gibbous blue afterimage of the exploding Typhon from his vision, surveyed the scene. As the smoke that shrouded the plain thinned, he saw carnage. He saw bodies spilled around patches of scorched ground. He saw a Scarab tank cracked open, eviscerated, like a beetle crushed underfoot. But, to his eyes, the damage seemed considerably less significant than it could have been. The troops were still in their lines. There were still four C39s left, now descending, their vanes making whorls in the smoke. The Nephthysians had tried their damnedest, but the Lightbringer's army had held out.

If only he hadn't known that the air raid was only the beginning. A softening-up exercise.

A ground assault was on its way, soon. Very soon.

26. ARMED

THE LIGHTBRINGER GOT swiftly out there, crossing the plain, assessing the state of play, seeing what had been lost and what was still intact, redeploying his resources, shoring up gaps in the lines, and, wherever he went, strengthening his troops' resolve with a few well chosen words, a congratulation here, an encouragement there.

"Remember," he said, at every opportunity, "it's not the size of the army in the fight, it's the size of the fight in the army. Which makes us the strongest army there's ever been."

He also oversaw the burial of the dead and the triage of the wounded. Anyone too badly hurt to engage in combat again was pulled back to the field hospital that had been set up on the northern side of Mount Megiddo. The rest were treated on the spot and offered a choice of recuperation behind lines or staying put. Invariably they plumped for the latter, much to their leader's delight.

When the Lightbringer returned from his tour of inspection, David was all set to challenge him about the Zafirah incident. He headed for the command post, intending to intercept him and demand a private audience. It seemed churlish under the circumstances – petty, even – but he had to know if what he'd seen earlier that morning was what he thought he'd seen. The Lightbringer's army had just skirmished with the enemy, and a bigger, fiercer battle was looming, but something important was at stake here: his faith in his brother, what remained of it.

The Lightbringer appeared with an entourage of warlords. He greeted David with a weary wave.

"Planning meeting," he said. "Coming?"

David hesitated. A planning meeting could go on for hours, and all that time he would be sitting there, listening to conversations conducted in rapid-fire Arabic, with the Lightbringer clueing him in on what was being said, but only now and then, during infrequent lulls in the proceedings. He couldn't see himself waiting that long to have his man-to-man with Steven. Instead, he could see himself quietly fuming in a corner of the room, getting more and more agitated until in the end he stood up and said or did something rash and regrettable.

He swallowed hard. Much though it pained him, he would have to put the matter on hold. For now.

"No," he said.

"No?"

"You don't need me. I'd be better off finding myself some weapons and getting down there." He nodded towards the plain. "That's where I'm needed, I think."

A heartbeat pause. Then: "Fair enough. If you say so."

"I do," David said, and left.

He made a beeline for the armoury, which occupied the husk of a building that had probably been Megiddo's main counting-house. The city, in its heyday, had stood at the nexus of several major trade routes and had raked in revenue accordingly, in the form of levies and handling fees. Now, in a hall where actuaries had once hunched over ledgers and money had been accumulated, an arsenal was stockpiled. Under the eye of a man called Farooq, who was, for want of a better job title, quartermaster, David browsed. Farooq recommended an Argentine pistol, a Horusite mace. He proffered David several types of sub-machine gun. "Very good, this one. Three-round-burst setting. Kill, kill, kill." With a gurning mime of firing the gun. "And save on ammo." But what David was after, and found, were an Osirisiac *ba* lance and a crook-and-flail set.

He hefted the *ba* lance, then the crook and flail. This was what he understood. This was what he knew. The weapons felt right in his hands. They were things he had been trained to use and knew he could rely on. A god rod and a pair of modified farming implements – tools of the trade.

He checked the charge in the lance. Three-quarters full. Not bad going. He strapped it on his back. He hooked the crook and flail onto his belt.

Then, tossing a "*Shokran*" to Farooq, he exited the armoury and set off down the mountain.

STEVEN HADN'T TRIED to stop him.

That was the thought that obsessed David as he headed south across the plain, past smouldering fields and around bomb craters, to the forwardmost line.

He'd said he was going down here, into the thick of things, and Steven had replied, "Fair enough. If you say so." As if meaning: *You go and face the enemy head-on, when he comes. Put your life in jeopardy. I don't care.*

Perhaps he'd been preoccupied, too many other things to think about. Perhaps he'd seen the determination in his brother's eye and known there was nothing he could to dissuade him.

Or perhaps letting David go to the battlefront, where he might well get killed, was convenient for Steven. His rival for Zafirah, eliminated.

No, Steven wasn't like that.

Was he?

David wasn't sure he knew his little brother any more. Steven hadn't simply changed into the Lightbringer. Being the Lightbringer had changed Steven. It was more than a role, more than the donning of mask, jumpsuit and gloves. As David walked across the plain, he looked at the Lightbringer's troops recovering from the raid and preparing themselves for the impending ground battle, and he admired them and pitied them in equal measure. The Lightbringer had given these Freegyptians something to believe in. He'd drawn them on with a vision of their god-independent way of life being spread across the globe. What they didn't understand, at least not at any conscious level, was that he had achieved this by behaving much like a god himself. He had bent them to his will, as a god would. He refused to show them his true face, keeping a godlike distance between him and them. He pretended to care about them, and perhaps he did, but in a lofty, aloof way, and it was important to them that they loved him as much as, if not more than, he did them.

And now they were cleaning their guns, checking the magazines, attaching grenades to bandolier belts, sharpening knives, sitting in tight-lipped anticipation of what was to come. Some had brought bleached-white cotton balaclavas with them, which they were wearing now, to resemble their leader. Some were smearing their faces with chalk dust or pale foundation make-up – war paint – for the same purpose. And some were so sick with nerves, their faces were ashen, whitened by natural means. It was all so brave. So wonderful. So inexpressibly sad.

He passed near the spot where he knew Zafirah and her fellow Liberators were positioned. They had come through the bombing unscathed. He saw Zafirah busy stripping a rifle down to its components, hunched over the task like a concert pianist tackling a difficult passage in a sonata. He slipped by without her seeing. He didn't want to face her at present. Whatever was going on between her and his brother, he didn't hold her to blame. To some extent it was his own fault. He'd had his chance with her and blown it. Talking to her would only remind him of that, and of Steven's underhand behaviour. It would deepen the mire of bitterness he was sinking into.

David's skull crackled with the onset of a hangover. Somewhere amid the brittle pain a voice was telling him that he could, should simply walk away from all this. Go west, the only direction from which the enemy hosts weren't approaching. Aim for the coast, get on a boat, find his way back to Cyprus and his garrison. Now was the time. His last chance, really. Wash his hands of this whole business. Forget Steven. Forget Zafirah. Return to the army and all he was familiar with. Return to his gods, Osiris of the Djed-pillar, Isis of the Harvest, begging their forgiveness with prayer and altar-sacrifice. Disentangle himself from the coils of a cause that he didn't truly hold with and a fraternal relationship that had turned upside down, with the older brother the thrall of the younger. Everything was wrong here. He knew it. He didn't belong. This was not his fight. He should quit while he still could. Getting through and out of Arabia would be difficult but not impossible. He was a smart and resourceful fellow. And if what was waiting for him when he rejoined the army was a court martial, so be it. He suspected, though, that in the light of its deeds at Petra the army might prefer to let him slip quietly back into the ranks. No questions asked, no awkward answers raised. Or else grant him an honourable discharge if he wanted it. Were he to leave Megiddo now, it would be to face an uncertain future – but there would at least be a future. Staying meant facing a very certain future, and a very short one.

He was tempted. But he resisted. And the temptation was unexpectedly easy to resist.

He would finish what he had started. He would fight here.

Not for the Lightbringer. Not for Steven.

For these people. The Freegyptians. For their sake.

He was David Westwynter, a paratrooper, a soldier, a good one.

His presence here would make little or no difference to the outcome of the battle.

But it would make all the difference in the world to him.

27. MEGIDDO

NO GROUND FORCE could hope to sneak up on an entrenched enemy unawares, especially not one of the size the Nephthysians had assembled. The Lightbringer's army had plenty of warning that the foe was coming. Scouts and spotters posted on hilltops radioed in with sightings of dust clouds on the horizon, then of long processions of troop transport bringing in men and materiel. They reported soldiers setting up tents, forward bases being established, Scarab tanks rolling to the forefront. Much of it was already happening before the bombing raid took place. After the raid, the pace of progress quickened. Infantry were organised into their regiments, drilled on tactics. Armoured divisions, meanwhile, headed out in formation to take up position at the foot of the valley. The grind of drive spheres drifted north towards Mount Megiddo like the rumble of a low-grade earth tremor.

A conservative estimate would put the total of Nephthysian troops at 20,000. Of Scarab tanks there were a good couple of hundred.

The Nephthysian generals had learned their lesson with the mummies at Suez, and had had it confirmed with the level of retaliation during the bombing raid. The Lightbringer was a wily and formidable opponent. His troops had spirit and bite. They were few in number but motivated. No chances should be taken. The generals had mustered many more troops than they'd thought they would need, but they would use them all. Absolute and overwhelming numerical superiority was called for.

And then there was the small matter of the Setic task force currently forging south, several columns of infantry and armour heading down through Armenia and Azerbaijan, skirting the eastern fringes of the Ottoman Empire to pass into Persia and Mesopotamia and beyond. They were still a day or two away from arriving, these reinforcements, and the Nephthysians were keen that by the time they got here the battle would be over and there would be nothing left for them to do, except maybe mop up the odd fleeing Freegyptian. It was a matter of pride. Intra-bloc politics. The Setics needed to be shown that the Nephthysians could handle things by themselves, thank you very much. A decree had come down from the Synodical Council to the generals: *Prove to the Commissariat of Holy Affairs that we're not the bumbling inferiors they like to think we are.*

The Lightbringer might have selected the battlefield but that was the only say he would have in determining the course of the battle itself. He and his troops were going to be wiped out. Instantly, decisively, devastatingly. A massacre.

BY MID-MORNING THE sky was overcast. Charcoal-smudge clouds moved in to hang low over the plain, blotting out the sun. Ra, it seemed, did not want to observe what was about to take place. A veil had been drawn.

The Lightbringer looked down from Mount Megiddo, scanning the scene with binoculars. His troops were in place. There was nothing else he could do except wait and watch, with his radio at hand so that he could give orders as and when necessary.

The grey sky pleased him. The Nephthysian Scarab tanks must be low on juice, having driven hard to get here, and now there was no sunlight to replenish their solar batteries, whereas his tanks had been sitting idle for days and were fully charged.

And that wasn't the only advantage he had.

There was still a trick up his sleeve. Something the Nephs simply wouldn't be expecting. A trump card.

He'd hinted as much to the warlords, and they had passed the word on down through the ranks.

The Lightbringer's small but resolute band of followers stood like a garden fence before an oncoming hurricane. It might just smash them to flinders. But if they could withstand it for a while, if they bent and broke but still stayed more or less intact, then...

Then...

Then everything would be very different.

THE NEPHTHYSIAN ARMOURED divisions began their offensive shortly after midday. Phalanxes of Scarab tanks crawled northward. Within an hour they were close enough to the Lightbringer's forward positions to open fire. Their initial salvoes were met by intense return fire. Mortars and rocket-propelled grenades hammered them, along with volleys of various-coloured *ba*. Several of the tanks erupted in domes of purple light.

But there were more behind. For each one the Freegyptians destroyed, another came forward to take its place. Slowly, persistently, the tanks gained ground, visiting considerable damage on the Lightbringer's men and machines.

The four remaining C39s roared into action, strafing the tanks and swiftly notching up several bullseyes. The gunships were low on ammunition, however. Soon their missile pods were empty and their *ba* cells had run dry. They pounded away at the tanks with bullets, but then these too were gone. The only things left to use as weapons were the helicopters themselves.

Nonomura and his men prepared themselves for their death runs. Each pilot aimed for a concentration of tanks, intending to take four, five or more with them. The choppers flew across the plain at full speed, swooping on the Nephthysians. Inside, the crews sang Anubis's praises, telling him how almighty he was and how happy they were to be coming to meet him. One of the C39s didn't make it to its destination. A bolt from a blaster nozzle evaporated it in midair. The others, though, danced around the incoming *ba* and struck dead-on. Cascades of purple light erupted upwards as the groupings of tanks exploded, one igniting the next in a chain reaction.

But more Scarab tanks came, and still more, bearing down hard on the Lightbringer's front ranks. Under pressure, the Freegyptians responded with street-fighting tactics. They were, many of them, veterans of guerrilla warfare. They knew that what could not be achieved by means of heavy artillery might be done with people on the ground, moving at speed and taking reckless risks. They darted out, scurrying from place of cover to place of cover and lobbing grenades at the ranks or loosing off with *ba* lances, shrieking battle cries as they went. The tanks' blaster nozzles swivelled in all directions, trying to track and eliminate these new, nimbler targets. Men died, incinerated by blasts of divine essence. But their constant harrying took its toll. Tank after tank ended up a burning wreck, or else lost a caterpillar track or had its drive sphere damaged so that it was rendered immobile, to be picked off at leisure. Several of the tanks destroyed each other, shooting wildly at a Freegyptian and hitting the machine next door instead. Two of them removed themselves from the equation by chasing after the same man so intently that they collided. The driver of another tank became so disorientated by the number of sources of hostile fire that he ploughed his vehicle nose first into a drainage ditch, leaving its drive-sphere high in the air, spinning uselessly.

It was touch-and-go for a while. The Scarab tanks came perilously close to breaking through the Freegyptian lines. In the end, though, the Nephthysian generals saw how their armoured divisions were taking a pasting, and how their numbers were being whittled down by the infidels, and ordered a strategic withdrawal. By now there were perhaps half as many tanks left as had set out, and the majority of them were low on battery power. It was time to get them off the field while they could still move. The tanks retreated, passing among a host of advancing foot soldiers. They limped back to base, drawing on their reserve batteries for the final mile or so of the journey. Several hours of basking in direct sunlight would be called for before they could make a return visit to the plain, and that couldn't even begin to happen while the cloud cover remained stubbornly in place.

Still, the Nephthysian generals were confident. Dozens of infantry regiments were now marching into the theatre of combat. There was going to be no let-up for the Lightbringer's forces, no reprieve. Within an hour of the tanks falling back, the first clashes between Freegyptians and Nephthysian troops had begun.

DAVID WIELDED HIS *ba* lance with precision, firing from behind a whitewashed farmyard wall, making every narrow-beam shot count.

He had fallen in with a small group of Freegyptians, among them Saeed and Salim, the cousins-who-could-be-twins. Together, they had been responsible for the destruction of five Scarab tanks and the crippling of three others.

Now they were holding a farmhouse against the oncoming Nephthysian infantry. The air rang with gunshots and the snap-crackle-zap of *ba* bolts. Cordite and the burnt-bone tang of *ba* were all that David could smell.

He was calm, his calmness the kind that often came in the midst of conflict, an eye-of-the-storm tranquillity. Everything outside his head was hellish and insane. Men were slaughtering men. Bodies were piling up in front of the farmhouse. Death reigned. But inside him there was only certainty, a sense of expediency, a simplification of self. He must fight and kill or he would be killed. This was what his world had telescoped down to. A Nephthysian soldier came lurching towards him out of a field of wheat. David took aim, pressed the trigger and the soldier's helmeted head exploded into a thousand fragments, disappearing as instantaneously as a popped balloon. The decapitated body stumbled on for several steps before sprawling flat over the corpse of a colleague. David scanned for the next enemy. A purple *ba* bolt thudded into the other side of the wall. He flinched and ducked. When the dust cleared, he aimed over the top of the wall and shot in the direction the bolt had come from. There was nothing else to do but this: fire, fire back, keep firing. Battle had such an awful purity to it. The terror and horror were so immense, they were like a flame, scorching existence down to its essence. He did not have to think about anything but the next moment and the moment after that. He needed to live, and stay alive. That was all there was to it.

Soon the gunfire and *ba*-fire dwindled. The time was coming, *that* time, the customary phase-shift in modern warfare when the fighting went from ranged weapons to hand-to-hand. David's *ba* lance was spent. He tossed it aside and reached for the crook and flail. He rose from behind the pockmarked, battered wall. Out in the fields, Nephthysians were approaching, hundreds of them. Literally hundreds. The Freegyptians with David had knives, and some of them had Horusite maces and Setic staves. Whether or not they were competent with these weapons, he didn't know. They had sidearms, too. Would they observe the niceties of battlefield tradition and keep them holstered from this point on? David didn't know that either, and didn't care. All that mattered to him now was the enemy. He moved out into the field, wading through thigh-deep crops, crook raised in right hand, flail whirling in left. His heart sang a song of dread and joy. The Nephthysians closed in, short swords drawn. He was numb, contented, and ready.

28. BARQUE

RA HAS SUMMONED *them. They come.*

Every god in the Pantheon, from the mightiest to the least, travels to the Solar Barque. Ra has sent out a message that has lit up in their thoughts like fire in the sky – an invitation, framed in such a way that it does not brook refusal – and they come immediately, without quibble or demur. For Ra sends out such messages seldom, once in an eon, and great would be his disappointment with those who ignore them, and great would be their shame.

The gods throng the deck of the boat, chattering loudly, full of speculation. Neith moves among them. The goddess of war seems brasher and bosomier than usual, and her armour and arms gleam dazzlingly and clank deafeningly. She boasts to anyone who will listen that she can't remember when she last felt quite so invigorated.

"Feel that," she says, offering a flexed biceps. "Go on. Give it a squeeze. Hard as rock. And the size of it. Put an ox to shame, a muscle like that would."

When Neith is in such fine fettle, woe betide the world of men.

Osiris and Isis, hand in hand, quiz Thoth about the convocation. What is its purpose? Why has everyone been called here with such haste, such urgency? And where is Ra?

"All will be revealed shortly," says Ra's vizier. *"The Sun God awaits below. He will appear once everybody is present and has settled down."*

As he speaks, Set and Horus pass each other on deck, and there is a not-quite-accidental butting of shoulders. Straight away both of them assume an aggressive stance, like tomcats in an alley, and there is name-calling. Threats lace the air between them. All the gods in the immediate vicinity move to one side, anticipating a scuffle. It wouldn't be the first time.

Then Nephthys intervenes, pulling Set away from his nephew. She tries to pacify her husband, but her tone is snappish. It seems she has reached the limits of her patience where Set is concerned. *"Always picking a fight,"* she scolds. *"Always on the lookout for trouble. What is wrong with you? Didn't you promise Ra you would turn over a new leaf? Well, didn't you?"*

Set glares at her, enraged. His eyes glitter, hot as coals. He looks as if he might hit her.

Then, all at once, he relents. Relaxes. Smiles.

"You're quite right, my dear," he says. *"I did tell Ra I would try to be a better person and kiss and make up with my enemies."* He chucks her under the chin.

Nephthys is pleased and relieved.

Set turns to his nephew. *"Horus…"*

Horus cocks his head, wary. *"Yes?"*

"I apologise."

"For?"

"For striking your shoulder with mine, for one thing. I was careless. I wasn't looking where I was going. I'm sorry, also, for everything I said to you just now. Most of all, though, I'm sorry for the discontent that has simmered between us since… since as long as I can remember. We have had our ups and downs, haven't we?"

In Horus's single eye there is a gleam of mistrust. His mouth twists. *"That's one way of putting it."*

"For instance, that time we lay in bed together and I ejaculated into your hand."

Horus looks down and shuffles his feet. "You don't have to mention that here, in front of all these people."

"No, no," says Set, "I do have to. I'm making a clean breast of things. It was wrong of me to do what I did. I invited you to join me in bed, and you did so in all innocence, and then while you slept I abused you. Abused your trust. I visited an indignity upon you in the hope of gaining advantage, so that afterwards I could boast, 'Look, I've spilled semen over Horus.' I wished to belittle you, but happily your mother managed to thwart my scheme."

"Indeed," says Isis. By now all the other gods on the Solar Barque have broken off their own conversations and are avidly following the exchange between Set and Horus. "I did what I had to, to spare my son from humiliation," she continues. "I cut off and threw away his hand rather than leave it in place, defiled by your seed."

Horus rubs his wrist, where a faint, bracelet-like scar may be seen. The hand he possesses now is a replacement, fashioned for him by Isis.

"You still boasted about your act of pollution," she says to Set, "but without proof, no one would believe you."

"I was outwitted," says Set. "And it wasn't the only time. Remember when I challenged you to a race in boats made of stone?"

"Oh ho, yes!" says Horus. "I built mine out of cedar wood coated in gypsum, and won."

"I was utterly taken in, nephew. Your boat looked like a thing of rock but floated beautifully, while mine, made from an actual mountain peak, sank like... well, what else would it sink like? I made a big fuss about it at the time, telling everyone how you cheated, but secretly I was impressed with your ingenuity. You beat me at my own game. Full marks to you, Horus."

"But why are you raising these age-old affairs, Uncle?" says Horus. "What has brought on this strange mood of yours?"

"I'm simply trying to tell you that I have wronged you, Horus – as you have wronged me, although that is of lesser importance. I'm trying, in my very clumsy way, to make you understand that I want us to forget all the bad blood between us and be on good terms from now on. I know that our disputes have sometimes been ferocious, and no less often been foolish, but I'm hoping we can put them all behind us and start afresh. I want to be less of an antagonist to you, more of an uncle. Do you... do you think that might be possible? At all?"

Set bends his head. He looks up at Horus, hands clasped together. It's quite a sight, the muscular Lord of the Desert humbly imploring his nephew for a second chance. Horus himself seems unable to believe it wholeheartedly. His frown and the narrowness of his eye say he's waiting for a sudden reversal. Surely Set is attempting to get him to lower his guard, in order to deliver a sucker-punch out of nowhere.

But no sucker-punch comes.

"If you're sincere in this desire..." Horus says slowly.

"Oh, I am. I am."

"Then yes, I could probably see my way to forgetting what is past and beginning again."

"Horus! Really?"

Horus nods.

"Come here!" Set springs forward and enfolds his nephew in a massive, manly hug. Horus's arms come up and he pats his uncle's back, tentatively at first, then firmly. Set draws back, studies Horus for a moment, then leans in and plants a kiss on his lips. Horus is startled, but after a moment his eye closes and the kiss is returned. Deeply. Lasciviously. Nephthys looks on, perplexed, while amongst the gathered deities there are wolf-whistles and a few cheers, and somebody advises Set and Horus to get a room. The source of this suggestion is, in fact, one of Horus's own children, all of whom are highly amused to see their father locked in an embrace with another male god.

Eventually the kissing couple break apart. Horus is abashed, his cheeks pink, while Set wears an air of triumphant satisfaction. He turns to his wife, and there is a glee in his voice as he says, "There. See? I've kissed and made up with Horus. Just what you wanted, isn't it?"

"Well, yes, maybe," says Nephthys. "If not quite... that."

"But my dear, is it so wrong to admit passion for another? Even if that other isn't one's own spouse?"

"Too late. You cannot shame me, husband," Nephthys retorts. Her expression is smug. "I have already begun making the rounds with a confession of my misdeed. Just a short while ago, in fact, I prostrated myself before Isis and her husband in their palace and told them everything."

"Did you now?" says Set, glancing toward their brother and sister. "And how did they take it?"

Isis, still holding Osiris's hand, reaches over and rests her other hand on the back of Nephthys's neck. "How would you expect us to take it, Set?" she says. "How, other than with understanding and forgiveness."

Nephthys gazes into her sister's eyes with gratitude.

"Nephthys made an error of judgement," Isis goes on. "Deep down I always knew she had slept with Osiris, but I chose not to make a fuss about it. 'Least said, soonest mended,' as the saying goes. She acted out of lust, not malice. Her intention was never to hurt me or my husband. If she is guilty of anything, it's thoughtlessness, and that is a sin I can easily pardon."

"And you, Osiris?" Set says to his brother. "How do you feel about all this?"

"Blameless," comes the reply. "Nephthys masqueraded as Isis. I was none the wiser."

Set raises one coppery eyebrow. "Honestly?"

"Honestly," says Osiris, with finality.

"Ha!" booms a deep, ebony voice from a corner of the Solar Barque. It is Anubis, who has been standing at one remove all this time, aloof from the rest of the Pantheon, as is his wont. "And I suppose, Osiris, if you deny you knew who seduced you, you would deny also that you are my father?"

Osiris regards the Jackal-Headed One evenly. "I would not deny that," he says, a slow and careful choice of words. "I would deny only that I have been a father to you. And it is an oversight for which I would like to make amends. All this time, we have been distant from one another, you and I, Anubis, each of us suspecting, *or knowing, the truth of our kinship and yet unable, or unwilling, to act upon it. It has pained me to be apart from one with whom I should be so close. I have discussed the matter with Isis, and she is of a like mind with me. If you are amenable to the idea, henceforth I would like to be able to call you... son."*

There is a collective exhalation from the audience of deities, both a gasp and a sigh. None of them, however, could look more surprised or moved than Anubis. His sombre features seem to quiver. For a moment it appears that his habitual mask of impassiveness might slip. He might even shed a tear. Soon enough, though, he has reasserted control over himself. He inclines his head towards Osiris and says, "I shall consider your request, He Who Is Called The Eternally Good Being. What you are suggesting does not strike me as an entirely undesirable proposition."

It is at this point – with peace having settled among the principal members of the Pantheon like a deep fall of snow, or so it would seem – that Ra at last makes an appearance. Despite not having been physically present on deck, he is nonetheless aware of all that has just occurred, having been eavesdropping through the boards from his berth below.

"My family, my kin, my fellow gods," he says, with warmth. "Here you all are. How good of you to come. And what a remarkable turn of events we have just witnessed. Set and Horus reconciled. Nephthys publicly declaring her transgression. Osiris acknowledging Anubis as his son. Truly it gladdens my heart."

His face darkens, just a little.

"If only," he says, "there were not a cloud on the horizon to mar my happiness."

"You speak of the Lightbringer," says Osiris.

"Indeed so," says Ra. "You are all by now aware of this upstart mortal and how he wishes to turn the entire world against us. And in case you haven't seen what he has done to us already... Wepwawet?"

Anubis's son drags himself over to Ra's side. He is all skin and bones, this godling. He creaks as he walks. Particles of skin flake from him like dust.

"Sobek?"

The crocodile god limps across the deck to join the parade of unfortunates. His scales are missing in patches, as though he has been afflicted by some kind of reptilian mange. His yellow eyes are dull, like pus.

"Of all those who have suffered at the Lightbringer's hands," says Ra, "these two have suffered the worst. The Lightbringer has picked on the least among us, the weakest, doing them harm even though they have done him none. Shameful coward!"

A ripple of assent passes through the crowd of gods.

"But my lord Ra," says Nephthys, "while I share your outrage, you must know that even now my worshippers are engaging in battle with the Lightbringer and his followers."

"And my worshippers are rushing to join in the fray," adds Set. "Victory is assured. It won't be long before this man and his revolution have been snuffed out."

"I know this, and it is good," says Ra.

Horus steps forward. "Though I doubt they need my help, I would be willing to back up my uncle and aunt in eradicating him," he volunteers. "It wouldn't be difficult for me to persuade my bloc to throw its weight behind theirs."

Set grabs him and gives him a hug, rubbing his hair much as an uncle would, then nuzzling his ear, much as an uncle wouldn't.

"And if Horus takes part, we could as well," says Osiris, with a nod at Isis. "Imagine: the whole world turning on the Lightbringer as one. What a message that would send. Never again would any mortal dare attempt what he has."

"I am prepared to get involved too," says Anubis. "A handful of turncoats from among my worshippers lent the Lightbringer assistance, and I'd like to make up for that in some way."

Ra studies them. "It is most gratifying," he says, "to see you all in agreement. I could not ask for more. You have rallied together in a way that not so long ago I would have thought impossible. This is truly a remarkable thing."

He hesitates.

"Which makes it all the more distressing for me to say what I have to next."

He heaves a sigh.

"Yes, O Ra?" prompts Isis.

A sadness dims Ra's sun eye and deepens the glow of his moon eye.

"One of you here is a traitor," he says. "One of you here is in league with the Lightbringer."

There is a massed intake of breath, followed by an outbreak of hubbub and consternation. God jabbers to god. Voices rise in protest and dismay. Someone exclaims, "No!" Someone else exclaims, "Why?" The uproar aboard the Solar Barque rises to such levels that the boat starts to rock in the water, and it's all Maat can do to hold the tiller steady and maintain a straight course.

Ra appeals for calm, and little by little is granted it.

"I do not make this accusation wildly," he says. "I have pondered the matter long and hard, and discussed it with the two sagest individuals I know, namely Thoth and Maat. Regrettably, I have been able to come to no other conclusion. The evidence is clear – or rather, unclear. By which I mean it is the very absence of clarity surrounding the Lightbringer which has led me to deduce that he is acting with divine help."

"But it's absurd!" exclaims Set. "What you're saying contradicts everything we understand about this person. The Lightbringer hates the Pantheon and wishes to overthrow us. Why would he then be in league with one of us? It makes no sense."

"True," says Ra, "but how else to account for the fact that I cannot see him properly? I cannot look at his face, or into his heart and mind. I, whose light penetrates everywhere, gaze and gaze at the Lightbringer and see only shadows, dark and unfathomable. No mortal has the ability to hide himself from me like that. Only one kind of power could produce such a phenomenon – divine power."

"With all due respect, Ra, my uncle is right," says Horus. "It makes no sense. There must be some other explanation."

"I wish there were."

"What if it is divine power that's shielding him," says Isis, "but none of ours? What if some other god, from another pantheon, is responsible?"

The First Family take immediate umbrage.

"Nonsense!" howls Shu, like a gale.

"Impossible!" rumbles Tefnut, like thunder.

"No other gods survive," says Nut.

"Killed them all, we did," says Geb. "Anyone who says we didn't is a liar and an idiot."

Osiris bristles. "Mind your tongue, Geb. That's my wife you're talking about."

"I was merely advancing a theory," says Isis.

"Well, don't!" the four members of the First Family snap in unison. "Our rivals are dead. All of them. Extinct. Gone. We did our job thoroughly, exterminating them one by one, till the very last of them finished squirming in our grasp and lay still."

"So there," adds Geb.

"Please, simmer down," says Ra, patting the air. "First Family, nobody is querying your rigour or denigrating your achievement. The question Isis raised is one that I myself felt obliged to entertain as a possibility. Perhaps, just perhaps, a god did manage to escape your attention and survive. However, I was forced to conclude that such a thing could not be. We would have known if there was even just one other god left. Somewhere, in some far distant outpost of the world, there'd have been worship – a temple, an altar, some earthly means by which that deity's existence was sustained. I, the all-seer, would have seen it, and I have not. Believe me, I wish it were otherwise. I wish some other god from some other pantheon were the culprit here. But the awful, inescapable truth is that it must be one of us. Standing here among us, at this very moment, is someone who has imbued the Lightbringer with his or her essence, in such a way as to occlude him from scrutiny. Someone here has enabled the Lightbringer to get as far as he has with his crusade against the Pantheon. And nobody is leaving this barge until I've found out who it is."

29. DELIRIOUS

DAVID. ALONE. PANTING. Drenched in blood.

He didn't know how much time had passed. The field around him was crimson. Trampled wheat stems, dripping gore. Bodies sprawled everywhere.

David stood, trembling with exhaustion, the flail drooping from his left hand, the crook in his right almost too heavy to hold up.

The blood on him – how much of it was his own? He knew he had received wounds. How many? How bad? He couldn't bring himself to look. He couldn't bear to move his head, or dare to. Simply remaining upright was as much as he could manage.

The dead were heaped two high, three high on all sides. Nephthysians mainly, many of them still clutching their short swords. Gobbets of flesh littered the earth, scraps of entrail. A shambles. Blood had made black mud of the soil.

David fought to stay conscious. There were more Nephs out there, circling beyond the perimeter of the killing ground, wary, watchful. Would they keep their distance? Or would they pluck up the courage to step past the piles of corpses and come at him? He was the only one left. The others, the Freegyptians, were all gone. Saeed, Salim, both dead. The rest of the group likewise. If the Nephthysians decided to move in on him, that would be that. He didn't have the strength left to fight them. He couldn't kill any more of them. They would bring him down. Perhaps, right now, one of them was unshouldering his *ba* lance, in frank disregard for battlefield etiquette. Taking aim. Finger tightening on trigger. A single shot to the head, to end it all.

David didn't want to die. But he couldn't see what else he could do. He'd given everything he had. He'd watched himself, as though from a distance, laying into attacker after attacker. He'd been like a dispassionate observer, admiring his own technique. The use of the flail to distract and stun, the crook to deliver a disabling or killing blow. How well the army had schooled him. Those countless hours out on the training ground, repeating the actions and combinations till they were enshrined in his muscle-memory, being barked at by instructors because he wasn't keeping his guard up, wasn't putting his weight on the correct foot, wasn't doing this, wasn't doing that. All so that he could become the man who could do what he had just done – slaughtered scores of foes with brutal, unremitting efficiency. And now he was finished. Every part of him hurt, a symphony of pain, from the bassy throb of sore muscles to the sharp high notes of slashed skin. There was nothing else for it but to stand and wait. Wait for whatever came.

He was David Westwynter, the brother of the Lightbringer, not that anyone knew that apart from him and Steven. He was a long way from home and from the aegis of Osiris and Isis. He was a success as a warrior and not much else. That would have to be his epitaph.

Finally the Nephthysians came to a decision. They started to close in. He counted at least ten of them. They were faceless to him, not individuals, just people in identical uniforms and rectangle-and-semicircle-crested helmets. He couldn't hold it against them, what they were about to do, any more than the condemned man could hold it against the executioner for wielding the axe. They would kill him because they must.

How many times had he faced death in recent weeks? Stared it straight in the eye? So many times that he was getting used to it. Starting to get bored of it, even. If Anubis wanted him so badly, he should stop pussyfooting around and just take him.

The Nephthysians formed a semicircle in front of him, swords at the ready. Each seemed reluctant to step within range of David's weapons, as if hoping another would be the first to take the plunge. What was their problem? Couldn't they tell he was past being capable of defending himself? What did they need, an engraved invitation?

Then one of them fell down.

The rest turned, startled.

Another of them looked down to find that the end of a crossbow bolt had sprouted from his chest. He keeled over.

A third had a chin. Then he had no chin. His jawbone was ripped away by a bullet impact.

The remaining Nephthysians scattered, trying to find cover. Bullets and crossbow bolts blizzarded at them. David heard gunshots and a diesel engine. Then there were Freegyptians all around him, hounding the Nephthysians through the wheat, scything them down. To use range weapons in a hand weapon situation was dirty fighting, but they didn't care. He recognised the faces of several of his saviours. Zafirah's Liberators. And here came Zafirah herself, dishevelled, caked with grime, but still in command.

"This way," she told David. "Come on. Don't just stand there. We have to fall back. The forward positions are overrun. There are Nephs everywhere. Come *on*!"

JOLTING AROUND IN the back of a ZT. Zafirah saying that the Lightbringer had ordered a retreat to the second line of positions on the plain. Hold that line till sunset. The Nephthysians would most likely halt their advance then and everyone could retrench overnight.

David didn't care. He had just one question to ask.

"Do you love him?"

Zafirah seemed not to understand. He wasn't sure he had asked the question correctly. He tried again.

"Do you *love* him?"

Even to his own ears the words sounded nonsensical, as though phrased in a foreign language neither he nor Zafirah knew.

She stared at him.

"Look at you," she said. "Delirious. You're barely here. We need to get you to the field hospital."

Barely here. She was right. David felt like a passenger in his own body, much as his body was a passenger in the car. And to lapse into unconsciousness, to go from *barely here* to *not here at all*, was easy, akin to agreeing to let someone else be the driver for a while. A surrendering of control. A case of: go on then, why not?

UNDER CANVAS. A large marquee-like tent. A place that reeked of excrement and death. Cries of distress that came as regularly and insistently as the tolling of a bell. Bodies lying on blankets, arranged close-packed and neatly like the blocks of a parquet floor. Men and women moving among them, ministering – people David knew to have been doctors back in Luxor, nurses, even a couple of veterinarians.

Steven, talking to one of them in Arabic. About him. About David down here on the ground, who didn't know what time it was or how long he had been there or whether the lack of pain he was feeling was due to analgesics or not and, if not, whether that was a good sign or a bad one.

Steven squatting down next to him. Whispering.

"You're going to be fine, Dave. They'll take good care of you. It's blood loss. The faintness? The disorientation? Blood loss. Nephs cut you up pretty badly, but you'll be OK. Just lie there and recover."

And with that, he was gone, quick as a snake slithering through grass.

AND DAVID SLEPT.

Profoundly.

30. TEREBINTH

Sometime during the night, a doctor came to check on him. The man's face, lit from below by the battery-powered lantern he carried, was familiar, even though he was not actually one of the Luxor medics. David recognised him at some whole other, deeper level. His bronzed, perfect features set off a chime within. So did the scars that laced his body. David knew he was looking up at Osiris, and knew he was dreaming.

Osiris did not speak, merely studied David from head to toe, examining him as a doctor might, diagnosing.

"I've strayed," David said. "I know that. And even though I have been killing your enemies, it's not been in your name or the name of your sister-wife. Please forgive me."

Still Osiris said nothing, and now he was holding a djed-pillar, the ribbed column that was his sacred emblem. It was a sheaf of corn. It was a leafless tree. It was a backbone. It was all three at once, and it was laid on its side, the position that symbolised defeat and death.

Carefully, gently, Osiris began rotating it from horizontal to vertical. The djed-pillar thickened and grew tall as it turned, sprouting fleshy vegetation. Osiris smiled as it came alive in his grasp, pulsing with vibrancy. He pointed with his free hand to the erect pillar, then to David.

He did this three times, then took his lantern and the pillar and strode off, disappearing with a halo of light around him into darkness.

Darkness.

Darkness.

Dawn.

David's eyelids fluttered open. A doctor, a real one this time, was bent over him, changing the dressing on the worst of his wounds, a deep gash in his left upper arm. She peered at him with the sore eyes of someone who hadn't slept for at least a day and a half. She finished her work, and later brought him some lamb broth in a bowl.

David slurped the broth and thought about his dream and knew it had been a true divine visitation, unlike the dream in which Courtdene and his parents had figured. In which case, it must mean something. It wasn't just some delusional brain-phantasm brought on by exhaustion and injury. The dream had to have contained a message. But what?

Osiris was the god of resurrection. Just as he had been restored to life after Set tore him to pieces, so he oversaw the transmigration of each person's ka to its new, eternal existence in the Field of Reeds, helping them surmount death as he had. He fulfilled a similar function in nature. In spring, Osirisiac farmers prayed to him to make their crops shoot up and be plentiful. From the dead winter earth Osiris generated life.

With his djed-pillar he had been illustrating… something.

My own life? David wondered.

When the doctor returned for the soup bowl, David asked her how he had been during the night.

"You lie very still all night," she replied in halting English. "Not good. We worry. But you are good now, I think. You are come through. Worst is over."

David had to admit that he didn't feel too bad. Felt better, in fact, than he had any right to expect. He ached all over, but the pains were external, superficial. At the core of him, where it counted, he felt hale and whole.

Osiris's doing? Or just the body's own healing processes?

He had the strength to sit up. Soon he had the strength to stand and walk about a bit.

Was *he* the djed-pillar Osiris had raised?

Perhaps he was placing too great an emphasis on his place in the grand scheme of things. Did Osiris care that much about him? Was the god taking a personal interest in him? If so, why? God dreams were meant to clarify your thinking. So how come his thoughts felt cloudier and more muddled than ever?

He exited the field hospital to get some air and shake off the stench of human suffering. Not far from the tent, a score of bodies lay on the ground, covered with blankets and awaiting burial – those who'd been wounded so severely, the doctors hadn't been able to save them. David moved away, shunning the bodies not so much through squeamishness but because they seemed just so mundane. So banal. The blankets shrouded them incompletely. Here a bare foot showed, there a hand. The meat that was left behind after the ka had flown.

His eye fell on a solitary terebinth tree standing proud at the edge of a field, straight-trunked, its leaves in full early-summer ripeness and roundly, succulently green. He went and sat in its shade. The tree's sharp, resinous aroma surrounded him. Nearby, a cicada began to chirrup.

He remained there for a while, with his forearms on his knees and his chin on his hands, inhaling the turpentiney smell of the terebinth and feeling its rough bark against his back and listening to the cicada's clicking, buzzing proclamation of territory and desire. He stared into space, and so deep was the reverie he sank into that a sudden uproar from the far side of Mount Megiddo, the sound of combat being resumed after the night's lull, barely impinged. His ear heard, but his mind was elsewhere.

Out on the plain, the armies clashed again. The Nephthysian infantry had regrouped overnight, drawing reserves up from base to bolster its main force. The Lightbringer's troops had distributed themselves along the second line of positions, in accordance with their leader's instructions. Rather than clustered in knots, the Freegyptians were now strung out thinly so as to afford fewer concentrated targets and a more even spread of resistance. Universally it was accepted that, in this formation, they could not hold out for long.

And they didn't. Within an hour the Nephthysians had broken through in several places. The order came down from the Lightbringer: retreat. Pull back to the third line at the foot of the mountain.

The Nephthysians powered onward, blasting at the Freegyptians, who mounted a rearguard action as they went, strewing landmines and tripwire-triggered grenades in their wake. These slowed the Nephthysians but didn't deter them. On they came, advancing with the stalwart self-assurance of soldiers who knew that victory was, if not at hand, then at least within reach.

The Freegyptians, bunching around the base of Mount Megiddo's southern flank, fought valiantly. The Nephthysians were brought to a standstill, though not repulsed. They hurled themselves repeatedly at the infidels but couldn't seem to make a dent in their defences. The gun emplacements atop the mountain poured bullets down on them. Still they pressed hard, not allowing the enemy one moment's peace. Their generals urged them on from the rear, insisting that the Freegyptians would be worn down soon. They couldn't keep taking this much punishment indefinitely. They must buckle under.

Thousands of Nephthysians made the journey to Iaru that day. Hundreds of Freegyptians, too, found themselves in the afterlife. Anticipating oblivion, it came as a shock to them to discover that the godless person possessed a ka and it lived on. Then, soon enough, they set to work harvesting reeds alongside the billions of other souls already there, and swiftly the rhythm of toil became all they knew. The capacity to feel surprise, or much of anything else, was lost to them, falling away like some surplus, vestigial organ. They were as happy as ants, wishing nothing for themselves but to be among others of their kind and contribute to the communal workload.

Meanwhile, in the world they had recently departed, battle raged on, and twenty miles to the north of Megiddo, one of the Lightbringer's scouts caught a first glimpse of the approaching Setic reinforcements.

The scout could hardly believe his eyes. At first he thought that what his binoculars were showing him must be the entire Setic task force, but he soon perceived that it was simply the vanguard. It alone stretched from horizon to horizon, and there was more behind.

This wasn't a mere handful of battalions. This was *everything*.

31. INFLUENCE

FOR THE FIRST *time in memory, Mandet, the night barque, has carried an onboard complement of more than two. Ra and lion-headed Aker, its usual crewman and passenger, have been joined by the entire Pantheon for the nocturnal journey through the realm of the dead. Their main aspects ride the boat, confined there in accordance with Ra's will, and none of the gods has enjoyed the voyage, especially not Anubis. The others grumble about the darkness and the bitter cold, their voices echoing sibilantly off the stone walls of the caverns through which they are passing, and Anubis grumbles about their grumbling. This is part of his kingdom, after all. Who are they to criticise it so? He doesn't go to their realms and complain about the brightness and warmth, does he?*

Arrival at the eastern gate of heaven and transfer to Mesektet, the Solar Barque, does little to lift anyone's mood. Suspicion and resentment continue to bristle among the gods. The traitor has not come forth. No one has made it known that he or she is the Lightbringer's divine ally. Ra expects the culprit to own up. It would be the proper thing to do. He cannot force a confession out of anyone, but he believes guilt must surely be preying on the conscience of the individual in question and will prick the truth out of him or her in due course. Everyone just needs to be patient.

Apophis rears out of the river, and Set duly leaps to grapple with him. As he does so, one of Horus's children, Hapi, can be heard to remark, "There's your man, if you ask me. Great-Uncle Set. Who else could it be? A known deceiver. A prince of lies. With a track record like his – of course it's him."

When Set returns to the boat, bloodied from battle, he heads straight over to Hapi. Grabbing the androgynous young godling by the throat, he hoists him off the deck. Hapi's long hair flaps around and his pendulous breasts quiver as Set holds him aloft.

"I have sharp ears, girly-man," he says. "If you have an accusation to make, make it to my face, not behind my back."

Hapi gargles, clutching his great-uncle's forearm, trying to claw his way out of Set's grasp.

"Reckon I'm the one, do you?" Set goes on. "Well, think about it. The Lightbringer's people hurt Wepwawet. My grandson. Right now they're fighting Nephthys. My wife. Why, then, would I be collaborating with him? Eh? Eh?" He shakes Hapi about like a dog with a rabbit. "Why? What do I gain? It makes no sense."

In a paroxysm of fear, Hapi's bladder lets go. Urine sluices down the insides of his legs.

Set sneers. "The God of Inundation. Bringer of the Flood. Pissing himself. How apt."

Horus appears at Set's side and appeals to him to put Hapi down.

"I thought you couldn't abide your children," says Set.

"Can't control them," says Horus. "Not quite the same thing. Besides, I am still their father. Hapi spoke foolishly. He meant nothing by it and regrets it now. Don't you, Hapi?"

Hapi nods as best he can with Set's hand locked around his neck.

"So, my dear Uncle, begging you kindly, would you let him go?"

Set glares at Hapi, then with an inclination of the head to Horus, a mark of his newfound esteem for his nephew, does as asked. Hapi tumbles to the deck and lies there in a heap, wheezing for breath. Set turns smartly on his heel and makes for the bows, where he keeps a basin of water so that he can wash off Apophis's blood.

Ra scowls. A disagreeable episode, and there will be more of its kind if matters continues as they are. Tempers are fraying. But he cannot back down. His path is set. He must stand firm. The guilty god will be identified. It is only a matter of time.

Meanwhile, Osiris has drawn Isis aside for a quiet word.

"I don't know about you, Isis," he says, "but I'm not prepared to sit around on this boat for who knows how long, waiting for something that might not ever happen. I won't have it. Ra cannot treat us in this way. Keeping us here like a teacher holding the class back after school because someone placed a tack on his chair…"

"It's a little more serious than that, dear."

"Even so, I find it insulting. Demeaning."

"It's Ra's will," Isis counters. "He is the All-Father. We must do as he asks – however misguided what he asks may seem."

"If we were to just up and leave, though, how could he stop us?"

"He couldn't. But think about it. Anyone who left would immediately have suspicion fall on them. It would be seen as being tantamount to an admission of guilt."

"A fair point," says Osiris. "Then let me confess something to you."

Isis's jaw drops. "Osiris! It isn't you, is it? You're the one who's been helping the Lightbringer? It can't be. Why?"

"No. No! It isn't me. And keep your voice down, will you?" Osiris glances around. Luckily no one appears to have overheard his sister-wife's outburst. "Just listen for a moment. I did leave the boat last night. Only briefly. I sent out a tiny aspect of myself to the mortal realm. It was such a minuscule amount of my essence, nobody could have noticed."

"I certainly didn't, and if I didn't, I doubt anyone else did. Where did you go?"

"To where the Lightbringer is battling with Nephthys's worshippers, at Megiddo."

"Why?"

"One of ours is down there. Can you not feel him? An Englishman. He's embedded among the Freegyptians."

Isis turns her gaze inward, searching. "Yes. I feel him. There he is. His name is David Westwynter. I see… I see he has been such a troubled man. A conflict in him, between what he feels he ought to be and what he is. Given so much by birthright yet always wanting something else, something both more and less. Assured and accomplished on the outside, but like an unhappy boy within. A slave to his own sense of duty. What is he doing there, fighting alongside the Lightbringer?"

"That I can't work out. They seem to be related somehow, but everything connected with the Lightbringer is so imprecise. As Ra says, there is an opacity about him, and it extends to those around him. But when visiting the Westwynter man in his sleep, I detected within him a simmering dislike of the Lightbringer. There is bad blood between them, and it is something I thought I could exploit. And did."

"Osiris, what have you done?"

"Not much," says Osiris. "Merely planted the germ of an idea in his mind. He was once quite devout. Then he drifted from our influence. I have tried to anchor him once more, remind him of certain values."

"How will that help us?"

"It may not help at all. Mortals have free will. They do not always do as we desire. But if everything works out as I hope, we shall soon be off this barge and able to return to our palaces."

"The Westwynter man..."

"... has become a potential catalyst for change. If human nature takes its course, and I think it will, the Lightbringer will soon be out of the picture."

"And with him gone, the stalemate that reigns here will be resolved," says Isis, understanding.

"Just so. No Lightbringer, no need to worry about which of us has secretly been helping him. The point will be rendered moot."

"Ra will still want to know who it is. He won't just let the matter drop."

"But it won't be of such urgency any more, and Ra will be hard pushed to continue to justify keeping everyone here. He'll have to let us go, and if he wants to pursue his detective work, he can do it in his own time."

"It may be," says Isis, "that once the Lightbringer dies, his godly benefactor will realise that the game is up and admit responsibility."

"That may happen too. Either way, this will all be over."

"Osiris." Isis clasps his face and kisses him hard. "You're a cunning so-and-so. I love you."

"And I you, sister-wife. Now, let us rejoin the others and wait to see how things play out."

32. REFUGE

PASTOR-PRESIDENT WILKINS DELIVERED a televised statement from the Oval Office, and what he said caught North America on the hop. He announced that, as of this moment, there was to be a cessation of hostilities between Horusites and Setics. Already, Horusite naval units were being recalled from the Bering Sea and the Sea of Okhotsk. The entire North Pacific Fleet, in fact, was heading back to base in Vancouver and San Francisco. Similarly the Setics were pulling their ships back to Murmansk and Tsingtao.

This move, which he acknowledged was a surprising one, although the adjective he preferred to use was "neat", came about as the result of a single phone call to Vladimir Chang, in which Wilkins had informed the Commissar that the White House's high priests had all received dream visions unequivocally urging a peace settlement with the Setics. Chang confirmed that Setic high priests had received similar instructions, and thus, in a matter of a few hours, with top-ranking diplomats rushing around various capitals in a flurry of ambassadorial activity, a deal was sealed.

"Our gods have willed it," Wilkins said, flashing his trademark aw-shucks smirk at the camera, "and so it must be done. What's more, as a sign of our spirit of co-operation with the Setics, I've agreed to assist them in their campaign against this Lightbringer fella who's causing such a ruckus in the Middle East right about now and giving the Nephs such a headache." The Pastor-President's advisers had told him never to refer to Nephthysians by their full name. Not only did this do wonders for his down-home image, but he couldn't actually pronounce the word. "We haven't yet ironed out the detail on what form this assistance is gonna take. But Commissar Chang and I have agreed that it'd be good for us to show the Setics some support, so after his troops have hit the guy, our boys are gonna be close behind. It kinda feels like we should've been doing this all along, dontcha think? Leastways it does to ol' Jeb here. Like maybe the Setics and us have more in common than we thought, that's why we've been scrappin' so much."

A slippery argument, doctrinally speaking, but it carried some emotional heft.

"Ain't it funny how the words 'competition' and 'coalition' sound so much alike?" was how Pastor-President Wilkins signed off his broadcast, along with another of his just-a-regular-guy smirks.

The Osirisiac Hegemony was quick to proclaim that it was behind the Horusites in their decision, and that for the time being all military operations against the Setics in Eastern Europe and the Mediterranean would be suspended. As a mark of earnest, all Osirisiac troops were withdrawn from the Vistula flashpoint to a point five miles outside Warsaw. The Setic army reciprocated.

All eyes, then, were on Megiddo and the events unfolding there. International conflict had been shelved, if only temporarily. Hatchets had been buried. The global war drums had stopped beating. The world was watching.

AND AS THE world watched, the Lightbringer was forced to give the command for one last retreat. His beleaguered troops surrendered their positions at the foot of Mount Megiddo and scrambled up the mountainside to the ruins of the city, their last redoubt. The Nephthysians gave chase, but the limited width and number of the pathways that led to the top meant they couldn't do so in significant strength. The Freegyptians were able to ward them off the whole way up, and once they had gained the advantage of level high ground they were even better placed to keep the enemy at bay. Again and again, Nephthysian infantrymen filed up the paths. Again and again, the Lightbringer's troops picked them off from above, ending their sallies and sending them back downhill in a tumble of panic.

On the other side of Mount Megiddo, the medics set to work dismantling the field hospital and transporting it and its patients to the relative safety of the city. With Setics approaching from the north, there was no alternative. The field hospital could not remain where it was, as clemency for the wounded was not a given in a situation like this. In the course of a normal war, convention had it that one side spared the other's injured soldiers, although the dead, of course, were another story. But this was not a normal war, so there was no guarantee the convention would apply. The city offered refuge, and in the short term that was all that mattered (and no one now was thinking in anything but the short term).

The wounded who could walk, walked, or in many cases limped. The rest had to be carried, and the doctors spent several hours doing just that, using blankets as makeshift stretchers. David joined in. He paired up with one of the veterinarians to lug casualty after casualty up a narrow track that zigzagged back and forth across the mountain slope. It was a punishing slog. His hands cramped, his back ached, sweat stung his eyes, his wounds burned, and the groaning burden in the blanket grew heavier with ever step. Each time they reached the summit, the vet advised David to stop. He had done enough. He was still recuperating from his own injuries. He should leave the helping to someone else. But David insisted on going down to fetch the next patient.

Life.

Life was what counted.

Life and the living.

During each of his trudges downhill, David would reflect on his dream of Osiris and how he had felt sitting in the shade of the terebinth earlier on, at no great distance from the yet to be buried – and still not yet buried – Freegyptian corpses. Sitting with his back to a tree that was burgeoning with life while the cicada trilled and flies buzzed around the laid-out dead and alighted on their exposed, unfeeling toes and fingers or crawled under the blankets to get to the good stuff beneath, the eyes, the orifices.

It wasn't remorse, as such. David didn't feel a sudden wave of guilt over the Nephthysian soldiers he had slain yesterday or the many other enemy troops he had despatched since joining the army. He could safely rationalise everything he had ever done in combat. Them or him. Kill or be killed. The brute equation of war, the zero-sum balance of the battlefield: one soldier + another opposing soldier = one soldier. That was acceptable to him, a necessity of the way the world was and of his chosen role in it.

What seemed less acceptable, if not downright *un*acceptable, was the sheer inanity of so much death. From Petra onwards, it seemed that corpses had littered his wake. Every paratrooper in his stick, from Sergeant McAllister down. The Nephthysian ambushers, including Captain Maradi. The Bedouin, none of whom had really deserved to die except Uncle Chessboard Smile. The Liberators whom the Bedouin had killed during their raid. The Wepwawetian monks. And now all these Freegyptians, and yet more Nephthysians. Death was shadowing his footsteps like some big dumb brute of a dog that had latched on to him even though he was not its owner.

Well, enough. He was fed up. Sick of it. He would not be a part of it any more.

Once the field hospital was re-established in its new location on the mountaintop, David went in search of the Lightbringer. He didn't have to look far. Steven was standing, alone, on one of a pair of stone plinths that had once formed a gateway. He was surveying the scene to the north and to the south – the Setic armies rolling inexorably towards Megiddo, and the tattered remnants of his own army fending off Nephthysian attacks from below. David strode up, grabbed him by the sleeve and yanked him down from his perch.

"Dave! You're up and about. Fantastic. Knew you'd be OK. Takes a lot to put *you* down. So what's up?"

"This." David gestured, indicating the predicament they were in. "What is this?"

"What do you mean?"

"What is going on here?" David said. How hard it was not to shout. "Your troops are on their last legs, ammo's running low, the Setics are just about on top of us, and the Nephs aren't going to sit down there for long without launching a full-scale assault or else calling the bombers back in."

"Your point being?"

"What kind of half-arsed plan are you working to? You've lost nearly two-thirds of your army and you've got about a thousand able bodies left who are willing to lay down their lives for you, but what for? What's to be gained? Attrition warfare only works if you're grinding down the enemy to the same extent that he's grinding you down, and that certainly isn't the case here. Anyway, soon as the Setics arrive we're dead. All of us. What'll have become of your dream of liberating the world then?"

"First of all," said the Lightbringer, "these people *are* willing to lay down their lives for me, yes. And that's something. That's an inspiration to us all."

"You glib bast—"

"Second of all, Dave, the situation isn't nearly as bleak as it looks to you."

"It couldn't look much bleaker, frankly."

"But there are certain things you don't know. Things which make all the difference."

"Oh yes? Such as?"

"I don't have to tell you. You'll find out soon enough."

"I think you fucking should tell me, as a matter of fact. Because right now, Steven, the only hope I can see of any of us getting through this alive is to surrender. Give up while we still can. Unless you've got something pretty damn amazing up your sleeve, I'd recommend that we do just that. And if you don't want to follow that recommendation, I can make you."

"Oh yes, big brother?" said Steven with scorn. "Really? Make me how? What are you going to do if I don't, run to Mum and Dad and tell on me?"

"Beat the living shit out of you, for starters."

"I'm so scared."

"You should be."

"What's got into you, Dave? Something's eating at you. What is it? Don't you trust me any more?"

"I'm not sure I ever did."

"Then why, can I ask, have you come all this way with me? Helped me at every turn? If you've never trusted me, why have you stuck by my side ever since I beat you hollow at senet?"

"Because," David replied, "I thought you needed me. And because these Freegyptians have such faith in you. And because, I don't know, but... I fell for it."

"For...?"

"Your vision. Of a god-free world. It was... attractive."

"It still is."

"No, I think not," David said, shaking his head. "Not any more. The gods use us. They don't care about us. We're nothing more than a convenient power source to them, like batteries in a radio."

"Which is exactly what I've been saying."

"*But*. We can live with them. We just don't have to live *for* them. We can get on with being who we are, without compromising in any way to them. The gods pay little attention to us. We can return the favour."

"We all just turn our backs on them? Not going to happen."

"Maybe we can't collectively. Individually, though..."

"So that's it?" Steven cocked his head in an inquisitive fashion. "That's Dave's great change of heart? 'I give up. I'm not taking sides any longer. Leave me out of this.'"

"More or less. I can do it. And you could too. Standing against the gods is just as bad as kowtowing. It validates them. Surrender now. Call it quits."

Steven laughed. "If only it were that easy."

"If not for your own sake, then for all of these people, your followers, what's left of them. They don't have to die here today. It would be senseless if they did."

"Their job is to hold this city," said Steven. "That's all they have to do. For as long as possible..." A rattle of gunfire from a nearby emplacement served as punctuation, placing an ellipsis at the end of Steven's words.

"While the Nephs lay siege, and then the Setics come in and polish us off? Steven, I'll say it again, in case you didn't get it the first time. What's to be gained? What is the point?"

"You simply cannot understand, Dave. But that's not your fault. You're too limited in your outlook. You always were. You'll never see the bigger picture the way I do."

This was said so smugly, so patronisingly, David was enraged. How dare Steven – his little brother! – how dare he talk to him like that? Four years his junior, and acting as if he had a lifetime of experience over him. This little brat who had come along and intruded on his firstborn, only-child existence, whom he'd done his best to accommodate, whom he'd defended and protected and (as it turned out, in vain) mourned bitterly, whom he'd opened up to about Zafirah only to have this act of confiding abused and thrown back in his teeth...

Nothing changed. Lightbringer or not, Steven was still the same snotty, ungrateful little sod he had always been.

The urge to punch him was strong. Almost overwhelming. Smack him in the face with a blow that was freighted with years of feelings of injustice and aggrievement. It would be all Steven deserved and more.

Instead, softly, almost to his own surprise, David said, "Take the mask off."

Steven cupped hand to ear, an impression of someone mishearing.

"The mask. Take it off. I need to see your face."

"No way, Dave. I can't show you."

"I need to look you in the eye. See who you are."

"You know who I am."

"But not who you've become. Come on. It isn't much to ask."

"It's more than you realise."

"The mask is your advantage over me. It allows you to hide everything from me, while I can't hide anything from you. We need to be equals. Take the mask off."

"Can't it at least wait?" said Steven. "Please. Give me a day or two, then I'll happily do it."

"No. I've waited long enough. Now."

"It's not a pretty sight."

"Don't care."

"Dave, this isn't something I can just—"

David lunged, catching his brother off-guard. He got a hand to the side of the mask, gripping a fold of fabric. Steven tried to wrestle him off. David held fast. Steven pummelled his forearm, yelling at him to let go, not to do this, not now. David began to tug the mask upwards. Steven wrenched his head away, to counteract the move.

There was a rending sound. David staggered back with a scrap of the mask in his hand.

Steven screeched in frustration and clamped a hand over the section of his face that was now exposed by a jagged hole in the mask – his left cheek.

But too late. A fraction of a second too late.

David had glimpsed what lay there, and Steven knew it.

The burned skin, the scarring...

Had a shape.

Formed a pattern.

Was a picture.

Seared into the skin of Steven's face: an image. One David recognised. It was well known. The emblem of one of the gods. It wasn't an exact representation, but close enough. As close as one could expect from puckered scar tissue.

"You. Fucking. Twat!" Steven snarled. "What have you done?"

"No," said David, numb. "You. What have *you* done, Steven?"

33. REVELATION

STEVEN LED DAVID to the old storehouse that was now the Lightbringer's war room. They could be alone there. He covered the side of his face with a hand the whole way, in case anyone saw.

In the storehouse, he slumped into a folding chair. David remained standing. There was silence for a while, broken only by the sporadic percussion beats of the battle going on outside. Steven sat with his head bowed, his back bent. Finally he straightened up and, seizing the top of the mask with one hand, pulled it off in a single, decisive movement.

His hair was shaggy and unkempt but otherwise much as David remembered, except for the few strands of grey that now salted its sandy-brownness. His face, so much like David's own, showed few signs of the years that had passed other than a slight pouching around the eyes and the first shallow etchings of wrinkles across the forehead. There was the Westwynter nose, sharp and plain as ever, almost too pointed for its own good, as though it were more a tool for hacking with than an organ for smelling with. And there were Steven's long-lashed eyelids, which brought a touch of their mother's femininity to the masculine family features.

David found himself shocked – moved, even – to see his brother once again, after all this time of not quite seeing him, of knowing he was there beneath the mask but not having the knowledge confirmed beyond all doubt by the evidence of his own eyes. It was the difference between looking at a pencil study for a famous painting and the painting itself, with all the colour fleshed out and the depth shaded in.

A painting that had been vandalised.

"*Desfigurado*," Steven said. "See? Like I told you."

David was transfixed by the scarring. Couldn't tear his eyes from it.

"And you can also see the reason for the mask," Steven went on. "The real reason. One look at this" – he circled a finger at his cheek – "and the Lightbringer's reputation, his whole ethos, wouldn't mean a thing."

"You said people did see it," David said. "You told me you had the mask yanked from your head at gunpoint, several times, when you were going around Freegypt recruiting for your cause."

"I lied about that. I – I may have lied about quite a lot of things."

"No shit."

"But I'm prepared to be honest with you now, Dave. Tell you everything, straight. And you know you'll have to believe me, because there's nothing to be gained from lying to you any more."

"Isn't there?" said David.

"Oh, just bloody give it a rest, won't you?" Steven snapped. "We don't have much time, and anyway events are going to bear out everything I'm about to say. Listen to me. Let me get through this quickly without you interrupting. This is the truth. What really happened to me after the Battle of the Aegean..."

WHAT REALLY HAPPENED to me after the Battle of the Aegean was much like I said, to begin with at least. I did get thrown clear when the *Immortal* blew up. I did float for a night in the sea. I did gaze up at the stars and have my moment of epiphany. I did wash up the next morning on the shore of a tiny, uninhabited island smack dab in the middle of bloody nowhere.

There, though, is where the version I gave you deviates from the way things actually went.

I described that island as a Robinson Crusoe kind of place, didn't I? Tame rabbits hopping about, olive trees, a freshwater spring, a cave – the basic necessities for living, all present and correct and strangely convenient.

Fucking crap.

It was a rock. A bare hunk of rock sticking up out of the ocean. Not a scrap of shelter to be found. Not a hint of vegetation. Nothing to eat, nothing to drink and nowhere to hide from the elements. I made it sound like it wasn't such a bad spot to have wound up in – you know, could've been a lot worse.

Well, it *was* worse. It was a fucking sight worse.

After three days I was half-crazed with thirst and hunger and thinking about throwing myself into the sea. The sound of the waves beating against the island was like a mallet to my skull. The sun scorched down and I could feel myself cooking in its heat; could smell my own skin burning. At the middle of each day, when the sun was at its height, all I could do was lie in a ball with my navy tunic over my head and wait for evening.

On the fourth day, or it might have been the fifth, I managed to catch a crab that had scuttled up onto the island. I tore it apart and sucked out its insides like it was an oyster. It was the foulest thing I have ever tasted but I could've eaten a hundred more if I'd had the opportunity.

That kept me going for another day or so. Not so much the nutrition I got from the crab, more the possibility that more might come my way and I'd have a regular source of food. But the crab was a one-off. No other crustacean was stupid enough to come up onto that barren no-place. Only one living creature had the sheer dumb bad luck to be there: me.

By the end of the week I was in very bad shape indeed. I could barely move. My brain felt like a dried walnut. Parts of my skin were so badly sunburned, they looked as if they'd been flayed. I was delirious, imagining things. At one point Mum and Dad came to visit. Boy, were they disappointed in me. "And what sort of a farrago is this?" Dad demanded. "You're a disgrace, Steven, a disgrace!" Like I'd had a choice about getting shipwrecked on that island. Like it was nothing but some sort of poor career move. And Mum not much help, twittering on about how I'd upset my father and why didn't I ever think about anybody but myself? I'd have cried, except my body couldn't spare the moisture for tears.

The sea was looking even more tempting by then. If I'd had the strength to crawl down the rocks and slither in, I would have. It'd have been quick, and far better than slowly roasting to death out in the open. Just float along till I sank.

I held on for a couple more days. By which I mean I remained alive not through any great effort of will, but just by happening not to die. Humans. We can be killed in an instant. *Ba* bolt, bullet, car crash, falling off a cliff – *bang*, we're gone, just like that. But, given the option, life doesn't depart that easily, does it? It hangs on. It fights to the last, even when the fight isn't worth winning any more. Like Gran. How long did she have cancer for? Six months? For six whole months she just kept on going while the cancer ate her up from the inside. She was a shell by the end, a hollow thing that only looked like our grandmother. There was nothing beneath the skin. It looked like you could touch her and she'd disintegrate. But dammit, she was still alive. She could still talk, now and then. Still tick me off for slouching or tell you you were her favourite grandson, which you were, Dave, don't deny it. Frail in her bed, like she was made out of paper, but still refusing to go. Stubborn old cow.

And that stubbornness was in me, too, whether I liked it or not. I needed to die. I wanted to die. But life wouldn't let me.

And then *he* came.

He came in a dream, and at first I thought he was as much a hallucination as Mum and Dad had been. Why not? If I'd imagined them, why not him?

But there are dreams about gods and then there are god dreams. It's not only priests who get the latter. Ordinary people do, every so often, and you can tell the difference. One sort of dream, the gods just drift in, don't do much of anything, or maybe they look like someone you know and someone you know looks like them, and quite a lot of the time they resemble famous sportsmen and film stars, did you know that? True fact. It's funny.

But a god dream, a proper divine visitation – that's a whole different kettle of fish. There's nothing random or casual about it. You feel it deep down. It touches some part of you way below the normal level of consciousness. And your life changes.

So I soon figured out I was really in the presence of a god, and then he asked me how much I wanted to live. Not *whether* I wanted to live, note. How much. And of course my answer was: *a lot.* I mean, I'd been wishing I could die, but that was to escape the hellish hopelessness of my situation. Offered the chance, I'd have much preferred not to.

"What would you do, to live?" was his next question. "What would you be prepared to give in exchange?"

I thought about it, but really it was a no-brainer.

"Anything," I told him.

"Are you sure?" he said.

I said I was.

"We'll see," he said, and then was gone.

The next day, clouds gathered and it rained. For the first time since I'd pitched up on that wretched island, the sun wasn't broiling me. Soft rain was coming down from the sky. It washed me and cooled me and bathed me, and it gathered in dimples in the rocks, giving me thimblefuls of fresh water to slurp up. I went down on all fours and lapped away like a dog.

The god came again when I next slept. I was pathetically grateful. "You brought me that rain," I said, almost slobbering in my delight.

"It happened to rain," he replied with a shrug. "Are you still ready to live?"

"I am," I said. "I'll do whatever it takes. Even though you aren't my national deity, I will serve you."

"You say that. You'll need to prove it."

And off he went again.

And the following morning, would you believe it, a wave came along and threw a big old shoal of sardines up onto the rocks, and most of them flopped and flipped themselves back into the sea, but a couple of dozen were left stranded there, high and dry, gasping their last, and I gathered them up and ate one raw and laid the rest out to cook in the sun, because those rocks could get as hot as a griddle, and bingo, within an hour or so I was snacking down on baked sardine flesh and it was sweet and juicy and my mouth's watering even now at the memory of it.

Third dream. He was back.

"Give me a few years of your life," he said, "and in return I will give you power. Power over men. I will make you as close to a deity as any mortal may get. But the condition is that you must work for me. You must act according to my wishes. Your time will not be your own. Your every waking hour will be spent pursuing my goals. Do this, and when you have finished you will be free. Free to pursue your life as before."

As bargains go, it didn't seem a bad one. Not that I was in any position to haggle. It was clearly a take-it-or-leave-it arrangement, and since leaving it meant dying a slow horrible death and taking it meant survival, what else was I going to do? Already he'd proved himself with the rainfall and the sardines. He'd shown me he meant what he said. He was serious.

"It will not be pleasant," he added. "I will be bestowing a minuscule portion of my essence on you, and make no mistake, it will hurt. The mortal frame was not designed to be a receptacle for such power. In order to fit you for it, you will first need to be broken in... toughened."

"I can handle it," I told him. "When do we start?"

"Now," he said, and...

He thrust into me. That's the only word I can think of. Thrust his *ba* into me. There's no other way of putting it. It wasn't gentle. It wasn't subtle. It was like... I was crouching there on those rocks and there was this enormous, penetrating, agonising influx of... of force. Sudden, and overwhelming. My mind went blank, as though every fuse in my body had blown. I remember waking up, screaming. Clawing at the rocks. Blood trickling from my mouth because I'd bitten my tongue and from my nose because I don't know why. Everything hurt. I was tingling all over, and not in a nice way. Like pins and needles times a hundred. All I could do was lie there sobbing. The pain faded after about an hour, but the sense of intrusion – violation – didn't. I felt... different. Changed. Strange inside. I couldn't put my finger on how, precisely. I just knew I was no longer who I had been.

It happened again, next time I slept. And again. And again. I came to dread closing my eyes, knowing what was to come. But I knew I had to endure it. This was all part of the deal. The receiving of power. The breaking-in. The toughening. And it didn't get any easier with repetition. Each time, in fact, it was worse. More painful. More humiliating. Each time, I was left feeling raw and used and a little less the person I used to be. Degraded. As though the old Steven, happy-go-lucky Steven, irreverent and impulsive Steven, was getting seared away layer by layer, to allow this new thing into me, the Steven I was to become.

Rain showers provided me with drinking water, just enough of it when I needed it. I soon had the strength and the mental wherewithal to lie on the rocks by the sea and catch fish with my bare hands. It's not an easy skill to master, since the angle of refraction through the water makes things look like they're somewhere when actually they're just to the side of that, but I found that if I dipped my hands under the surface and held them there long enough, the fish stopped being suspicious and swam close enough to grab. I even managed to haul out a lobster once.

Five and a half weeks I lived like that. Forty days and nights. I kept track of the time like prisoners do, scratching marks on a rock in batches of five. By the end, my uniform was in tatters, just rags hanging off me. I had a hermit's hair and beard. I was skeletal, and tottery on my pins, and stank like a cesspit.

But I had power. It thrummed inside me, the god's gift. Gift? No, I earned it. It wasn't handed to me. I paid for it, every bit of it, with suffering.

On the last night, the fortieth night, the god told me he was done with me. He had infused me with as much of his essence as I'd need.

"With this power," he said, "you will be able to bend people to your will. They will cede authority over themselves to you, and do it voluntarily, bowing to you in the same instinctive way that they do to the gods. You will not be able to make anyone do anything that goes against the grain of their own wishes. By speaking to them in the right way, however, with coaxing words and wily flattery, you will be able to mould their wishes to match yours."

What I had now, in other words, was the silverest of silver tongues.

"You will also," the god went on, "be invisible to the rest of the Pantheon. You will be able to carry out your work in secret, without fear of their intervention."

In other words, he'd made me the human equivalent of a *ba*-infused amulet. Instead of priests, I was a blur to the gods.

"But," he said, "you must use these abilities only to further *my* ends, and in order to ensure you keep to that, I am going to mark you. Mark you in such a way that there is never any doubt who is your master. Hide the mark from others by all means, but you will always know it is there and you will not be able to avoid it. Every time you look at your own reflection, the mark will look back at you. Others may not recognise it for what it is. Some may take it for just an unfortunate scar. But you will know, and I will know, and it will signify the compact we have sealed."

Like I said last time, I had been hit in the face by shrapnel from the exploding *Immortal*. I had had my face damaged. But the god took that damage and transformed it. The scarring twisted and reshaped itself into what you see before you now. I felt it happen, and it hurt too, surprise, surprise.

Dawn the next day, a fishing boat was pulling up to anchor beside the island. I staggered down to it. A Greek fisherman was urinating over the guardrail. Iannis.

I told him to take me off the island. It was the very first time I exercised my power. I spoke commandingly, as a god would. Iannis agreed instantly that I could hitch a ride on his boat. We set off, and I never once looked back. I kept my face turned away from the island till I knew it was safely out of sight. That fucking place... I still have nightmares about it, you know. Every now and again I dream I'm stuck there and will never get off and everything that's happened since, *that's* the dream. In reality, I'm dying there on those rocks, fantasising the next few years of my life. All this, the chair I'm sitting on, the room we're in, you, Dave – it doesn't exist. Bizarre, eh?

From then on, the story goes much as I told you. I stayed with Iannis and did the drug-running thing with him and all that, in order to give myself time to recover from my ordeal and plot and think and scheme. I knew what the god wanted from me. I just had to figure out how to bring it about in the most effective fashion.

Freegypt was the obvious place to set up shop. There, apathy towards the Pantheon was a way of life, and apathy can be turned into antipathy without much effort, like sharpening a blunt pencil. Plus, with all the militias and infighting in Upper Freegypt, they had the ready-made raw material for an army. I formulated a plan. Learn Arabic. Then create an image for myself. The mask was obligatory, to disguise the god's mark. I'd tried growing a beard but it didn't really work. Didn't obscure enough of the scarring. Also, if I wore a mask that covered my face completely it would make me a blank canvas, something people could project their own dreams and ideals onto. I'd be both less of a man with it, and more. And the name? That just popped into my head one morning. Al Ashraqa. He who brightens. The Lightbringer. Why not? It summed up what I was pretending to do, bring illumination to a benighted world. Kind of arrogant, I appreciate, but then I saw the Lightbringer as quite an arrogant character. People like arrogance in a leader, anyway. They're drawn to it. They want a leader to have certainty and guts and ambition.

And the Lightbringer had those – *has* those – in abundance.

"PRETENDING," SAID DAVID. "Pretending to bring illumination to the world."

"Yes."

"You're a fraud. This whole 'crusade' of yours – nothing but a sham."

"Harsh words. Not how I'd put it."

"How would you put it?"

"This is just a job, Dave," said Steven. "Something I have to do. I'm discharging an obligation. I made a deal, and this is my side of it."

"A deal with a god."

"Yes."

"Who you can't even bring yourself to name."

Steven looked away. "You can't understand what it was like. He treated me like... like..."

"A slave?"

"No, worse than that. A dog."

"Or how about like his property?" David offered, recalling the image that had sprung to mind when he'd caught that glimpse of the edge of the scar back at the Temple of Hatshepsut – a cattle brand.

"Ha," said Steven, an empty laugh. "Yeah, that'll do."

"You should say his name, though. If he's your owner, you should be prepared to admit to it."

"Why? It's obvious who he is, isn't it?"

"Still. For my sake. Say it out loud. Say who you submitted to."

Steven said the name, softly, not even quite a whisper.

"Again," David said. "Properly."

"What for? Look. Look at this." Steven gesticulated at the scar. "What does it look like?"

It looked like the head of some kind of animal, a creature with no direct analogue among the fauna of earth. It had a long, pointed snout, pricked ears, and horns like an antelope's. The name it had been given was the Typhonic Beast, after a malevolent fire-god of the Ancient Greeks.

"I know what it is," said David. "Whose emblem is it? Come on. Loud and clear. *Say his name.*"

Steven sighed, then loudly, clearly, uttered the word.

"Set."

34. BEAST

"THERE," SAID STEVEN rancorously. "Happy now? It's Set's emblem. Set is my master. I have been doing the bidding of the Lord of the Desert. Set rules me. How many other ways can I phrase it? Set saved my life and I've been working for him ever since. You got it out of me. Congrats." He stood up. "Now, if it's all right with you, I'm going to find a spare mask, put it on and go out there and be the Lightbringer for a little while longer."

"No." David thrust him back down into the chair. "We're not done yet."

"But the people out there," Steven protested, "*my* people…"

"You don't care that much what happens to them."

"They need to see that I'm there, looking out for them."

"A few more minutes, that's all."

Steven glared, but did not try to get up again. "All right. Have your big moment. Lecture me on what I've done wrong."

"I said a few minutes. *That* lecture would take several hours."

"Oh, ha ha."

"Steven, don't you see what you've done? The enormity of it? You've led three-thousand-odd people to their deaths. You've abused their trust and sacrificed them to save your own skin. You've deceived them with a lie which you don't even believe in yourself."

"You – you can be such a high-and-mighty prig, Dave," his brother snapped. "Don't you dare judge me. You weren't on that island. It wasn't your life hanging in the balance. If you'd been there, suffering like I was, you'd have done the same. You'd have leapt at the chance Set was offering you. Don't tell me you wouldn't."

"I wouldn't."

"Come off it."

"No, really, I wouldn't. I'd have thought through the consequences and said no."

"And died? Lingeringly? Agonisingly? Yeah, right, fuck off."

"You forget. Not so long ago, I got lost in the desert. I went through pretty much what you did. I know exactly how you felt, and if Set or any other god had come to me with a bargain like that, even when I was at my lowest point, I know what my answer would have been."

"You can't say that for certain."

"I think I can."

"Well then, doesn't that make you the nobler, better one of us?" Steven spat out. "You're the upstanding older brother, never knowingly unheroic, and I'm the weakling, the runt, the disappointment, Westwynter Minor in every way. Glad we've established that – or rather, re-established."

"What gets me is that you gave in so easily. You didn't put up a fight. You didn't hesitate. Set barely had to ask and you were his."

"Isn't that how it is? A perfect illustration of the relationship between the Pantheon and humankind. They screw us, and we bend over and take it."

"You feel no shame?"

"I left shame behind somewhere in the middle of the Aegean."

"Yes, I reckon you did and all." David scratched his chin. "Tell me, this gift Set gave you…"

"Not a gift."

"The prize you won, then. You used it on all the Freegyptians?"

"Yep. In my speeches, or on a one-to-one basis. All I had to do was sound convincing, and they'd be convinced. You could call it a heightened form of my natural charm. Sometimes it was almost too easy. They wanted what I was promising them, wanted it so much. First of all peace in Upper Freegypt, then the opportunity to spread their national philosophy – their belief in unbelief – to the rest of the world. In a way, what they were looking for was a prophet, a secular evangelist. And they got one."

"No, they got a false messiah."

"More harsh words."

"Just telling it like it is, Steven."

"Look, Dave, you can accuse me of misleading people, toying with their hopes, throwing away their lives, whatever, but as far as I'm concerned I've done nothing wrong. I've been acting on a god's commands. You do that. Everyone does that! Slag me off if it makes you feel better, but you're not going to make *me* feel bad."

"Fine," said David. "Then I won't try. There is one thing I'd like to know, however."

"What?" said Steven with an exasperated huff.

"Did you use it on me at any point? Your power?"

Quickly: "No."

"You're sure about that?"

"No! I mean, yes I'm sure. No, I didn't use it on you."

"Not in order to get me to tag along with you, for instance?"

"No." Steven chortled. "You definitely did that all by yourself. Remember what I said? I said Set told me that I won't be able to make anyone do what they didn't want to. I can encourage people along, I can facilitate their own desires, but I can't force them to act against their will. I meant it earlier, when I described the Freegyptians as being willing to lay down their lives for me. They are. And they wouldn't if the cause I stood for wasn't one they felt was worth dying for."

"You made them feel that way. Manipulated them."

"I simply showed them that that was how they felt."

"So you never once did the same to me? About anything?"

"Why does this matter to you so much, Dave?"

"It just does."

Steven looked him in the eye. "I did not, I swear," he said, and David couldn't help noticing how the Typhonic Beast on Steven's cheek writhed as he spoke, as though the words were coming as much from it as him. "Everything you've done has been of your own free will. I haven't tried to influence you in any way."

David thought of Zafirah. He thought of Steven telling him, *She's not for you.* He thought of how the admonition had stuck with him, like some sort of imperishable creed in his brain. How it stood now like a screen between him and her.

If Steven was telling the truth, then he only had his own timidity to blame. Deep down he was afraid of Zafirah. Not of who she was but of how she saw into the heart of him and didn't hesitate to tell him what she found there. Women he had gone out with in the past had been superficial women. He'd known that and liked that. They wanted nothing more from him than to be what he appeared to be, rich and debonair David Westwynter, a man with a family cartouche and a wallet to match. Zafirah didn't care about any of that, which made her dangerous to him. As dangerous as she was alluring. With her, he had to be who he was, and what he was wasn't something he was all that comfortable with.

That was if Steven was telling the truth.

If Steven was lying...

Then on one level it didn't make any difference. He still had only himself to blame. Steven couldn't have made him shrink from Zafirah if that wasn't what he himself, whether he knew it or not, wanted.

It did, though, make a difference on another level. It meant Steven had used his power to reinforce David's self-doubt, in order to guarantee nothing would happen between him and Zafirah.

"I don't believe you," David said at last.

"Fair enough, then don't."

"You haven't been straight with me this whole time. Why should things have changed now? You've kept so much hidden from me..."

"For a good reason. If you'd known everything, you'd never have stuck around, and I wanted you to stick around. We'd been brought back together by some incredible quirk of fate. We'd become the closest I can ever remember us being. There were times when I wanted to come clean with you, really I did, but I was just so happy to have you back and have you respecting me for once. It seemed daft to put that at risk."

"Good reason? Selfish reason, more like."

"If that's how you want to see it, Dave, then you have something seriously twisted in your head. Anyway, I've had enough of this conversation. I need to go. Let me."

Steven rose and waved at his brother to move aside.

David didn't.

Steven made to push past him.

David grabbed him by the shoulder.

Steven brushed his hand off.

David grabbed him again.

They stared at each other, and in each other's eyes saw twenty-plus years of brotherhood, of shared blood and experience. They saw a love that was so old they took it for granted and scarcely noticed it any more, and a rivalry that became only fresher and sharper with every argument they had, every set of insults they exchanged, every lie one or the other of them told. The bond between them was so ingrained – so familiar, in every sense of the word – that it was easy to forget it existed, while the things that separated them grew ever more numerous. Suddenly, now, more divided them than joined them. The canyon between them had grown wider than the span of its bridges.

Neither of them threw the first punch. Or rather, they both did. It happened spontaneously and simultaneously. David swung for Steven; Steven swung for David.

And then they were grappling, brawling, sprawling on the floor, rolling in the storehouse dust, now David on top, now Steven, and the blows came thick and fast, delivered with fury and scorn, and they were boys again, the children they used to be, as though years had not gone by and nothing had changed. They hated each other with the intensity of boyhood hate. All either could think about was hurting the other, physically expressing his contempt for the other.

Briefly David gained the upper hand. Straddling Steven, he pounded him with everything he had. Then Steven grabbed David's injured arm and squeezed the wound till several of the stitches burst and blood erupted, soaking through his shirtsleeve. David roared, and Steven shoved him off. Standing, he started to kick David in the stomach. David grabbed his foot, twisted it, and sent him spinning over onto his belly. Then he dived onto Steven's back and slammed his face against the floor repeatedly. Steven elbow-jabbed him in the nose. More blood gushed. David got an arm around his brother's neck and wrenched his head backwards. Steven gasped and gargled. David locked his other hand against Steven's temple and increased the pressure. Steven's face reddened, then purpled. Spittle flew from his mouth, snot dribbled from his nose. He flailed at David helplessly; clawed at his arm. David continued to lever his head backwards and sideways, aware he was preventing Steven from breathing properly. Aware he was asphyxiating him. Killing him.

"Dave... don't..." Steven choked out.

Servant of Set. Betrayer of trust. Liar. Deceiver. Man who would be god.

In his mind's eye, David saw Osiris smiling. This was what *his* god wanted. The Lightbringer, the earthly agent of Osiris's despised brother, must die. And who, then, could be better suited for the role of assassin than the Lightbringer's very own brother?

"... Daaave..."

A few more seconds, that was all it would take. David had a firm grip. Steven's windpipe was being crushed. He was struggling to breathe. His throat was making a series of wet, glottal noises like hiccups crossed with grunts, but no air was getting in. A few more seconds, and then it would all be over. The Freegyptians could surrender. The Nephthysians and Setics might not treat them kindly as captives, but at least they'd have a chance of surviving. Otherwise they were as good as dead. By taking this one life, David might save a thousand others.

"... d..."

No.

David let go. Steven slumped face first on the floor, wheezing hard.

No. David had had his fill of killing. He remembered the terebinth tree and the corpses. Life, not death.

He sat in a corner while Steven recovered. Slowly the colour left Steven's face and his breathing began to come evenly, less harshly. He rolled onto his back and looked at David. His eyes were craze-patterned with broken capillaries.

"You fucker," he rasped, hoarse-voiced. "You were going to do it, weren't you? You really were."

David said nothing, just examined his hands. There was blood on them but only his own, stray spatters from his nose and his sodden shirtsleeve.

"I knew you were a heartless bastard," Steven went on. "But even so. Fuck's sake, I was halfway to Iaru. What got into you?"

David wiped his hands on his trousers. He checked his nose. Not broken. The blood there was starting to coagulate. His arm throbbed exquisitely. The reopened gash would need attention. New stitches. His knuckles ached. Bad punching. In his blind, all-consuming rage he'd forgotten his training. He'd hit too hard. He was lucky not to have broken a finger.

Sitting up, Steven probed his neck in a gingerly fashion. "Suppose I should just be thankful you stopped."

David completed his self-inventory. Bruises, abrasions... He'd been in worse shape than this.

"You not talking to me any more? Is that it?" Steven said. "Bet you're not. Bet you're too fucking ashamed to. Psychopath. Honestly, David, if I were you I'd seek professional—"

"Shut up."

"Don't tell me to shut up, you ruddy lunatic. There's you going on about how I don't care about other people's lives, and then you go and—"

"Shut up and listen, Steven."

"To you? No thanks."

"No. *Listen.*"

Steven cocked his head.

Outside, there were shouts of alarm, and a low, distant grinding drone.

"That sounds like…"

"Bombers," said David. "From the south. Neph Typhons again, I'd guess."

"Holy shit," Steven breathed. "This is it."

35. TYPHONS

THEY STUMBLED OUT of the storehouse, Steven pausing only to find a spare Lightbringer mask and pull it on.

The Typhons were coming up the valley, eight of them in a straggling line. They flew at their usual ponderous pace, and today there seemed a kind of sinister unhurriedness about it, as though the planes knew they could take their time. Their infidel prey were all in one place and far weaker than before. Almost out of ammunition. No Anubian gunships left to defend them. A single Typhon, with a full payload, would have been sufficient. Eight assured absolute annihilation.

A Freegyptian manning one of the gun emplacements opened fire, but it was a token gesture of defiance. The Typhons were too far off and were coming in too high anyway. The Lightbringer ordered the man to cease fire. Everyone. Cease fire. There was no point.

One of the warlords came over and asked the Lightbringer what they were supposed to do now. His face showed anxiety but also hope. Al Ashraqa would have a solution. He must do.

The faces of all the other Freegyptians displayed the same mixture of emotions: fear overlaid with faith. The Lightbringer would steer them out of this predicament, surely.

If only you knew, thought David.

He scanned around for Zafirah. Couldn't find her. Had she even made it to the mountain? He had no idea. She could have died down there on the plain during the final retreat, for all he knew.

In these, his last moments of life, he would have liked to see her again, one last time. Just so that he could say he was sorry for being such an idiot. Sorry, too, for everything his brother had done to her and her countrymen.

The Lightbringer called out to everyone within earshot. As far as David could glean, he was telling them not to worry, help was at hand.

Help? David thought. *You lying sack of shit. What help?*

There was no one nearby who was going to come to the Freegyptians' rescue. To the west David could see the forefront of the Setic task force, consisting of several dozen Scarab tanks and some heavier-duty artillery units, including a number of mobile rocket launchers. They were all in position, ready for an assault on Mount Megiddo. Doubtless the Nephthysians had called up the bombers to pre-empt that. They were determined that credit for the final quashing of the infidel uprising would be theirs, not the Setics'.

As David looked down at the Setic battalions, the word that sprang to mind was overkill. The KSD must have been truly unnerved by the Lightbringer to send down a task force as immense as this. Either that or it was an expression of how little confidence they had in their Nephthysian allies to do the job properly. But still, David was struck by the inordinate levels of manpower and firepower the Setics had committed to the field. It was a mark of how the Lightbringer had got under their skin, or, to be accurate, the skin of their god.

But then that was Steven for you. A man with a true talent for annoyance.

David felt an odd, mental snagging sensation. He reviewed what he had just been musing on. Something was there, in the train of thought that had just gone by. Something that might explain Steven's current state of confident calmness. Something that would account for it, other than that the Lightbringer dare not show uncertainty in the presence of his followers, even in the face of certain doom.

Mark. Skin. God.

Of course.

Of course!

David could have slapped himself. It was blindingly obvious. He would have realised it sooner had he not been so preoccupied with bullying the truth out of Steven.

The nearest of the Typhons was almost level with Mount Megiddo. Bomb bay doors open. Bombs at the ready.

Steven had allied himself with a god.

Which god?

Only the member of the Pantheon who ruled the bloc that presently had a vast army assembled to the north, east and west of the mountain.

Only Set himself.

A moment later, a surface-to-air missile was snaking its way up from the Setic ranks towards the leading Typhon.

A moment after that, the Typhon was a ball of reddish-purple light.

And a moment after *that*, the other seven bombers were on the receiving end of a blitz of long-range ordnance. One after another they popped like bubbles in the air, bathing the plain in shades of scarlet and magenta, cherry and lilac, burgundy and mauve. The echoes of eight massive detonations rippled along the valley and across the land, and as they faded an astonished cheer went up from the top of Mount Megiddo, a chorus of relief and disbelief.

Saved.

By the Setics?

The Freegyptians turned to their leader, looking for an explanation.

But the Lightbringer said nothing, and his masked face was inscrutable.

Only David understood, and even he wasn't entirely sure what was going on.

Meanwhile the Setic task force swung into action. It flowed around the mountain like floodwater and poured into the valley to smash into the Nephthysians, who could not resist, who barely had a chance to defend themselves. One army swept the other before it. Hapless, helpless, taken completely by surprise, the Nephthysians were driven back, back, back down the plain, and the Setic task force rolled on, wave after wave, southward and further, leaving debris and bodies and a shredded-to-ribbons pact in their wake.

36. SET

NEPHTHYS SUDDENLY CLUTCHES her chest.

"Wha—?" she gasps. "What is this? I feel..."

Her eyes roll. She swoons. Isis is there to catch her and lower her to the deck. Cradling her sister's head in her lap, she fans her face. "Water!" Isis calls out. "Somebody fetch some water."

Bast arrives with a pitcher and cup. She pours from one to the other fastidiously, careful not to let a drop fall on herself, then hands the cup to Isis. Isis tips water between Nephthys's lips, and gradually, eyelids fluttering, the stricken goddess comes round.

Nephthys searches the faces of the gods who are standing around her. Her gaze finds the only one that isn't showing concern.

"You," she hisses. "This is you, isn't it?"

Set cannot hide his mirth. "My dear sister-wife, are you not feeling well? You seem to have had a nasty turn. Whatever can it be?"

"You... are hurting me. On earth. Your mortals... attack mine."

"Now why would that be?" Set says, feigning puzzlement. "Oh wait. Could it be because you're a treacherous, adulterous slut? Because you slept with our brother and then denied it? Because you gave me a son who isn't even mine but whom you expected me to call my own? Because you shun me in favour of our sister? I very much think it could be."

"Set, you have turned on your own wife?" says Osiris, aghast.

"Yes, brother, that is precisely what I have done," says Set. "For someone as uxorious as yourself, I know that seems like the worst crime anyone could commit. For me, it's just long-overdue payback. How long have I had to endure marriage to this conniving, two-timing bitch? Too long! And with no end in sight. An eternity of wedlock stretching before us. I couldn't take it any more. Nephthys has made a laughing stock of me. I heard you, all of you" – he wheels around, glaring at all the gods on the boat – "whispering about me, passing comment behind my back. Set the cuckold. Set the unwitting stepfather of a bastard. Finding even more reason to spurn me and mock me. And it was all her fault!" He jabs an accusing finger at Nephthys.

"And so now you're killing her?"

This comes from Ra. His face is pale, so pale it nearly matches the colour of his moon eye. He trembles with sorrow and indignation.

"I don't know about that. Maybe," says Set. "Certainly the armies of my kingdom have begun making inroads into hers, and there will be slaughter. Whether or not Nephthys dies from that remains to be seen. What I am doing is punishing her. For a long time my sister-wife has treated me abominably. I have borne it with as much restraint as I can, but enough is enough. Now, at last, I am returning the compliment."

"Set, please..." Nephthys begs. "I'm sorry. I'm sorry for everything I did. Stop this now."

Her brother-husband shrugs. "Stop? When I have hardly even started? I don't think so."

"Father," says Anubis, stepping forward. "To deal with my mother in this way – it is unnecessarily cruel."

"On the contrary," says Set. "Never has cruelty been more necessary. Now all of you will learn that I am not to be trifled with. I am not to be looked down on and used as a general whipping-boy, the butt of everyone's contempt. After this, when you see what I am prepared to do to my own wife, my closest of kin, my own flesh and blood, you will no longer be so quick to belittle me. You will look at me with new eyes, and in those eyes there will be respect."

His irises glow like twin volcanoes. The light in them is terrible to behold, as vindictive as it is self-righteous.

Ra groans like someone who has been punched in the stomach. "You are the one who created the Lightbringer," he says. "All along it was you. Here on the Boat of a Million Years, right under my nose, you were carrying out all these machinations."

"Of course, Great-Great-Uncle. Who else could it have been? We are what we are. Each of us has his or her own nature and cannot help but be true to it. I am Set, who beguiles and dupes, and you are Ra, whose kind, forgiving temperament blinkers him to the dark secrets that lie in others' hearts."

"But allying yourself with a mortal and sparking an infidel revolt – what for? What to gain?"

"A ruse," says Set simply. "To camouflage my true intentions. The Lightbringer has been, if you will, a smokescreen. His crusade was nothing more than a means of manoeuvring my mortals and Nephthys's into a position where mine could strike against hers with maximum effectiveness. But do not judge me too harshly, O Ra. You sought peace among us, and for a time the Lightbringer gave you just that. We all rallied together against him, and your dearest wish was granted." A crowing laugh. "But only for a time."

Ra is fuming. He cannot remember when he last felt so abused and debased. He strides up to Set and – unable to help himself – lashes out at him with a backhand slap. The blow catches Set by surprise and he falls to his knees. He rises instantly, poised to retaliate, but before he can both Bast and Neith have pounced on him. They wrestle him back down to the boards of the deck. Bast yowls a warning at him, slashing the air in front of his face with fingers like talons, while Neith just gruffly tells him to stay put or lose his balls again.

"I... regret that," says Ra, ashamed. "It was wrong of me. I lost control."

"Do no berate yourself, All-Father," says Isis. "You only did what the rest of us wanted to."

"Even so. Unforgivable." Ra squats down on his hunkers, so that his face is close to Set's. "What you have done is unforgivable too, Set."

"So?" Set sneers. "Punish me then. Oops, no you can't. You're already doing that, twice a day."

"I want you to rethink all this. Leave Nephthys be. You've made your point. You'd like the rest of us to respect you? Do the decent thing, call off your armies, and we will."

"No one will respect an act of weakness like that."

"Then you'd rather your fellow gods went on hating you? Even more than before? Because that's what will happen if you continue to harm your sister-wife."

"I can live with it. Besides" – Set twists his head to look at Horus – "not all of you hate me. Eh, Horus?"

The one-eyed god, once Set's most implacable foe, nods conspiratorially. "Your ruthlessness is to be admired, Uncle," he says. "I could learn a thing or two from your example. Perhaps we should try to forge a closer partnership. At the earliest opportunity we must get together and have a free and full exchange of... ideas."

The two share a lustful smile. Meanwhile Nephthys moans. Her fate, it seems, is sealed.

Ra straightens up, despondent. It is the worst outcome possible. Nothing is any different. The Pantheon is still at war with itself. The allegiances may have changed but the antagonism remains. Peace flowered briefly, and has withered and died.

There is nothing he can do. Nothing but let his hands drop to his sides and say, "That's it, then. I give up. I tried my best. I failed. Enough. No more. It's over. You may all go. Return to your palaces. Resume your feuding if you wish. Somehow I think you're happier that way. Contentment, consensus, harmony – you say you want them but you don't. They only bore you. Go. Now. Go!"

Thus commanded, the gods disperse. Osiris and Isis take the ailing Nephthys with them. Anubis storms off, his expression saying that he has much to be morose about and will take great pleasure in wallowing in that moroseness. Horus and Set depart together, inevitably. Set leaves with an insouciant wave, promising he'll be back to face Apophis at sundown.

Soon there is no one on the Solar Barque but Ra, Bast, Maat, Ammut and Thoth.

Thoth says to Ra, "So what now, my lord?"

Ra eyes his wizened vizier.

He sighs, bitterly, resignedly.

"You know what, old friend?" he says, after a long silence. "I think it's time for a change. I'm done with all this. I'm weary. I feel twilight upon me, an evening of the soul, a lengthening of the shadows. I've done as much as I can do, and I have no more to give."

"This talk smacks of defeatism."

"No, of pragmatism. The time has come for something new. I need to step aside. Just as I gave up being King of the Earth, now I must give up being ruler of the gods."

"Must you?"

"I must."

"But if you do," says Thoth, worry adding to the many wrinkles on his face, "who will replace you? You are Ra, the greatest of us, whose brightness has warmed us since time immemorial, whose light is our benison. To whom will you pass on the crown?"

"To whom?" Ra pats his vizier on the shoulder. "As wise a head as yours can surely figure that one out, Thoth."

37. GAVRILENKO

SETIC TROOPS STORMED Mount Megiddo, crowding onto the summit from several sides at once and converging on the Freegyptians. They met no resistance. The Lightbringer had instructed his followers to lay down their arms. The fighting was over, he said. Everything that had needed to be done, they had done, and he was grateful to them. They had been brave, they had been loyal, and he would ask for nothing more from them.

The Freegyptians sensed a valedictory note in their leader's words. They were already perplexed, and this perplexed them further. Among some of them it had begun to dawn that the Lightbringer was not quite what he had made himself out to be. Others simply remained baffled. The Setics had attacked the Nephthysians? How could that happen? Did it mean the Setics were on *their* side? Were they joining the Lightbringer's crusade? Surely not!

A Setic colonel took charge of the scene. First he had his men round up the Freegyptians and make them sit in groups at gunpoint. Next he identified the infidels' leader, which was, of course, no great challenge. The Lightbringer was brought forward to meet him. He went passively, prodded along by a couple of Setic soldiers with their *ba* lances.

The colonel and the Lightbringer spoke together for some time. David, sitting cross-legged among the Freegyptians, strained to hear what they were saying, but there were too many other competing noises: the Freegyptians murmuring to one another, the clatter and clank of the Setic task force still passing around the foot of the mountain, and the far-off tremors of the battle being conducted to the south.

It was a long conversation, and the longer it went on, the uneasier David became. Finally the colonel nodded to the Lightbringer, who offered him a salute in return, not a snappy military one, a casual tapping of fingers to forehead. Then the Lightbringer turned and made his way back to the Freegyptians – specifically, to David.

"A word," he said, beckoning.

David stood, conscious of the *ba* lances that were aiming his way, each with a gape-mouthed Typhonic Beast head at its tip. He joined Steven, who led him back to the Setic colonel.

"Colonel Gavrilenko," he said. "This is David."

The Setic had a lugubrious Russian face but eyes like a jackdaw's, pale, beady, and quick.

"The colonel speaks English," Steven added. "Better English than he does Arabic."

"Colonel," David said.

Gavrilenko drew on a cigarette and puffed the smoke out in such a way that it didn't quite go straight in David's face.

"Your friend here says I can be trusting you," he said in a gravelly voice. "You are good man."

"That's kind of him," David replied, shooting a glance at his brother. The mask was still on. No way of fathoming what Steven was up to here. "You realise, Colonel, that under the terms of the Global Convention for—"

The cigarette waved from side to side. "No Convention here. Is not proper war. You are not proper prisoners."

"Nevertheless we expect to be treated—"

Again the cigarette cut him off. "You will be going home. All of you. I am giving my word on that to Lightbringer, and to you.

Transportation will be arranged. A day, maybe two days, you will be returning to Freegypt."

"Thank you, Colonel," said David. "These people are civilians. Your soldiers should bear that in mind when dealing with them."

"From what I am having seen, they do not fight like civilians. Fight better than soldiers. Like warriors. But yes, they will be looked after as well as can be expected. Setic high command is not interested in Freegyptians. We have, how is it you are saying? Bigger fish for frying."

"The Nephthysians. Can I ask, Colonel, what's happened to the Bi-Continental Pact? How come the Setics have turned on their allies?"

Gavrilenko gave a shrug, his mouth turning down at the corners like a sad clown's. "How am I knowing? I am not KSD. Not Commissar Chang. I am just soldier. High command says we launch attack on Nephthysians on Megiddo Plain, so we launch attack. Send Nephs scurrying like frightened mice. Horusites are also attacking Nephs."

"Really?"

"Offensive has begun on western Africa. Horusite Atlantic fleet is bombing Congo. Marines landing at Guinea and Ivory Coast. Two-prong assault, us here, them there. Africa and Arabia crushed in the middle. Like in pincers of crab."

"Horus... and Set? Together?" said David. It seemed inconceivable.

"I know. And Osirisiacs not happy, saying maybe they come to aid of Nephthysians," said Gavrilenko. "The gods, they spin and pirouette like the ballerinas. Dancing together, then apart. One moment one way, next moment another. What can we do? Everything has changed, and yet everything is still the same. New enemies, new allies, but war goes on."

He dropped his cigarette butt and ground it out under his heel.

"So now you must wait here," he said. "One day or two, like I am telling you. It will be OK. Is not so bad a place for waiting. Nice views."

David felt that they had been dismissed. He turned to go. Then, noticing that Steven hadn't moved, he halted.

"Coming?"

Steven slowly shook his head.

Gavrilenko raised an eyebrow. "Lightbringer did not explain?"

"Explain what?" said David.

The Russian's lugubriousness doubled, every muscle in his face seeming to sag.

"I am having orders," he said. "These things must be done. Freegyptians are civilians, not soldiers, but still, an example must be made. So this thing will never be repeated. Is just how it is. I will give you a moment."

He went off to consult with a junior officer, leaving David and Steven alone except for the two Setics guarding them.

David looked at his brother and saw that he was trembling. He looked at him again, and suddenly the penny dropped.

"Shit, Steven..."

"It's OK, Dave. It's my own fault, really. I should have foreseen this. It's a shock, but actually it makes a kind of sense. What am I going to do, go back there to all my followers? They're already starting to suspect I've sold them a lie. Give them time and their suspicions will harden into certainty. Then what? They won't forgive me. They'll round on me like dogs on their master. Some of those warlords are not nice men. They'd make sure I paid for misleading them. It wouldn't be quick."

"But..." David indicated his own left cheek, meaning Steven's. "This. What about this? You're Set's servant. Therefore you're on his" – meaning Gavrilenko's – "side."

"Yeah, funny, that," said Steven. "The colonel's orders come right from the top, I mean high-priest high. In other words, straight from the divine horse's mouth. So it would seem that I've been sold a lie as well, just like I sold everyone else a lie. Now that I've done what I was supposed to, I've outlived my usefulness. Set has decided it's better not to have me around any more."

"No. This can't be. This is stupid."

"I thought the Setics might hail me a hero. I was expecting a nice apartment in Moscow, a dacha on the Black Sea coast, all the caviar I could eat, all the vodka I could drink, all the Natashas I could shag. So many medals I could barely stand up. But hey, like the colonel said, an example must be made."

"Speak to him," David urged. "You know, *speak* to him. Use your power on him. Get him to change his mind."

"Doesn't work that way, remember. I can talk someone into doing something, but as long as it's not against their nature. Does Gavrilenko strike you as the type to disobey an order? Not me. He's a soldier to the marrow."

"You could try."

"But don't you get it, Dave? He's not the problem. Set himself has decreed what's to be done with me. Nothing's going to change that. If it isn't Gavrilenko who does the dirty deed, it'll be some other mortal flunky."

"But why? Why has Set just... abandoned you?"

"Hmmm, the least trustworthy of all the gods, notorious for his tricks and lies – why would he suddenly toss me aside like a used handkerchief? I don't know, Dave. Because he's Set, perhaps? Or perhaps because, as I am, I'm too dangerous to leave be. I'm carrying some of his essence around inside me. I could do all sorts of things with that, things that might throw a spanner in the works, especially now I know how expendable I am to him. He's played me, now he wants me off the game board, simple as that."

David glanced around. The two soldiers guarding them weren't paying much attention at present. The other Setics seemed preoccupied, Gavrilenko included.

Lowering his voice, he said to Steven, "We'll make a run for it. Hit those two, grab their god rods, blast our way out of here."

"Dave." Steven's tone was warm, almost tender. "No. I appreciate the gesture, but look. This – this whole escapade – has come to an end. We both know it. Your idea will only get the both of us killed, and that would be pointless. I'm all right with what's about to happen. I'm not saying that to sound brave. I really am. Maybe if I had longer to think about it, I wouldn't be. But look at it this way. I've had a few more years of life that I otherwise wouldn't have, and they've been fun ones. Exciting. An adventure. *And* I've had a chance to be reconciled with my big brother – even if it ended up with us beating seven shades of shit out of each other. By the way, sorry about what I did to your bad arm. Try and get that fixed as soon as you can, will you?"

"Steven, don't give in like this. There must be something we can do. Think."

"Amazing," Steven said. "Less than an hour ago we could've killed each other. Now you don't want me to die."

"Maybe I just don't want someone else to kill you. It should be my job."

A brittle laugh. "Yeah, fraternal prerogative or something. Dave, do you think you're going home after this?"

"England? Haven't thought that far ahead. Why?"

"If you do, tell Mum and Dad everything. Eventually it's going to become known who the Lightbringer was. Someone somewhere is going to figure it out. Some journalist will dig around and get to the bottom of it and name and shame me. So perhaps it would be better if you told our parents first, rather than have them find out about it in a newspaper. But whatever you do, tell them the truth. Tell them why I did everything I did. Maybe Dad will somehow find it in his heart to sympathise."

"Not the Jack Westwynter I know."

"True. Then at least maybe Mum will. Oh, and Dave? Zafirah. Tell her..."

David gritted his teeth. *Tell her what? That you love her? That you don't love her but wanted her anyway to spite me? What, Steven?*

"Tell her how you feel about her," Steven said. "Just come out and say it. If she's still alive, if she's up here somewhere, find her and talk to her. She may not be right for you, but who am I to judge? At least give it a shot with her."

David was dumbfounded.

Steven turned. "Colonel? Colonel Gavrilenko? We're done. Let's get this over with, shall we?"

He tugged off his mask. His eyes were wide and shone like glass. His mouth was tight. The scar on his cheek looked, at that moment, like nothing but a scar, like a random pattern of injury, which only through happenstance, and with some imagination, resembled a Typhonic Beast.

He thrust the mask into David's hand and, bareheaded, naked-faced, strode over to the Russian officer.

IT WAS SUMMARY. It was swift. Five Setic soldiers lined up with their *ba* lances. Steven stood against a half-tumbled wall, facing them unflinchingly.

David turned away at the very last second, covering his ears. He looked out across the plain, which was burning. Smoke rose everywhere, from bombed-out farmhouses, from fields that were smouldering down to stubble, from the shells of wrecked vehicles. A brown haze filled the air, dimming the light of the low afternoon sun.

A flash of red flickered on the stones of the ruined city. Some of the Freegyptians who had a view of the execution winced and cried out in dismay. Others were flinty-eyed.

David raised the Lightbringer mask to his nose and inhaled the smell of his brother's hair and sweat.

Briefly, for a handful of seconds, Steven lived on in this world.

38. DETAINEES

SHE FOUND HIM.

Late in the evening, Colonel Gavrilenko had granted the Freegyptians some freedom of movement around the city ruins. The Setics distributed military rations among them and escorted those who needed toilet breaks. A cautious trust had been established between detainers and detainees.

Zafirah approached David as one of the Freegyptian medics was inserting fresh stitches into his arm. David's smile of greeting was a contorted thing, the best he could manage with a large curved needle worming its way through his flesh, unmitigated by any form of anaesthetic.

"You made it," he said. "You survived. I was about to start looking for you."

"I've saved you the trouble," she said. There were cordite burns on her face and a patch of scorching on her neck – a near-miss from a *ba* bolt, it was safe to assume – but otherwise she was unharmed. "Is it true? We're all going home?"

"If Colonel Gavrilenko is to be believed, and I think he is. He says he's ordered up some troop trucks from the rear. Should have them here by the morning."

"Unexpected kindness from our enemy."

"I'm not sure the Setics *are* our enemy," David said. "Frankly, I stopped being clear on the whole business of friend and foe a while back."

"I've heard rumours. Horusites fighting in league with the Setics. The Hegemony offering to help out the Nephthysians."

"It's an unholy mess. Or maybe a holy one, I don't know. All I know is, even though we helped trigger this turnabout, no one seems to be holding us to account for it. We were the catalyst, we did our bit, and already we've almost been forgotten."

"The Lightbringer..." Zafirah began.

David set his jaw. "What about him?"

"I didn't see... how they killed him. I was over on the far side of the mountaintop. They had us huddled together there. It was a firing squad, yes?"

"Yes."

"And he... People are saying he tricked us. Used us. All his talk of ridding the world of the gods – it was all lies."

David picked his words with care. "It seems that way. He was playing a different game."

"But we believed him!" she exclaimed. "We believed *in* him."

"I know. And many of us died for him."

"How can someone do that? How?"

"Maybe... maybe because he had no choice. He couldn't see what else to do."

"No, that is too generous. Too forgiving. He had a choice. He chose to deceive. And now he's paid for it, and good riddance." She spat on the ground. "I only wish I'd been there, at the execution. I wish they'd let me have a *ba* lance. I wouldn't have been merciful and aimed for his head, either."

The jewels of her eyes blazed, and David knew that, even if the medic hadn't been there, this would not have been the moment to tell her everything he knew about the Lightbringer and reveal the truth of his relationship with him. That would have to wait till later, assuming he and Zafirah had a "later". He hoped that she would see that he had been misled by Steven as much as anyone, if not more than anyone.

"One good thing he did, though," she said. "He explained you to me."

"Me?"

"About how you were. I went to see him yesterday morning. I wanted to talk about you. I thought he might be able to give me some insight into you. Tell me what made you tick. He was an Englishman, so are you, and the two of you appeared to get on well. I felt, if anyone could help me, he could."

She was referring to the meeting that David had, by chance, spied on, while drunk. The one he'd taken to be the aftermath of a lovers' tryst.

So it wasn't?

"And did he?" he said. "Help?"

"He said you were inhibited. You had emotions, buried deep down inside you, but you didn't always know what they were or how to deal with them. He said what made you happy was when you didn't have to think about things too hard, when everything was stripped down to the basics. That made you good at being a soldier, he said. Good at being a schoolboy too, and a son. But not so good in more complicated situations, when the rules weren't so clear cut."

"Ah." David gave a slow nod. "Well, he might not have been wrong."

"He was very gentle about it. These weren't criticisms. He just described the sort of man you were, and then ended it by touching my cheek and telling me to be patient with you, not to put pressure on you. You'd sort yourself out, given time."

"Just touched your cheek?"

"Like so." She pressed the palm of one hand to the side of David's face, softly, warmly, for several seconds. "To reassure me. He was..." She thumbed at the corner of each of her eyes. "I hate him. I'm glad he's dead. But he was sincere then, I'm sure of it. He wanted me to be able to understand you. And he wanted to give me the courage to be able to do this, something I promised myself I would do when I next saw you."

She leaned forward and kissed David. Her mouth was hard against his, unequivocal. He closed his eyes. He heard the medic chuckle beside him. The kiss ended. He wanted it to go on. His lips tingled with it. He wanted Zafirah to kiss him again. He opened his eyes, and she was walking away. She didn't look back. She had made her point, and now it was up to him. What happened next was up to him.

"Finished," said the medic, tying a knot in the surgical thread. "Go now. Go after the woman."

David stood. His arm throbbed and he felt woozy.

Steven, faintly, like an echo of an echo: *She isn't for you.*

Protecting him. Unselfishly. A younger brother looking out for the older.

And everything he'd seen when paralytic on sake was not what he thought he'd seen. He'd assumed the worst, and overlooked the alternative possibility.

"Go," urged the medic, jabbing the needle in the air, like an incentive.

David tottered forward.

39. COURTDENE

A BLUSTERY SUMMER afternoon on the south coast of England. A pebble beach beleaguered by the Channel, wind-whisked waves rising and lapsing against the breakwaters. A triptych of warships – frigate, destroyer, frigate – steaming from east to west, their grey silhouettes perched right on the horizon line, as though sailing on a knife-edge.

David stood at the midpoint of the mile-long strand, staring off into the distance. At his back rose the chalk cliff that denoted the southern boundary of the family estate. In front of him, at his toes, was the beach's high tide mark, sketched in skeins of dried-out bladderwrack. The wind buffeted him. He shivered inside his jacket. It wasn't at all a cold day, not by British standards, but he'd spent the past few weeks in far hotter climes and his skin had thinned as well as tanned.

He observed the warships' progress, and the mirroring glide of the clouds above. British navy vessels, out of Chatham, bound for the Bay of Biscay. Once assembled there with the rest of the Osirisiac fleet, they would be heading down to the Gulf of Guinea to engage with the Horusites. It was already being heralded as one of the greatest sea battles of all time, a clash that would make the fracas in the Aegean look like model boats bumping into one another on a park pond.

Horus in direct conflict with his own parents.

Under any other circumstances, David might have found that amusing.

He was in the country for just a week, here on a false passport that a friend of a friend of Zafirah's had whipped up. He'd come to visit his parents, gather up a few personal belongings and go. He'd phoned ahead, rather than turn up unannounced, and consequently his father was not at Courtdene. Jack Westwynter was making a point of not being there for that period, electing to board at his London club instead. David's mother, on the other hand, had stayed, and spent the time roaming the corridors of the house, alternately trying to be helpful and trying to talk David out of leaving.

"We've only just got you back," pleaded Cleo Westwynter at one point, holding out his monogrammed hairbrush for him to put in his suitcase. "Back from the dead. Can't you stay a little longer?"

He told her he couldn't. She must see that. He just couldn't. If nothing else, the surname Westwynter was not a comfortable one to have in England at present. The family cartouche had lost its cachet. A Moscow newspaper had unearthed certain facts about the Lightbringer's true identity, embellished them as only a newspaper could, and generated a scandal that had spread across the world. Stock in AW Games had dropped sharply, and David's father was constantly under siege from reporters wanting to know what he thought of his younger son and indeed his older son, who was alleged to have aided and abetted the Lightbringer. Jack Westwynter disavowed his children as vehemently as possible. "If one could legally divorce one's own offspring," he told one journalist, "I bloody well would."

There would be no rapprochement, David knew that. Nobody could hold a grudge quite like his dad could, and besides, the man's anger was justified. Steven and David had done nothing but bring shame on the family. It was regrettable, but it was also irremediable. Everyone would simply have to live with it.

David was about to turn and head for the set of concrete steps that climbed the cliff face when he caught sight of someone making their way along the beach towards him. It was an old man dressed in a shabby long-coat and carrying something bundled to his chest. It was only when he saw the bundle writhe that David realised it was alive. Some kind of small animal. A cat.

The man puffed laboriously over the pebbles. Now and then he missed his footing, and pebbles would tumble against one with a sound like the clatter of castanets, and the cat, startled, would tighten its claw-grip on his coat.

David decided to wait and say hello to the man as he passed. After all, they were alone on the beach, the only two people within sight. It would be impolite simply to walk off.

In the event, the old man got in first with a greeting. "Lovely day for a stroll!" he called out.

"A little bracing for my liking," David replied.

"Oh, I don't mind a bit of a chill," the old man said. "I'm always warm inside."

He had olive skin, a Mediterranean complexion, and a hint of an accent, although David couldn't pinpoint what country the accent belonged to. He also had one eye that was much paler than its counterpart. Its iris was so mistily pale, in fact, that David wondered if the man didn't have a cataract. Partial albinism, at least, if there was such a thing. As for the cat, it was delicately slender, with a smooth, light-brown pelt that showed just a hint of tabby stripes. The man halted beside David and set the animal down at his feet. The cat yowled plaintively, then set to washing itself.

"Unusual," David said. "Taking a cat for a walk."

"Ah, can't bear to be parted from her. She comes with me everywhere, don't you, Bast?"

At the sound of her name, the cat glanced up, blinked at the old man, then carried on with her ablutions.

"Bast," said David. "If I had a penny for every cat I'd met called that."

"Apologies for the lack of originality," the old man said genially. "I like to think this one, though, has a special connection with the feline goddess."

"If I had a penny for every time I'd heard that too."

"Ha! Yes." The old man glanced out to sea, eyeing the warships, which had by now almost disappeared from view past the next headland. His face grew sombre. "There they go," he said. "Bad business. Another few thousand young men and women destined for the seabed. And nothing will come of it, you mark my words. After the battle's over, nothing will have changed. More warships will be built to replace the ones lost. More young men and women will volunteer to man – and indeed woman – them. The cycle will go on. It's sad. So sad."

David grunted.

"You don't agree?"

"Huh? No. No, I do. Very much so. It's futile, utterly futile. Achieves nothing. But you have to be philosophical. This is how it's always going to be. Unless we can tell the gods to bugger off and leave us alone, this is the future, for all time. We'll keep fighting in their name, killing each other with their *ba*. I can't foresee an end to it."

"I can," said the old man. "Or at least, I hope I can. It may not seem that way right now, but I honestly believe a change is coming. I have grounds for optimism."

"I wish I did."

"Not that long ago, you see, one man stood up and led a rebellion. You know who I'm talking about, of course."

David half laughed. "I have a fairly shrewd idea."

The old man looked at him sidelong. "Thought you might. And although this man turned out to be a charlatan, and the poor people who followed him just a bunch of well-meaning dupes, he nonetheless proved a point."

"He did? And what was it? There's a sucker born every minute?"

"He proved that it was possible. Possible to stand up and tell the gods to, as you so decorously put it, bugger off. Possible to do that and have a significant number of others fall in line behind him."

"But he was a fake. An opportunist. They're also saying he was a Setic stooge. The Setics set him up as a patsy, then shot him down once he'd done what they needed him to."

"Maybe so," said the old man. "But, for all that, he got a message out to the world. And perhaps someone, somewhere, has heard that message and been inspired by it. Perhaps, even as we speak, there's a young man, a young woman, who's seen what the Lightbringer stood for, not what he was, and is thinking, 'Yes, I understand. I refuse to be dictated to by the gods.' And that person will gather like-minded individuals around them, and another revolution will begin. A quieter, non-violent one this time. The kind of revolution that has a chance of success precisely because nobody has to die to promote it. A movement that spreads via word of mouth rather than the sound of a gun. And gradually, but in increasing numbers, people will turn their backs on the Pantheon, until a time will come when the gods have no more power here and there will be peace."

"You're quite the dreamer, aren't you?"

"I am. Oh, that I am. But my feeling is, if I say this sort of thing to enough people, spread a message of my own, then I'm doing my bit. With every stranger I speak to, such as yourself, I'm helping pave the way for this other revolution to happen."

"You do this a lot, then?"

"All the time now, my friend. All the time. It has become my vocation. Once I was quite an important chap, you know. Held high office. But I gave that up to become this. A wanderer. A traveller. From king of the earth to king of the road, you might say."

David grinned. "I could spin you a similar yarn. About giving up status."

"Tell me, did you do it for a good cause too?"

"I thought so. The first time. I'm sort of doing it again now, and this time I *know* it's for a good cause."

"Love?"

"How did you guess?"

The old man tapped his forehead. "I'm smart. And, you have that look about you. It's in your eyes. You're seeing beyond that horizon over there. You're seeing something – some*one* – far away. And that's where your heart lies."

"Couple of days and I'll be back there. Freegypt."

"Freegypt? Fine place to be. Been meaning to visit it myself again, one day."

"Again?"

"Oh, I was there. Long time ago. Before you were born. If I could call anywhere home, that's it."

"Maybe we'll run into each other there, sometime."

"That would be nice, I think."

"I'm down Luxor way."

"I like Luxor."

Bast the cat let out an impatient meow.

"All right, little one, all right," the old man said, picking her up and stroking her. "Let's move on then, if you insist. No manners, cats," he said to David. "They do as they please. Mind you, they let you do the same. They don't judge. They don't make demands. That's why I like them."

He held out a hand to David.

"Nice chatting with you," he said, as David grasped and shook it. "And don't forget what I said. It's not hopeless. This age we're in – the age of Ra, I suppose you could call it – it won't last. The time has to come when an age of wisdom and clarity takes over, an age of Reason. We just have to keep hoping and trying, and it will happen."

He shuffled away, petting his cat. David watched him and watched him till he was a dot at the far end of the beach.

He didn't know what to make of the encounter, or of the man himself. Crazy tramp with delusions of having been some sort of dignitary once? Eccentric ex-dignitary with delusions of being a tramp? Who could say?

The wind continued to bluster and the waves to crash, and the glitter of sunlight on the sea deepened from platinum to gold. David kept wanting to turn and head for the house, but his feet seemed entrenched in the pebbles, stuck fast. The tide crawled in. The day ebbed.

Soon the sky was red and the sun was setting.

David thought of Ra on his barge, and Set slaying Apophis.

And then, with an effort, but not a great one, he banished the thought.

And the sun went down like...
... like...
... like the sun going down.

ACKNOWLEDGEMENTS

I'D LIKE TO thank many of the usual suspects. The author friends who've shared thoughts, ideas, jokes, whinge sessions, alcohol, and games of online Scrabble with me: Keith Brooke, Eric Brown, Pete Crowther, Roger Levy, Adam Roberts, not forgetting the mighty Vole Pogrom. The non-author friends who've done much the same, especially Ariel, Beak, Chris, Johnny, Larry, Ron, and Tim. The brilliant blokes at Solaris – George, Christian, Mark – for giving me this opportunity. And Lou, of course, for the continuing love, support, and inspiration.

ABOUT THE AUTHOR

JAMES LOVEGROVE PUBLISHED his first novel at the age of twenty-four and has since written more than fifty books. He has been shortlisted for numerous awards, including the Arthur C. Clarke Award, the John W. Campbell Memorial Award, the Bram Stoker Award, the British Fantasy Society Award and the Manchester Book Award, and his work has so far been translated into fourteen languages. He is a regular reviewer of fiction for the Financial Times. In 2011 he became a *New York Times* best selling author with *The Age of Odin*.

www.jameslovegrove.com

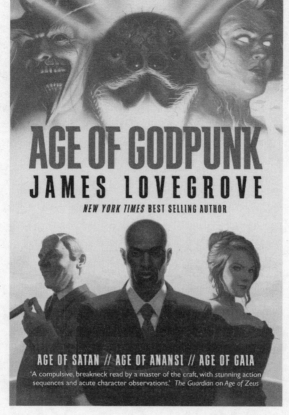

AGE OF GODPUNK

JAMES LOVEGROVE

NEW YORK TIMES BEST SELLING AUTHOR

AGE OF SATAN // AGE OF ANANSI // AGE OF GAIA

'A compulsive, breakneck read by a master of the craft, with stunning action sequences and acute character observations.' *The Guardian* on *Age of Zeus*

UK ISBN: 978-1-78108-128-0 • US ISBN: 978-1-78108-129-7 • £7.99/$8.99

**'Lovegrove is vigorously carving out a 'godpunk' subgenre –
rebellious underdog humans battling an outmoded belief system.
Guns help a bit, but the real weapon is free will.' *Pornokitsch***

Age of Anansi: Dion Yeboah leads an orderly, disciplined life... until the day the spider appears, and throws Dion's existence into chaos...

Age of Satan: Guy Lucas travels the world, haunted by the tragic consequences of a black mass performed as a boy, but the Devil dogs his steps...

Age of Gaia: Energy magnate Barnaby Pollard has the world at his feet, until he meets Lydia Laidlaw, a beautiful and opinionated eco-journalist...

WWW.SOLARISBOOKS.COM